THE
DWELLING
OF
EKHIDNA

LAUREN JANKOWSKI

Crimson Fox
PUBLISHING

TURNER, OREGON

THE DWELLING OF EKHIDNA: Book Five of the
Shape Shifter Chronicles
Copyright © 2017 by Lauren Jankowski.

Published by Crimson Fox Publishing
www.crimsonfoxpublishing.com

Cover art by Najla Qamber Designs.

ISBN: 978-1-946202-20-8

To Allison,

Be wary when you walk in Seelie Court.

Never trust a trickster!

DEDICATION

To my beloved Border Collie, Turbo, who taught me to never take myself too seriously. I miss his goofy sideways smile and our daily wanderings. He was a very good boy.

All the best,

Lauren Jankowski

CHAPTER ONE

It was a warm morning. The streets were still quiet as the newly risen sun beamed down on the city. The air was starting to grow heavy with humidity. Only a few small cafés were open in the square as loyal patrons arrived for their daily coffee. In one café, a single woman sat by herself at a table just outside the building. She wore all black and her eyes were concealed by sunglasses. The woman had arrived right when the café opened and hadn't moved since. She had her back to the window frame behind her and kept her eyes forward.

Isis didn't react when the young waiter placed the small espresso in front of her. The younger man was the only waiter at the early hour. It was a warm day and Isis could smell the drops of perspiration starting to form on the young man's dark skin. She kept her attention on the quiet streets.

"Puis-je vous offrir quelque chose d'autre?"

"Non," she responded without looking at him. Turning her gaze up, she looked at a few open windows in the building across the street. It wasn't unusual for the warmer seasons. Her sharp eyes could pick out silhouettes moving about in the various apartments. Two members of her

1

team were in one of the windows. In the unlikely event she needed a sniper, Malone and Devin were standing by.

"A little politeness goes a long way, Blitz," Nero's voice filtered in through her earpiece and he finally remembered to use her codename. She ignored him as she continued watching the street. He and Ajax were in a surveillance van with Radar, an experiment who was staying at the mansion, keeping an eye on the streets. Jensen was nearby with Shae in another small café. They were watching the alternate routes their mark occasionally took. Alex and Jade were patrolling the streets, also keeping watch on possible routes.

"Radar, do you see anything out of the ordinary?" Isis asked under her breath, making sure she remained inconspicuous. For the past couple years, the Four had traveled all over the globe, following up on leads about the Grenich higher ups, who had been unusually quiet. It was a lot of reconnaissance and the normals found it terribly dull. Thankfully, they had some training. Isis would have preferred a team of experiments, but she could work with what she had.

"Streets are clear, as we anticipated. Nothing out of the ordinary to report so far," Radar responded. She had been one of the first experiments to volunteer to help the protectors bring the fight to Grenich. Her almost supernatural ability to override firewalls and hack into security systems frequently came in handy. Radar had been modified to be the perfect hacker as well as a fighter. She was one of the few experiments who experienced genuine love for what she was good at. Technology was a language Radar was fluent in and the world in which she was most comfortable.

Isis glanced down at her espresso, watching the steam curl up from the small white cup. They were currently in France. One of Milo's sources had informed him that Carding had been spotted with one of the more important investors recently. The investor, a Mr. Kelton, was a notorious Francophile, and according to Milo's sources, he was also being groomed to run a larger laboratory. There was one in France, but Milo had never been able to pinpoint the exact location. Tailing Kelton might lead them to that laboratory or it would lead them to another Grenich bank. If nothing else, he would make a worthwhile hostage. All possibilities offered something useful and so Isis convinced the others it was worth pursuing.

She looked across the street again, spotting Jade casually turning a corner as she did another sweep. The shape shifters had spent the past week memorizing the man's routine and preferred routes. It had given Jack, Isis, and Radar enough information to map out the best strategic positions. He always got a cappuccino from the tiny café that Isis currently sat outside of and always early in the morning, early enough to avoid any kind of crowd. She had done her best to alter her appearance so he wouldn't recognize her as an experiment. Her short dark hair was dyed a metallic blue color and she wore the contact lenses that concealed her glowing eyes. As an added precaution, she also wore her dark sunglasses. Investors rarely interacted with experiments, but he would likely have some idea what she looked like because of how valuable she was. The same went for Jack, who was currently with Orion in their base of operations.

She heard the fans in the café and someone turning the page of a newspaper, but paid it no mind. As usual, her senses were flooding her brain with information. Isis was able to block out the unimportant bits and focus on the useful data. She crossed one leg over the other, furrowing her brow.

"It's much quieter than it should be, even at this hour," she observed, glancing to the side. Since the announcement of the lab escapes, shape shifters found it much harder to blend in among humans. People were on edge, which made them a lot more paranoid and even volatile. There were also random virus outbreaks, which were brief but brutal and stirred up more fear. The people's fear fed into the shape shifter populace, and many shape shifters blamed the experiments. Protectors were starting to turn against Jet and Lilly, which was making the whole situation even more difficult. Set was playing a long game and he was a master at it.

"Do you think he's aware of us?" Ajax's calm voice filtered through her earpiece. She took off her sunglasses and laid them on the table. It wasn't out of the realm of possibilities, but she didn't know how he would have noticed them. They took every precaution to make sure their presence would go undetected. Kelton wasn't an experiment and therefore shouldn't be a difficult mark to approach or observe.

"The noise levels are much lower than they should be and I don't like that. We should consider aborting," Radar mentioned. Isis was about to respond when the hairs on the back of her neck suddenly stood on end. An unnatural chill swept over the café and all around Isis, things seemed to slow down and the normal sounds became muted. A familiar scent reached her nose, one she hadn't encountered in years.

"Now where's the fun in that?" a silky masculine voice came from her right. Isis' entire body went rigid and she swallowed. She heard Radar's sharp intake of breath in her earpiece and imagined Jack had a similar reaction. Isis felt something akin to fear as she cautiously turned to look at the speaker.

Standing there, a few feet away, was Set. The former guardian was dressed in fine clothes, which stood out among all the plainly dressed people on the street. His gold cufflinks were in the shape of the Grenich symbol and glistened in the sunlight. His expensive cologne burned her sensitive nose and Isis fought not to grimace. Set was wearing his older appearance, which made him look deceptively harmless. His snowy white hair and lined face completed the illusion of an elderly man. His sharp blue eyes, fixed solely on her, were a little too bright and aware. Set could never entirely hide how powerful he was, even when he concealed his younger visages.

Isis looked to his right, to the woman wearing a red dress and a large fancy hat, Pyra. She had blonde curly hair and cold brown eyes. She wore a thin gold necklace about her throat with a charm, also in the shape of the Grenich symbol, and a small diamond ring on her right ring finger. Whereas Set looked at Isis like a valuable jewel, Pyra looked at her with disdain, as if Isis' very existence offended her. She stood a little taller than Set, partly due to the heels she wore. When Set pulled out one of the chairs at Isis' small table, the woman folded her body down into it without taking her eyes off Isis. Out of the two of them, Isis found Pyra to be the bigger threat. She was unpredictable and Isis did not like unpredictable.

"So, where are your little protector friends? I would love to meet the team," Set began in his friendly manner, flashing a toothy grin as he sat next to Isis.

"Scatter," Isis ordered calmly into her earpiece before quickly pulling it out of her ear, crushing it in her palm, and dumping the now-useless equipment into the espresso. Sitting back in her chair, she watched him defiantly, awaiting his reaction. Set only laughed softly, picking up the cup and swirling the hot liquid around a little.

"Bit overdramatic, don't you think?" Set asked, still grinning as he placed the cup down and raised his hands. "Relax. I come in peace and good faith. I merely wanted to see how my wayward experiments have been adjusting to life in the outside world."

Isis didn't respond as she kept her gaze on him, subtly dropping her hand to where she kept her garrote and a throwing knife. Silence pervaded everything and Isis noticed the entire square had become stationary. People were frozen in mid-step, some in the middle of turning a page in a paper or lifting a cup to their lips. *How is he doing this? He shouldn't have this much power on Earth. There are too many variables.* Isis' mind raced as she tried to think of a way out of the dangerous situation. It was one of the very few circumstances where retreating was the wisest course of action, but the temptation to eliminate the threat before her was almost overpowering. If she timed her action right, she could at least take out one. The other would kill her more likely than not, but if she could just eliminate one, the other might act rashly. The protectors and guardians would have a fighting chance.

"Now, now, let's not act hastily," Pyra warned calmly, as if reading her thoughts. "Your little friends wouldn't want this place and everyone in it to burn. It's quite a painful and violent way to die, not to mention the massive amount of collateral damage."

As if on cue, the espresso caught on fire with a quiet whoosh sound and Isis instinctively slapped the cup away. It fell off the table and shattered on the paved ground, the breaking sound echoing as if in a cave. After a moment, the tiny red flames sputtered out in the sludge. Isis kept her attention on the two who sat before her. Her eyes flicked to the side when she saw movement. The waiter shook his head a couple times as if dazed. He looked around, obviously confused about the strange scene.

"You have been quite the busy bee, my dear. Causing an absolute ruckus and being quite a nuisance. A lot of my investors are rather unhappy with your antics, not to mention Mr. Chance. Tracy finds that most amusing," Set continued conversationally, motioning for the waiter, the sun glinting on his expensive watch. "Myself, I find I'm at a bit of a loss in regards to your motivation. Don't get me wrong, I find this little teenage rebellion adorable, but I don't understand the reason behind it. What do you hope to achieve from all this destruction, all this death?"

Isis remained silent and motionless, trying to figure out why the two heads of Grenich would take such a risk to approach her in the open. She was no match for them, but they had no idea how much backup she had. Supernaturals wouldn't be as susceptible to their abilities and they had to know she had allied with many of them. This was a foolish move, one no experiment would ever consider.

"Café au lait, deux," Set ordered and waved the waiter away like he was shooing a fly before turning his attention back to Isis. "7-299, I must insist on your coming home. You've had your fun, but it's time for you and the others to return. You were made for order and —"

"You made the experiments to further your own agenda," Isis interrupted, fixing her eyes on him. "As I told Chance, I will not be your weapon or your cannon fodder. I will not allow others to be either."

The toothy grin spread across Set's features again. "You think Jet isn't using you to further an agenda? Or the good doctor? How about the guardians? You think they're not using you and the others as their own personal weapons and living shields? It is a simple fact of life on this world and the others: everyone and everything has a purpose. Some people are made to be used, but they help others achieve such glorious things when they acknowledge their place and serve their purpose."

Set leaned forward as if he were going to tell her a secret, one gloved hand sliding close to hers. "You were made to be used, 7-299. I think you're smart enough to recognize that."

Isis held his gaze, her face not betraying anything. "Are you going to try to kill me?"

Set chuckled and sat back, reaching into an inner pocket. "Not today, no. I have brought you a small gift. How much do the protectors know about your time at Grenich? You were my best operative, by far. Even the newer series haven't come close to reaching your success rate, though they tend to be a little less brutal."

"I don't remember —"

"Don't lie to me, 7-299. We both know the seven series don't undergo mind-wipes; too much risk in removing a lot of valuable information in those little noggins of yours," Set reached into an inner pocket and Isis' hand instantly went to her throwing knife. Pyra's eyes flashed and she rotated her wrist so her palm faced upwards, heat waves starting to form over her hand. The corners of Set's lips curled upwards as he removed his hand from his pocket. He held what looked like some kind of high-tech flashdrive between his fingers, which he placed on the table and pushed toward her. Isis looked at the dark gray stick, recognizing the Grenich symbol etched at the top.

"From the Corporation's records, a few of your greatest hits and some of 7-295's as well, including some video footage of the two of you in the field. I thought your new pack would be interested in what their new weapons can really do," Set nodded at it. "Go on, take it. Unless you worry about how they'll react. Hmm, quite a pickle isn't it? You might lose the few allies you have, which you sorely need if you have any hope of surviving this fight."

Isis took the flashdrive off the table and tucked it into a pouch on her belt. Set began to take off one of his gloves, looking off down the street as he tugged at the fingers.

"Do not mistake this temporary truce for surrender, 7-299," Pyra warned, drawing Isis' attention to her. "You're the one who started this fight. You know things are only going to get even more unpleasant."

"You should have brought guards," Isis responded as she dropped both feet to the ground, preparing to spring from the chair. Pyra smiled and Set chuckled, glancing over to the approaching waiter. Isis could hear someone running up the nearest street. It was likely a member of her team, disobeying direct orders. Typical. The normals had almost no sense of self-preservation and it could be quite irksome at times.

"Well, it has been fun catching up, but I'm afraid we have to go," Set said. "The Grenich Corporation isn't going to run itself after all."

Set suddenly lunged for the waiter with his bare hand.

Isis moved faster and shoved the waiter out of the way, causing him to drop the tray with the two cappuccinos and sit down hard on a chair. She was not able to move out of the way of Set's hand, which touched the bare flesh of her arm. Isis couldn't prevent the scream that passed her lips as agony lit up every nerve in her body. The world faded in and out of focus as she collapsed to the hard ground, curling in on herself and tightly grasping her arm. It felt like the muscles were being painfully compressed and the bones were grinding together. She gasped for breath as she tried to get the pain under control. Looking up, she noticed Set standing just outside the fence around the café. His face was a portrait of shock as he looked down at her, an expression she had never seen on him before. Pyra dragged him out of her sight and Isis swallowed, pressing her forehead against the rough pavement as she focused on remaining conscious.

"Isis!"

She felt a strong hand grasp her shoulder and gently help her sit up. The subtle scent of nice soap filled her nose. Of course it would be him. She briefly allowed her head to rest against his chest, focusing on breathing and getting the pain under control. The smooth fabric of his shirt felt nice against her skin and she concentrated on that sensation.

"Guardians, what the hell happened? Is she all right?" she heard Shae's concerned voice somewhere above her. "Jade, we need help. Isis is down."

"Help me up," Isis got out between gritted teeth, tightly gripping the tailored shirt with her good hand. She turned her head so she could look up into Jensen's concerned sky blue eyes. He hesitated, but then carefully helped her to her feet. She heard the crackle of flames nearby and took off running toward it, not even looking back to see if Jensen and Shae were following.

Isis quickly ran to an alleyway, taking a shortcut that would allow her to approach her adversary from the side.

Slipping a throwing dagger out of her belt, she held the grip tightly in her good hand. She could hear Nero swearing in her earpiece and Radar ordering them not to open the doors. There was a lot of static and Isis didn't know how long the earpieces would continue working.

When she saw the warm reddish-orange glow and smelled the acrid smoke, Isis picked up her pace even more. Those windows would burst with the intensity of Pyra's flames. Sliding to a smooth stop, she hurled the throwing knife straight at the former guardian. Pyra turned at her approach and the knife sunk deep in her shoulder, sending her stumbling back a few steps and causing her flames to extinguish. A shadow crossed over her face and she raised her good hand in Isis' direction. Isis turned swiftly and grabbed Jensen with her good arm as he skidded to a halt next to her. Yanking him into the relative safety of a doorway, she shoved him to the ground and shielded him with her own body as the stream of flame scorched the walls around them. In the distance, she heard Shae yelp and hoped the protector had enough sense to avoid the infuriated former guardian. Isis could feel the heat on her back and heard her skin start to sizzle as it blistered. The scent of burning hair and flesh assaulted her sense of smell as she closed her eyes against the onslaught. It was mercifully short as she heard Set snap at Pyra to get in the car. The flames abruptly disappeared and then there was the sound of tires screeching away, fading off in the distance.

Isis quickly lifted her head, twisting to look over her shoulder. Her shirt was smoking and her bare shoulders had turned an angry shade of red, the skin blistering, but quickly fading as her body repaired the damage. Surprisingly, it seemed that she had only sustained some second degree burns. Jensen also looked up, sweat beading on his face and brow. He stood up when Isis did, smoothing his sleeves and shirt, and coughed a little. He waved off Isis' questioning look, signaling that he was okay.

"Is everyone all right?" Jade jogged over to them, Alex and Shae following close behind. Isis twisted when she heard Jensen run down the alley toward where the surveillance van was parked. She turned and followed him with the other three on their heels.

The back of the van was still on fire and the taillights had already melted. Jensen shouted the two protectors' names, obviously concerned, as he tried to figure out a way to open the back doors. Isis approached the vehicle and pounded twice on the side, making sure to avoid the unnaturally red flames. A few seconds later, the driver's side door opened and Ajax jumped out, followed by Nero, and then Radar. Nero and Ajax were both coughing harshly and drenched in sweat. Radar looked unfazed, not a drop of sweat touched her dark skin as she walked a few feet away and sat on the curb, opening up a small netbook. The quiet sound of keys clicking was lost to the crackle of the flames. Her glowing brown eyes remained glued to the screen.

"Guardians have mercy," Ajax managed to cough out. "I thought she was going to roast us alive. I have never experienced anything like that, even when we've gone into burning buildings."

"She killed him. She killed Beowulf," Nero said mournfully. "Jensen, hold me."

The Four looked over at him and Ajax just shook his head, muttering something about his youngest brother being a child. Jensen supportively patted his friend's shoulder, smiling in amusement as Nero continued pretending to grieve the van. Alex moved over to the van and climbed in the driver's seat. She emerged a moment later with a fire extinguisher.

"Was anything savable?" Jade asked no one in particular, watching as Alex set about extinguishing the flames.

"Most of the equipment in there was pretty cooked,

nothing's really salvageable," Radar answered without looking up from her small laptop. "Van's still drivable though."

"His name was Beowulf!" Nero insisted loudly, drawing irritated looks from both Ajax and Jade. He spread his hands and offered a crooked smile.

Isis moved over to Radar's side, peering intently at the screen and the security footage the young experiment had managed to find in the short time she had been sitting. As expected, the two Grenich heads were gone, seemingly vanished into thin air. Isis held her still-throbbing arm gingerly. Every small movement caused it to ache, though it was gradually fading. She flexed her fingers and her vision blurred briefly from the resulting pain, but she managed to suppress any outward indication of discomfort.

"Anything on the cams?" Shae asked, looking over to Isis and Radar. She frowned when she noticed Isis was still holding her arm. Isis saw the look Shae was giving her and shook her head, waving her off with her good hand. They had more pressing matters to worry about. Shae opened her mouth to protest, but was cut off by the distant sound of sirens. Radar immediately stiffened and sprang to her feet, closing her netbook. She didn't have much experience being on the front lines, or in the outside world in general, having operated almost solely within the walls of Grenich laboratories.

"We need to get back to the safe house," Isis said, looking over to where Alex had finally managed to extinguish the last of the flames. Pyra hadn't had enough time to release a full-powered flame. If Isis had arrived a minute later, the van's occupants likely would have roasted alive. Her back still stung faintly, though it was nothing compared to her hurting arm. Isis glanced down briefly at the limb, noticing the skin had turned a strange ash gray color where Set had touched her.

"Agreed," Jade said. "Ajax, take the van and meet us

back at the safe house. Jack and Orion might have seen something on their feed."

"All right, come on Wiglaf," Ajax called to Nero, motioning for him to follow. Radar moved over toward them.

Jensen nudged Isis with his shoulder, smiling when she looked over at him.

"Thanks for saving my skin," he mentioned. "I fear I'm destined to forever be your damsel in distress."

It is unlikely either of us will live forever, Isis thought, answering, "Damsel is a feminine term. Bachelor is the masculine equivalent. I am unaware if there is a gender neutral term."

Jensen snickered. "Bachelor in distress doesn't have quite the same ring to it though."

"I don't believe the phrase is strictly meant to be poetic."

"Jensen, Isis, get moving," Jade called over to them as she ducked into her car with Alex in the passenger's side. Shae hurried over to Jensen's car while Isis moved toward the alley. She peered at the blackened wall one last time, taking out her phone and snapping a few pictures for later examination. After slipping her phone back into one of the pouches on her belt, Isis turned and swiftly jogged back to Jensen's car.

~~*~*~*

Isis watched as Orion sucked in air through his teeth as he examined her arm. It had taken them a couple hours to return to the guest house they were using as a base of operations, which was located on a chateau owned by a prestigious protector family who had always been loyal to Jet's family. Jensen and Nat had briefly sought sanctuary on the grounds when they had been fleeing for their lives. Isis tried to stay as out of sight as much as she could. The owners seemed rather nervous about the experiments and so limited interaction seemed to be a wise course of action.

"How bad is it?" Jade asked from where she leaned against the table Isis sat on. Orion shook his head, his attention not moving from Isis' arm.

"This is where he touched you?" Orion asked, studying the angry red welts that ran down Isis' flesh. He was wearing latex gloves to avoid contact with the affected area, a simple precaution. Isis nodded in response to his question, her gaze drifting over to where Jack stood against the opposite wall. He focused on her phone, scrolling through the pictures she took of the damage and occasionally squinting at the small screen. Shae was leaning against the wall next to him, her eyes focused mostly on the ceiling. She pursed her lips, blowing her bangs out of her eyes. Alex sat across from Isis, paging quickly through an old book she had brought with her.

"Does it still hurt?" Orion asked, drawing her attention back to him. He spread his fingers over the four welts as he measured the width between them. They were fading at a slower rate than was normal for an experiment.

"Not really, since I cut away the affected skin," Isis responded, flexing her fingers. "There's a faint stinging, but I expect that will stop when the welts heal."

"Yes, if you could please refrain from performing surgery on yourself, it would be much appreciated," Orion muttered as he tested the range of motion in her arm.

"I second that," Shae chimed in.

"The problem needed to be remedied and I was capable of doing so," Isis replied, looking back to Orion. He had been on the phone with Jet when they returned and Isis was frustrated with the continuing discomfort in her arm so she had done what she was trained to do: fix the problem using the method most likely to work. The affected area seemed to be inhibiting her healing, so Isis had decided to cut it away to see if that would revive her regenerative abilities. It had, though the red welts had appeared after her skin healed.

She had not expected the normals to overreact as much as they did. Nor be so loud. Shae had walked in as she was in the middle of cutting away some of the affected area and immediately started yelling, which attracted the other two. Their combined shouting had brought Jack and Radar, as well as Orion. He had been as equally disturbed as the three women, whereas the experiments were quite dumbfounded. Then again, the reactions of normals were often rather strange to them.

"Why would they come out in public like that?" Jack asked quietly, looking up from the phone. Isis shrugged as she gently pulled her arm away from Orion. He put his hands on his hips, his brow furrowing as he thought about Jack's question.

"From what you've told us, that did seem uncharacteristically bold," Jade mentioned. "Did you see anything on the surveillance feeds?"

"The screens went to static shortly after Set and Pyra sat down," Jack answered as he handed Isis' phone back to her.

"Do you think he affected the security cameras?" Alex asked, not looking up from her book. She grabbed a pencil from behind her ear and scribbled something in the margin.

"It is unlikely. I suspect he used an experiment, probably another E-series like Radar," Isis said quietly as she slipped her phone back into a pouch on her belt. "He would have needed all his power to affect as large an area as he did."

"How do you know?" Jade asked, looking over at her. Isis shrugged.

"I don't, not for sure. It's a hypothesis based on what little information the guardians have on him and whatever Milo knows. However, if he is more powerful than we suspect, it means we're at even more of a disadvantage than we originally thought. I will need some time to figure out better strategies," she explained, looking up when

Radar entered with her tablet.

"No reports of any kind of disturbance at the café or surrounding areas," she reported as she handed the tablet to Isis. "Grenich cleaners, I suspect."

Isis handed the tablet to Jade, who scrolled through the various reports, some which had obviously been obtained using less than legal means. Alex looked up from her book and moved over to where Jade was sitting, looking over her shoulder at the tablet.

"Jet thinks things have calmed down enough that you can return home, though I would recommend you and the others keep a low profile," Orion mentioned as he pulled off his gloves and balled them up. "He also needs to hear of our findings in order to address the concerns of protectors and their allies."

Jade looked up sharply at that last statement. Out of the others, she and Jensen had been the most against leaving the mansion. There had been rumors of protectors forming anti-experiment groups. Shocker had seen evidence of shape shifters approaching the power plant where some experiments sought refuge. There hadn't been any confrontation, but it felt like one was inevitable. In the midst of this unrest, there had been a few challenges to Jet and Lilly's leadership and a lot of protectors were questioning the wisdom of offering sanctuary to experiments rather than locking them up. Jensen and Jade didn't like leaving the protector leaders while there was a brewing conflict.

"Jet wanted me to remind you that you have the Changing of Seasons celebration tonight in the Meadows. And yes, you do have to go," Orion interrupted Isis before she could protest.

"Our work here isn't done," she stated, standing from the table. Orion gave her a skeptical look as he tossed the gloves into a wastebasket.

"If Set is aware of our presence, he'll have taken precautions. We need to regroup and figure out our next move," he countered.

"It has been a while since you've seen Electra," Shae added. "She misses you, Isis. Besides, we're all going to be there. We normals do need a break every now and again."

Isis rubbed the back of her neck, trying to figure some way out of attending a pointless ceremony. The normals' celebrations meant crowds and crowds meant disadvantages. She had gotten out of going to the last Changing of Seasons ceremony because she had been tracking a potential lead, which required her to go undercover for a short amount of time and she had to keep communication to a minimum.

"Very well," she relented. "I do not understand the purpose of my attending. Many of the guardians are uneasy around experiments. From what I understand, your revelries are not supposed to be stressful."

Alex, Shae, and Jade couldn't help but laugh at that. Even Orion smiled a little. Isis was unsure what they found so humorous, but that was usual. She glanced over to where Radar was taking the tablet back from Alex.

"Anyhow, the ceremony begins at sundown. My brothers and I shall be Appearing back at the mansion within the hour. You should do the same."

"I will not wear a dress," Isis stated firmly. "Formalwear presents severe disadvantages in a fight and inhibits my ability to move. It is also difficult to conceal weaponry."

"Yes, Isis. Everyone is fully aware of your feelings on formalwear," Orion said tiredly. "No one is going to insist on your wearing a dress. Wear whatever you like."

Isis nodded and watched as he left, followed shortly by the other three and Jack. Radar was about to follow them, but Isis put a hand on her arm. She glanced over to the door, making sure the normals had left. After their footsteps had faded to the point where they couldn't overhear the two experiments, Isis turned her glowing eyes to Radar's own.

"I need you to look at something, but you must be discreet," Isis explained, reaching into one of the pouches on her belt, pulling out the flashdrive. "Set gave this to me at the café. I don't want the normals to know about it until we know exactly what's on it."

Radar took the flashdrive Isis held out to her, twisting it around her fingers. "Did he tell you what was on it?"

"Files on Jack and I," Isis answered. "He indicated it was information on missions we were on, perhaps some video footage as well. I believe he's trying a divide-and-conquer strategy, among others. If that's the case and the information on that stick furthers his agenda, I will not show it to the normals. However, if there's something valuable on it, we should do so."

Radar nodded, continuing to rotate the flashdrive around her fingers. "If they find out you kept this from them, they will not react well. Normals value transparency."

"I am aware of that, but this is for their own good," Isis replied. "Let me know what you find."

"I'll start working on it tonight."

Isis stepped past Radar and out into the brightly lit hall, heading toward the stairway that would bring her to the main floor of the guest house. Ajax and Jensen were going over something at a large table. Both looked up when she emerged from the lower floor, offering her a friendly smile of greeting. She dipped her head, her usual acknowledgment, and continued on her way.

~~*~*~*

Passion bit her lower lip as her lover went down on her, smothering her moans of pleasure. The last thing the guardian needed was for one of the damn muses to wander past her room door and hear her in the throes of pleasure. She gripped the hook on the door with one hand while the other ran through the long dark hair of the woman in front of her. Hera raised her eyes, a mischievous glint in her dark brown gaze. She stood up again and ran a hand through Passion's hair, both women smiling and panting. Sweat glistened on their skin.

"We should really be getting ready for the Changing of Seasons ceremony," Hera mentioned. "We've been going at it for close to two hours."

"Means we have at least another hour left," Passion said breathlessly as she captured her lover's mouth with her own. She wrapped her legs around Hera's large waist and Hera spun around, bringing her to the bed. A knocking at the door interrupted the moment and Passion groaned as she reluctantly lowered her feet to the ground. She motioned for Hera to go into the bathroom, which the other guardian swiftly did. Passion caught the robe Hera tossed out to her and pulled it on, cinching the sash with an aggravated growl as she moved across the room to the door. Pulling it open, Passion resisted the overwhelming urge to roll her eyes.

"Good morning, Mother," she greeted as she brushed some hair out of her face. Artemis arched an eyebrow as she took in Passion's appearance.

"You know it is the Changing of Seasons celebration tonight, right?" Artemis said in a tone that indicated she knew her daughter was fully aware of the fact. Passion slapped her hand to her head, gasping overdramatically.

"Guardians, is that tonight? I completely forgot," she said, faking shock. Artemis shook her head and bit the inside of her cheek. Passion smiled slightly, enjoying her mother's exasperation.

"The protectors will be here in a couple hours and Jet and Lilly need you to accompany them so they can review some footage with Roan. Apparently Set made an appearance in Paris and approached Isis."

Passion was sure her heart stopped and she gripped the door tightly. "Is everyone okay?"

Artemis nodded. "Isis was injured, but not severely.

Though, with her, she's practically indestructible."

Passion crossed her arms over her chest and shook her head. "She's not, but the High Council keeps treating her as if she is. And one of these days it's going to get her killed. Again."

Artemis glanced down the hall when Electra approached. She was already dressed for the celebration in a long dark purple gown with silver designs sewn into the fabric. Electra didn't look overly happy with her attire and she likely wasn't. Under one arm, she held a small silver bag. Electra smiled in greeting at the two women.

"Hello, Grandmother. Mother," she said as she stopped by Passion's door. "Can you help me with my hair, Mom?"

Passion nodded and opened her door a little wider, allowing Electra to duck under her arm and enter her quarters. She looked back to Artemis.

"I'll see you at the celebration, Mother. And before you say anything, yes, I will be on time," Passion said. Artemis gave her an incredibly skeptical look.

"Don't worry, Grandmother, I'll make sure she's there," Electra called over her shoulder as she pulled out a couple brushes and some hair clips from her small bag. Artemis turned her dark blue eyes back to her daughter.

"No leaving either, Passion," she warned as she turned and started walking away. "I know how much you enjoy sneaking away from the celebration."

"Yes, Mother," Passion said as she watched Artemis disappear down the hall to her own room. She waited a few moments before leaning back.

"All clear," she called over her shoulder. Electra barely even looked up when Hera emerged from her Mother's bathroom.

"Hello, Hera," she greeted politely as she started brushing her long hair out.

"Good morning, Electra," Hera responded as she approached the door. She captured Passion's lips with her own in a deep kiss. Passion smiled at her as they pulled back and Hera stepped out of the room. Passion shut the door and turned to her daughter, who grinned at her mother.

"You've certainly been celebrating early," she commented. Passion swatted at her playfully, laughing.

"I haven't seen Hera in quite some time. She's one of the busiest guardians in the Meadows," she said as she started toward the bathroom. "I'm going to take a quick shower and then I'll help you with your hair."

Electra nodded and Passion shut the bathroom door. When Passion finished showering and stepped back out into her room, scrubbing a towel through her wet hair, Electra was still sitting in front of the mirror.

"I hear Isis can't get out of this ceremony," Electra mentioned as she handed her mother a different brush and watched Passion brush her own hair.

"That's what Jet tells me," Passion replied, setting down her brush. "She does seem rather . . . uncomfortable when she's here."

"It's an unfamiliar place, one that's more static than she's accustomed to," Electra said, watching her mother approach her. "According to Alex, experiments have difficulty with peaceful settings. It's completely different from what they're used to."

Passion started brushing her daughter's hair with the comb Electra handed her. "You've been learning a lot about experiments?"

Electra shrugged. "I don't like the way the High Council treats them. We shouldn't use them like Set did. We should try to learn about them and their needs and desires. Even though it's almost impossible with how aloof they can be, I feel like we should at least make an effort."

Passion smiled and leaned down, kissing Electra's head. "I don't tell you often enough how proud I am of you."

Electra snickered. "You're getting quite sentimental, Mom."

Passion laughed as she reached toward one of the drawers, pulling it open. "How are the preparations going in the main hall?"

"Some of the guardian men have already arrived and are criticizing everything, the poor messengers," Electra reported, watching as her mother drew out a few autumn-colored ribbons. "The guardian men from the water lands are here with the royal line. They're quite insufferable, as usual. Do guardian men from the water lands ever do anything other than sulk?"

Passion smiled. "I wouldn't know. I try to keep my association with guardian men in charge of water to a minimum. They were never really fond of me to begin with and then I sided with Jet during his courtship of Lilly, favoring him over the water guardian whom Lilly was originally supposed to wed. That cemented my place as their least favorite guardian, but it wasn't any great loss in my opinion."

"I'm inclined to agree with you," Electra grumbled. "I should probably warn Isis to steer clear of them. The way they were looking at me, I have a feeling they aren't her biggest fans."

Passion laughed softly as she continued braiding her daughter's hair.

~~*~*~*

Isis stared at Nero, wondering how he could manage to be so energetic in such a formal setting while wearing restrictive clothing. He was doing a rhythmic rolling motion with his arms and hadn't stopped moving since they had arrived back at the mansion. He would occasionally pause whenever Jade or Ajax looked at him, but the moment they looked away, he was back to dancing. He suddenly grabbed Shae, wrapping an arm around her waist and holding her hand with his free one, pulling her into some sort of ballroom move and spinning her around.

"Save it for the party, Deverell," Shae laughed, her eyes sparkling.

"Ah come on, Shae. We're going to a fairytale ball, live the fantasy," Nero replied, a playful gleam in his eyes.

"Most fairytales are morality tales that end in mutilation and disfigurement, unless you're referring to the sanitized updated versions, in which women are typically rewritten in subservient roles," Isis mentioned. "I don't understand the appeal of either."

Both Nero and Shae stared at her while she could hear Jensen desperately trying to stifle laughter behind her. Isis turned her attention back to observing the main hall of the mansion.

All the protectors had changed into their formalwear and they were preparing to Appear at the Meadows. Isis melted back into the shadows, quietly moving away from the small group and headed for Jet's study. She passed an open door to the smaller library, noticing Remington and Orion playing a game of chess inside. Isis could see the steam wafting up from their mugs of tea. She focused back on the end of the hall, blocking out all the other meaningless information buzzing about her head.

The door was open a crack, warm light spilling out of the doorway. Inside, Isis could see Lilly standing by her husband's chair, helping him with something. As Isis stepped into the room, she saw that Jet was fiddling with a cufflink.

"Jet, stop fidgeting," Lilly laughed as she attempted to fix the cufflink.

"Honestly, I should call Jensen in here to help me with these damn — oh god!" Jet started when he looked up and saw Isis standing in the room. "We are definitely investing in some kind of bell for you to wear."

Isis tilted her head. "That would be inadvisable. I rely on stealth for a number of things. A bell would inhibit an incredibly valuable skill."

Jet closed his eyes and massaged his forehead. "What

can I do for you, Isis?"

"I understand that you and Lilly are going to speak with Roan about the Paris operation," Isis mentioned. Jet nodded as he finally fastened the bothersome cufflink.

"Orion has provided me with a few questions and notes," he stated, nodding toward the desk at a legal pad. Isis glanced at it and then bent down to retrieve a flashdrive that was tucked into one of the straps on her boot.

"This is all the footage Radar managed to retrieve," she said as she approached the desk, holding the flashdrive out to Lilly. She took it and smiled in gratitude, tucking it into one of the sleeves of her dark green dress.

"I know you would prefer to sit in while we're questioning him, but the guardians do have their traditions and since you're half-guardian, you have obligations," Jet spoke apologetically.

"I understand," Isis replied, moving to leave. She paused before the door and glanced back at them, wondering if there was any way she could get out of going to the ceremony. The Meadows was a peculiar place, one that was much too quiet for her. Serenity and peace made her uncomfortable. The guardians were also a strange race that she had trouble figuring out and their mannerisms around her made her even more uneasy. *It would probably be beneficial to spend some time observing them,* she thought, glancing briefly to the ground.

"Isis?"

She looked up at Lilly's voice, noticing that both of them were looking at her with concern. Shifting her weight slightly to give her posture a more relaxed appearance, Isis waited for one of them to speak again.

"Is something wrong?" Lilly asked when she realized Isis wasn't going to speak.

"No," Isis answered. "I will be out in the foyer."

She turned and stepped out into the hall, sticking to the shadows as she made her way back toward the group. As she continued walking, a movement in the kitchen caught her attention. Changing her destination, she swiftly and silently strode toward the open door. As usual, it smelled pleasantly of fresh bakery and assorted spices.

Dane was in the kitchen, as he almost always was since recovering from the fight at the Grenich laboratory. His face was the portrait of intense concentration as he whipped a mixture in a large bowl. Isis approached him and stood near the island, where the remnants of the ingredients he was using were left: egg shells, assorted packages and wrappers, and various discarded utensils. On the main counter, there were a number of elaborate dishes set out, many cooling. Isis reached out to lift a corner of paper that was peeking out from under a bowl on the island, likely the recipe he was currently working on.

"It's a soufflé," Dane said without turning around or looking up from his task. "Chocolate at the moment. I plan on starting the cheese one when this is in the oven. I'm going to make a croquembouche at some point tomorrow. The small-ish normal challenged me."

Isis dropped her arm and moved around the island. Dane looked over at her when she approached him. Their glowing eyes were bright in the dimness of the kitchen. Dane hadn't turned on many lights. Experiments rarely did, but Dane seemed to have a particular affinity for darkness.

"Are you speaking of Hunter?" Isis asked, watching as Dane resumed beating the mixture. "I thought she and Milo were still in Monte Carlo, following up on a possible lead to Grenich funds."

"They are. She called to give a status update to her parents and since I picked up, I asked her to give me a challenge. Most of the normals' recipes are so simplistic. I need something stimulating, before boredom drives me mad," Dane said, glancing at Isis when she leaned against the counter near him. "Since your ill-advised crusade against Grenich means I can't do what experiments are made for, I've had to settle for a hobby."

"If you're looking to be useful, Shocker could use help at the old power plant," she pointed out, disregarding the coolness in his voice. "You're fully recovered, so you're able to hold your own."

"Shocker is what the normals often term a dickhead," Dane dismissed as he put the bowl down and grabbed another bowl with ingredients in it, carefully combining the two. "I have no intention of spending any measurable amount of time with him."

Isis raised her eyebrows briefly and then looked off to the side. Dane finished combining the ingredients and started to fold them together. He caught her gaze and nodded toward some ramekins that were sitting nearby. Isis pushed them closer to him.

"I know about the confrontation you had with Set," he said, not looking up from his work as he started to pour the mixture into the dishes. "And I know that he gave you a flashdrive. I happened to see Radar working just now. You can't give the normals that information."

"They already have some idea of our pasts. Set is going to keep dangling that over our heads. I prefer not to give him any more leverage on us," Isis replied. She watched as Dane finished pouring out the soufflé and opened the pre-heated oven, sliding them inside. He straightened up and she stared at the plain grey apron he wore, which was speckled with flour and powdered sugar.

"Are you absolutely determined to burn down every potential safe haven we find? We are fighting a war, Blitz. There's enough unrest already and Set's continuing to add to it. Don't do his work for him," Dane warned. "I would prefer not to lose yet another living space, especially one that has a kitchen like this."

"If you're so concerned about that, you could always help us fight," Isis mentioned, looking over her shoulder when she heard Jade call her name. "You are a possible Key."

"Yeah, and I'm not suicidal either. You and Jack go running about the world, kicking over whatever rocks you can find. It's only a matter of time before you kick a landmine," Dane stated, moving over to another oven when the timer dinged. "You two are like big juicy steaks and you're just dangling yourselves in front of countless hungry wolves."

Isis watched as he pulled a Baked Alaska out of the oven and set it on the stovetop, shaking his gloved hands. "I really don't give a damn what happens to Grenich. Whether it falls or becomes stronger. All I care about is survival, something you should think about as well."

Dane looked over to the door when Alex poked her head in. Isis turned her head, glancing over her shoulder. Alex was wearing a pale gold dress, simply cut. It glistened a little, even in the dim lighting.

"We're almost ready to Appear," Alex reported, looking over at the multiple dishes set out around the counter. "I see your hobby is still keeping you busy, Dane."

"For the most part," Dane replied, looking over at Isis. "Have fun avoiding the normals. Do think over what I've said while you're there."

Isis looked at him and pushed off the counter, turning toward Alex. She moved over to the door and stepped around Alex. Behind her, she could hear the faint sounds of Dane cleaning up the island. Out of all the experiments, he had proven to be the most frustrating. He was uninterested in taking any active part in fighting or helping the experiments. On the rare occasions he wasn't cooking, he was observing the mansion's occupants. Isis didn't really know what to make of him, but he stayed out of her way so she didn't concern herself overmuch with him.

When they emerged in the foyer, Isis saw Sly coming down the stairway. She was wearing a dark-colored dress with a large slit going up to her thigh. The mysterious shape shifter reached the bottom of the stairs and approached Jade, kissing her in greeting. Jade smiled and whispered something to her, which made Sly laugh quietly and nod. Her emerald gaze met Isis' and she dipped her head in greeting, wrapping her arm about Jade's waist. Isis looked further down the hall when she spotted Jet and Lilly emerging from the dark hallway.

"Finally!" Nero exclaimed. Isis looked to her left when Jensen strode up beside her. He looked every inch the gentleman in his finely-tailored clothes.

"Is everyone ready?" Jet asked, ignoring Nero. Isis glanced at the group, taking a mental note of who would be there. She planned on staying near the shape shifters for the most part, but also wanted to stop by the massive library in the Meadows at some point. Having read all the shape shifters information on Chaos, Isis wanted to see what the guardians wrote of him. There were numerous accounts of historical events like the War of the Meadows. If she had any hope of getting a complete picture, Isis needed more information than she had.

The Pearl Castle was lavishly decorated. The warm colors of autumn adorned every wall and pillar. Roan couldn't help but be amused as he watched two messengers paint some guardian potion on the walls of the dungeon, which sparkled briefly before forming vines with leaves that were autumn colors. Roan lay on his back, his eyes following the messengers as they left the dungeons. He never did understand why the guardians insisted on decorating every last inch of the Pearl Castle for a Changing of Seasons celebration, including the dungeons. His musings were interrupted by the sound of the dungeon door opening.

"Always early," Roan said to himself with a quiet laugh. He listened to the two sets of footsteps approach his cell, but didn't bother getting up. Roan closed his eyes and wondered if he could fool the protectors into thinking he was asleep. How his elder brother could have worked at Grenich for as long as he had and yet still be lacking so much information on the heads was beyond Roan's understanding. *Then again, Set does know how to keep himself hidden,* Roan thought. Hell, he still had no idea how the labs and experimentations worked. That was Orion's area of expertise.

"Roan?"

Roan opened his eyes and turned his attention to the clear wall of his cell. Jet and Lilly stood there, both dressed in fine clothing for the celebration. Jet was holding a tablet, which he was staring at intently. The screen lit up his features with a bluish light.

Lilly stood next to him, looking radiant as ever. The dark green dress enhanced her golden hair. She looked at Roan with her bright sapphire eyes, studying him. She really was quite a capable leader and one of the few who had earned Roan's respect. Jet was certainly lucky to have her at his side. Lilly turned to Jet and handed him a flashdrive.

"I assume Astrea informed you we would be visiting and why," Jet mentioned as he slid the flashdrive into the slot of the tablet he held. He tapped a few spots on the screen before looking up to Roan. The former assassin stood from the bed and approached the glass wall.

"She did. The Four had a run-in with Set?" he asked.

"And Pyra," Lilly added. Roan's eyebrows rose briefly. That was quite unexpected. Set enjoyed flirting with disaster every now and again, but Pyra was more inclined to play it safe. In fact, Roan couldn't recall a time when he actually saw the former fire guardian in person. As far as he knew, she had never been to Earth outside the Grenich laboratories.

"That surprises you?" Jet asked, noticing the change in Roan's expression.

"It's certainly not something I would have expected,"

he admitted. Jet turned the tablet so Roan could see it. The shape shifter stared at a picture of a blackened wall, his eyes widening slightly. Judging from the amount of damage, Pyra had unleashed a powerful flame. There was a massive amount of scorching around a doorway. Roan couldn't help but whistle as he studied the blackened wall.

"Pyra's work, I take it," Roan said and Jet nodded. "Any casualties?"

"Thankfully not. Isis' back was burned, but it healed within minutes," Jet said as he turned the tablet back toward him and tapped a few more spots on the screen. "However, her encounter with Set is what has me puzzled and I thought you might be able to explain what happened."

"We weren't able to retrieve much," Lilly added. "Even with Radar's considerable talent, most of the footage was corrupted."

"I assume Grenich cleaners sanitized the scene and the surrounding area?" Roan asked, to which Jet nodded. It figured, Grenich was good at covering its tracks. Since the Meadows wasn't in a state of complete meltdown, Roan assumed Grenich had suppressed whatever had happened. The world continued on in blissful ignorance.

Jet turned the tablet so that Roan could once again see the screen. He focused on it, watching the fuzzy black and white image. Jet was explaining something, about the lack of sound or quality, but Roan tuned him out as he kept his attention on the footage. He watched as Set and Pyra took a seat near Isis, who appeared completely unfazed by their presence. *Atta girl*, Roan thought as the video skipped, allowing himself a tiny half-smile. Knowing her defiance must have pissed off Set and Pyra amused Roan. The screen became a little wavy and then steadied itself again. The former assassin noticed a waiter approaching the table and he squinted as he stared at the screen.

"Guardians have mercy," he breathed, looking up sharply to Jet. "Rewind it a bit, to where the waiter is approaching."

Jet turned his attention back to the screen, rewinding the footage and showing it to Roan again. Roan leaned forward as he watched the footage again, crossing his arms over his chest. He could feel a tendril of unease creep up his spine as he watched Set grab for the waiter but latch onto Isis' arm instead. Bare flesh met bare flesh and Isis collapsed, curling in tightly on herself. This was not good. Turning his eyes back to Jet and Lilly, he rubbed his chin as he thought over how to explain what they were looking at.

"Is Isis all right now?" he asked.

"She is. There were welts on her arm for a while afterwards, but they've healed completely," Lilly answered.

"She's very lucky," Roan mentioned as he turned a little so he could lean against the glass wall. "She survived something I didn't think possible. Judging from Set's reaction, what little we saw of it, he didn't think it possible either."

Jet looked at him expectantly, waiting for an explanation. Roan briefly looked over at Lilly. Judging from her expression, she had some idea of what he was talking about. That wasn't overly surprising, seeing as how she had once been a guardian.

"Set used to be a guardian of death and now he's a necromancer. Death is naturally part of who he is. He has some powers, some sway over life and death," Roan began. "One of the most dangerous is his ability to drain the life out of any living thing within seconds with a mere touch of his hand. You'll notice he was wearing gloves, which he took off just before he lunged for the waiter. My guess is he was conserving his power, building it up in preparation to make an escape. Isis got in the way. By all rights, she should be dead."

Jet's face was the portrait of shock as he stared at Roan. He and Lilly exchanged a look and Jet swallowed, turning his attention back to Roan. The former assassin had a feeling the protector now felt the same unease he did.

"What do you think that means?" Jet asked quietly. Roan shrugged and tapped his fingers on the glass.

"It could be luck, could be due to her guardian blood, or . . ." Roan trailed off.

"Or it could be more evidence pointing to her being the Key," Jet finished, running a hand through his dark hair. Roan nodded once, continuing to drum his fingers on the window. To the best of his knowledge, the protectors had put the issue of the Key on the backburner since retrieving the three suspects. Roan had repeatedly warned his older brother about ignoring the issue, but Orion had his own methods. *Ineffective though they may be,* Roan thought as he watched a series of looks pass between Jet and Lilly. Their options were quite limited: without the prophecy, they had no way of deducing which of the three seven series was the Key. However, Set was also working with limited options, since he had none of the Key possibilities.

"I'd start taking more action, Jet," Roan suggested. "You have a fairly large advantage over Set at the moment, but it won't last. He's going to be much more aggressive now that you have his ultimate weapon. Don't act rashly, but don't make the mistake of being timid either. And make sure to utilize the experiments whenever possible. At the moment, they're probably your greatest asset."

Jet glanced at Roan. "I am not naïve, Roan. I'm aware of how men like Set operate and how to counter that. Thank you for your insight."

He turned to Lilly, who was looking at Roan thoughtfully. She looked over at Jet and wrapped her arm around his. They both took their leave of Roan, who watched them go. He looked back to the orange, red, and yellow leaves painted on the wall across from his cell. They glistened in the fading afternoon light.

"Guardians," he said derisively with a shake of his head.

CHAPTER TWO

The main hall was decorated with ribbons and leaves, everything reflecting the upcoming season. Large trees lined the towering walls, blossoming with the last remnants of summer; many had owls hidden among their branches. The large birds watched everything with their enormous eyes. Vines covered the walls, decorated in brightly-colored leaves. Brown, orange, yellow, and red streamers hung down from the elaborate chandeliers high above their heads, reflecting the overall color scheme in the castle. The messengers were even dressed to match the upcoming season. Fall fruits and vegetables were spread about the base of each tree and giant pumpkins sat upon the stairs. A giant amber ball hung overhead, symbolizing the harvest moon. The walls had been painted in shades of yellow, red, and amber. It looked nothing like it typically did and there wasn't an inch of space that wasn't decorated for the upcoming celebration.

The main hall was more crowded than Isis could ever remember seeing it. The autumn Changing of Seasons celebration tended to be much larger than the others. The guardians all wore elaborate butterfly masks and their clothing was elaborate and colored in the warm shades of autumn. The women wore their hair in extravagant styles, most decorated with jewels, beads, or ribbons. The men wore crowns of autumn leaves about their heads. Younger guardians chased each other around, laughing joyfully. Isis glanced behind her as two young women dashed past the group. There was a muted hum as the guardians conversed among themselves, a few glancing up at the newly arrived shape shifters.

"Are you okay?" Alex's voice came from her right. Isis nodded once, her eyes traveling over the large gathering again. She glanced briefly over her left shoulder, where Jensen was standing. He was standing out of her personal space, but near enough that she could sense him. His presence was oddly . . . comforting, as was the presence of the other shape shifters. Shae stood next to Alex, her green eyes sparkling with excitement. She was practically bouncing on her heels, looking around eagerly. Out of the Four of them, Shae was the only one who enjoyed such elaborate parties. Jade stood next to Shae and had her arm around Sly's waist. Sly was studying her nails, obviously uninterested in the spectacle. Jack had his back pressed against the wall behind them, his mouth set in a thin line. Shae had asked him to come as her friend, knowing about his curiosity when it came to normals. Judging from his rigid posture, Isis could tell his senses were as overwhelmed as hers. He might have been more open to the event, but it didn't mean he was any less uncomfortable in such a setting.

The shape shifters soon dispersed to talk with the guardians they knew. Both Shae and Jensen hung back. Shae went over to Jack to make sure he was okay while Jensen moved over to a table full of wine glasses, lifting a fancy glass of deep red wine. Isis noticed Jet and Lilly emerge from the hallway that led to the door to the dungeons. She started forward, intent on finding out what information they had received from Roan.

"I'm going to speak with Jet and Lilly," Isis informed

Alex as she walked past her. Alex merely nodded in response as she turned back to the woman she had been talking to. The woman beamed at Isis and she recognized her as Phoenix, the young fire guardian she had met a time or two in the past.

When she was about halfway across the hall, the guardians all gathered in a large cluster, looking up to the balcony. A loud cheer rose from the crowd, as Adonia and Artemis emerged. Isis rubbed her forehead in frustration for a moment before looking around the crowd she found herself engulfed in. Her eyes scanned for any openings in the throng of excited guardians. She could easily use her sense of smell to find Jet and Lilly, but the issue was reaching them. Looking around her, Isis realized that she had lost sight of almost all the other shape shifters. For a moment, she wondered if she were violating the terms of her release. Then she caught a glimpse of Ajax, who was standing a few people away from her. *Close enough,* she decided as she turned her attention back to figuring out how to get through the crowd.

"Welcome, everyone," Adonia greeted warmly, her strong voice traveling over the crowd. "Tonight, we celebrate one season ending and the beginning of another."

Isis slid her body around a guardian and narrowly dodged an elbow to the face when the man raised a glass of wine. The guardian turned to apologize, but went wide-eyed when he saw her. *Probably should have worn the contact lenses,* Isis realized as she refocused on weaving her way through the guardians. Most of the normals she lived with had grown accustomed to her glowing eyes, but the guardians hadn't. Isis paused when she noticed something odd out of the corner of her eye.

Tilting her head down a little to allow her to turn her neck ever so slightly for a better view, she observed the one guardian in the crowd who wasn't looking up to Adonia. He was a younger man and his attention was fixed on her, not even attempting to be discreet. The different shades of blue identified him as being from the water lands, but the absence of a ring on his left finger indicated he wasn't a head guardian. The stranger was standing near Merrick, the head of the water lands on the male side, and the other leaders. *An apprentice perhaps,* Isis theorized, wondering about the crown of dead leaves on his head. He had a strange expression, one she couldn't clearly read. The stranger's hand rested on something near his right hip, something gold and roundish in shape. Some of the guardians wore ceremonial weapons as part of their celebration clothing, but any kind of weapon was a potential danger. Isis had agreed to leave her firearms at home, but she had more than enough blades on her to neutralize a threat. Her own hand drifted to the hilt of a large knife in a scabbard that was strapped to her upper leg.

"And now, let us celebrate," Adonia finished her speech to thunderous applause and the main ballroom doors were pulled open, allowing the guardians to filter in. Beautiful melodic music, mostly from stringed instruments, drifted out. Isis soon lost sight of the strange guardian man as she was engulfed in a sea of colors. A few flashes of blue drifted past her, lost among the other colors. Her senses became even sharper and she tensed up as she prepared for a surprise attack.

The feeling of a hand on her shoulder caused Isis to move instinctively as she grabbed the wrist and leaped up, wrapping her legs around the person's neck. She threw her body forward, violently pulling the person to the ground. Tightening her legs so that the person's air was cut off, Isis pinned the arm in a painfully tight joint-lock. She could almost hear the bones creak under the pressure she put on them and heard the quiet whimpers of pain.

Lucky gave a strangled yelp and tried not to move too much, his free hand smacking the ground as he squirmed uncomfortably. Isis soon found a pair of spears pointed at her face and her mind quickly sped through different strategies for how to disarm the wielders. She unconsciously tightened her grip on Lucky, causing him to let out another cry. The main hall had gone eerily silent as everyone who was still in the hall watched the unfolding scene in horror. There were a few grumbles of disapproval and a few guardians grumbled about the animal and other less than flattering terms, which she was more than used to. Isis heard a familiar voice swear somewhere near the stairs as well as the voices of the other shape shifters, who were desperately trying to diffuse the situation. Isis released Lucky and rolled away from him, springing to her feet with an unnatural ease, hearing a few startled gasps around her. The guards' weapons followed her every move, a few of the younger ones' trembled, and she stood in a ready stance, fully prepared to fight. Lucky coughed and gagged, holding his sore arm as he sat up. He glanced over at Isis, shock reflected in his expression.

"What do you think you're doing? Put those away."

Isis turned at her twin's infuriated voice, watching as Electra smacked one of the guard's spears away as she moved to stand in front of her sister. Isis raised her eyebrows briefly before turning her gaze to her wrist. She was the last person in the main hall in need of protection. If anything, the guards needed protection from her. Isis focused her attention on the garrote she had disguised as a bracelet, fiddling with the small grip and pulling the wire out slightly. If the situation got uglier, she would snatch one of the younger guardians to use as a shield. That would cut down on the casualty count.

As her sister exchanged heated words with the guards, Isis looked about the main hall. Most of the guardians had gone into the ballroom and the others who had stayed to watch the incident were gradually dispersing. The other members of the Four were standing close to her as were Jensen and Nero, all of them incredibly tense as they watched the loud exchange between Electra and the guards. Jack was massaging his brow, but kept his distance, not wanting to add to the conflict. There were a few more guards around, but they hadn't completely encircled her. Had she wanted to retreat or attack, Isis could do either. The sound of ruffling feathers drew her attention over to one of the trees where a large great-horned owl was shaking out his wings. Letting out a quiet hoot that was lost among all the other noise, the bird quickly went back to quietly observing the goings on.

"Look, it was my fault, not hers. She's fine," Lucky assured the stone-faced guards, stepping up beside Electra. "I'm fine. No harm done. Let's just enjoy the celebration, okay?"

Isis heard some uneasy muttering, which she disregarded as she slid the garrote wire back into place. It wasn't new or useful information that many guardians were troubled about her. As Electra shooed the crowd away with her typical boldness, Isis studied her twin. She was wearing a dark purple dress with some faint hints of silver threads sewn in, giving it a subtle sparkle and making it resemble the night sky. She wore an elaborate mask about her eyes, a darker butterfly than most of the other guardians and it glistened when the light caught it. Her hair was done up in simple braids, but had a hint of waviness to it. It was the most dressed up Isis had ever seen Electra and it looked odd. After she finished chasing guards away, Electra turned back to Isis.

"Are you all right?" she asked. Isis nodded once in response, leaning back slightly to look toward the ballroom. The pleasant music of lyres drifted out from the room; they were the most prominent of the instruments being played. A strong melodic feminine voice was soon heard, singing of the great deeds of guardians throughout history. Isis imagined it was probably one of the muses. She couldn't see Jet or Lilly and the room looked crowded. *I suppose I will have to wait for that information,* she thought with a little vexation. Had she really needed the information, she would have slipped into the ballroom and located the protector leaders. Isis had no intention of entering another crowded space unless she absolutely had to.

"Shame. A brawl would liven up this dull excuse for a party," Sly commented somewhere nearby. Isis looked over to her and saw she had a flute of what looked like champagne. Jade gave her a warning look, to which she just smiled pleasantly.

"I'm sorry about touching your shoulder," Lucky apologized, his eyes reflecting remorse. "I forgot that you were ah . . . um, that you didn't like being touched. Electra was looking for you and I saw you, so I figured I could get your attention faster."

Isis looked at him, tilting her head a little. "It was a mistake, normals are prone to them. I apologize for any injury you sustained from being thrown."

Lucky smiled, his eyes reflecting a feeling of relief as well as the usual amount of shyness. Though he didn't seem to be scared of her, Lucky did strike her as unusually bashful for a guardian. Isis turned her attention back to Electra, who was smiling at her.

"May I hug you?" she asked, to which Isis stared in response. After a moment she nodded and Electra all but launched herself at Isis.

"I have missed you so much," Electra stated, a hint of enthusiasm in her voice, as she gently held her twin, making sure to not constrict her. "It has been such a long time since we've seen each other."

Isis thought about what to do, still a little unaccustomed to the normals need for affection. She settled on returning the embrace lightly with one arm.

"It is good to see you as well," she replied as Electra stepped out of the hug. "You look . . . healthy."

Electra laughed softly at the attempt at pleasant small talk. "You have been spending at least some time with Nero."

Isis nodded. "On missions. How is Passion?"

"She's good. She's with Donovan right now, walking in the gardens," Electra said with a conspiratorial smile and wink. Isis considered attempting to smile back but decided against it. Physical expressions still felt uncomfortable and it probably reflected on her face. The last thing she wanted was the normals acting melancholy. Shifting her weight, Isis looked over to where Jensen was standing next to Nero, who was talking to a younger male guardian. Jensen met her gaze and smiled a small, almost mischievous smile.

"My presence would be unsettling to those in the ballroom and I wouldn't enjoy the sensory overload of such an environment," Isis said, turning her attention back to Electra. "Would you mind if I spent some time in the library? There is something I would like to look up."

Electra looked disappointed, though she did her best to mask it. "Of course. I'll tell grandmother and great-grandmother. You will try to make it back before the closing ceremony? I would like to catch up a little, if you would like to, I mean."

"I will try," Isis assured her, then turned and started toward where the other members of the Four were standing. They all looked over to her when she stopped next to them. Swallowing, Isis clasped her hands behind her back and studied them for a moment.

"I would like to spend some time in the library and would require an escort. However, I understand if —"

"I'll go with you," Alex hurriedly interrupted. Shae chuckled, her eyes twinkling with amusement.

"You never were one for social gatherings," she stated fondly, with a hint before turning to Alex with a devilish grin. "And from what I've been told, neither are you."

Alex laughed sarcastically as Isis turned away from them, making her way in the direction of the library. She could hear Alex's soft footsteps just behind her. The protector had an interesting gait, always quick but not heavy. Isis found she actually had to focus on hearing a bit more in order to pick out Alex's gait. It was an interesting anomaly.

It didn't take them long to reach the massive doors of the library. They passed by Silver, who sat in the windowsill, paging through a book. Her silky hair sparkled in the moonlight, as did the goggles on her head. She smiled at them as they passed by.

"So why the library?" Alex asked curiously as Isis pulled open the heavy wooden door. She briefly closed her eyes and tilted her head a little, listening. There were a couple soft giggles, likely young guardians engaging in intercourse of one kind or another. Opening her eyes, Isis stepped into the library and moved confidently across the enormous space. It was relatively dark, most of the lights having been extinguished since the librarians and caretakers were at the Changing of Seasons. The smell of old books filled the air and the quiet was a welcome change from the assault on her senses. Peering up, Isis studied the stained glass windows, which glowed in the moonlight. For a moment, she just studied the different scenes of heroic guardians from history. Shocker was right: art had a certain aesthetic pleasantness to it.

"Isis?"

"I'm looking for different accounts of the War of the Meadows, preferably from different races," Isis paused and turned her gaze to Alex. "You enjoy books. You must have visited this library fairly regularly during your upbringing."

Alex looked at her, puzzled. "Remington didn't make regular trips to the Meadows, but I've been here a few times in the past. Why?"

"Do you think you could locate books concerning the War of the Meadows?"

"Maybe," Alex answered hesitantly with a shrug. "I can try."

"The more you can find, the better," Isis said. "I'll meet you at the tables shortly."

Alex watched as Isis disappeared in the shadows before making her way over to the stacks. It took her a while to figure out the layout of the enormous library, but she managed to track down a few books about the War, mostly those written by protectors but she managed to find a rare copy of an account written by a seductress. She made her way to the open part of the library, where the large tables were, and was unsurprised to find Isis already seated at one. What did surprise Alex was the enormous tome she had in front of her, one of the sacred texts.

"Isis, you can't just," Alex began as she set the books in her arms down, pausing. "Wait a minute, how did you even get down to that area of the library. It's supposed to be locked to everyone but —"

"But librarians and the royal line," Isis finished for her, gently turning a page in the enormous tome. "The physical locks were easy enough to open. The protection spells took a little finagling. I had to sacrifice some blood, but it was a small price to pay."

"Yours?"

Isis looked up, noticing the concern on her teammate's face. "Of course."

Alex looked relieved as she sat down near Isis. She quietly watched her for a moment, biting her lower lip. Alex looked down at her nails, which were painted a burnt orange, for a moment and then continued fidgeting.

"If there is something you wish to ask me, which it seems like there is, feel free to do so," Isis mentioned without looking up from the book. "I can assure you that I am incapable of taking any kind of offense. You needn't feel any hesitancy or discomfort."

Isis leaned down and ran her fingers over the binding, her brow creasing as she studied a page in the book. Alex stared at her, obviously taken unawares by her statement. Both women looked up to the second floor of the shadowy library, noticing a few figures moving on the second level followed by quiet giggling. Alex shook her head and looked back at Isis.

"Do you know how Set chooses shape shifters to experiment on? The ones not born in the Corporation?" she asked. "Orion doesn't, neither does Milo, so I thought —"

"I do not," Isis answered as she reached over the book and grabbed one of the books Alex had retrieved, studying the cover for a moment. "No one at the Corporation does, except for Set and his immediate kin. Information that sensitive would not have been shared with anyone, least of all their products."

Alex watched as Isis flipped through the pages, going quiet for a moment. "I might have a theory."

Isis paused, her eyes rising to study Alex. As usual, her expression betrayed nothing but Alex's statement had caught her off guard. Slowly, she closed the book though she kept a finger in it to hold her place as she continued watching the protector.

Alex swallowed, uncomfortable under the intense glowing gaze. "I don't have nearly enough information to be certain and I want to talk to a few more experiments to make sure I'm actually onto something, but I think I found a kind of pattern."

"If you have figured out how Set chooses what shape shifters to experiment on, that would be quite advantageous for us," Isis said, looking back down at the book. "However, it would also be quite dangerous for you. How many experiments have you spoken with?"

Alex shrugged as she picked up a book and fingered the binding. "Just Coop and Jack. I already know you fit the pattern just from knowing you before you underwent experimentation."

Isis sat up straight, her entire body rigid when she noticed a picture on the tome she had opened in front of her. It was a picture of a field in flames, guardians and protectors writhing in agony while others continued fighting just outside the inferno. It had been one of the last assaults during the War of the Meadows and one of the most devastating. The necromancers had set off a weapon no one had ever seen before, one that contained Pyra's flames. Pyra and Set had killed as many of their own troops as they had the guardians and their allies. Every single account had made mention of it; the fire that devoured. The red flames could not be extinguished, not by normal means, and it was not something Isis was sure she could counter. What made her blood run cold was the small gold ball in the picture, a harmless looking thing, except for the flames pouring out of it and reaching toward the sky.

Alex looked over at the book, alarmed at the sudden change in the other woman. She was asking her something but Isis' attention was fixed on the pages in front of her. Reading the text on the opposite page, her glowing green eyes strayed back to the horrific picture.

"What? What is it?" Alex craned her neck, trying to see what Isis saw. Isis didn't even glance at her as she dashed away, bolting to the door. The only thought in her head was that she had spotted it too late, much too late. Alex barely had a chance to stand up before Isis had yanked open the heavy door and sprinted out, leaving a confused protector alone in the shadows of the library.

~~*~*~*

Jade and Sly sat on the main steps, neither one overly eager to join the other shape shifters in the ballroom. Sly leaned back on her elbows, stretching her long legs in front of her. Jade had one leg drawn up and wrapped her arms around it. She had chosen to wear dress pants so that she could move around a bit more freely. Glancing over at Sly, she smiled a little and leaned over, kissing her neck gently. Sly laughed quietly and nudged Jade with her shoulder.

"Darling, we'll corrupt the impressionable baby

guardians," Sly teased, arching a suggestive eyebrow. Jade nipped at her flesh, causing Sly to shiver in pleasure. They both glanced up at the sound of an overdramatic gasp. Nero stood at the foot of the steps, one hand on his chest as he played at being offended.

"Two fine upstanding ladies, canoodling in public. If I had a monocle, it would have dropped into the glass of champagne I would have been holding," Nero teased as he dropped on the steps below the two women.

"Already on your brothers' nerves, Nero?" Jade asked as she changed her position so she could lay her head on Sly's lap.

"I'm always on Ajax's nerves. I swear, he and Orion are actual carbon copies of each other. They both just give me that wet cat look whenever I so much as breathe," Nero laughed before making an over-exaggerated grumpy expression. Jade snorted and Sly chuckled as the youngest Deverell reclined on the steps so that he was resting on one elbow.

"I swear, you and Jensen are the worst influences on each other," Jade commented with a rueful shake of her head.

"How do you know Jensen was involved?"

"Because when is he not?"

Nero couldn't help but laugh at her reply, shaking his head as she looked out over the main hall. Reaching over to a pumpkin resting on hay, Nero pulled out a thin golden reed and began playing with it, twirling it around his fingers. Jade crossed one leg so she could rest her ankle on her bent knee. All three looked over to where the ballroom doors opened and Shae twirled out with Phoenix. Her face was lit up with pure joy as she spun Phoenix, who also laughed happily. Phoenix's dark red gown swept out in a circle around her feet, making her appear to be the very embodiment of grace and elegance.

"Jade, the guardians are the absolute best dancers," Shae called over as she wrapped one arm around Phoenix's waist, pulling her close, and held her hand with the other. "No offense, Nero."

Nero laughed again. "It is well-known that women guardians tend to be better dancing partners. I'm good, but I'm afraid even I will never be able to compare to the glorious young Phoenix."

The two women laughed as they continued carrying on. Jade looked over at Nero, turning so that she was on her side. She draped one arm over Sly's legs, smiling at Nero.

"Is there anyone you won't flirt with?" she teased. Nero merely smiled and waggled his eyebrows in response, causing her to playfully swat at him. Though Jade wouldn't admit it to them, it was nice having the Deverells around again. Not only were they good allies, they were also entertaining. Sly's slender fingertips traced small circles on Jade's back, traveling over muscles that were well-known to her.

A flash of black sped out from the hallway and dashed toward the ballroom door, throwing it open and disappearing inside. *Uh oh,* Jade thought as she slowly sat up. Both Shae and Phoenix's hair and dresses had been whipped up when the figure dashed past them, as had a lot of the decorations that covered the main hall. When the two women turned to look for the source of the unexpected breeze, the figure had already disappeared inside the ballroom. Shae let go of Phoenix and looked over to Jade, spreading her hands in question.

"Was that Isis?" Sly asked with a hint of amusement.

"That can't be good," Jade said as she slowly rose to her feet. Sly just leaned back on her elbows, a faint smile playing across her lips. She was probably the only one who enjoyed when the experiments got up to shenanigans. Alex soon emerged from the hallway leading to the enormous library, looking almost as puzzled as her teammates felt.

"Okay, what happened?" Jade asked, massaging her forehead. She really didn't want to deal with this shit right now. *Can't I have one night off? Just one,* she thought.

"I don't know. She was looking at a book about the War of the Meadows and then —"

Alex was cut off when the windows of the ballroom exploded outwards, followed by a loud roar of fire. The force behind the explosion knocked Alex, Shae, and Phoenix to the ground. Sly immediately stiffened and Jade sat up straight.

"Jesus!" Nero shouted as he jumped to his feet, hurrying over to where the three women were on the ground. Jade followed close behind him, but paused briefly to observe the strange red flames. She wanted to get an idea of what they were dealing with.

The unnaturally red flames took the shape of thick tendrils and crawled along the wall, climbing toward the ceiling and spreading across the bricks, devouring everything in its path: decorations, jewels, ribbons, paintings, tapestries. The fire moved and behaved more like a fast-moving fungus than a flame, except for the searing heat it gave off. The bright light dimmed considerably as it was engulfed by the strange red flames. Soon the hall was lit only by an eerie blood-colored glow. The crackling of flames was drowned out by the cacophony of screams echoing throughout the castle.

~~*~*~*

The dungeons were quiet during the Changing of Seasons celebration, for which Roan was grateful. He enjoyed the peaceful stillness of the evening. Stretched out on his comfortable bed, he held a book upright on his chest. His green eyes slowly roamed over the neat black script. It was a book of shape shifter tales, records of their great deeds. *Guardians, we do love to embellish things,* Roan thought with a small smile as he turned a page. Truthfully, the stories bored him, but he wanted to keep his mind occupied with something that wasn't revolving solely around Grenich. Unfortunately for him, he could see Set's and Pyra's fingerprints all over the history of shape shifters. A missing hero here, a sudden disappearance there; all of them sprinkled with little skirmishes and strife. Grenich had been in the shadows, but it had always been there, pulling various strings. *If only our ancestors had the wisdom to see what was right in front of their damn noses,* Roan thought as he closed the book and set it off to the side. Part of him wondered just how many shape shifters, and protectors in particular, were complicit in Grenich deeds. It wouldn't surprise him in the slightest if some of the most revered heroes and loyal families had known more than they recorded. Roan even suspected some Deverells could potentially be involved with the necromancers, which could explain how the family line continued to survive.

A rushing sound followed by muffled screaming overhead made him frown and sit up. *That most certainly isn't the sound of a joyful celebration,* he realized. On the wall across from his cell, the sparkling leaves on the vine began to sway as if disturbed by a breeze and then began trembling violently. Slowly dropping his feet to the cool floor, Roan stood up and made his way over to the glass wall of his cell. Backing up so that he could see a little further down the hall, he caught a glimpse of a dull flickering in the rotunda. It was similar to firelight, but that was impossible . . .

Trying to change his position for a better look, the door was suddenly pushed open and a guard backed into the cell block, spear held in front of her. Roan kept his attention on the strange glow. He watched in horror as bright red tentacles of pulsing flame oozed under the door and then crawled up. It started to creep along the walls, engulfing the vines and leaves, turning them into ash. The guard stood in the center of the hall, her spear held at the ready. When the flame began to glow brighter, Roan immediately pounded on the wall.

"Hey! Hey!" he tried to shout a warning to the guard.

"Don't touch the —!"

The red flames on the walls suddenly burst inwards, swallowing the guard where she stood. There was a brief scream before the body fell to the ground, the weapons and flesh instantly incinerated by the fire. Roan ran his hands through his hair and backed away from the glass. He had only seen Pyra's flames once or twice in the past, during simulations, but it was enough to show him that he wanted nothing to do with them.

The flames soon spread over the walls and covered the glass, but it couldn't get through the glass barrier. Roan almost laughed at the situation: at the moment, the safest ones in the Meadows were the prisoners in their cells.

The flames suddenly separated to form the shape of two hands on the still clear glass. The hands danced across the glass, as if someone were pressing their hands on it to see inside. Roan gave a cocky half-smile, carefully approaching the glass wall. He was safe, but physical contact with the glass would likely burn the flesh off his palms.

"That's a cute little spell," Roan commented smoothly. "Manipulating your flames from another plane is impressive, but it's really just a very complicated illusion. You may not know me very well but you know me well enough to realize games don't impress me, Pyra."

One of the fingers waved back and forth in a chastising gesture. Roan could hear distant shouts and wondered how long it would take the guardians to put out the fire. Did the experiments know? If they did, would the guardians be smart enough to listen to them? The situation could turn out very ugly, especially if the male guardians acted like bullheaded jackasses. Thoughts of Passion danced in his head and Roan swallowed, hoping that she and her daughters were okay.

Looking back to the window, he saw a strange thin red flame, almost like a cobweb, formed the outline of lips on the glass as if someone had laid a fiery kiss on the surface.

Then the hands and the thin flame disappeared. Roan quickly grabbed the blankets off his bed, crouched on the floor, and wrapped them around himself. It never hurt to take precautions. He could hear the soft roaring of the flames just outside his cell.

~~*~*~*

"Spending the night in *really* would have been the wiser choice," Sly commented dryly as she pulled Alex to her feet. The protector held one of her arms, clenching her eyes shut in pain.

"Not helpful, Sly," Jade replied as she and Nero helped Shae and Phoenix to their feet. Most of the decorations had already been reduced to ash and the temperature in the hallway was rapidly climbing. Jade could feel the air getting choked with heat, though there wasn't any smoke. *Guardian fire,* she realized as she shook Shae who looked dazed. The younger shape shifter had a hand to her temple and shook her head, likely trying to clear the stars from her vision.

"Hey, Phoenix, look at me."

Jade looked over at the sound of Nero's voice. He was gently holding the young guardian's arm and snapped a couple times in front of her face, drawing her attention to him. She appeared to have taken the worst of the powerful explosion. The younger guardian's face and arms were cut up from the glass as was Shae's. Phoenix looked completely disoriented and was obviously having trouble focusing. Jade turned her attention back to Shae, who seemed to be more alert and nodded at the questioning look in Jade's eyes, lightly squeezing the other protector's forearm to reassure her friend that she was okay. Jade nodded once and looked back to Nero, who had taken off his jacket and wrapped it around the young guardian's shoulders.

"Phoenix? Yeah, there we go," Nero continued

speaking to Phoenix, who finally looked at him. "Hey, I need to help the others, okay? I'll be right back, yeah?"

Jade watched as Nero continued talking to Phoenix as he led her to the stairs and gently guided her to sit down. Once she was sitting, Phoenix covered her ears with her hands and clenched her eyes shut. Nero straightened up again, keeping one hand on her shoulder, and looked over to Jade and Shae.

Jade and Shae turned to the side when Jack burst out of the ballroom. A number of guardians ran after him, wide-eyed in fear. The sound of terrified screaming combined with the roaring fire echoed throughout the large castle. The seven series made his way across the main hall, his stride as confident as ever. His glowing brown eyes stood out, enhanced by the unnatural dim lighting.

"Get the guardians to safety, make sure no one touches the red flames," he said to Jade as he passed by, barely glancing at her. His attention was on the guards standing in front of the main entrance, shouting, "Open the doors! Use your spears, don't touch the flames!"

The guards turned to the doors, which were already swallowed up by the strange red flames. Jack reached them as they attempted to push open the doors. When he saw they were struggling, Jack took a few large steps back.

"Jack, no!" Jade shouted when she realized what he was planning to do. He ignored her as he ran forward and slammed his body against the flame-engulfed doors, which finally burst open, allowing the dark red flame to spread out and up. Jack let out a yell of agony and curled in on himself where he had fallen, small tendrils of smoke rising up from his burned clothes and flesh. Behind them, Jade could faintly hear Isis shouting not to use water. Outside, she could hear the guardians who were lucky enough to have been out there shouting in alarm. Both Shae and Jade looked behind them, uncertain where to focus their attention. Shae grimaced a little, one hand protectively holding her side.

"Go help Jack," Jade yelled over the roaring flames and terrified screaming. "Alex and I will help in the ballroom. Nero, you and Sly get the guardians outside!"

Shae nodded and ran to where Jack had fallen while Nero and Sly started herding the panicking cluster of younger guardians toward the opened doors. Jade turned to Alex, who was already making her way into the ballroom, one hand held up to protect herself from the deep red flames. There were surprisingly few bodies on the ground, but Jade focused first on finding Isis. In the center of the ballroom, there was an enormous pillar of bright red flame that roared louder than anything she had ever heard. It sounded like an enormous train was barreling through the Pearl Castle. Flames ran out like tendrils from it, both at the base and at the top. There were thin, almost translucent wisps of flame floating around the area like loose spider webs or dandelion seeds.

"Jet? Lilly?" Jade yelled out, squinting as she tried to find the protector leaders or the other Deverell brothers. It was difficult to see and most forms were mere silhouettes in the dark red glow of the flames.

"Jade, over here!" she heard Lilly yell. Jade reached behind her and grabbed Alex, trying to pull her through the chaos that surrounded them. A few younger guardians suddenly collided with the two protectors, knocking them down in a tangle of limbs. Jade was elbowed in the face but quickly found her feet, narrowly avoiding getting trampled. Sniffing back the blood from her aching nose, she looked over to Alex, noticing she had also gotten to her feet, though she was looking toward the ceiling with wide eyes. Jade followed her gaze and was sure her own heart stopped for a moment. She swallowed as she instinctively moved closer to her friend, staring up at the image that looked like it had emerged straight from a nightmare.

At the top of the pillar of flames, there was a pair of large and disturbingly human eyes. They were currently focused toward the side of the two women. As if feeling their gaze, the eyes turned on them and fixed on the two protectors. The flames beneath it formed into a grotesque mockery of a mouth, which twisted in what was probably meant to be a smile.

"Get down!" Jade heard Isis's shout about a half-second before she was shoved to the ground, knocking Alex down with her again. Jade pushed herself up on her elbow and watched as a flame in the shape of a fist smashed into Isis, who was standing where Jade had been a moment ago. The woman went flying and collided with the wall, falling to the ground. Her features were twisted in pain and she gritted her teeth as she struggled to push herself up, her clothes smoking a little. Some debris rained down on her from the newly formed crack in the wall. Isis shook her head, one hand reaching up to protect the back of her neck. Her glowing green eyes turned back to the strange eyes in the flames.

The eyes fixed on her and another fist of flame sailed toward her, but she was ready. Isis rolled forward and pulled out her sais, stabbing and slashing at the flame when it came back at her. The fist disappeared and an inhuman shriek sounded from somewhere in the pillars. A large flat wall of fire, almost like the flat of a palm, sliced down toward Isis. The woman smoothly dropped to the ground and rolled under it, got to her feet, and backed up a few steps. Isis spun the sais, holding the points down as she waited for the next attack. Jade couldn't help but stare at the woman, who was completely unaffected by the chaos that surrounded her or the smoke rising from her clothes from where it had been burned by the unnatural flame.

Isis stared up at the eyes and the grotesque mouth, striding toward the pillar of flame, completely unafraid. Pausing a few feet from the enormous pillar, Isis held the gaze of the strange disembodied eyes. They seemed to glare down at her. In the pillar, some of the fire began to curl as it started forming another fist. Isis quickly got into a fighting stance, moving faster than anyone could see.

"Now!" Isis yelled, adjusting her grip on the sai in her left hand. Jade could just make out two forms on the opposite side of the ballroom as they stepped out of the shadows. Two arrows suddenly sank deep into the eyes and a deafening shriek echoed throughout the castle, and probably throughout the Meadows, as the flames flickered. Jade winced as her ears began ringing painfully. The shriek seemed to drill straight through her brain. Next to her, Alex cringed and raised her hands to cover her ears. Jade looked over to Isis, who threw the sai toward the center of the ballroom. There was a metal clanking sound and the red flame suddenly became less vibrant. The enormous pillar of flame seemed to deflate and collapse in on itself, splashing tiny flames outward.

Two fire guardians, Blaze and her eldest daughter, Calida, hurried forward to the walls and held out their hands, palms flat. A stream of orange flame spread over the now weak red flame, quickly swallowing it up. Ocean stepped up next with a few of her apprentices and they put their hands over the orange flame, careful to avoid contact with the red flames. Water spread over the walls, swallowing up any remaining traces of flame and extinguishing the fire.

Jade looked toward the front of the ballroom where Artemis and Electra lowered their bows. Artemis blew a strand of short hair out of her face and Electra looked mildly shell-shocked as she turned her attention to her twin, who still stood near the middle of the ballroom. Isis met her gaze, her chest rising and falling steadily as she panted for air. She moved toward the center of the room and retrieved the sai she had thrown, pulling it out of the strange gold circular object it had pierced. Spinning both weapons, Isis slid them into their scabbards on her belt. Jade swallowed, noticing how much she was sweating for the first time. Her clothes were soaked and mildly singed.

Next to her, she felt Alex shiver.

The few remaining figures were scattered around the mostly empty ballroom, surrounded by the faint screaming of the panicking young guardians outside and the moans of the wounded still on the floor. Looking around and noticing there were a few casualties, Jade glanced behind her when she heard quiet steps. Sly stood in the doorway of the ballroom, her eyes wide and her mouth opened in shock.

"What the fuck was that?"

CHAPTER THREE

Isis looked over to where Jade and Alex were, watching them for a moment in the charred remains of the ballroom. An eerie quiet had fallen over the formerly lively space, broken only by an occasional soft sob. Jade ran the back of her hand over her brow, wiping away the sweat that coated her skin, and climbed to her feet. Horror was reflected on both Jade and Alex's expressions as they surveyed the ruins. Their faces were streaked with gray and black from the falling ashes caused by the fire, which still drifted about in the air. Isis glanced around at the few bodies of the guardians that had been consumed by the flames, nowhere near as many as she expected. The remains were curled up, indicating their last moments were agonizing. Death by Pyra's flames was not a good way to go. In fact, it was the most agonizing way Isis knew of and one that she definitely didn't want to experience.

Looking across the ballroom, she saw the Deverell brothers slowly climb to their feet. Malone was coughing harshly and Ajax had a nasty looking burn on the side of his neck and another running down his arm. Devin was focused solely on the young guardians, who were still huddled in the corner. The Deverells had apparently been shielding the guardians who had frozen in fear. All the protectors were in a state of shock, which was not helpful.

"Jade," Alex coughed, moving around Jade. Jade turned and cursed under her breath when she saw Jensen toss his nice jacket off his shoulders, which he had been using to cover himself as well as Jet and Lilly. Lilly was hovering over Jet and cradling his head in her lap. She didn't even glance up when Jade and Alex approached. Even from where she stood, Isis could see the tears glistening in the blonde woman's eyes as she focused on her wounded husband. Jensen looked over at Isis, who briefly met his gaze before turning her attention back to the small gold device at her feet, untouched by the flames it had released. She crouched down to get a better look, rubbing the bottom of her chin.

"What in the name of all the guardians happened here?" the booming voice of Aneurin thundered through the ballroom. Isis' brow creased as she tried to figure out where Aneurin had been. She hadn't seen him when she ran into the ballroom and she found that peculiar. At the moment, it wasn't a terribly pressing matter so she pushed it to the back of her buzzing mind. Sniffing the air above the gold device, Isis smelled mostly bleach but there was the faint hint of saltwater.

"Oh look, the men show up in the aftermath to ask the obvious and be completely useless," Sly muttered under her breath. Isis ran a hand over her short hair, struggling not to wince at the pull on her healing wound. The fiery fist had severely burned her flesh and though her clothes had mended, the flesh was taking a little longer. Even her broken and fractured bones had already healed, but those hadn't been inflicted by a guardian or necromancer magic. Pyra's flames were powerful enough to harm even the most advanced products, as almost all Grenich experiments knew from firsthand experience.

"Get the healers," Artemis ordered a few messengers, surveying the damage. "Ready the healing wing, there are many wounded."

Isis had tuned out the moans of the wounded and the sobs of the fearful. Their pain was not useful for piecing together what had happened and figuring out how to respond. She heard her twin approach and looked over to the entrance to the ballroom. There was the sound of light footsteps, likely more guardians coming to see what had happened. Soon, Amethyst and the head male healer, Eshmun, entered and their jaws dropped open as they stared at the scene. They quickly began directing their apprentices to help move the wounded to the healing wing.

"Isis?"

Isis looked over at her twin, who had removed her mask as soon as the fire had started. Tears glistened in Electra's eyes and Isis could see she was distressed. Isis turned her attention back to the gold device, which was still smoking from the power of the flames it had released. She clenched her jaw, running her thumb over her bottom lip. It had been a bold move, but it didn't make sense. They still couldn't enter the Meadows, the casualty count wasn't as high as it would have been had the device been set off so as to trap the guardians in the ballroom, and surely Set knew she would be able to pick out the culprit almost immediately. They sacrificed a valuable inside source, but for what purpose? Nothing the necromancers were doing made sense to her. She couldn't figure out their strategy, not even a theory. It was bothering her and she knew it was a dangerous position to be in.

"What's that?" she heard Alex's voice come from over her shoulder.

"A fairly brutal weapon that was first used by the necromancers in the War of the Meadows. Don't touch it until the smoking stops," Isis warned as she stood up. "It contains flames created by Pyra and when released, it devours whatever is in its path. It's devastating when used outside, but indoors . . . nowhere near as effective. It has a fairly limited range, but the flames can burn forever if not properly stopped."

Electra put her bow over her shoulder. "Do you know how it got here?"

Isis nodded, toeing the device carefully. "I saw a male guardian apprentice from the water lands holding it earlier, just before I had the altercation with Lucky."

"Which one?" there was a change in her sister's voice, but Isis disregarded it.

"I don't know. He was standing near Merrick, light hair and eyes, medium build. The designs on his clothing indicated he was an apprentice. The device smells faintly of saltwater, so likely someone from the seas or oceans," Isis glanced up to where a couple healers were carrying a stretcher. "I will be able to identify him."

Turning to leave, Isis heard Electra following right behind her. The two moved through the main hallway, among the charred trees. The hay had been reduced to blackened ashes, as had most of the fruits and vegetables. There were no more streamers or ribbons and the fire had scorched everything. The hall was left in shades of ash gray and white, making it appear dead. Isis glimpsed Amthyst and Eir carrying out a stretcher that Adonia lay on, which made her pause briefly. Something was tugging at her mind, an uneasiness, but she couldn't think of a reason for it.

After a moment, Isis continued walking, pausing briefly when she noticed Shae and a young healer helping Jack, who appeared to have sustained some serious burns. Electra passed by her, but Isis focused on Jack and Shae. Shae was attempting to reassure Jack from where she sat next to him, both of them sitting with their backs resting against the stones behind them. His eyes were closed and he rested his head back against the smooth stones. Jack grunted quietly when the healer gently rubbed some kind of salve on the burns on his arm and neck, a pained grimace briefly twisting his features. Shae gritted her teeth in sympathy and looked over at Isis, who turned her attention back to the night and moved away from them, continuing on her way.

Isis stepped out into the cool night, quickening her pace to a jog when she spotted Nero standing a few feet away. The sweet clean air felt good in her lungs and on her face, stark contrast to the heat and falling ash in the Pearl Castle. It was also much quieter outside, which was a welcome relief. She looked around for her twin, who had moved past her when she paused before exiting, but Isis couldn't find her in the large crowd of guardians who milled about outside.

Stopping next to Nero, who didn't notice her, Isis observed the scene before her. Many of the younger guardians were huddled together, shaking and crying and comforting each other as best they could. The more experienced guardians looked stunned and unsure of what to do. *Useless,* Isis thought as she put her hands on her hips. For all their wisdom, many of the guardians led dangerously sheltered lives. It was going to be a severe disadvantage in the future.

"Jensen and your brothers are inside. They appear to have only sustained minor injuries," Isis reported and Nero jolted in surprise, obviously not having heard her approach. "Have you seen Electra?"

"Yeah, just a moment ago," Nero said, coughing briefly and then gesturing in the general direction of the crowd of guardians. "She was looking for someone. Uh, a water guardian I think."

There was a shuffling to her right, but Isis pretended not to hear it. She just needed the person, a male guardian from the sound of it, to get within kicking distance, which would have the added bonus of giving him overconfidence. It would make it easier to take him down. Without warning, he changed his direction and moved into the crowd of older guardians standing nearby. Isis finally spotted her sister and began moving toward her when

Electra suddenly ran toward a male guardian who Isis recognized as the one who had stared at her earlier in the evening.

Electra reached him first and he turned around just in time to be struck with a strong left hook that dropped him like a sack of doorknobs. Electra straddled him, grabbed a fistful of his tunic, and punched him in the face, again and again. Isis began running to her sister, as guardians started shouting in protest. A few moved to intervene, but Electra just continued hitting the light-haired guardian, who raised his hands in a vain attempt to protect his face from her merciless blows.

"You traitorous fuck, you damn animal! I'm going to kill you! I'm going to fucking kill you," Electra snarled in a tone Isis had never heard from her before. She continued to relentlessly beat the male guardian, who kept trying to protect his face from her fist. Isis reached them and grabbed Electra's arm, halting her attack and trying to pull her away. Her twin briefly stopped to turn and shove her sister away, which surprised the seven series so much that she actually took a couple steps back.

Isis set her jaw and moved forward, grabbed her sister's arm again, and forcefully yanked her off the male guardian, dragging her a few feet away from him and locking her arms around her, holding Electra back. Looking back to the water guardian, Isis observed the damage. His nose was a bleeding pulp, obviously broken, and his lower lip was split and swollen. He was going to be sporting a pair of black eyes in the morning. Thankfully, Electra hadn't broken his jaw. *At least he'll still be able to talk,* Isis thought, as she looked over at the large group of guardians. She scanned the crowd for the head male guardian of water, but didn't see him. Many of the older guardians had gone back inside the castle to help in whatever way they could.

Isis focused on holding her sister back as Electra continued to thrash around, clawing at her arms and fighting against her grip. The guardian was quite formidable, but she was a normal and therefore incapable of breaking an experiment's hold. Isis looked over to where Nero was running to help, but she shook her head and he immediately stopped.

"Get the guards to take care of him," she ordered firmly, moving her head a little to keep Electra's long hair out of her face. Nero nodded once and ran back to the castle where Nemesis was just emerging. *Well at least that's convenient,* Isis thought as she refocused on preventing her twin from murdering the water apprentice.

"You're a fucking monster, Aegaeon!" Electra continued screaming curses at the water guardian, which echoed in the quiet night. He laughed at the statement, sniffing and thumbing at some blood from his damaged nose. His clothing was ruined and blood continued to drip from his face, staining the blue tunic.

"I'm a monster? Oh no, lady Electra, the monster is the one you would call sister. The creature with more blood on her hands than all the necromancers in history combined," he sneered, spitting a mouthful of blood at their feet. "That *abomination* behind you."

Isis raised an eyebrow at the word Aegaeon all but spat at her. It was not a term often used by guardians, not even the ones who didn't like the experiments. That made it a minor anomaly and Isis stored it in her memory for later use. Electra let out a cry of frustration and anger, clawing even more aggressively at her twin's arms as she tried to get her grip to loosen.

"You sick, twisted, depraved thing! How dare you call yourself a guardian!" Electra snapped, pulling against her sister's hold. Her struggles were gradually ceasing and Isis estimated that she would wear herself out soon. Normals had such little stamina and seemed incapable of saving their energy. Isis looked around for any sign of Nemesis or any of the other guards, wanting to get the water apprentice away from her twin. She didn't normally think Electra was capable of murder, but her protectiveness toward her loved ones could cause her to act rashly. Aegaeon was a potentially valuable lead and Isis didn't want to lose him.

"The women of these lands have left us vulnerable with their weakness and soft heartedness, allowing their emotions to dictate their actions. And it started with your whore of a mother. She should have been banished. Instead she's allowed to keep her title and her two bastard half-breeds run around, sullying our once great land," he continued, wiping some blood away from his lip, spitting more out on the ground. "Set will restore The Meadows to its former greatness."

Electra let out a furious laugh, still fighting against Isis' unbreakable hold. "Are you really so damn naïve? Set hates all the guardians! He seeks to annihilate us! Look what he did to my sister, what he turned her into! She's a guardian!"

Aegaeon looked at Isis with an expression of pure disgust. "That creature isn't a guardian and never was. She's not even a shape shifter anymore. She's an animal that needs to be put down before she has the chance to kill again, if she hasn't already. You worry about Set bringing us to ruin, but the bigger threat is that thing behind you. She will destroy all of us if given the chance."

Nemesis finally arrived on the scene, followed closely by a male guardian Isis didn't recognize. He carried himself with confidence and wore the colors of the royal line, so she assumed he was Aneurin's apprentice or heir. He had youthful features, though his eyes told her he was ancient, and he carried a torch. The male guardian looked nothing short of furious as he glared at the young water guardian, but Nemesis' expression was impassive. The guards were trained from a young age to not display any emotion when working. The male guardian gave a short nod and Nemesis stepped forward with a pair of heavy iron shackles, which she quickly affixed to his wrists. Aegaeon sneered at Isis one last time before Nemesis turned him around and pushed him forward, ordering him to move, the male guardian with the torch following close behind them. Isis watched as the younger water guardian was led away then turned her attention back to Electra, who was still trying to lunge out of Isis' grip to go after him.

"Let me go," she hissed. "I'm going to kill him."

"I fail to see the purpose in that. He may have valuable information —"

"I don't fucking care!"

"Well you should," Isis responded, her voice remaining even. Electra was still struggling against her, snarling curses. Isis watched as Aegaeon disappeared inside the Pearl Castle. Many guardians watched him go. A few glanced nervously at Electra, shuffling their feet uncomfortably. Isis finally let go of Electra once Aegaeon was out of sight and looked off across the lands. A cool breeze swept through the night, brushing against her face. Electra turned back to look at her, her fists clenched and trembling. It was obvious that she was still upset.

"After all he did?" Electra demanded, accusingly, drawing Isis' attention back to her. "He allied with the man who wants to murder our people, who experimented on you, who *tortured* you and countless other shape shifters! He deserves to die and you just want me to let him go!?"

"I do not require you to fight my battles for me," Isis said calmly. Electra was taken by surprise by the statement and stared at Isis, obviously unsure what to say. Isis looked over at the remaining guardians, most of who were now staring at the two of them.

"You claim Set took away my choices and freedom and you believe that to be reprehensible, an unforgivable act. Yet you would act in a similar manner and seek out revenge on my behalf when I neither ask nor want you to," Isis continued. "We cannot fight Set if you kill everyone complicit in Grenich's crimes. That's not even feasible because a great many are involved in Set's deeds."

Isis looked back over her shoulder, wanting to go back

inside and get a better idea of the casualty count before listening in on the interrogation. Even if she weren't allowed in the room, she would find a way to get the information she wanted. The Pearl Castle was relatively easy to infiltrate.

"You can't let him get away with what he did," Electra protested softly. Isis played with the garrote wire on her wrist.

"I highly doubt that is possible. The dungeons are more than capable of holding him. They held me without a problem," she responded with a shrug. "An eternity in a cell seems adequate punishment by guardian standards."

"It's not," Electra said, swiping at her face with one hand. "Not for what he did."

Isis shook her head, not really in the mood to deal with the contradictory ways and beliefs of normals. It would be the wise course of action to eliminate Aegaeon once they finished questioning him, but that went against the sacred laws of the guardians. Isis didn't understand their morality, but she knew it was important to them. At the moment, it wasn't interfering with her own strategies, so Isis would follow their decision. Maintaining a relatively civil alliance with the guardians was in her best interests anyway. Fully turning to face her twin, Isis slipped the garrote back into place.

"No? Then what punishment would you assign to me? Because I have done *much* worse than he has," she pointed out, placing her hands on her hips. "You know what I have been modified to do, what I am. Aegaeon is correct about my being a monster by your definitions, Electra. You may think you know what I did at the Grenich Corporation, but I guarantee you I've done worse than anything you could possibly imagine."

Electra stared at her, unsure of how to respond. She shifted her weight and swallowed, letting out her breath. Isis watched her, looking her over to take in her state. Her respiration was regular and her complexion was normal again. Isis turned her attention to just over her sister's shoulder, catching a familiar scent on the air.

"Electra! Isis!"

Passion practically knocked her daughter down when she ran into her, wrapping her arms around her tightly, and letting out a sob of relief. She put one hand on the back of Electra's head and gently kissed her temple before burying her face in the space between her neck and shoulder. Passion tilted her head up slightly and her eyes traveled over to Isis who took a step back and nodded once at Passion to reassure the guardian she was unharmed. Passion closed her eyes again, tears escaping from behind her closed lids as she buried her face in Electra's hair. Electra held her mother just as tightly, closing her eyes in relief.

"I have some things I need to do in the Pearl Castle," Isis stated as she turned to make her way back to the castle.

"Can we talk later?" Electra asked, her voice raspy from screaming.

"If you wish," Isis answered without turning around. She moved through the grass, heading for the enormous doors. The few guardians she passed nervously shuffled out of her way, fear reflecting in their eyes as they tried to avoid her gaze. Pausing briefly and looking back to her sister, Isis noticed Donovan slowly moving to Passion's side. Nero was approaching her from the left, but she paid him no heed. She watched as Lucky ran over to Donovan and wrapped his arms around the guardian, who stared at him in surprise and a bit of exasperation for a moment before gently patting his shoulder, an obvious gesture of reassurance and even affection. Isis doubted she would ever understand the need normals had for comfort after trauma.

"I wasn't trying to eavesdrop, but I . . . um, I overheard a bit of your conversation with Electra," Nero began, scratching the back of his head in discomfort. "You don't believe that, do you? About being a monster?"

"It is the truth," Isis replied easily. "But monsters have their uses."

She turned and continued on her way to the Pearl Castle, noticing the bright light spilling out. They had apparently relit the torches to keep out the night. Isis wasn't sure which was preferable. After a moment, she heard Nero turn and follow her. They passed by some messengers, who were dragging out burned debris from the castle. A few were already starting to scrub the scorched walls, attempting to restore some sense of order to the Pearl Castle.

~~*~*~*

Artemis stood in the healing rooms with her arms crossed over her chest, watching the healers continue with their work. Amethyst was working on a patient in the closest bed and she glanced up, exchanging a look of concern with Artemis. She had ordered the healers not to use their magic after the first couple victims had been helped. Something didn't feel right, but neither woman could figure out what it was. Artemis had sent Silver and Blaze to do some research on Pyra's flames to see if they could figure out if there were any lingering effects or dangers. Many of the healers were unhappy with their orders and Artemis could see it in their faces.

Adonia had been severely wounded and was the first one healed. She was resting in her living quarters and Artemis was acting in her stead while she recovered. The healing ward was still overflowing and their healing herbs and potions could only do so much. Many of the wounded were still in danger of fading away and the ones who were still conscious were in agony, requiring heavy doses of painkillers and muscles relaxants. The soothing subtle scent of assorted flowers from the different worlds helped cover up the smell of burned flesh and blood, as did some of the herbs that were soaking in hot water in different pots in the back of the enormous healing ward. Both Amethyst and Eshmun knew how to make a safe and comforting environment for healing.

On the opposite side of the room, Eshmun was helping the healers with the most severely wounded. He straightened up and ran the back of one hand across his brow before placing his hands on his hips, one finger tapping his left hip. The younger healers and the apprentices were doing an admirable job seeing to their patients, but they could only do so much without magic.

Artemis turned her attention to where Jet lay asleep on a bed, his head on Lilly's chest. She was dozing lightly, her arms wrapped gently around him. Jet had extensive burns on his back and had suffered a concussion, both sustained while he and Lilly had been attempting to help save some of the younger guardians. *Always a protector,* Artemis thought as she looked over to the door of the healing wing as a healer and Shae helped Jack inside. The experiment looked as if he had seen better days. The right side of his face was burned and his entire right arm had been wrapped. It looked like his wounds were gradually healing, but she could still see pain in his glowing brown eyes and in the stiff way he moved. Artemis' heart was breaking at the sight of so much suffering, but she kept her face devoid of emotion. She had to be strong for her people. Her eyes roamed over the beds, searching for any sign of her daughter. It was the first time Artemis had ever prayed that Passion had snuck out of a celebration.

"What is the meaning of this, Artemis!?" Aneurin's bellow echoed throughout the room, causing many of the conscious patients to cringe. "Merrick tells me you have ordered the healers to not help the wounded?"

"I ordered no such thing. I ordered them not to use their magic for the time being. We have plenty of herbs and medicines that are being used," Artemis said calmly, having expected this confrontation. Aneurin stormed over to her, looking toward Eshmun.

"Use your magic and any means necessary to save as many as you can, that is an order," Aneurin commanded the healers, turning to leave the room. Passion and Electra entered the healing wing, looking between the two guardians. Artemis glimpsed Donovan over Passion's shoulder and felt a weight lift off her shoulders. Passion was alive and unhurt. *And we need more hands in here. My daughter's timing is impeccable for once,* she thought as she dropped her arms and turned to address the room.

"Ignore that order," Artemis stated. Aneurin turned around and Artemis could almost feel his fury. He stood rigidly, his eyes darkening a shade as he glared at her.

"You would let our people suffer and die," he began and Artemis turned to face him fully, striding forward so she was a few feet away from him. Squaring her shoulders and lifting her chin so that she stood her full height, Artemis set her jaw and pinned him with a glare.

"I am trying to save our people, as is my job. Something doesn't feel right and Amethyst shares my concerns. Until I know for certain that Pyra hasn't laid some other kind of trap, I will not put any more guardians in danger," Artemis explained coolly, her eyes narrowing. "And I would thank you to remember that I am acting queen while Adonia is recovering. I am of equal rank and position to you and you will respect me as such. If you question me like that again, I will see you brought before the High Council if I have to drag you there myself."

Artemis took a step back and looked to the healing wing again, ignoring Passion when she began clapping. Aneurin was practically trembling with anger, but Artemis didn't care. She wasn't going to risk any more lives unless she had no other choice.

Aneurin swallowed and smoothed the front of his tunic. "We are a culture who follows our conscience. The healers must act in their best judgement and in the best interest of their patients. If that requires them to not use all their resources, so be it."

With that, he turned and strode out of the healing wing. Artemis closed her eyes briefly, resting a hand at the base of her throat. She exchanged a look with Amethyst, who reached out to Eshmun as he was passing her by to retrieve more supplies. Like the other guardians, the healers hadn't changed since the fire. However, their clothing wasn't as singed as most of the other guardians since the flames had not reached inside the healing rooms.

"Don't use your magic," she warned, her violet eyes meeting Eshmun's dark gaze. "Something isn't right and I know you feel it too. There is some evil at work."

Eshmun glanced around the healing wing, looking back to Amethyst. "Do we just let them continue to suffer, risk losing even more lives? I'm not comfortable with that, Amethyst."

"We help in whatever way we can, but I agree with Artemis that exercising caution is the best course of action right now," Amethyst responded. The two head healers looked out over the crowded healing wing and Artemis followed their gaze where some healers had started using their magic again. Artemis turned to the side when she felt a soft hand on her shoulder, looking into the eyes of her daughter.

"What do you need?" Passion asked softly. Over her shoulder, Artemis could see Electra looking at her expectantly. She offered them a weak smile, grateful for their help.

"Amethyst, show Passion and Electra how they can help," Artemis said, turning to Donovan, who stood off to the side. "Astrea mentioned that you had caught the culprit?"

"Actually, your granddaughter did that —"

"As long as we have him in custody," Artemis interrupted. "I assume Alister is prepared to begin the interrogation?"

"Alister and Nemesis brought Aegaeon to the

dungeons," Electra replied. "So he's probably waiting for you."

Artemis strode across the warmly lit space to where Lilly had woken and was sitting up on the bed. Her dark sapphire eyes met Artemis' and she gently maneuvered out from under Jet, making sure he was comfortable before getting off the bed and smoothing her dress.

"It is your right to sit in on the interrogation if you like," Artemis began, but Lilly shook her head. She looked back at Jet and then to Artemis again, smiling shakily.

"I need to get back to the mansion and let everyone know what happened. Undoubtedly the protectors will want to figure out what to do next," she replied softly. "Perhaps Isis could sit in for Jet and I? She will likely be able to pick up things that we might not notice."

Artemis nodded. "That is probably a wise course of action, though I'm sure Aneurin will not be happy with it."

Lilly offered Artemis a sympathetic smile, glancing over her shoulder to her husband again. Artemis could see the uncertainty in the normally confident woman. Lilly didn't like the idea of leaving while Jet was still in a vulnerable state, even if her husband was almost fully recovered. Artemis reached out and gave her arm a supportive squeeze.

"Try not to worry too much. The healers will look after Jet and send him home once he awakens," Artemis said softly, glancing over Lilly's shoulder to where Jet lay. Passion was standing at his bedside, checking to make sure his wounds had been fully healed. "You know my daughter would die before she let any harm come to him."

Lilly laughed quietly and brushed at her cheek. "Thank you, Lady Artemis."

Artemis nodded and stepped back, watching as Lilly disappeared in a bright shimmer of blue light. She made her way out of the healing ward, scrubbing her hands over her face and letting out a long breath. Pausing briefly, she wondered where Isis would be. The woman was like a phantom, coming and going with few people seeing her. The messengers were cleaning up the hall and the main part of the Pearl Castle was mostly quiet except for the quiet scrapping of brushes and brooms. Artemis smoothed the front of her dress and started for the dungeon area.

"Lady Artemis?"

Artemis turned and Astrea stopped, bowing her head respectfully, her hand resting on the pommel of her sword. The head dungeon guard was dressed in her ceremonial uniform, which still glistened even in the dim light. Artemis waved a hand, indicating the formality was unnecessary. Astrea stood at ease, meeting Artemis' gaze with her dark eyes. She brushed a few strands of black hair behind her ear.

"Lord Alister and my sister are waiting for you in the interrogation rooms," Astrea reported. "And your granddaughter is also there."

Artemis' brow furrowed. "Isis is there?"

"Not in the room, but just outside of it. I believe she is listening," Astrea replied.

Artemis smiled and nodded in gratitude, looking around at the strangely quiet main hall. It was eerie to see it so bare and Artemis didn't like it. It felt cold and barren; lifeless.

"Thank you, lady Astrea. You may take the remainder of the night off," Artemis said. Astrea bowed her head again and walked away. Artemis moved toward the dungeons, staying out of the way of the messengers cleaning up the hall.

~~*~*~*

Isis sat in the dungeons, high up in a niche beside a marble sculpture of one of the justice guardians. She was just outside the interrogation room where Aegaeon was with Nemesis and the guardian man, who Isis now knew was Alister. Oddly enough, the interrogation rooms hadn't been touched by the flames and most of the walls weren't as scorched as the main hall and ballroom. The door to the interrogation room was open and light spilled out into the mostly dark hallway. The two guardians were awaiting Artemis and probably Lilly, seeing as how Jet was probably still resting after being healed. The only sound in the dungeons was Aegaeon tapping his finger on the table.

Isis listened to the tapping as she stared at the vines and bright leaves traveling over the wall across the way, thinking about the attack and replaying it in her mind. It was either the least successful attack of the necromancers or there was some important detail she was missing. She had done a quick sweep of the dungeons, checking for anything out of place. The guards hadn't seen her and neither had the prisoners. She'd wager Roan suspected she had been there, but he didn't visibly react at all. His block was the one of the very few that had been scorched in the main part of the dungeon. Isis hadn't gone down to the lower levels, which would have required picking a few locks.

The tapping paused and then Aegaeon tapped seven times rapidly, before going quiet again. She raised an eyebrow, wondering if he genuinely believed that would unnerve her. The tapping began again, but it was calm and measured, steady. Isis pulled her leg up to her chest so she could rest her chin on her knee, listening for the soft steps of the guardian woman they were awaiting. One of the guardians in the room shifted their position, likely the man. Nemesis never moved without purpose and she was obviously used to remaining completely still for long periods of time. Out of all the guardians, the guards would probably be the most formidable opponents. After briefly studying them, Isis could see some parallels to experiments and she was sure Set had based some of their training on the guards' training in the Meadows.

Soon, she heard the door open to the dungeons and soft footsteps descend the stairs. She instinctively pressed her slender body back even further into the shadows, patiently waiting. Artemis soon stepped into view, looking lost in thought. Isis watched her as she continued approaching the door, unaware of her presence. She was still dressed in a royal purple dress; the darkest color Isis had ever seen her wear. It was an elegant but simple dress; nothing garish about it. It didn't shimmer like the other guardian dresses and it made Artemis' dark blue eyes stand out. It was streaked with ashes and singed in a few spots, but it still made Artemis look like the powerful guardian she was. The guardian woman paused just outside the door, running a hand through her dark hair. She looked around the hallway, as if searching for someone.

"The other two are already inside with him," Isis spoke just loud enough for Artemis to hear her. The older guardian's eyes widened and she whipped her head around to look up to where Isis was. Isis pushed off from the edge of niche, dropping straight to the ground and landing in a crouch. She straightened up and met Artemis' gaze before looking over at the room.

"He has been tapping since he was brought in," Isis reported, looking down the way Artemis had come from. She frowned when Lilly didn't follow. Jet would still be recovering from his wounds, but Lilly had been mostly unharmed. Surely she would sit in on the interrogation, or perhaps she would send Jade.

"Is he nervous?" Artemis asked, drawing Isis' attention back to her.

"No," Isis replied, looking back to the guardian. "I thought a protector would be in there while he's being questioned."

"Yes, I would like a protector in there with us," Artemis said as she watched Isis. "You're probably aware that Jet is still in the healing wards. Lilly has returned to the mansion to let the others know what happened. The Deverells have also returned, as have Jade and Alex. Lilly requested you sit in for her."

Isis stared at her, looking for any signs of deception. When none were forthcoming, Isis put her hands on her hips and looked toward the interrogation room. The tapping continued unabated.

"I will do as you request, but I must once again remind you that I am no protector," Isis said quietly. "Your sacred laws are very clear about the role of non-protectors in guardian matters, especially ones such as these."

Artemis was quiet for a moment, studying her granddaughter, and then stepped forward to the open door. The tapping stopped briefly and Isis crossed her arms over her chest, listening to Artemis request the male guardian's presence outside. He stepped out and Isis briefly sized him up. He was wearing a nice tunic that had more earthy tones than was typical of the dress for the autumn Changing of Seasons ceremony. He had dark eyes and was a little shorter than most of the other guardian men, though he still stood a couple inches taller than her. His dark hair was quite short, which made his head look a little rounder.

"Isis, this is Alister," Artemis introduced and Alister offered his hand, which Isis looked at before turning her eyes back to his. She didn't like shaking hands, but found she frequently had to do so in order to put the normals at ease. Lightly, she put her hand in his and shook. His grip was firm but not too tight or constrictive.

"It is a pleasure to finally meet you outside the High Council," Alister said with a soft smile. Isis turned her head slightly, keeping him in her line of vision as she looked back down the hall to where the guards were changing shifts.

"Alister, I've requested Isis sit in on the interrogation. I believe she would have some valuable insight," Artemis said and Alister looked over at her. "The other protectors have already returned to the mansion, except for the wounded. Lilly has asked that Isis take her place in the interrogation and I agreed. Isis pointed out that her presence may be at odds with our sacred laws and I wanted to know if you had similar concerns."

Alister smiled at Artemis. "Well, the section of the sacred laws you're referring to can have a number of different interpretations. Given the circumstances, I feel we should take that into account. I have no objections to Isis sitting in, so long as she follows our rules in regards to prisoner treatment."

Looking back to the two guardians, Isis nodded once and watched as he turned back to the room. She wasn't going to press the issue, not when she had exactly what she wanted. They could deal with the ire of the more old fashioned guardians on their own.

Stepping into the well-lit room, Isis noticed Nemesis standing in the corner a few feet away from the door. She held her staff at her side and her expression was unreadable. Like the other guards, Nemesis wore her uniform instead of a fancy dress. She had removed the mask some time ago. Looking around the room, she remembered the last time she had been in an interrogation room. Her eyes turned to the chairs and she thought back to when she had killed Onyx. It seemed like a lifetime ago, but it was seared in her memory. Isis turned her attention to Aegaeon, who was smirking at her as he continued to tap the table with one long finger.

"I see we're disregarding even more sacred laws," he commented, his eyes never moving from Isis. "No matter. This will be fun."

Isis moved over to the corner on the other side of the room, raising one foot to rest on the wall behind her. She crossed her arms in front of her and leaned back, relaxing her posture so that she appeared at ease. Artemis and Alister sat down across from Aegaeon, but his eyes never moved from hers and she kept his gaze. In her mind, she debated the benefits of acting timid. It might cause him to drop his guard a bit, if she could trick him into overconfidence.

"I suppose we should start with why," Alister stated, pulling out some parchment and a nice pen. Aegaeon broke his gaze to look at Alister.

"I'll answer all your questions, but I'll only talk to her," he said, pointing at Isis, his shackles rattling every time he moved. Alister looked up at the guardian apprentice.

"I beg your pardon?"

A feral grin spread across Aegaeon's face again as he continued looking at Isis and he leaned forward. "In for a penny, in for a pound. We might as well disregard all our sacred laws. I'll talk to that creature and you can even stay in the room, if you wish. But I want her to sit here, across from me. Surely you're expecting her to read me, Lord Alister, my imperceptible tells. Why not give her the full advantage and a clear view?"

Alister looked to Artemis and then twisted in his chair to look back at Isis. She could see the hesitancy flicker across his expression. Isis raised an eyebrow and lowered her foot to the ground, recognizing the strategy of the apprentice. She wasn't sure if Set had ordered it or if Aegaeon was improvising, but either way, she knew how to counter it. Hopefully they would allow her to do so. Artemis also turned to look back at Isis, a question in her eyes. Isis lifted her chin up, giving her consent, and Artemis turned back to Alister, nodding once.

"Very well, Aegaeon," Alister conceded and Aegaeon couldn't hide his surprise. Alister stood up as did Artemis and Isis stepped forward as they moved back to where she had been standing. She cautiously approached the table, attempting to paint uncertainty in her expression as she pushed the seat Alister had occupied aside and moved the seat Artemis had been sitting in to the center. Lightly sitting down and folding her fingers together, she leaned forward and studied Aegaeon. He mirrored her actions, but started tapping the table again with one finger.

"How many died?" he asked, his gaze not moving from Isis.

"That's not how this works," Alister stated firmly from behind her. "Where did you get the device?"

"I guarantee you it's nowhere near her body count. I would bet the casualty count is under ten," Aegaeon ignored him as his gaze remained fixed on Isis, who arched an eyebrow. "Not so with you, is it? Your body count could fill a small continent. You don't even care, do you? All that blood on your hands, mostly innocent, it doesn't even faze you. To you, all of us are just expendable pawns, right?"

Isis looked him up and down. A healer had bandaged his nose, but his clothing was still bloodstained and his lip was still swollen. Large splotches of blood marred the otherwise finely-made blue material he wore. She watched him, trying to figure out how much he knew.

"Aegaeon, you said you would answer our questions."

"I can answer that if you wish," Isis said without looking away from Aegaeon. "Set and Pyra likely caused a small anomaly that he would have been sent to investigate. Normally guardians have protector escorts, but they're easy to sneak away from if one is truly determined. He would have been approached by an associate, probably one of their sons or maybe their grandson, and given a pitch. Obviously whatever they offered he accepted. This likely would have been sometime in the last three to five years, based on how they operate."

Aegaeon's eyes widened slightly for the briefest moment and Isis knew she had been mostly right. She tapped her thumbs together, biting the inside of her cheek.

"By my count, at least ten guardians were killed," she began, her eyes not moving from Aegaeon. "But it will increase, probably over the next few days. You didn't know that, though, did you? You're an insignificant pawn, a means to an end, so they wouldn't have told you everything they had planned."

Isis paused and leaned forward slightly, her eyes never moving from Aegaeon's face. "You're right about my being a killer, and that is precisely why I know you're not. I recognize killers and threats; you are neither. You ran from the flames with all the other young guardians and you stayed in the Meadows. You have nowhere to go. Your confidence now is false, the last attempt at some kind of control. You may be bitter and you may even hate the choices and actions of the guardian women, but you are no killer."

Isis lowered her head a little, still looking at Aegaeon and noticed a small bead of sweat crawling down his temple. "You are scared and you should be. This bravado is a smokescreen, one that is useless and reveals just how weak you are."

Isis stood from the table and turned to leave the room, ignoring the questioning looks the three guardians sent her way. She paused at the door, not bothering to look at Aegaeon.

"I would recommend cooperating with the guardians. They are the only chance you have to survive, seeing as how you've served your purpose in the eyes of the necromancers. Set doesn't like loose ends and his reach is far."

With that, Isis pulled open the door and stepped out in the dark quiet hall. Closing the door behind her, she leaned back against it and let out a long steadying breath. Almost immediately, she picked up the scent of saltwater in the hallway. She turned her head in the direction of the main part of the dungeon and saw Merrick, the head guardian of water on the male side, standing at the end of the hall, framed in bright light from the entrance. Isis swallowed and started moving in his direction, her movements as silent and stealthy as ever. He held his hands behind his back and looked incredibly proper, even in his singed clothing. His blue eyes studied her for a moment and he opened his mouth to speak.

"I don't have any proof and the guardians don't use aggressive interrogation techniques, so your apprentice probably won't give you up, but I know you're also allied with the necromancers," Isis said as she approached him. "An apprentice wouldn't act alone, not without getting caught. The chances of a head guardian not noticing an incendiary device are infinitesimal."

Merrick blinked at her a couple times. "I have no idea what you're talking about, protector. I recommend exercising caution when making such serious accusations."

She paused when she stood in front of him. "You will slip up eventually."

Crossing her arms in front of her chest, Isis watched him closely, looking for any sign of hesitation or fear. She saw none, indicating he was a much more dangerous opponent than Aegaeon. He didn't even flinch at the sight of her glowing eyes and made no attempt to goad her. Merrick just stood there, watching her with an unreadable expression.

"I am deeply ashamed that my apprentice and heir was corrupted so, but you cannot think that I would betray my own people in such a way," he said, a hint of pain in his words.

Isis' eyes followed him as he stepped past her, moving toward the interrogation rooms. Her hand slid down to the butterfly knife on her belt. The wise course of action would be to take care of the threat immediately, before any more damage could be done. Unfortunately, it was a poor strategy, one that would result in a number of messy complications. It wasn't worth it, Isis decided as she dropped her hand to her side.

"If you lay a hand on Passion, Electra, or anyone else I share genes with, I will rip your spine out," she warned calmly, just loud enough that he could hear her. Merrick stopped, his posture going rigid for a brief moment.

"Be careful, shape shifter. You're starting to sound like your father," he responded, just as quietly. Isis looked over at him, watching as he took a seat on the bench just outside the interrogation room the guardians were in.

Turning back to the hallway, she continued out into the round room and moved to leave the dungeons.

~~*~*~*

Shae inhaled deeply as she woke up from a light sleep. Her face scrunched up as she stretched her stiff limbs and took in the darkened healing wing. A few feet away, she saw a healer standing near a bed with her back to Shae. It was eerily quiet in the wing and Shae shivered, glancing over to the bed Jack was in. His eyes were still closed, but the burns had almost completely vanished. *Nice ability to have,* Shae thought with a smile. She turned when she heard a groan on her other side. Jet raised a hand to his face, rubbing his eyes. He blinked a few times and looked over at Shae.

"Welcome back, sleepyhead," Shae said softly, making sure not to disturb any of the other patients. Jet looked around the healing wing before turning his gaze back to Shae.

"How long have I been out?" he asked as he rubbed his temple. He gratefully accepted the glass of water Shae held out to him, nodding his thanks and drained the glass in one gulp.

"A while," Shae answered, unfolding her legs so she could rest them on the floor. "It will be dawn in a couple hours. Most of the others went back home to take care of things, make sure everything's okay there. I hung back to wait for you two sleeping beauties to wake up."

Jet let out a huff of laughter, which turned into a grimace of pain. Shae shook her foot, which felt like it was being jabbed with hundreds of pins and needles. She took the empty glass Jet handed back to her and set it on the table next to the bed.

"You feeling okay?" she asked Jet, resisting the urge to stomp her foot to rid it of the annoying sensation. Jet nodded and leaned back so he was resting on one elbow.

"Well as can be expected. My back still feels a bit tight, stings a little," he said, nodding over at Jack. "How is he?"

"He got burned pretty bad, but as you can see," Shae gestured to him with a sweeping motion of her arm, "those super experiment healing abilities have taken care of most of it. He'll probably wake up soon and then we can —"

A bloodcurdling shriek echoed throughout the healing ward, causing all three shape shifters to stiffen in surprise. Shae jumped to her feet and Jack sat up in the bed, his glowing brown eyes snapping open. Shae looked over to where the healer had been standing, watching as the young woman crumpled. Another shout, from closer, echoed throughout the large space as a young male apprentice fell, dropping the tools he had been carrying, which clattered noisily on the ground. A cacophony of screaming began echoing throughout the healing wing.

Shae swiftly started toward the woman healer as Jet threw the covers off his legs and hurried over to where the second healer had fallen. Shae knelt beside the young woman, her eyes widening when she saw the growing puddle of blood.

"My hands, my hands," the girl whimpered, her entire face contorting in pain. Shae looked at her hands, which were clenched tightly. Blood was leaking out of her fists. Shae gently grasped one arm, intending to get a closer look at her hand. She was stunned with the flesh of the arm slid off as if it were tissue paper. Shae cringed and immediately dropped the flesh, brushing it off her hands. She struggled not to vomit or react too much, though her stomach was doing flips. The girl cried in pain as Shae tried to figure out what to do. Looking up, she saw Jack standing nearby. He was looking around the healing wing, unaffected by the horrible wails of pain.

"We should get the healers," he stated. Shae nodded and was about to get up to do that when the doors burst open and Amethyst walked in, followed closely by her apprentice, Eir. Both women stared at the sight before them and then Amethyst whispered something to Eir. As the apprentice dashed off to carry out whatever she had been told, Amethyst approached Shae and knelt beside the ailing healer.

"I think I may have hurt her more," Shae whispered apologetically as Amethyst inspected the girl's arm. The healer shook her head, stripping off the silky lavender-colored robe she had been wearing over her nightclothes.

"It's not your fault. You could not have known, especially if what I suspect is correct," Amethyst responded, looking to the side when Eir re-entered with a few other healing apprentices and healers. Their arms were filled with various supplies, which they promptly laid down on the tables at the back of the room.

"Bring me a blanket," Amethyst ordered and Eir hurried to comply. Amethyst turned her attention to Shae. "We're going to roll her onto a blanket and then carry her over to that empty bed over there."

Shae nodded, looking over her shoulder when Eir returned and unfolded the blanket, laying it beside the fallen healer who was still whimpering in pain.

"Eir, send some messengers to check the healers quarters and send one to get Artemis. Tell her to have a messenger contact the men, see if something similar is happening there," Amethyst ordered and then turned back to Shae. "Ready?"

Shae nodded and helped Amethyst with the fallen healer. Once they had gotten her to a bed, Amethyst turned her attention to the other healers.

"Shae?"

Shae looked over to the doors when she heard Electra's voice. The young guardian moved over to her, followed closely by Passion. They both looked alarmed and stared at the chaotic healing wing. All of the previously empty beds were now filled with writhing healers. The patients who had been ordered to spend the night in the healing wards were now awake and sitting up, distressed by the scene before them.

"What happened?" Electra and Passion asked at the same time. Shae shrugged and spread her hands. The lights in the healing wing suddenly brightened significantly and if it were possible, it looked even worse in the light.

"I-I don't know. One minute it was quiet and the next . . . this."

Shae looked down, noticing the blood on her hands again. She swallowed the warm feeling in her throat and tried not to be sick. Electra noticed her discomfort and moved over to a table, dipped a small towel in water and returned to the shape shifter's side, offering it to her. Shae smiled in gratitude and scrubbed her hands clean. She looked over to the entrance when Artemis strode inside, walking straight to Amethyst.

"Will this nightmare never end?" Electra asked, running a hand through her hair. Shae noticed that Electra was in her sleepwear, as were most of the other guardians. She couldn't remember ever seeing a guardian in sleepwear before. Jet moved over to them, scrubbing a hand through his hair.

"You're looking better," Passion commented with a small smile, patting his shoulder as she and Electra hurried over to Amethyst. They were soon helping with the healers, who Amethyst ordered brought over to one side of the room. Jet looked over to Jack, who was standing a few feet behind Shae. He was watching everything intently, not moving at all.

"Is this Grenich?" Jet asked. The experiment glanced over at him before looking back to the room, scratching the back of his head.

"I don't know. It's not like anything I've ever seen before," he answered. The doors opened again and Silver moved inside. The light sparkled on the goggles atop her head and in her small arms was an enormous tome. Both Amethyst and Artemis looked over when she approached them. She pointed to something in the book and both women read what she was directing their attention to. The color seemed to drain from Artemis' face and she covered her mouth with one hand.

"That does not look good," Shae said under her breath.

"It's not," a soft voice came from behind them. Both Jet and Shae turned, surprised to see Isis standing there. Neither had heard her approach or even realized she was still in the Meadows. She stood with arms crossed, her gaze fixed on Silver. She turned her attention to Jet and Shae.

"The impulsiveness of guardian men may have just killed us," she said.

CHAPTER FOUR

Isis sat next to Jet and the Four, waiting for Amethyst to give her testimony before the High Council. Her glowing green eyes wandered over all the stern-looking guardians in the towering seats at the front of the room. The few guardian healers who hadn't been afflicted had spent most of the night caring for those who were and Isis could faintly hear the moans of the sick and dying in the healing wing. Amethyst had wisely instructed the uninfected healers to not use their magic. No one objected to or questioned her orders this time.

Looking around the room, Isis took note of how bare it was aside from them. In the row behind them, Jensen and Malone were sitting quietly, but the rest of the room was empty. The guardians were all helping in the now overcrowded healing wing, as was Orion, who had been summoned to help in the early morning hours. Many of the members of the High Council were still wearing bloodstained clothes, having come directly from their healing wings. The compassion of the guardians was possible to exploit, but it also provided some very valuable advantages. Isis looked over to her left when Shae crossed one leg over her other, shifting her position again. She was very uneasy, likely rattled after seeing the gruesome effects of the mystery illness up close. As if feeling eyes on her, Shae looked over at Isis and offered a thin watery smile, leaning back in her seat. Isis let her gaze roam over the high vaulted ceiling before it returned back to the High Council.

"Lady Amethyst, thank you for being here today," Aneurin began, tapping his thumbs together. "Could you please inform us of the situation? As best you understand it?"

Amethyst crossed her arms over her chest and narrowed her eyes at the members of the High Council. "Were I a lesser guardian, I would respond that a fool ordered healers to go against common sense and now we find ourselves in an even worse situation than we had been in."

There was some grumbling among the guardians and even Jade's eyes widened a little at the head healer's icy tone. Eshmun, who was leaning against the table a few feet behind Amethyst, looked over at the head healer but remained quiet. Donovan, ducked his chin briefly, and he looked rather impressed with the defiant healer.

"Amethyst, please," Adonia spoke softly, but still with an authoritative edge. Though she looked a little tired, she was as intimidating as ever. Amethyst rubbed the side of her neck briefly, closing her eyes and dropping her head for a moment. Isis studied the head healer, reading the frustration she was feeling.

"Please forgive me, it has been a very long night and will almost certainly be a very long day," the healer apologized. "The healers are afflicted with a sickness that hasn't been seen since the third generation of guardians. One of the symptoms is that it causes the flesh to thin so much that it slides off at the gentlest touch. Aside from that, it also causes a high fever and pain and it drains the healer of their abilities. The disease is fatal if not treated and the afflicted can last for months, always tormented by the pain."

Amethyst paused briefly, looking back to where the shape shifters were and then to the High Council again.

"This sickness has only ever afflicted healers. As the High Council knows, healers absorb the harm done to their patient. Our bodies are stronger and more able to repair damage or illness. The only thing we've ever been susceptible to, aside from weapons, is this virus. It lies dormant in a patient until a healer absorbs it and then it becomes active. I had the messengers collect the accounts of witnesses to last night's attack and every single witness spoke of seeing what they described as wisps or webbings of flame in the air. Astrea and Nemesis spoke with the prisoners in the areas of the dungeon where the flames reached, all of whom reported seeing something similar. I believe this was how the virus was released."

Isis looked over her shoulder when the door opened and Lilly entered quietly. She moved over to the wall and then proceeded up the aisle to the row in which they were sitting. Taking a seat beside Jet, she gently kissed his cheek before turning her attention to the High Council.

"We lost eleven guardians in the attack," Eshmun spoke up, shifting his weight a little. "There are 27 afflicted male healers and 22 women; most of them are apprentices or messengers. We're the immune system of the Meadows as well as Earth. If we don't find a way to remedy this, we won't be able to keep the illnesses in check. Already we're struggling."

Isis looked over to where Donovan was sitting, his head resting on his hand. He had been doodling on his writing pad as he usually did, but had stopped the second he heard the number of healers afflicted. His attention was now fixed solely on the two head healers. Isis heard Jensen lean forward behind her.

"We have to talk after this," he whispered next to her ear. She nodded once and turned her attention back to the proceedings. Amethyst took a step forward and folded her hands in front of her, swallowing. Isis raised an eyebrow and sat up even more, noticing the change in body language.

"We have only ever had one remedy for this illness, Betha's tears," she began carefully and instantly the High Council members began murmuring, most of them in disapproval. Adonia ran a hand over her face before resting it on the side of her mouth. Artemis looked as uncomfortable as Isis had ever seen her look. Adonia glanced over at her and the two women exchanged a look.

"Uh oh," Jade whispered next to her. Both Alex and Shae looked bewildered. Jet's jaw clenched and Lilly looked worried. Isis glanced behind her at Malone and Jensen, both of whom looked as though their mouths were about to drop open.

"That was lost back in the eighth generation, after the incident we unanimously agreed never to speak of again," Aneurin said firmly. Donovan rolled his eyes over in his direction but remained quiet. Isis pursed her lips, wondering exactly what it was she had somehow missed in her research. Judging from the reaction a simple suggestion got, it was something rather important. Her gaze next turned to the apprentices, who looked just as lost as Shae and Alex.

"It was lost, not destroyed," Amethyst answered just as firmly, crossing her arms over her chest once again. "It was in the Box of Original Elements, which was stolen and hidden. There is one who knows where it is. We were lucky, for centuries, but now I believe it is time for drastic action."

"Amethyst, if you're about to suggest what I think you are," Aneurin said, closing his eyes as he massaged his brow. "We cannot risk more guardian lives on what might be a fool's errand."

"No, we cannot spare any more guardians," Amethyst agreed. "However, I was thinking the protectors could help us. They are better qualified for what I have in mind."

She gestured to Eshmun. "We discussed this at length last night and concluded that this is our best and quite possibly only chance. Eshmun will explain our idea while I talk to the protectors. I suggest we meet in about fifteen minutes to see whether or not we're all in accordance."

"I believe that is acceptable," Adonia said, rising a little stiffly. "We'll meet in the adjoining chambers."

Isis watched as the High Council filed out the door to the side, disappearing in the adjoining room. Nemesis and another guard stood in front of the door, fixing their eyes on the opposite wall. She was intrigued to hear Amethyst's plan and turned her attention back to the head healer who stepped through the gate and approached the protectors. She sat on the bench in front of the Four, twisting herself so that she was facing them and folding her legs under her.

"Amethyst, you cannot possibly think you can trust her," Jet began. Amethyst looked over at him.

"Would you mind actually listening to my idea before jumping to conclusions?" she asked, but it sounded more like a statement. Isis recognized the edge in her tone. There was a similar one in Orion's whenever he spoke with Shocker, which wasn't that often. Amethyst turned her attention back to the Four.

"Aside from Jade, do any of you know about Eris?" Amethyst asked, drumming her fingers on the back of the bench. Both Shae and Alex shook their heads, but Isis didn't respond. Amethyst glanced at her, but didn't comment.

"Eris was Artemis' eldest daughter, disowned for crimes against the Meadows and Earth. She was born with the ability to influence people's wills and their perception, a very dangerous skill and one that's strictly regulated. To take away a person's free will is considered a heinous act, as you're all aware. Eris was born a trickster, but she went too far and forced a number of people on Earth to worship her as a goddess," Amethyst paused, picking at her dress. "The guardians were able to repair much of the damage she did, but Eris' actions were deemed unforgiveable and she was sentenced to life in the depths of the dungeons, which is reserved for our most dangerous adversaries. She has been there ever since."

"And she knows where the Box of Original Elements is?" Isis asked.

Amethyst nodded. "When her crimes were discovered, she fled the Meadows and for a great many years, she managed to evade both our trackers and the protectors. Before she was caught, Eris managed to steal the box and took it to the Seelie Court, where she used her abilities to gain access to one of their sacred islands. By the time the trackers were able to find her, she had already hidden it and hasn't ever revealed where it is. Time passed and many guardians forgot about the Box of Original Elements, since it was basically a relic."

"That was unwise," Isis observed and Amethyst nodded in response. She was one of the few guardians who didn't take offense at the bluntness of experiments. In this case, Isis thought it was likely the healer agreed with her.

"Unfortunately, now we urgently need what's inside that box," Amethyst continued. "I hope we have something we can offer Eris, some kind of bargain we can strike for her cooperation."

"And if you can't?" Jade asked, sounding as if she really didn't like Amethyst's idea. Isis looked between her and Amethyst, noticing the head healer's eyes briefly traveling over her.

"Then I don't really know —"

"I could make her talk," Isis interrupted, causing all the protectors to look over at her. "If it came down to that, I could make her take us to the box."

The other members of the Four looked at her, horrified, while Jet ran a hand over his face and shook his head in disapproval. Isis shrugged and leaned back in her seat. She knew they didn't like being reminded of what she was, but they didn't have the time for mollycoddling. If she had to use more aggressive methods, than she would.

"Unfortunately, any use of force is considered torture and therefore strictly forbidden by our sacred laws," Amethyst was quick to remind her. Isis studied the head healer for a moment before her gaze traveled to the guards, who still stood in front of the door.

"Your sacred laws, not mine," she pointed out, looking back to Amethyst. "You might need an experiment, whether you like it or not."

Isis got to her feet and made her way out of the row, not looking back at the protectors as she stepped into the aisle. From what she had observed of the guardians and the High Council, Isis was almost certain they would approve Amethyst's idea. Protectors were somewhat expendable and in their eyes, she certainly was. It wasn't the best plan, but at the moment, it was the only one they had. Isis didn't like the idea of going to a strange world, but she could work with it. She was modified to be adaptable.

Isis could hear the quiet whispers of the protectors and the head healer behind her as she pulled open the door and stepped out into the hall. She moved away from the door and waited patiently, watching the other end of the hall. After a moment, the door opened again and Jensen stepped out. He noticed her and closed the distance between them, moving to the other side of the hall so he stood across from her. She watched him, waiting for him to speak.

Jensen glanced back to the High Council room, sticking his hands in his pockets. "Why don't you just do what you did back at the bank, when I was wounded?"

Isis half-smiled and leaned back against the wall behind her, holding her hands behind her back. She had anticipated the question and was thankful only a few shape shifters knew about that particular ability. If the guardians found out, Isis wasn't sure how they would react and she didn't like dealing with uncertainties.

"My ability to heal others is different from guardian healers," she explained quietly, keeping her senses sharp for any unwanted company. "Theirs is innate and linked to their natural compassion. They absorb damage and repair it. Mine is most likely a result of the modifications. I have to spill blood and sacrifice energy in order to heal wounds. While it might heal this sickness, I would probably only be able to help four healers, five at most. I don't believe that would remedy the problem or make any kind of measurable difference. The cost would almost certainly outweigh the benefits."

Jensen stared at her. "You can't heal others without harming yourself?"

"As far as I can tell, that's accurate."

Jensen briefly looked at his feet as a messenger passed by them. Isis turned to watch the woman disappear around a bend, likely heading for the stairway. She looked back at Jensen, noticing a faint hint of guilt in his expression.

"You needn't beat yourself up. I healed you of my own volition and incurred no lasting harm," Isis said, attempting to be reassuring. She didn't enjoy when protectors experienced guilt and self-condemnation. It was so unnecessary.

The soft sound of moaning from the healing wing could be heard a little more clearly out in the bright hallway. She moved further down the hall, heading for the balcony. Jensen followed her and they soon stood in the bright natural light, out of the gloom. Isis closed her eyes and lifted her face up toward the ceiling, allowing the pleasant coolness of the Pearl Castle to wash over her.

She glanced at Jensen in her periphery vision as they stopped to lean on a railing. Turning her attention back out over the castle, Isis observed the messengers in their pastel-colored clothing below them. There were fewer due to the early hour. Most of the damage from the previous night had been scrubbed away and a few messengers were sweeping up the last remnants of fire. Now the main hall just looked unusually bare.

"You had a very strong reaction to Amethyst's suggestion," Isis observed, drawing Jensen's attention to her.

"Did I?" Jensen asked in a way that suggested he knew exactly what she was talking about. Isis turned so that she fully faced him.

"You have heard of Eris before," Isis mentioned. Jensen ran a hand through his hair and nodded, grimacing as though the very idea of Eris was unpleasant.

"Nero and I only heard stories from his older brothers," Jensen said with a shrug. "And of course, Jet has a few opinions on her and I have always trusted his judgment. She's trouble, Isis. I don't think Amethyst's idea is a good one."

Isis straightened up, running her hands over the smooth railing. "It's not ideal, but it's the only one we have at the moment. The protectors and guardians don't have the time to come up with a better one. The situation needs to be remedied as soon as possible, before Set and Pyra can press their advantage."

Jensen leaned down on the railing and pressed his hands in front of him and Isis noticed the tension he was holding in his shoulders. She drummed her fingers on the railing, contemplating the possible advantages she might find. Taking a powerful and potentially volatile guardian into an unfamiliar land was not the best situation. But it was exactly the kind of adversity she was conditioned to make the most of.

"I'm sure Jet and the guardians will take all possible precautions," Isis mentioned and Jensen looked over at her. He offered her a half-smile, obviously not reassured.

"If the High Council decides in favor of Amethyst's plan," he pointed out softly. Isis shrugged, already certain the High Council would rule in favor of the head healer. They really had no other choice and their history suggested they saw protectors as disposable. Isis looked up when the door to the High Council meeting room was pulled open and Jet stormed out, looking irate. He didn't even glance at Jensen when the younger protector called his name. Isis watched as he descended the stairs, disappearing in the direction of the healing wing.

"Where can I find out more about Eris?" Isis asked, looking over Jensen's shoulder to where the other three of the Four were exiting the meeting chamber. Alex and Shae looked a little worried, but Jade had an expression of anger.

"I imagine the guardians will have some information on her. Remington and the Deverells will also know a fair amount," Jensen replied, straightening up. He met her gaze and tilted forward slightly. Isis also leaned forward, resting her head against his. She briefly closed her eyes and focused on the warmth of his skin. It was pleasant.

"See you back at the mansion?" Jensen whispered and she nodded. As they broke contact, Jensen offered her one last smile and turned to the stairway, moving toward the healing wing. Isis turned to where the other three were standing a few feet away. Jade's stiff posture practically radiated fury and her nostrils flared a little.

"I take it the High Council has accepted Amethyst's plan," Isis stated, holding her hands behind her. Jade nodded once, massaging the back of her neck.

"I understand why and I know it's a necessary evil, but that doesn't mean I like it," she said quietly. "It cost a lot of protectors' lives to capture Eris. She is cunning and smart, not to mention powerful. Letting her out is opening Pandora's Box."

"So what is the plan?" Isis asked, disregarding Jade's concerns for the time being. Until she knew more about Eris, she really couldn't speak to how justifiable they were.

"Hecate and Jet still need to contact the Seelie Court, which they'll do this afternoon," Alex answered, shifting her weight and crossing her arms. "If all goes well, which it likely will, we leave in three days with a small group yet to be decided."

"It would be wise to bring at least Jack with us," Isis remarked. "And Radar would also be a valuable asset."

"We'll probably decide that tomorrow," Jade said. "But that definitely seems like a good idea."

Over Alex's shoulder, Isis could see the rest of the meeting hall slowly filter out of the room. Nobody looked overly happy with the decision and Isis resolved to learn as much about Eris as she possibly could before meeting her.

~~*~*~*

Deep in the depths of the dungeons in the Pearl Castle, most of the cells were empty. There was one cell in particular that was unlike the others, separated in its own section so the prisoner had no contact with other prisoners. The cell sat alone in the center of an enormous well-lit room. Everything around the single cell was painted in different shades of gray and in the ceiling high above, skylights beamed down the warm rays of the sun, ensuring the prisoner received an adequate amount of natural light. When the sun set, there were torches on the wall. The room with the single cell was never to be entirely engulfed in darkness or shadows. She knew how to use unlit areas to her advantage.

The inside of the cell resembled a lavish bedroom, with towering bookcases and comfortable furniture. There was a desk complete with stationary and a variety of writing instruments, all of which were often used as were the paintbrushes and canvases. A number of enormous paintings were resting against the walls. There was a closet on one side of the cell and a bathroom on the opposite side. It more resembled a room for royalty than a dungeon cell.

A single woman occupied the opulent cell and she was often found stretched out across the chaise lounge, engrossed in a book. Aside from the guards, few guardians came down so deep in the dungeons. Only Astrea and Nemesis were permitted to interact with the woman regularly, who was considered one of the most dangerous prisoners in the Meadows.

Passion followed Nemesis silently down the stairs, her mind racing as it had been since the High Council meeting the previous day. She almost laughed as she remembered when she dreaded seeing Roan in the dungeons. Given the choice, she would have talked to him for hours rather than see her older sister for even one minute. She hadn't seen Eris since she had been recaptured and brought back to the Meadows after her rebellion. That had been more than two-hundred years ago by Earth measures, Passion realized with surprise. She tightened her already-tight ponytail and smoothed her dress. Passion knew her mother visited Eris every decade or so. It was the only time she ever saw Artemis look sad.

"I apologize for all the precautions," Nemesis spoke, bringing Passion out of her thoughts. "I assure you they are all quite necessary."

Passion nodded, keeping her eyes forward on the long steep staircase they were descending. "Nemesis, I haven't seen her since . . ."

Nemesis looked over her shoulder when Passion trailed off and Passion was sure she could read the uncertainty in her expression. Passion looked out one of the windows in the stairwell before meeting Nemesis' gaze again.

"I don't know how to talk to her," Passion finally admitted under her breath. Nemesis paused and leaned back against the wall, her dark brown eyes fixing on the younger guardian. Passion didn't flinch under her scrutinizing gaze.

"Lady Electra had a similar concern about her twin. I could see it when I first started training her. She didn't know how to talk to her, yet she found a way. Though she has time on her side, whereas you do not," Nemesis said, looking down the stairway, a thoughtful expression on her face.

"I regularly see your sister and she is a very angry individual, as she always has been. She frequently lashes out at the guards and your mother and I will not lie, her tongue is as sharp as her mind. Yet, that anger covers a lot of hurt. I don't believe Eris is malicious at heart, though she would like everyone to believe otherwise. More than anything, I think she desires what most of us do: acceptance. Her pride prevents her from reaching out and you must tread carefully because of this. Keep in mind that our survival rests on Amethyst's plan."

Passion stared at Nemesis. "Right. No pressure."

Nemesis laughed. "I have faith in you, Passion. Just listen to your heart and the words will come."

Nemesis offered her a small smile and nodded over her shoulder. The two women descended the rest of the stairs. When they reached the bottom, Passion looked over to the skylights, which filled the room with a soft natural light. There was a quiet scraping sound and Passion noticed a few messengers scrubbing the last evidence of the flames on the far wall, supervised by a very stern-looking guard. She let out her breath and walked forward toward the glass cell, heading to the spot where visitors normally sat, while Nemesis stayed back by the stairwell.

There were two comfortable-looking chairs sitting across from one of the walls with a small wooden table between them. *They must have replaced whatever burned during the celebration,* she realized as she admired the new furniture. Passion ran her fingers over the smooth table briefly before gathering her nerve and looking toward the glass wall towering in front of her.

Eris was hanging upside down on a bar, her back to Passion. Her arms were stretched out, slowly moving in a slithering motion. The sunlight gleamed on the guardian glisten in her flesh. The controlled movement was oddly hypnotic and Passion couldn't help but stare. Eris was dressed in dark-colored clothing and her long black hair flowed down over her head, almost touching the dark blue carpet beneath her.

"Last time I checked, it's too early for my next meal and I don't have any visitors scheduled for another few years. Though granted, my sense of time is a bit skewed thanks to being locked away like some animal in a zoo," Eris spoke without turning around. "What do you want?"

Passion stared at her and opened her mouth to speak, but hesitated. None of the memories she had of her older sister were pleasant. Truth be told, she had been glad when Eris had been locked away and stricken from most of their books. Passion couldn't help but feel some small amount of guilt for that relief. Her eyes wandered over to the large canvases resting against the opposite wall of the cell. They fell on a remarkably realistic painting of three golden apples on a simple plate in front of a mirror. Passion raised an eyebrow briefly, unsurprised that her sister would paint something like that. Eris was known for needling people in any way she could.

"Either speak or go. You are ruining my meditation," her voice was husky, similar to Passion's. The younger guardian turned her gaze back to her sister.

Passion swallowed, steeling her nerves. "Eris."

Eris turned her head to the side, looking at Passion out of her peripheral vision. She reached up for the bar and swung her legs over her head, somersaulting off the bar. Spinning around, she stared at Passion and smiled widely. Her icy blue eyes sparkled with amusement and something else that Passion couldn't identify. She had painted her lips the brightest shade of ruby red and eyeliner with smoky eyeshadow made her eyes stand out. Passion noticed she wore pants and a tight undershirt, obviously still having an aversion to dresses.

"If it isn't my baby sister," Eris cooed lightly, cocking her hip. "My how you've grown."

Eris wandered over to the table in her cell, where a

decanter of water and glasses sat. She poured herself a glass, swished the water around briefly, and looked over at Passion, sipping the clear liquid.

"I'd be lying if I said I wasn't surprised," Eris commented after swallowing the water and putting the glass aside. "I'd almost be touched if I didn't suspect the hand of another behind this impromptu visit."

Passion licked her lips and smiled slightly. "How are you?"

Eris' arched an eyebrow. "I haven't seen you in over two hundred years and now you're suddenly curious about my welfare. Really, Passion?"

"You're my sister —"

"Oh if only I weren't in this cell. I'd make you smash your head against that wall to be spared your nauseating sentiment," Eris commented wistfully as she moved across the cell and grabbed a cerulean blouse that was draped over the lounge. "You wouldn't be down here unless ordered to be, so do tell. What exactly does the High Council want?"

Eris smiled craftily as she buttoned up the blouse, watching her new visitor like a cat watching a mouse. Passion looked over to the base of the stairs where Nemesis still stood watch. She cautiously took another step closer to the glass that separated her from her sister.

"You undoubtedly saw the red flames during the Changing of Seasons ceremony. The guards reported that it reached the dungeons, as did some of the other prisoners," Passion began. Eris moved over to a chair in the cell, lightly trailing her fingers over it.

"Yes, it was boring, an old fire guardian trick. Though it did make for some pretty colors," Eris mentioned, tilting her head toward a canvas. Passion looked over at it, noticing the brightly colored canvas was glistening, indicating the paint was still wet. It was another impressively realistic image, one that could almost pass for a photograph. The image was of Eris standing in front of blood red flames, which towered behind the glass. Eris looked demure, a small smile playing on her lips, and she held her arms crossed over her chest. She wore an emerald green shirt, which stood out from the bright red flames.

"You painted a selfie," Passion said slowly, not believing her eyes. "The castle was on fire, people were dying, and . . . you painted a selfie?"

"Is that what they're called these days?" Eris asked as she studied the canvas. "Cute."

Passion ran her hands over her face, not understanding her sister's indifference or why she would want to capture such a horrible moment. Eris truly mystified her and Passion once again questioned the wisdom of asking for her help. Looking to the side, she watched as the messengers and guards left, obviously for a break. They passed by Nemesis, who nodded in greeting. Turning back to the cell, Passion saw Eris was also watching them go. Turning her blue gaze back to Passion, a crafty smile split Eris' bright red lips.

"I am aware of the whole tiff with the Grenich Corporation, so let me guess: Pyra was the culprit," Eris said as she dropped into one of the chairs in the cell, crossing one leg over the other. "Things have certainly been rather interesting in my absence, according to the little gossip that reaches my ears. I heard you're now the mother of two bastards, twin girls. Never one to do anything half way, are you? Artemis must be *so* proud. Tell me, little sister, did Chaos really kill and resurrect one of your daughters? Is she truly the dangerous little fiend I have heard so many nervous whispers about the past few years?"

Passion felt her breath freeze in her chest and she forced herself not to react to Eris' words, knowing that was exactly what the other guardian wanted. Eris' eyes widened briefly and her mouth dropped open. She threw back her head and laughed, resting a hand on her chest.

"So it is true then. Oh that is *amazing,*" Eris leaned

forward as if she were about to share a secret with Passion, her eyes sparkling with amusement. "I must know: does it hurt every time you see her? Is she a reminder of just how much of a failure you are? Or do you fear that your daughter has become a monster just like her —"

"Stop!" Passion snapped, her eyes blazing. Her voice echoed about the empty room, a hollow sound. Eris' grin became a little more subtle, but still sharp as a knife as she slowly straightened up and sat back in the chair. Passion remained quiet, refusing to give her elder sister the satisfaction of seeing how deeply her words cut. Eris looked so much like their mother, save for those pale blue eyes. How they could be so different, Passion had no idea. She and Artemis had a volatile relationship, but Artemis had never been outright cruel to her nor did she ever take pleasure in Passion's pain.

"It would appear I've touched a nerve. How interesting. Predictable, but still interesting," Eris observed, pursing her lips as she rested her head between her index finger and thumb. "Will you ever get to the point of this little visit? The anticipation is killing me."

Passion crossed her arms over her chest and thought over her words again. It seemed a few degrees colder in this room, but she theorized it was her mind playing tricks on her. At least she could feel the warm light on her from the skylights. It was a small comfort, but a comfort nonetheless.

"Timidity doesn't suit you, Passion," Eris warned, annoyance lacing her words. "Speak your peace and be gone. And be sure to take that damn statue with you."

Passion looked back to where Nemesis stood, unbothered by Eris' words. *She must be used to this by now,* Passion thought. She looked back to Eris' newest canvas, noticing the small wisps drifting by in the flame. Her sister obviously still had an incredible eye for detail.

"There was a virus in the red flames, one which affects only the healers and it hasn't been seen in many years,"

Passion began and Eris chuckled bitterly, rising to her feet. She sauntered over to the glass wall, studying Passion. The other guardian met her sister's gaze, not flinching. After a moment, Eris mirrored her sister's stance. She was a couple inches shorter than Passion, but held herself confidently.

"Ah, I understand now. The High Council needs Betha's Tears and you're here to convince me to reveal where I hid the Original Elements, right? Are you going to try appealing to my better nature?" Eris asked, raising an eyebrow. "Or is there going to be torture? Are you going to try to force the answer out of me?"

"No, never," Passion said, aghast at the suggestion. Eris looked disappointed and glanced down at her nails, examining them briefly.

"Shame. What fun we could have had," she sighed as she turned back and began to walk around her cell. "If you're here to ask nicely, you've wasted a trip. I have no intention of telling any damn guardian where the box is. The healers can rot for all I care."

Passion licked her lips again, knowing Eris was still trying to get under her skin. The guardian leaned down and plucked a thick book off a lower shelf, opening it and flipping through the pages.

"The High Council would never be able to trust your word, even if you were being cooperative, so a team of protectors will accompany you to the Island of Avalon in the Seelie Court, where you'll show them to the box," Passion continued, massaging the side of her neck. "Jet and Lilly will be negotiating with the Seelie Court. We have a truce with them, so they will likely be amenable. If they agree to allow us to investigate, you'll be leaving with the protectors in two days."

Eris scoffed as she turned a page in her book. "Adonia must be *incredibly* desperate if she agreed to such a poorly conceived plan."

"In exchange for your help, the High Council will

consider reducing your sentence and I will support such a reduction, as will mother," Passion continued, ignoring Eris' bitterness. "We will also support your name being rewritten into the family tree. You will be recognized as being from the line of Betha again."

Eris snapped the book shut and the sudden loud noise caused Passion to flinch. She stared at Eris, whose eyes narrowed. Though her eyes didn't change color like Passion's, they did darken significantly when she was angered.

"I don't care about nor want empty titles or some meaningless lineage. And the High Council's opinion means less than nothing to me," Eris growled, her eyes flickering with rage. The lights around them brightened and then dimmed before returning to normal. Passion swallowed and nodded, unnerved by the sudden change in Eris's demeanor. Her sister's moods could change in the blink of an eye and it was one of the reasons Passion had always feared her.

"Well, it seems we actually have something in common," she offered with a small smile. Eris let out a huff of breath, leaning back against her desk as she reopened the book and turned her attention back to its pages. Her posture became relaxed once again and the anger disappeared from her face as she turned a page.

"This team of protectors who will escort me, I assume it includes one of my nieces?" Eris mentioned, a cunning smile dancing across her face. "A little bird told me she's one of the Four spoken of in guardian prophecies."

"Eris, we really don't have times for games —"

"Dear sister, there's *always* time for games," Eris interrupted without looking up from her book, lazily turning a page. "What is she considered anyway? A zombie? Perhaps a revenant? Cannon fodder for the High Council to use as they see fit?"

Passion's fist clenched briefly. "Why are you like this? Is it not enough that your people are suffering? Do you have no heart?"

Eris slowly closed the book and set it off to the side, resting her hands in her lap. The corners of her lips curled up in a bitter smile, which more resembled a sneer, and she turned her attention back to Passion. "First, the guardians are not *my* people, something they have made crystal clear practically since the day I came into this world. Even before my alleged crimes, they were looking for a way to be rid of me. Do not insult my intelligence by acting like I owe some kind of loyalty to them. Second, you question whether I have a heart? That's a bit hypocritical of you, dear sister, who never once came to see me after my imprisonment. How many times have you visited your lover, I wonder? And yes, I am aware that the assassin is in a cell in the upper level of the dungeons."

Passion looked off to the side, "I didn't think you wanted to —"

Eris suddenly moved so that she was directly across from Passion and slammed her hands on the glass, causing Passion to flinch again and take a small step back. "Your attempt to assuage your own guilt bores me, Passion. I don't like being bored. If you're going to try to manipulate me into helping, you damn well better put more effort into it."

Passion clenched her jaw, feeling her frustration build. "Fine. What do you want, Eris? What can the High Council offer you?"

Eris dropped her hands from the glass and stepped back, moving over to the lounge and dropping down on it, lying on her back. She trailed her fingers on the floor, leaving sparkling streaks behind her fingertips. The cell dampened her abilities, but didn't strip them from her.

"Who says I have a price? I may be perfectly content in my cage. It has a certain je ne sais quoi," Eris mused, crossing one leg over the other. "At least it's better than running around with a bunch of shape shifters. You might as well lock me in a barn with livestock. Speaking of:

bestiality? Really, Passion? Now that's one thing I certainly didn't see coming."

Passion ran her hands through her hair as her sister snickered, realizing she was getting nowhere. She breathed in and out, glancing once more at Nemesis.

"Eris, I didn't have to come here and I realize I probably shouldn't have," she began carefully. Eris rolled over so she lay on her stomach, turning her face toward her sister. Passion was struck by how extraordinarily young Eris looked. Most would think she was Isis and Electra's age. Eris had always had very youthful features and looked younger than Passion. Eris knew it and had learned long ago how to use it to her advantage. Even now, Passion was sure she knew how to manipulate the guards tasked with watching her.

"I know I have no right to ask you for any favors and I know you are not likely to grant me any," Passion continued, keeping her voice calm and even. "But I . . . Eris, I beg you to cooperate with the protectors and help us stop this virus. If not for us, do it for yourself. I know you have no love for the guardians, and perhaps that's justified, but the necromancers would be even worse. I don't want to see any harm come to my daughter or to you. If I lost either one of you, it would crush me. And I don't think Electra could survive losing her sister a second time."

A small half-smile split Eris' bright red lips. "My, my, my, Passion, is this humility? Apparently an old dog can learn new tricks. Your abilities to manipulate are close to being promising. I almost feel bad that they're wasted on me."

Eris closed her eyes and turned her face toward the ceiling. "You know as well as I that I have no choice in this matter, so I am puzzled as to what exactly you're asking of me. Mere cooperation?" She clicked her tongue and shook her head. "Cooperation is not in my nature."

"I'm aware," Passion said under her breath, feeling

frustrated. "I'm sure I'll see you again in a couple days, if I'm not busy in the healing wings. Please at least think over what I've said and what's at stake."

Eris waved a hand dismissively and Passion walked away from the cell, moving to where Nemesis still stood watch. They moved up the stairs in silence. Each step felt heavier than the last and Passion found herself getting tired just thinking about the long day ahead. With the shortage of healers and the overcrowded healing wing, many guardians were pulling double duty and filling in for the fallen healers.

"Try not to let your heart be troubled, my Lady," Nemesis said as they continued up the stairs. "As I mentioned earlier, your sister isn't malicious, just angry. She may yet do the right thing, but perhaps in her own way."

"I wish I shared your faith, Nemesis," Passion replied as they stepped out into the small area leading to the stairs. "But from what I've seen, Eris hasn't changed at all since her imprisonment. That does not bode well for us."

Nemesis opened the door and Passion stepped out, watching as Nemesis locked the door behind them with a key from the large keyring she was wearing on her belt. Passion wished the guard a good day and continued on her way to the busy healing wings, where she knew Electra would already be helping. Many of the younger guardians had immediately volunteered to help with the sick and wounded, which took some of the burden off the older guardians. It was a small comfort in the face of such suffering.

~~*~*~*

Late at night, all was quiet in the mansion. The halls had been emptier than usual for the past few months, since the war with Grenich had intensified. Shape shifters were coming and going constantly, leaving the large dwelling silent. The staff often worked shorter days.

A dark blue light appeared in the mostly empty kitchen as Lilly returned from a long day in the Meadows. After setting up the meeting with the Seelie Court, Jet had returned to the mansion to begin working on what they would need for the negotiations while Lilly hung back to help with the sick healers. Once she Appeared, Lilly all but collapsed in a chair at the small table toward the back of the kitchen. Her hands were clean, but her dress was a mess, stained with blood and other fluids. Her normally immaculate hair was loosely held back in a messy braid. Pressing the heels of her hands against her eyes, Lilly could feel warm tears gathering in them. Three healers had died that afternoon and their last moments had been agonizing. It seemed that nothing could comfort them, the pain was so intense. Their skin was so thin that no one could even hold their hand. Lilly would never be able to forget how they cried and then gasped for breath as they struggled to breathe.

Lilly was startled when a plate of brightly-colored vegetables slid under her face. The vegetables were atop a mountain of rice and the dish smelled as heavenly as it looked. She looked up into Dane's glowing light brown eyes. He had a small hand towel slung over one shoulder, and flour mottled his clothes and arms.

"Jet was waiting for you, but I believe he fell asleep. Seemed pretty exhausted," Dane mentioned as he sat down across from Lilly, nodding at the steaming dish. "Vegetable stir-fry. I know you're a vegetarian and I had some time to kill while waiting for the fucking brioche to finish. Figured I could whip up a small dish for any straggling protectors. You normals have the strange tendency to forget to eat when under high amounts of stress."

"Thank you," Lilly said quietly as Dane offered her a fork. He nodded and stood up, making his way over to the sink. There was a multitude of used dishes on the counter tops. He turned on the water and grabbed a large bowl. Lilly poked at the food, moving it around with her fork.

"Blitz, or Isis if you prefer, was in here earlier," Dane mentioned. "She told me what happened. She's probably in the library, going through books for more information on Eris. That one does enjoy her research."

"I'm not sure she'll find much, aside from in the old journals," Lilly replied. She wasn't sure if Eris ever interacted with shape shifters enough to be mentioned in their books. *At least, not before her crimes and subsequent capture,* Lilly thought as she recalled the chase a number of protectors had taken part in to find Eris. She hadn't made it easy and many still bore scars from her traps. There would likely be a wealth of information about that chase and Eris' capture.

"She'll make do," Dane said, bringing Lilly out of her thoughts. "So things have taken a turn for the disastrous?"

Lilly swallowed a bite of food, looking over at Dane who put the pot off to the side to dry. He turned the water off, turned around, and looked over at Lilly. She turned her eyes back to the steaming vegetables on the dish, trying to think of another time the guardians had been attacked. Dane was drying his hands with a towel, watching her intently with his glowing brown eyes. After a moment, he approached the table again and sank down in the chair across from her, putting the towel on his shoulder.

"Figures. Normals have always had the uncanny ability to get themselves into rather unpleasant situations," he said with a quiet huff of laughter. "Blitz is right about one thing: you'll need the help of experiments to get through this one."

"If you're worried about —"

"I don't worry, Mrs. Monroe, I merely observe and, on occasion, predict," Dane interrupted, turning his gaze to Lilly as he crossed his arms on the table. "You can't fight Grenich without using experiments, I know that for certain."

Lilly stared at him, smiling a little. "I don't think you're offering to help."

Dane looked off into the shadows, going quiet for a moment. Lilly studied him and wondered what was going on in his head. It was unnerving how impossible it was to read experiments. Dane was strange, even for a seven series. She was convinced that she, Jet, and Remington were the only mansion occupants who didn't want to wring his neck. Dane enjoyed observing the normals and would occasionally press their buttons, as if to see where their limits were. That was on the very rare occasions that he wasn't in the kitchen, cooking. When he had first woken up after the destruction of the Grenich laboratory, Dane had wandered into the kitchen and just watched the staff, which made them a little nervous. They had gone about their business and tried to ignore the strange quiet man, but then he had regained his strength and started going out of his way to be a nuisance. On top of everything else, Jet and Lilly often found themselves dealing with a deluge of complaints about Dane.

Dane's shoulders slumped after a moment. "You normals are just determined to pull me back into the midst of this unending war, aren't you?"

"That is entirely up to you," Lilly said quietly. "No one is going to force you to do anything you don't want to do. You have been through more than enough and deserve some peace."

"Peace," Dane scoffed, meeting her gaze again. "I don't think that's in the cards for any experiment. I have no interest in taking an active part in this fight. However, I do owe a debt to you and your husband. Probably to Coop and Blitz as well, though I don't intend on letting them know it. I will help you in any way I can, but I will not die for you. I can offer you my knowledge and experience, but I don't intend to be part of any firefights."

Lilly smiled. "I believe we can agree to that."

Dane stood up and went back to the sink, turning on

the water again to continue washing the dishes. Lilly turned her attention back to the food in front of her. The kitchen remained quiet except for the running water.

~~*~*~*

Early the next morning, Isis was practicing kickboxing on a punching bag. Every controlled punch and kick made the bag rattle wildly. Isis was holding back a little, just enough to not break the chain the bag hung on. Orion had Copper make heavier and stronger chains to hold the bags up, after a few unfortunate incidents where the original chains snapped when the experiments attempted to practice on the punching bags.

Hearing pronounced footsteps descending the stairs, Isis remained focused on the bag. Soon enough, she heard Remington step into the training room. She kept hitting the bag, raising her leg in a strong roundhouse kick.

"Have Jet and Lilly returned yet?" she asked as she spun into a powerful kick that made the bag swing like a pendulum. Remington was quiet for a moment, watching her.

"You know, it does concern me how much time you spend on your own," he mentioned and she turned around to look at him, jerking her elbow back to strike the center of the bag. He was dressed in his casual clothes, what he usually wore around the mansion, and his wise eyes traveled briefly around the room before resting on her. Out of all the normals, he was probably the one who woke up the earliest. For a few hours every morning, it was only the experiments and Remington who were awake.

"I am around others frequently. I sometimes desire solitude," she answered.

"I see. That would be the reason for the very large knife," Remington said, looking pointedly at the combat knife she wore in a scabbard on her belt.

"Experiments are never unarmed," she replied. "Did

111

they return yet?"

"They have. The Seelie Court has agreed to grant the protectors temporary access to the Island of Avalon, though you're to respect their sacred lands and make sure Eris does the same," Remington reported, looking over to her as if he expected some kind of protest. She remained quiet and patiently waited for him to continue.

"Jet wants the four of you to choose your team. His only request is that you keep it reasonably sized. Obviously the Seelie Court wouldn't be thrilled with an army of shape shifters marching into their world."

"No, allies would not react well to such an act of aggression," Isis responded and Remington stared at her. Isis stepped past him and moved toward the stairwell. They only had a short amount of time to prepare for what would undoubtedly be a difficult excursion. She intended to make the most of that time.

CHAPTER FIVE

Isis watched her three teammates as they checked their equipment one last time. They were standing in the castle of the women night guardians, waiting for Nemesis to arrive with Eris. Studying the enormous stone walls, Isis remembered Electra telling her that the night guardians were the only ones who painted the walls of their castle. They were made to resemble the night skies and Isis could pick out most constellations, both from Earth and the Meadows. There were a few she couldn't identify and assumed they were from other worlds she hadn't been to. The silver stars on the wall glistened and glowed with light from actual stars. Like the rest of the lands of night, the castle was dark and no daylight ever touched it.

In the two days since Jet and Lilly had met with the Seelie Court, the situation in the Meadows remained mostly unchanged. The afflicted healers were declining steadily and Isis agreed with Amethyst's estimates of three to six months before they reached a point of no return. It was of the utmost importance to find the box as soon as possible. Any delay would result in more lost lives.

Isis looked over to where Radar was standing next to Jack, her small bag slung over her shoulder. She was fiddling with her tablet, her fingers occasionally dancing over the screen. Nero, Alpha, Sly, Steve, and Jensen rounded out their small group. They would remain on the ship while the Four went with Eris to retrieve the Box of Original Elements. The Seelie Court was quite adamant that only the Four and Eris set foot on the island, which the fey considered sacred land. It had taken a lot of convincing on Jet and Lilly's part to even get that much; and they had to agree to two elf escorts accompanying the group. The elves weren't even allowed to set foot on the island and would remain on the ship with the other shape shifters.

Isis glanced to her left when Electra let out a huff of breath and ran her fingers through her wavy hair. She had been fidgeting since they had arrived in the Meadows and Isis could see how much she disliked the situation. Isis turned her attention to the many weapons she was carrying, most of which she had hidden. She also had a small bag of personal items, mostly more weapons and tools for sharpening her blades.

"This is a bad idea," Electra grumbled under her breath as Isis pulled out a knife, checking the edge. When she was satisfied with its sharpness, she tucked it back into its sheath.

"Unfortunately, it is the best we have at the moment. The unaffected healers can only do so much without using magic. We need to neutralize the virus somehow," Isis replied, catching Alex's eye and tilting her head toward Radar. Alex nodded and approached the young experiment, who looked up when Alex said her name.

"What's that about?" Electra asked, noticing the wordless exchange.

"She has a theory about how Set is choosing the shape shifters he experiments on," Isis answered with a small shrug. "She wants to talk to a few more experiments before sharing her theory. She hasn't spoken with Radar yet and now seemed to be a good opportunity."

"Oh," Electra said, looking over to where Alex was talking with Radar. Isis glanced at her twin before looking out across the hall. She had tasked Dane and Coop with protecting the mansion and its inhabitants in her absence. Jet and Lilly had seen the small group off earlier that morning, as had Orion and Remington. Much like Jet, many older protectors were incredibly uneasy about Eris' temporary release. Isis hadn't been able to find out much about the woman, but wasn't really concerned as the trip to the island would likely tell her all she needed to know. It was much easier to observe someone in person than it was to read accounts of said person. There was too much bias in recorded accounts, even among the guardians.

A bright silver shimmer started to form in the middle of the hall, drawing everyone's attention. Within seconds, Nemesis stood there with Eris, who was wearing heavy shackles on her wrists. Once they had fully formed, Eris shivered a little as a sharp smile curled her bright red lips. Isis studied her for a minute, noticing that she didn't wear the typical guardian woman clothing. Instead, she had opted for tight pants and a dark purple shirt, partially unbuttoned. She had also used eyeliner and eyeshadow to give her eyes a smoky appearance. Her long dark hair was draped over one shoulder in a braid. Isis noticed that Eris was a couple inches shorter than guardian women typically were, though she held herself with the same amount of surety. *More,* Isis thought as she observed the woman's natural stance. The guardian's eyes rested on where Hecate was standing in the doorway leading to a long hallway.

"Lady Hecate, still shacked up with Vespera, I see. How *very* progressive of you two," Eris purred with a crafty smile. Hecate merely arched an eyebrow and remained silent. Tapping her fingertips together, Eris' eyes traveled over the small group in the throne room.

"Is this my personal band of merry men?" Eris asked as she raised her wrists up without looking at Nemesis so the guard could undo the shackles. "What fun we're going to

have. Nemesis, be a dear and take these things —
guardians, is that another damn Deverell?"

Nemesis withdrew something from her belt and
snapped it around Eris' upper arm, causing the younger
guardian to jolt in surprise and then sneer. Isis tilted her
head a little to better see what had been attached to her. It
appeared to be a thin gold bracelet in the shape of a vine
of leaves. The leaves were made of emeralds.

"Darling, I really don't need any more sparkle," Eris
commented as Nemesis unlocked the shackles and
removed them from her wrists. Nemesis merely raised her
eyebrow in response to Eris' comment and then turned to
the Four.

"She's wearing the Leaves of Ivy," Nemesis explained,
holding out what looked like a small compass on a string
of guardian silver. "If she should wander off or get lost,
you can find her using this. The Leaves can only be
removed by another guardian, so she can't slip out of it."

"Is that a challenge?" Eris asked with an impish grin as
she encircled her left wrist with the fingers of her right
hand, gently massaging it.

Jade took the compass from Nemesis with a grateful
nod as Eris' eyes wandered over to Electra and Isis, a small
half-smile tugging her lips. She sauntered closer, studying
the two women intently. The sisters looked back at her,
neither averting their gaze from the disgraced guardian.

"Are these my beautiful nieces? My, what fine creatures
they've grown to be," Eris spoke smoothly, glancing at
their exposed skin. "No guardian light though, what a
shame. They could almost pass for full-blooded."

Out of the corner of her eye, Isis noticed Electra go
rigid and could practically feel the anger radiating off of
her. Eris' attention snapped to Isis and she studied her
glowing green eyes. Isis held her gaze, surprised at the
absolute lack of fear or shock in Eris. Usually it took
normals a while to get used to her eyes, especially when
they had never encountered an experiment before. Eris

moved so that she stood directly in front of Isis, dangerously close to crossing into her personal space.

"You're even more interesting in the flesh, I daresay," Eris said, thinking out loud, her scrutinizing eyes roaming over Isis' face and body, sizing her up. "Hmm, I bet there are some juicy secrets swimming around in that steel trap of a mind. I can see all the little wheels and gears spinning behind those pretty eyes."

She raised a hand as if to touch her temple and Isis' hand moved of its own accord as it shot up and latched onto Eris' wrist. Eris' eyes widened briefly and then a look of triumph spread over her face. After a beat, her smile dropped as she looked down to where Isis' fingers were wrapped tightly around her flesh. Isis noticed Eris' skin was brightening almost imperceptibly in a pulsing pattern. Eris looked back to Isis' face, surprise reflecting in her wide eyes as her smile reappeared.

"Well, isn't that interesting," she whispered, her eyes not moving from Isis. Isis pushed Eris' wrist away and stepped back. She didn't know what had just happened, but judging from the guardian's reaction, Isis had unintentionally revealed something.

"I would advise you to be aware of my sister's personal space," Electra warned from next to Isis. "She doesn't like being touched, especially not by strangers."

Eris rolled her eyes over to Electra. "You'd be my other niece then. Quite the pretty little thing you are, both of you actually. However you've obviously been raised in the Meadows with the boring old guardians. I have to dislike you a little for that, purely out of principle. You understand, don't you?"

Electra arched an eyebrow and Eris scoffed, stretching her arms over her head and cracking her back.

"Your mother has that exact same look. Now I definitely don't like you," she remarked as she dropped her arms again, snapping and clapping rhythmically. "Can we get moving? I have been in that cell for ages. I need some fresh air and new scenery."

At that moment, the doors to the main hall were opened and Artemis entered, wearing a dark blue gown. Eris rolled her eyes again and grumbled under her breath, rubbing her eyes. Isis took the opportunity to move closer to the other members of the Four. She saw Hecate standing near the door to the stairs that led to the hall of doors.

"I wanted to see all of you off," Artemis said, looking over to Eris. "Hello, Eris."

"Mother," Eris responded, a clear edge to her voice. "Come to put on a nauseating display of familial love? Shouldn't my sister be with you? I would have thought she would want to see her one daughter and wish her luck or something equally asinine."

"Luck is a superstition and has no point or purpose," Isis mentioned from where she stood by Shae and Alex. Eris laughed loudly as she looked over at the woman.

"I like you," she purred, her eyes briefly dancing to where Jensen was standing near Nero. Eris tilted her head a little and pursed her lips. Raising her eyebrows once, she turned her attention back to Artemis.

"Passion is busy in the healing wing. Amethyst and the other healers require all the help they can get, which is why I can't stay very long," Artemis responded to Eris' earlier question, ignoring Isis' statement. "But she sends along her wish that all of you have a safe journey."

"No Adonia either? That's entirely unsurprising. Can we please get on with this show? Your saccharine emotion is tedious," Eris replied dismissively as she began to wind her braid into a tight bun, stepping closer to the shape shifters. She scrunched up her nose with a faint expression of disgust, obviously not thrilled with her company. Artemis moved closer so she stood near her daughter and Eris rolled her eyes over to her mother.

"Relax, Mother. It's a few days' trip to an uninhabited island. You needn't make a scene. I will be back in my cage soon enough where you and the guards can gawk at me to your heart's content," she said. "If the guardians were truly concerned with my safety, they would have provided me with a weapon or two instead of a pack of guard dogs."

Jade rubbed her forehead and muttered something about how it was going to be a very long trip. Isis glanced at her briefly before turning her attention back to Eris and Artemis, focusing on the interaction. Artemis wrapped her arms around Eris, who merely stood stiffly as if she weren't used to physical contact. Artemis kissed the side of her head.

"You know you will always have my love and I will worry about you until you return to us," Artemis whispered to Eris, so quietly Isis was sure only the experiments and Eris heard her. "Take care of yourself and please do not torment the shape shifters. They are good people."

Eris was quiet and her rigid posture didn't change. Artemis released her and stepped back, nodding to the shape shifters. Eris turned away from Artemis, her expression reflecting irritation as she moved over to where the protectors were standing. Isis noticed Electra step back from where she had been saying her goodbyes to the protectors, gently punching Nero's shoulder as he chuckled at an in-joke he shared with her. Her green eyes reflected worry and Isis wondered if her twin were capable of concealing any emotion she was experiencing. Electra stopped when she stood across from Isis.

"I know it's an uninhabited island and it's perfectly safe, probably safer than here or Earth anyway," she started with a quiet laugh, her eyes dropping briefly to her feet as she swallowed. "But I still worry."

"It is to be expected. You are a normal, your bonds are stronger than an experiment's," Isis replied with a slight shrug. "It is part of having emotions, to the best of my understanding. You needn't be concerned. We shall probably be back in a couple weeks, depending on how cooperative Eris is."

Electra offered a watery smile, glancing over to where Artemis was standing before looking back to Isis. "I brought you something."

Isis' eyebrows rose briefly as Electra produced a sheath from behind her back. Recognizing the designs as Silver's work, Isis looked back to her sister.

"The guardian smiths aren't supposed to make tools of war in large quantities. They only make ceremonial weapons and the ones we use to practice self-defense," Electra explained. "But Mom and I talked Silver into making this dagger. I know you already have a lot of weapons and don't need any more, but this one has magic in it. If you cut my name into any sort of reflective surface, we will be able to talk. I have a matching one. They glow when one of us is calling."

Isis tucked the dagger and sheath into the back of her belt. "I have a sufficient number of weapons already, but I suspect this was more a gesture. So, thank you."

Electra smiled again and Isis heard Eris start whistling as if she were calling to a dog. Isis twisted a little to look behind her and Eris started patting her leg, occasionally whistling and calling to her in a high-pitched voice. The other protectors already looked fed up with her antics, except for Nero and Jensen who were struggling not to laugh. Isis turned back to Electra, who looked rather irritated with Eris.

"I should go," Isis said.

"May I hug you?" Electra asked and Isis nodded. She waited patiently as Electra wrapped her arms around her and held her tightly for a moment. Isis didn't understand the normals need for physical contact or affection, but at least they weren't springing it on her anymore. There had been some rather unpleasant incidents early on. Giving her a warning allowed Isis to keep her instincts and reactions in check.

After a moment, Electra stepped back and smiled at

Isis. "Be safe. And be careful around Eris. She's very cunning and she still has her abilities, tempered though they may be."

Isis dipped her chin to her chest and moved to join the other protectors. She exchanged a brief look with Jensen as she walked past him. He had insisted on coming and Isis had agreed since it was a relatively low risk assignment. Eris was a concern, but she was a factor who could be controlled. Isis reached the Four and they followed Hecate into the hall just off the main room. She led them down a long, winding stone staircase that curled around an enormous pillar. Isis looked up at the lamps that contained starlight, which lit the enormous stairway with a bright silver glow. They soon reached the bottom of the stairs and walked into the Hall of Doors, which stretched for farther than the eye could see.

"Je-sus," Nero breathed behind them and Alpha whistled, which made Hecate smile faintly. It was obvious many of the shape shifters had never seen the hall before. Isis looked over her shoulder to Jensen, who was also staring in wide-eyed amazement at the numerous doors, all unique and reflecting the world they opened up to. Eris yawned in boredom as she glanced at her nails and pursed her lips. Sly also looked rather unimpressed and Isis again wondered why she had agreed to accompany them. Jet had needed a couple non-protectors to accompany the Four, mostly to assuage the concerns of the rebels. Alpha was there to make sure everything stayed on the up and up. The rebels were valuable allies, so Isis didn't mind her presence. Sly didn't owe loyalty to any group and though she was a good fighter, she was also the most difficult shape shifter to get a read on. Isis was still unclear on her motivations and found her difficult to predict.

They stopped in front of an elaborately decorated wooden door. It was molded and carved to look like a tangle of vines and leaves. A rainbow of different kinds of jewels was embedded deeply in the bark and lines of gold sparkled in the wood. Hecate put the key in a hole hidden in the cluster of vines and they curled away, folding inward, leaving a rectangular opening large enough for a tall person to easily walk through. On the other side, Isis could see a smooth stone floor of what looked like some sort of palace. Bright natural light illuminated the enormous room beyond the door and there were two tall elves standing inside, both wearing plain guards uniforms.

"I wish you luck and a safe journey," Hecate said from where she stood beside the door, her hands folded in front of her. "One of the elves will have a key to open the door when you're ready to return."

Jade, who had been leading the group, turned to address them. "Okay, everyone knows the plan and what they'll be doing?"

Everyone nodded in response, except for Isis and Eris. Jade turned and stepped through the doorway, followed by the rest of the group.

~~*~*~*

"The selkies will be waiting on the ship. They're the ones who can best navigate the waters, other than the merpeople. I think you will quite like the harbor, many do."

Isis barely heard the conversation between Jade and one of their elf escorts, the woman who had introduced herself as Maeve. She had a very outgoing personality and had been conversing with the protectors since they had stepped through the door. The guard seemed incredibly interested in the visitors and quite excited to show them around her homeland, which she obviously loved and took pride in. Like most non-fey though, Isis sensed a hesitance in Maeve. The crimes of the past were not forgotten by any, except for most fey nobility.

The other elf, a man named Keane, hadn't said much and remained silent at the end of the line. He did seem intrigued by the experiments, but thankfully didn't stare much. Isis occasionally looked back at him and noticed he was usually looking out over the lands, a small smile playing across his lips. From her research, Isis had found the elves to be an interesting dichotomy. They were fierce warriors, the best in the Seelie Court, hence their serving as guards to the fey. However, they were also the most open-minded of the races inhabiting the Seelie Court, often described as "friendly" and "good-natured" by their allies. They weren't as isolated as most other members of the Seelie Court and, from what she had read, they genuinely liked others.

Isis looked out over the sprawling hills of bright green and gold grass. The moment she had set foot in the Seelie Court, Isis experienced something akin to what the normals called déjà vu. It was a faint feeling, just something that tugged at the back of her mind, but it made her uneasy nonetheless. They had been walking for close to three hours by her estimates and she was just starting to notice the faint scent of seawater on the air. Isis remained toward the back of the line, just behind Eris, so she could observe the others in front of her. The sound of bleating drew Isis' attention to the left where a herd of pastel-colored deer pranced through the open field. Glancing up, she felt the sun warm her face.

"Ah, there is the harbor."

Isis looked down the hill they had just crested, noticing the large bustling harbor where a number of impressive-looking ships were docked. There was a lot of activity among the massive ships. On the land, there were numerous stalls and practically every race found in the Seelie Court was wandering around the harbor: shopping, bargaining and buying from the various merchants. They looked like tiny ants from where the group stood.

Isis looked to the side when Maeve made some gestures to Keane and he nodded his understanding, making a few gestures in response. Judging from the interactions Isis had already witnessed, the two elves had been working together for quite some time.

"Ugh, why can't we just Appear at the damn island? I'm going to reek of fish and elf and selkie for months," Eris griped as she glanced at her nails. She looked over at Keane, who was watching her. She rolled her eyes and made some gestures, which were similar to the ones the elf had exchanged with Maeve earlier. Isis noticed the elf's eyes widened a little in obvious surprise, but he made some gestures in response, his grin growing a little.

"Yes, I'm aware of your rules," Eris said as she also moved her hands, a little less surely than she had earlier.

"Are you following any of this?" Shae whispered as she moved over to Isis.

"Partly. It looks to be a form of Seelie Court sign language. Judging from what I've observed, it appears Keane is probably Deaf," Isis answered, glancing at Shae before stepping forward and pulling Eris away from where she had been reaching for Keane. Eris looked over at Isis, who just shook her head.

"No touching," Isis warned, looking over to Jack. "Can you watch her? Make sure she has no physical contact with anyone."

"You're no fun," Eris pouted, sticking out her lower lip as Jack led her away. Isis turned her attention to Shae, who couldn't hide how impressed she was.

"You know Seelie Court sign language?" she asked and Isis shook her head.

"Not fluently, I can only make an educated guess based on the little I've seen. It's unimportant," Isis said dismissively. "Normals need to avoid physical contact with Eris. I believe it's one of the ways she's able to affect people's free will and perception."

"Yeah, we picked up on that," Shae said, glancing at the guardian as a cool breeze swept over them. "She's really going to be a pain in the ass."

Isis looked over Shae's shoulder, noticing Radar approaching them. Shae twisted to follow her friend's gaze. Radar paused and looked between the women, her tablet in hand. Shae gave Isis an understanding smile and turned to join the rest of the group. Isis turned her attention to Radar, who watched Shae as she passed by.

"Is something wrong?" Isis asked, drawing the woman's attention back to her. Radar's skills were invaluable, but she was still uncomfortable about going out into the field. She was also incredibly wary of the normals and Isis was unsure how much contact she'd had with them in the laboratory. The E-series line very rarely had contact with others outside their series.

"I'm not entirely certain," Radar replied as she ran her finger over the back of her tablet. "I brought this to work on the flashdrive encryption while you're on the island. I was still getting a weak signal in the Meadows, which isn't surprising because it has a direct connection to Earth. Given time, I probably could figure out a way to strengthen it. The Seelie Court doesn't have as direct a connection to Earth, except for the one door. So it follows that I would have lost the signal once we entered this world."

Isis moved closer as Radar turned the tablet so she could see it. Radar ran a hand through her short hair and looked out over the vast colorful fields of the Seelie Court.

"I'm picking up a signal, it's weak but it's there. Based on what I've read about the Seelie Court, they don't have any sort of internet and don't rely on electricity as much as we do on Earth," Radar continued as Isis examined the screen. "There's a network here, somewhere, and it requires a password to access, but I think we should wait until the signal is stronger. *If* it gets stronger."

Isis handed the tablet back to Radar. "Keep an eye on it and let me know if anything changes. Hold off working on that flashdrive for the time being."

Radar nodded once and went to join the others, who were already starting to descend the hill. Isis moved to the edge and looked down to the harbor. The wind picked up, pushing against her, and she closed her eyes and inhaled deeply. Isis opened her eyes and turned when she heard Jensen approach, noticing his nice suit. Practically everything he owned was tailored and Isis still didn't understand why he wore such hindering clothing. Glancing out over the harbor once more, Isis began walking to meet Jensen.

"Is this the first time you've been to the Seelie Court?" she asked as they walked in the direction of the group.

"It is," Jensen said, adjusting the pack on his back. "I wish it were under different circumstances. This is an interesting place, very colorful. I hear the gem caves are astonishingly beautiful."

Isis looked over toward a tree with rainbow-colored leaves and could feel Jensen's eyes turn to her briefly. Lately, she had found herself curious about the way the normals saw the world. They had such a wide-eyed sense of awe about them, something they seemed to enjoy. Isis had never questioned or wondered at the world, nor seen the point in doing so, but she had always experienced some faint curiosity about things. She turned her eyes forward again.

"You know, if we finish this mission in a reasonable amount of time," Jensen began, sounding oddly unsure. "We could send the Box of Original Elements back with the group along with Eris, and maybe spend a little extra time here. Perhaps see the gem caves. Unless the enclosed space is too unpleasant for —"

"I would like that," Isis said softly. "If time allows."

Jensen couldn't keep the surprise from his face and seemed uncertain of what to say as they continued down the dusty path. Isis brushed her hands together, paying close attention to her surroundings. The sound of voices was becoming clearer the closer they got to the harbor. There was also an assortment of bird calls and some hypnotic singing drifting on the breeze.

"I read extensively about the trafficking scandal of the

Seelie Court," Isis stated as they descended the hill. "Your ancestors had a very active role in stopping the fey abducting other supernaturals. It was one of your father's first missions, according to what I read."

Jensen smiled in a melancholy way and looked down. "Ah yes, we Aldridges did have a reputation for meddling. It's one of the traditions I fear I'm carrying on."

Isis nodded to where Maeve was speaking with Alex, both women smiling. "The elves were also instrumental in bringing down the trafficking ring. There was an underground resistance, which is how the protectors first became aware of the fey's actions. In the aftermath, the elves were seen as traitors in the Seelie Court, for turning against their leaders. It's why they shall never again hold high office."

Jensen's eyes widened briefly. "I remember reading something about that. From the few memories I have of my parents, I remember my father always speaking fondly about elves. You're certainly thorough when it comes to research."

Isis shrugged. "If I were not, I likely wouldn't survive very long."

As they continued walking, her mind soaked up the information that surrounded them. The sound of the water was now the clearest sound and lavender-colored birds flew overhead, occasionally swooping down into the water and emerging with a fish. They resembled gulls in size and shape.

As they set foot on cobblestone roads, the noises and smells of the harbor greeted them. Isis' eyes darted around as she took in the lay of the land. Almost every single race in the Seelie Court could be found in the marketplace, most of them dressed in incredibly bright, elaborate clothing. As they walked through the place, they passed fey, elves, leprechauns, pixies, sprites, and even a couple dwarves. Isis didn't fail to notice how the dwarves shied away from her. Most of the others looked uneasy or intimidated by her, which was to be expected, but the bearded dwarves actually turned away and quickened their pace at the sight of her. Isis pretended not to notice and looked over at Jensen, who nodded politely at everyone they passed, whether or not the gesture was returned.

There were stalls set up all around the harbor, selling various goods and wares as well as a wide array of fruits and vegetables. Many stalls had an entertainer in front to draw in crowds, demonstrating some eye-catching talent like juggling or contortion. A number of youth ran around the different stalls, squealing in delight and occasionally being given a toy or sweet. Each stall had a flag hanging at the corner, identifying the race of the merchant. Jewels sparkled in the bright sunlight and the shimmering crests stood out even in the bright light. The quiet murmur of various conversations filled the air, as did the occasional laugh or merchant shouting prices. At the sound of fire, Isis' hand instinctively went to the gun she wore in a holster on her waist and she twisted around, noticing a pair of fire breathers in front of a stall at the end of the pathway. Turning back, she ignored the soft whoosh of fire and forced the rigidity out of her muscles. Glancing up when a fey on stilts walked by, Isis continued moving down the path.

A group of small pixie children ran past the two shape shifters, squealing in delight as they stopped in front of a stall selling toys. Looking around, Isis realized how much she stood out in her odd attire. Her shiny black catsuit was unlike the fine dresses worn by the majority of women in the Seelie Court and everyone wore bright vibrant colors. None of them wore weapons openly either and she had noticed that raised a few eyebrows. *I should have just gone with my concealed weapons,* she thought as she kept pace with Jensen.

Isis looked around at the selkies who were working in and around the massive ships, noticing most of them didn't have many typical gender markers. Some had more feminine traits and features, but the majority of them were androgynous. Their skin was dark from long hours in the intense sunlight and it appeared to be a little smoother than typical of normals. The selkies were also very sleek and their dark eyes glistened with intelligence. Mostly they went about their business, unbothered and uninterested in the newcomers. They didn't mingle with the other Seelie Court inhabitants either, which was the selkie way based on her research. The selkies were thought to have been one of the first inhabitants of the Seelie Court, older than even the fey. Not much was known about them, other than they preferred to be left to their own devices and were very protective of other selkies.

"Apparently, there's a special room on all the ships where the selkies keep their skins," Jensen said, nodding in polite greeting to a couple selkies who passed by them, one of whom turned to continue looking at Jensen, raising their eyebrows and nodding in approval. "At night, they take turns putting on their regular skins and swimming in the sea. They have a fascinating culture, though they are quite isolated by choice."

"They're fearsome in naval battles, not so much on land," Isis replied, noticing a mermaid sunning herself on a large boulder in the water, topless, as was common for mer-people. Her dark purple tail fanned out into fins, slapping the rock once, and her long brown hair just barely dipped into the water. Isis preferred to avoid water, due to the disadvantages it presented, but was more than capable of drowning a foe if push came to shove. Jensen chuckled beside her, playfully bumping her with his shoulder.

"Guardians have mercy, you take after my sister."

Both shape shifters looked over to Eris, who was now standing in front of them with her hands on her hips. She looked between the two of them, her eyes fixing on Jensen. Running her eyes over his body appraisingly, she nodded once and stuck her lips out.

"I mean, you could do worse, but still," she shuddered.

"That's just gross."

Eris turned and blew on the ear of a selkie who had been approaching them. Isis noticed something glisten in the air briefly, disappearing in the selkie's ear. The selkie froze mid-step and a tremor went through their body. Turning their attention to Eris, the selkie looked like a statue. Eris' lips curled upwards.

"Hello there, little otter," she whispered sweetly, but was cut off when Isis grabbed her arm and dragged her away roughly, pulling her into an alley between the stalls and slamming her against a rocky wall. Yanking out her butterfly knife, Isis had it open and at Eris' throat in the blink of an eye. She pressed on the blade just enough to be uncomfortable.

"I want you to understand one thing, I cannot kill you but I will use excessive force if I deem you a threat to the group's safety. Believe me, Eris, there are things much, *much* worse than death," Isis warned, glancing around briefly to make sure no one would try to interfere. "Antagonize whoever you like, but no magic and no manipulating people's wills. Do you understand me?"

Eris smiled, her icy blue eyes lit up with amusement. "Ooooh, you play rough. I daresay more of your father's blood runs in those veins. Very well, I agree to hold back on the games, for now. But tell me, baby shape shifter, do you think this will make me talk when we get to the island?"

Isis took a step back and with a few deft flicks of her wrist, closed her knife. She pushed it back into its place on her belt. Eris stepped away from the rock, massaging her throat.

"Let's go," Isis said, motioning for Eris to lead the way. Jensen stared at the guardian, leaning back a little as she passed by him. She kissed the air as she walked by, but continued on her way. Jensen looked to Isis, who followed a short way behind the woman.

"Shall we?" Isis said as she continued walking, heading

to the massive ship where the rest of the group had already started boarding.

~~*~*~*

Once the ship set sail, the day passed quickly. It was massive, large enough for each member of the group to have their own cot in the huge sleeping space, though there weren't any dividers. The ocean was calm and the gentle motion was relaxing to the passengers. The selkies were master seafarers and the ship ran like a well-oiled machine. The crew knew their jobs and did them well.

After putting their stuff in the sleeping space, the shape shifters spent the rest of the day wandering the ship and exploring. Eris was strangely quiet and remained on deck, sketching in a notebook she had stuffed into the small bag of clothing she had been allowed to bring. Occasionally she would just stare out over the blue waters.

After finishing dinner, the three women sat around the table while Steve and Jack cleaned up. It was quiet except for the faint sound of lively music that drifted down from the deck and the occasional lapping of the waves. Alex folded her arms on the table, glancing around surreptitiously. Shae grinned and playfully mirrored Alex. Isis looked up from a book of selkie stories she had been paging through when Jade entered the small kitchen area, brushing a strand of dark hair out of her face.

"Eris didn't want dinner, no surprise there," she grumbled huffily. "I left Sly and Nero in charge of her, though I really wish this ship had some kind of room we could lock her in. I don't like her wandering around."

"She's got nowhere to go," Shae pointed out.

"It's not her escaping that concerns me. If Eris wanted to, she could sway the crew to mutiny," Jade said, sinking down in the empty seat next to Alex. "Knowing her, she'd do it just for a lark."

Isis raised an eyebrow, but remained silent. She looked

over at Alex, who was chewing her lower lip. Alex had been silent throughout dinner and had been rather uneasy ever since they arrived at the Seelie Court. The protector glanced over at Isis and swallowed.

"I've noticed the experiments have something in common," she said quietly, drawing the attention of the three women. Out of the corner of her eye, Isis noticed Jack stop wiping down the counter and look over to the table. Steve paused from putting away clean dishes and also looked over to the table. Isis turned her attention back to Alex, waiting for her to continue. Alex was fiddling with her hands.

"Go on," Jade said, curiosity reflecting in her expression. Shae leaned forward expectantly. Alex looked between them and then looked over at Isis, who put her book down and turned her eyes to a small porthole, gazing at the night sky. The stars were mostly rose-colored and green in the Seelie Court and there were two moons, one a pastel pink and one periwinkle blue.

"Keep in mind I've only talked to several experiments," Alex reminded her as she folded her arms on the table. "Coop, Isis, Jack, Radar, Dane, and Shocker all had different lives. They were all recruited, for lack of a better term, in different ways. There was no obvious intersection, but there was one trait I found that Isis and Jack shared."

Alex looked over at Jack, who was partly leaning over the counter, his attention fixed on the four women at the table. "In my brief conversations with the experiments, I found they all fell on the asexual spectrum."

"And exactly how did you even think of that?" Jade asked, confused. Alex shrugged and leaned back in her seat.

"I'm not entirely sure. I remembered that Isis once told me that she identified as Gray-A, and as an aromantic asexual woman, I know how exceedingly rare that is among shape shifters in particular. It's practically unheard of among us. When they first came to the mansion, out of pure curiosity, I asked Jack how he identified," Alex looked back to Jack again.

"The Grenich Corporation didn't really allow for socializing and we weren't allowed to have identities outside of aliases for missions, but by your standards and definitions, I believe I'm biromantic asexual," Jack stated. Steve looked intrigued as he crossed his arms as he looked at the experiment and then back to the people at the table.

"So two asexual shape shifters, it could be a coincidence," Alex continued with a shake of her head. "But it was a very interesting coincidence, one that was statistically unlikely. I talked to Coop next and found out he's demisexual. Dane is the same and Shocker is aromantic asexual. Radar believes she's homoromantic asexual."

There was quiet for a moment as the shape shifters all thought about the information Alex had presented to them. Alex glanced over at Isis, who looked contemplative. Jade drummed her fingers on the table, looking over at her teammate.

"It's an interesting theory, but there's one thing I am having trouble wrapping my mind around," she began, massaging her forehead. "How on Earth could anyone ever find that out?"

Shae looked between the two women, her gaze settling on Alex expectantly. Alex swallowed and opened her mouth to respond.

"Have you learned nothing from working alongside experiments?" Isis asked quietly, her glowing eyes fixing on Jade. The woman turned her attention back to Isis, a little surprised by her interjection. Isis rarely ever spoke and usually just responded when directly asked a question.

"Do you think our sole purpose was active combat?" Isis continued, running her fingers through her short hair. "Our most common missions were reconnaissance, finding out information on targets and potential recruits. Normals are open books to experiments and experiments are chameleons. We can blend into your life, manipulate you and those around you into telling us every secret, and all before you even know we're there. It's relatively easy to spot an anomaly and Set has eyes everywhere."

Isis shook her head and stood from her seat, suddenly desiring fresh air. She stepped out of the narrow open door. The faint sounds of laughter and music drifted down from the door leading out to the deck. Isis silently walked down the cramped hallway, walking up the few steps to the door leading out.

The night air was refreshing as it drifted over her face when she stepped onto the deck. On the opposite side from her, there were a few selkie musicians playing on relatively simplistic stringed instruments. The jaunty tune danced lightly on the air and a large group of selkies were dancing a fast group dance, which resembled the contra style on Earth. Isis' sharp eyes soon picked out Alpha who was being taught by a few selkies how to participate in the dance. They were obviously enjoying themselves.

Looking around, Isis spotted Eris, who was dancing separate from the largest group. She was teaching a couple younger selkies, who were bright-eyed with excitement. Eris' legs almost looked as though they moved separate from her torso, though every movement was controlled and she looked like she was gliding over the wooden floor. She would occasionally pause to make sure the two young selkies were following. Isis watched as Eris tapped the ground with her foot, instructing one selkie where to put their feet. The selkie quickly complied, laughing when they finally managed to complete the floating move. Looking to the side, Isis noticed Nero lying on a box, watching the dancers. A selkie sat near him, eating from a small dish of steaming food.

Satisfied that everything was fine, Isis moved over to the side of the ship so she could look down at the calm waters. Even in the dark, she could see the brightly-colored tails of mer-people who followed alongside the ship. They would be gone once they entered the sacred waters surrounding the Island of Avalon. Isis also noticed other marine life: rainbow-colored fish and mammals and even a couple selkies in their normal seal form. Leaning down on her elbows, Isis saw the reflection of her own glowing eyes. For a moment she studied them, noticing they stood out more clearly than the stars. Almost all experiments hated their eyes, which frequently presented numerous strategic disadvantages in the field. The glow was difficult to conceal, especially in darker settings.

Closing her eyes, Isis dropped her head and shifted her weight. There were so many different scents and sounds bombarding her senses. Her mind was racing with the possibility that she had been targeted for recruitment. Normals would probably expect her to have some sort of feelings about it, but as usual, she felt nothing. It was something from the past, something she had no power over.

"Why so glum, sugarplum?"

Isis opened her eyes as she looked over at Eris, who had approached her once the song had ended. Looking back over her shoulder, Isis saw the two selkies she had been dancing with had rejoined the larger group as another tune started up. Eris followed her gaze and scoffed.

"You thought I had them under a spell," she feigned offense, raising a hand to her chest. "I am *genuinely* hurt. You think the absolute worst of me. I am capable of interacting with others without the use of my abilities. Particularly if their existence doesn't annoy me."

Isis looked at her, raising a skeptical eyebrow, and Eris leaned back so she rested on her elbows, a crafty smile playing on her lips. In the short time she had known her, Isis had gotten used to the expression. Eris looked at the seven series.

"You place way too much stock in the High Council's opinions and recollections," she commented and Isis looked back down to the dark water. "Try to kill your sister a couple times, not even really good attempts either, and suddenly you're the bad guy. Honestly, the High Council can be *so* overdramatic. It's embarrassing."

Isis raised her eyebrows, but kept watching the waves. "I thought your sentence was for forcing a population to worship you as a goddess."

Eris scoffed as she turned her attention back to the dancing. "Darling, do you honestly believe the guardians give a damn about lesser species? No, my dear, the High Council's pearl-clutching is only when a guardian is dealt some injury or slight. No matter how inconsequential or minor, you can always count on them to overreact about it."

Eris looked over at Isis, who was still looking down at the water. "You didn't know about my other supposed crimes? The incidents with Passion? The wedding fiasco?"

Isis shrugged. "Contrary to what many normals seem to believe, I'm not omniscient. I only know what the shape shifters and guardians do. Normals are incapable of giving impartial accounts, so whatever I heard, I took with a grain of salt. I do the same with whatever you tell me. And right now, you're still searching for some weakness you can use."

Eris looked disappointed. "They didn't write anything about my exploits? That's rather disheartening. Such good stories shouldn't be forgotten. Oh well."

Isis turned her attention to Eris. "There is one thing I would like to know."

Eris smiled, brightening up as she turned to face Isis. "Really? Let's see, you're not dense, so you wouldn't ask me about that damn box. You're not a sentimentalist, so you wouldn't ask me about my sister or any other family. What does that leave? What question has that fascinating mind of yours thought up?"

"How do you know Seelie Court sign language?" Isis asked. Eris' smile dropped and her expression reflected irritation as she looked back toward the dancers.

"Well that's a let-down," she grumbled, running her fingers through her long hair. "I have spent over three hundred years in the lowest level of the dungeon. What do you think I do to pass the time? I read a lot, a truly absurd amount as a matter of fact. I went through a language phase some time ago, picked it up then. There are few things the guardians excel at, but they are masters at sticking their noses in other people's business and also recording things: there's a wealth of information on the languages of every known species. I'm fluent in quite a few languages, probably more than most guardians. Seelie Court signing is relatively easy to learn, since it was developed by commoners."

Isis turned her gaze back to the water and she leaned down on her elbows again. Eris looked over at her with her peripheral vision. She crossed her arms over her chest.

"You haven't told me why you're out here all on your lonesome looking like a kicked puppy," Eris mentioned with disinterest.

"I do not require company," Isis replied, ignoring Eris' question. She was uninterested in introspection and wasn't in the mood to play Eris' games. The guardian arched an eyebrow.

"My, my, my, you are a cold one," she observed with a faint smile and quiet laugh. "You're not doing yourself any favors with that detachment, especially not if you're planning to face off against a guardian of death."

"Set is no longer a guardian. He's a necromancer."

"Minor details, petal," Eris said with a dismissive wave of her hand. "You can never completely erase your past. Even exiled guardians were guardians at one time."

Isis kept her eyes on the dark water, watching the reflection of the periwinkle moon as it rippled in the gentle waves. The smell of the water was pleasantly sweet, different from the salty scent of the oceans on Earth. Even the playful music was nice to her sensitive ears. Yet she was still uneasy due to it being a strange place.

Eris leaned down on one elbow, her eyes fixing on Isis. "It goes against everything I stand for, but I'm going to give you a piece of advice: embrace your anger, whatever embers remain. Anger is a powerful tool and motivator, one that should never be disregarded."

"Emotion is weakness. It clouds your mind and hinders the ability to think rationally and strategize," Isis replied. "This is especially true of anger."

"Only if you let it consume you, dove. Control it and it's an incredibly useful weapon," Eris stated, straightening up again. "I can only tolerate so much moping. And this is definitely past my limits."

Eris strode away from Isis, who glanced over her shoulder to watch the guardian move back toward the dancing groups. She settled down on a step and lazily pulled her hair loose from its braid, shaking her head a couple times and running her fingers through her long locks. Eris then leaned back and turned her face to the sky, allowing her hair to cascade down behind her.

Isis straightened up, glancing to the side when she heard footsteps approaching. Shae's light-colored blouse stood out in the dark night and her shoes clicked on the floor of the ship's deck. Looking over to the dancing selkies, she smiled and then turned her attention back to Isis. The wind picked up and rustled through the sails, creating a soft flapping sound. Shae's auburn hair drifted about in the breeze as she stood next to Isis on the deck.

"You left quite abruptly, even for you," she observed quietly, gently nudging Isis with her shoulder. "I wanted to make sure you were all right."

Isis turned around and leaned back against the railing, crossing her arms over her chest. She was wearing her catsuit, which hid the charms she wore at her throat: Blitz's symbol and a small guardian emerald shamrock with her name and birthdate. Shae moved a little closer, leaning against the railing next to her. She watched the dancing, patiently waiting for Isis to say something. Shae dropped her head briefly when she realized Isis wasn't going to speak.

"I know you cope with things differently than us normals, but I want you to know you can always talk to me if you want," Shae said quietly. "No judgment and whatever you say stays between us."

Isis was quiet as she turned her eyes to the night, thinking for a moment. "Alex's theory is a sound one, but it is one that does cause me some concern. An experiment's memory is a peculiar thing. We have eidetic memories, but Grenich is able to adjust what we can recall. They take the information they need and strip sensitive intel from our minds."

Shae frowned. "I'm not following your train of thought."

"If Set is targeting shape shifters with a specific trait, it would require a lot of reconnaissance work. Work that the seven series excel at," Isis mentioned, watching as Eris lifted one hand in the air and created sparkles around her fingertips. She ran it over her dark hair, which soon glistened as if it contained millions of stars. Isis looked back to Shae, studying her expression for a moment.

"I am not like the rest of you, I never will be. And I have recently noticed that there are some ways I'm not really like the other experiments. I don't have any desire to blend in or experience things the way normals do," Isis said quietly. "However, I don't . . . the idea that I might have aided in the recruitment of shape shifters, it bothers me."

Shae smiled, though Isis could read her discomfort. "That's your conscience. It's a good thing. And you can make amends for your past actions. You're doing so every day you fight against Set."

Isis swallowed and looked back to the selkies. She didn't think it was in her best interest to further explain what was bothering her. She allowed the protectors to hold onto the belief that she had a similar morality to them. Guilt was not something Isis was capable of and it wasn't a beneficial characteristic from what she could tell. Looking up, she watched an enormous purple bird sweep through the sky. After a moment, the creature plunged down into the water and emerged soon after with a wriggling fish in its beak.

A sudden electric shock traveled through Isis' body, causing her to fall heavily to her knees and suck in her breath. She put a fist to her temple, trying to quell the headache that suddenly flared to life. Her entire body tingled and she felt the hairs on her body stand on end, though the sensation only lasted a split second. Isis' eyes widened as she got back to her feet and looked at the other people on the deck to see if any had a similar reaction. They were still dancing, completely oblivious to anything out of the ordinary, but a few selkies were looking over at her, obviously having seen her fall. Isis turned and looked down to the water, squinting as she tried to see below the surface. Almost all the marine life had completely disappeared and the fish had noticeably thinned. *The Seelie Court doesn't have a barrier or spell surrounding the Island of Avalon. Even if they did, we're still days from the island,* Isis thought as she looked up again. Hurrying to the other end of the ship, she leaped up the few steps and moved to the back. Isis jumped up on the railing and looked off into the night. There was nothing visible behind them.

"Isis?" Shae's concerned voice came from her left and Isis looked down to her. The protector looked worried and had one hand held out as if to steady Isis. The sound of quiet footsteps made Isis instinctively reach for her sais. She hopped off the railing and landed weightlessly on the deck. Moving back to the steps, she spotted Jack looking over the side of the ship. He looked up as they approached, swallowing and looking between the two women, his eyes fixing on Isis.

"You felt it too?" he asked and she nodded in response as she dropped her hands away from her weapons. Jogging down the few steps, she moved past Jack toward the door on the other side of the boat, which led to the sleeping area.

Opening the door, Isis descended a few more steps and moved through the unlit hall. She reached the wooden door, pushing it open. There was a single candle lit, but Isis' superior eyesight pierced the thick shadows. She first saw Jensen dozing on one of the cots, an open book on his chest. Looking over to the other side of the room, she spotted Radar sitting with her back against the wall. Her glowing brown eyes were wide and round. She immediately looked up to Isis and her body lost some of its tension.

"Did you feel that?" Radar asked.

"I did, so did Jack, but none of the normals were noticeably affected," Isis replied, looking over her shoulder when she heard Shae and Jack approach. Stepping into the room, Isis moved over to where the younger experiment was sitting.

"Do you know what it was?" Isis asked.

Radar shook her head. "It felt as though we passed through some sort of electrified barrier, but I don't know how that's possible. There was no evidence that I could see."

"I didn't see anything on the deck," Isis reported as Jack stepped into the room with Shae close behind him. All three experiments glanced toward Jensen when they heard a change in his respiration. Blinking a couple times, Jensen looked over to them and sitting up when he saw the small group.

"Uh oh. What did I miss?" he asked, his voice rough with sleep, as he sat up. Isis looked back to Radar, who was studying the glowing screen of her tablet. The blue glow illuminated her features as she brought it closer to her face, squinting.

"What is it?" Isis asked and Radar glanced at her before looking back to the screen.

"The signal I showed you before we left, the strength

was mostly steady throughout the day. It got a little weaker, but overall there was no significant change," Radar said. "For the past couple hours, it's been getting steadily stronger."

CHAPTER SIX

The rest of the journey was uneventful. The nearer they got to the island, the more uneasy the experiments became. They denied it, but there was a subtle change in their manner — one only the protectors picked up on.

Isis watched Maeve and Keane play a game of strategy with intricately carved pieces in the fading daylight. It looked a little like the Seelie Court's version of chess. The two elves had been playing for more than two hours. She turned her attention back to sharpening the knife she held, sliding it smoothly over the whetstone. Behind her, Steve and Nero were playing checkers with a board Nero had brought along in his bag. He had brought a number of games to pass the time. *If even a fraction of what we've been told about Eris is true, we're going to be here for a long time and I can only have so much sex,* he had explained when he noticed her looking at the various games and multiple card decks he dumped out on his bunk. The other normals were pleased that Nero had brought games and soon made good use of them.

"We should be within sight of the island in the next couple hours, probably at sunset," Maeve mentioned without turning her attention from the game. She drummed her fingers when Keane moved and took one of her pieces off the board. Keane looked up and winked, causing her to chuckle and gesture. Keane laughed quietly and raised his hands, shrugging. Isis slid the small knife in the scabbard that was hidden in her boot. She got to her feet and moved across the deck, her senses sharp for any anomalies. The fading scent of dinner was drifting out from the kitchen and she could pick up the faint musty scent of the selkies skins in the other direction.

Alex was walking about the deck, tossing a small ball up and catching it. Eris was painting her fingernails with black nail polish, uninterested in the others. Jade was sitting on the railing, looking out over the water. Sly and Alpha were cleaning their guns, which they had taken apart and spread out neatly in front of them. Radar was in the sleeping quarters, working on some small gadgets while keeping an eye on her tablet. The signal was still getting stronger and it was making her nervous. Truth be told, it was making Isis uneasy as well.

"How much longer until we get to this bloody island?" Eris called out, shaking her hand to dry her nails. "You know, according to the sacred laws of the guardians, I do still have rights. Being trapped on a ship with you commoners qualifies as torment and torture. It is bad for my mental well-being."

"Funny, I was about to point out something similar about being stuck on a ship with a spoiled guardian," Alpha grumbled as she continued assembling the gun and Sly couldn't help but chuckle. Eris rolled her eyes and rested her wrist on her knee, looking out over the water.

Isis turned her attention up to where Jack was crouching on a spar, his attention focused on the horizon. She could read the same unease she felt in his body language, though he balanced effortlessly. One hand rested on the smooth wooden spar and Isis noticed some of the selkies glancing up at the experiment, apprehension and awe plastered on their faces. It wasn't the wisest thing, to show their abilities around normals, but Isis trusted Jack's judgement. If he needed a better vantage point, they could take a small risk and the selkies weren't a pressing concern. They were a fairly isolated group, one who didn't often take part in Seelie Court matters unless asked.

Moving toward the door that led to the sleeping quarters, Isis opened it and slipped silently inside. As she moved down the few steps, she paused and listened for anything out of the ordinary. When she heard nothing unusual, Isis continued to the sleeping quarters. As she entered the large room, her eyes turned to where Radar was working on one of her electronics. She had set up a battery powered lantern on the small table. A plate of untouched fruit and vegetables sat on the end of the desk, well out of the way of what she was working on. Isis looked to the opposite end of the room where Jensen was laying on his side on his cot, reading a large book. A steaming mug of tea was on a nearby chair and Jensen reached over without looking up from his book, lifting the mug and taking a sip.

"The communication devices will be ready in approximately fifteen minutes," Radar mentioned without taking her attention off the small curved object she was working on. Isis looked at the small tools laid out before the experiment, some of which only Radar's skilled fingers were able to wield. Copper had made her a few different sets of tools, working off the specifications she provided. He had grumbled frequently to Orion, but never to the experiments. Copper never complained to the experiments or denied the few requests they made. He had even made Radar a nice and durable canvas tool roll, which was currently unfurled on the desk. Radar never went anywhere without her tool roll.

Isis turned her attention to Jensen, moving across the room and settling on the bunk next to him. He didn't look up from his book, but offered her the mug of tea. Isis closed her glowing eyes and inhaled the mildly sweet scent of jasmine and herbs. She didn't often drink tea, but she did enjoy the pleasant scent of the beverage. Jensen looked over the top of his book to where Radar was focused completely on her work.

"She hasn't touched her dinner," he mentioned. Isis glanced over at Radar again then shrugged, leaning so she could rest her back against the curved wall behind them. Jensen was uncomfortable leaving his back exposed when he slept in unfamiliar places, something Isis had discovered fairly early on. It was a trait they shared, though Isis didn't sleep. Jensen looked over at her and she arched an eyebrow, handing the mug back to him.

"Experiments rarely consume food or drink when we're being observed. It means a greater likelihood that it has been poisoned," she explained, watching as he sipped his tea before setting it off to the side. "Normals in particular have very voyeuristic tendencies, especially when they kill."

Jensen closed his book and put it aside. "Of course. Apologies, Radar."

Radar turned around in her chair, looking at Jensen quizzically from behind the magnifying goggles she wore. Isis tilted her chin up in the direction of the plate of food. Radar still looked puzzled but turned back to her work. Jensen laughed softly as he pushed himself up into a sitting position.

"I fear I'm a hopeless normal," he said as he leaned back next to Isis. "Are we getting close to our destination?"

Isis nodded once. "Maeve said we'll be in there in a couple hours."

"Ah. Well, I imagine this won't be a pleasant trip," Jensen chuckled. "Eris will make things as difficult as she possibly can. Such is the way of tricksters."

"I can handle Eris," Isis replied as she looked over at Radar. "Try not to worry. Radar's very adept at what she does. We'll be able to stay in communication."

Jensen leaned over and rested his head against Isis'. She turned her head slightly to the side, listening to the soft sound of the waves slapping the side of the boat, which rocked almost imperceptibly. Isis was beginning to wonder if she had ever been to the Seelie Court during her time at Grenich. Nothing indicated that she had been and she had no memories of the place, yet nothing she experienced so far was new to her senses.

"You have weapons?" Isis asked and Jensen sat up again.

"Always," he replied with a gentle smile. "Worried about something going sideways?"

"Everyone should be prepared for anything at all times," Isis said as she sat up again. Being sedentary didn't suit her and she needed to check on the others. She also wanted to do one last check of her weapons before they reached their destination. Next to her, she heard Jensen sit up and then get to his feet.

As she was about to move to the door, Jack appeared. Isis tilted her head and he nodded over his shoulder.

"There's something you should see," he explained as she moved across the room. Jensen followed behind the two experiments. As they emerged onto the deck of the ship, Jack led them over to the railing, where the other members of the Four were standing. Shae and Alex looked concerned and Jade looked curious. Isis turned her attention across the water and her own eyes widened for a split second at what she saw in the distance: an island.

"Maeve's already confirmed that's the Island of Avalon," Jade mentioned as Isis laid her hands on the smooth wooden railing. "Though she can't explain how we're already so close. According to her, it should have been at least another half-hour before we even caught a glimpse of the island."

"Missing time," Jack mentioned as Isis looked around the ship. The selkies all looked incredibly unnerved and the elves were having an animated conversation in sign. Their hands flew swiftly and smoothly as they conversed silently. Nero was sitting near Eris and shuffling a deck of cards. Sly continued cleaning weapons while Alpha listened to the small iPod she had brought along. Her head bobbed along with a beat only she could hear and her fingers lightly tapped the box she sat on.

"Isis?"

Isis turned when she heard Steve's soft question. He looked concerned as he looked over to the island in the distance and then back to her. Isis rubbed her hands together, turning her attention to Jade. The older shape shifter shrugged and shook her head, resigned.

"We don't have much of a choice," Jade said.

"I agree. We should adjust the strategy and proceed as though we're heading into hostile territory," Isis mentioned. "Just as a precaution."

Jade nodded and moved over to where Alpha and Sly were. Isis watched as she embraced Alpha and then passionately kissed Sly. As the two women exchanged a few words, Isis looked around the rest of the ship. The selkies were preparing to drop the anchor and the ship's speed was gradually declining. They dashed about as the captain called out orders, directing the crew and gesturing to various places.

Eris stood up and stretched, rolling her neck around a little and swinging her arms to loosen them up. Her flesh noticeably glistened with guardian light in the bright sun. It was even more noticeable due to Eris' dark clothing and sleeveless shirt. As though feeling eyes on her, Eris turned to look at Isis. After a moment, a small half smile curved up a corner of her mouth. Isis turned her attention back to the island and squinted, focusing on the shores. There didn't seem to be any movement or other signs of life.

Looking up into the colorful sky, Isis noticed it was empty. Most of the usual sounds had ceased and there were no mer-people in sight. They were officially in sacred waters and completely alone.

~~*~*~*

When twilight fell, the Four were in a small rowing boat with Eris sitting in the front. As they rowed, she rested her head on her folded arm on the side of the small boat and trailed her fingers through the clear waters.

"You know, you could help a bit, Eris," Shae mentioned as she continued rowing.

"I could, but I won't," Eris replied with a nonchalant shrug. "Your kind excels at manual labor and my nails look incredibly nice. To damage them would simply be a crime."

When they finally reached the sands of the island, Jade and Isis got out first to make sure they were truly alone. Jade had her gun out and pointed at the ground as she walked a short way from the boat. Isis calmly moved off in the other direction, her sharp eyes scanning the ground and trees for any sign of life. The colors struck her as a bit duller than was typical of flora from the Seelie Court, even in the rapidly fading light. The sand crunched lightly under her boots as she took a few more steps forward and the ground soon became rockier. The silence was not ideal and not something she often encountered.

Entering the dark forest, Isis moved over to a fallen tree and crouched down. Running her fingers over the ground, she examined the soil and the plants. Nothing was out of place or sticking out to her, but she still felt like something was off. Examining the fallen tree, Isis tried to figure out what had made it fall. As she inspected it, something cracked in the distance, causing her entire body to go rigid as she looked in the direction of the sound. There was the quiet chirping of insects and the occasional breeze rustling through leaves, but nothing unusual for the location. Isis stood up again, brushing the dirt off her gloves. According to the Seelie Court's accounts, there were some forms of wildlife on the uninhabited Island of

Avalon. Isis caught the faint scent of some sort of canid and a couple birds.

The sound of Jade's sharp whistle caused her to look back where she had come from and Isis realized she had wandered out of the sight of her teammates. Striding back out onto the beach, she noticed Eris sitting on the lip of the boat while Shae stood nearby. Isis looked to her left, where Jade was standing at the edge of the forest. Alex was near her, making a mark on a nearby tree with a stick of bright pink chalk, which stuck out even in the dim light.

"Aw, she comes when called. Just like a little dog," Eris said, delighted. Jade shook her head and rubbed her eyes.

"Anything out of the ordinary?" Alex asked, ignoring Eris.

"Nothing that I could sense," Isis answered, resting a hand on the pommel of her sai. "I will notify you should that change."

"I suggest we move out," Jade said, glancing up at the sky, which continued to darken. "We'll get as far as we can before it gets dark and then set up camp —"

"I really hope you don't expect me to sleep on the ground like an animal," Eris mentioned from over where she leaned against the little rowboat.

"Tomorrow," Jade continued, ignoring the petulant guardian, "we'll head out to the area near where Eris was captured, start searching there and work our way out. Unless she chooses to be cooperative."

Eris smirked. "How wicked you think me, Jade. I may want to save all those poor suffering wretches in the Meadows. Perhaps I will lead you right to the box, if only to be allowed to return back to civilization. I'm not an animal lover, unlike my younger sister."

"Okay, great," Jade said curtly. "I'll count on that. Alex, have you checked the communication devices?"

"Yeah, they're working perfectly. Tap the button once to turn it on, hold it down to switch the channel, and twice shuts them off," Alex replied as she tucked the chalk back into an inner pocket of her shirt, looking over at Isis. "Radar did a really incredible job. There's almost no static."

Isis barely heard her as she looked back toward the thick forest that stood a few feet away. It was dark and she thought it was possible there would be a few open areas, which didn't sit well with her. The whole island was a tactical nightmare, one she would have preferred to avoid. Looking back to the other three, she moved a little closer.

"So we're about a two to four hour walk from where Eris was captured," Jade began.

"Box isn't anywhere near there, sugarplum," Eris interrupted in a sing-song voice, looking down at her painted nails.

"That's a lie," Isis stated. "She has a tell."

Eris narrowed her eyes as she looked over at Isis. "I am insulted at the suggestion I would be so careless. That is absolutely not true."

"It's not one a normal would notice, but it is there nonetheless," Isis replied, unbothered by Eris' reaction.

"This is either going to be very interesting or very tedious," Shae mentioned as she rubbed the side of her neck. "Here I was hoping for a nice girls weekend, some time on the beach, maybe not a piña colada or daiquiri but the Seelie Court equivalent."

Alex laughed quietly as she turned her attention back to the digital compass she was holding, another of Radar's inventions. Isis inhaled the scents of the island, identifying something that smelled a little like eucalyptus. A lot of the scents were similar to the ones on Earth, though nowhere near as strong.

"Ugh, can we stop dawdling and just *go*?" Eris moaned as she hopped off the boat. "Come on, ladies. Those apprentices aren't getting any healthier. Your kind enjoys digging in the mud and filth, so let's go find some. I'll tell you whether you're getting hotter or colder."

"Isis, you're up front with me. Eris, you'll walk between

us," Jade instructed. "Shae and Alex, cover our backs. Let's move out."

Eris moved over to where Jade was standing and saluted her theatrically. Shae and Alex took up their positions. All four women looked expectantly to where Isis was still standing, eyes closed and head tilted. After a moment, her glowing green eyes opened again and she moved over to the group. Jade looked at her questioningly but Isis just shook her head, indicating that nothing was wrong.

After more than an hour of walking, night had fallen and a light drizzle started. The pattering of raindrops on leaves was a welcome change in the mostly quiet forest, though it made the leaves move and the entire forest soon looked as though it was trembling. Eris moved jauntily, practically skipping alongside the shape shifters. Isis remained silent, relying on all her senses to tell her exactly what was going on around her. Her sharp eyes pierced the murky shadows that surrounded them. The forest was briefly illuminated by a flash of lightning, followed closely by the quiet rumble of thunder.

"That one doesn't talk much, does she?" Eris observed after a while as they continued on their way, playfully bumping Shae with her shoulder. "You protectors are always so dour. It's rather sad."

Spinning one finger in a circular motion, the whole area became incredibly bright as if it was daytime and the sun was out. A carpet made of millions of bright red roses suddenly stretched out as far as the eye could see, the ominous forest transforming in an instant. Delicate pink and white petals showered down upon the women and multicolored butterflies flitted about. Jade glared at Eris while Isis held a hand out, trying to capture some petals in her hand. They felt and smelled remarkably similar to flower petals, ones found in the Meadows. She couldn't tell if it was an illusion or a conjuring trick. Either way, it was impressively complex and detailed, giving her some idea of how powerful Eris was. All the flowers felt, looked, and smelled real.

"Knock it off," Jade growled, her eyes flickering with anger. Eris sighed and waved her hand. The flowers and butterflies instantly vanished, leaving behind the dark forest and the approaching storm. The change in light was jarring and it took Isis' eyes a split-second to adjust. She looked off into the forest when she thought she saw a flash of movement in the distance, a ripple in the shadows. Instinctively, her hands drifted to her sais.

"Jade, you remain a boring old cu—"

Isis whipped around when Eris let out a strangled gagging sound. What looked like a stiff vine had wrapped around the guardian's throat and cinched tightly, cutting off her breath. It then yanked Eris off her feet and pulled her backwards, pulling her up so that she was hanging from an enormous ancient-looking tree. Lightning split the sky again, briefly illuminating the horrific scene. Eris gurgled and clawed at the coils around her neck, attempting to break the plant that was killing her. She kicked her legs as she thrashed about wildly, instinctively panicking. All four women moved at once and Alex positioned herself under Eris' feet, taking most of the guardian's weight onto herself.

Isis swiftly shifted into a panther and scaled the tree within seconds, her claws piercing the rough bark. Once she was out on the branch that the vine had coiled around, she shifted back into her human form and yanked out her knife, cutting at the rough wood. The bark smoked when the blade touched it, but the weapon didn't even leave a nick. Isis blinked a couple times, staring in disbelief at the unblemished wood. She looked at the sharpened blade she held in her hand, not understanding how that was possible. Her knife was made of guardian silver, which would cut through anything.

"Isis, hurry up!" Jade shouted from a thick branch directly below her where she was standing precariously while also attempting to slice the deadly vine. "Eris, dammit, stop struggling! You're making it worse!"

Isis looked down at her briefly before raising her hand, lightning splitting the sky again, and then stabbed deep into the vine. There was a sizzling sound as it pierced the bark; white sparks burst out from around the blade and a strange viscous fluid bubbled up around the knife. Isis could hear Eris thrashing about and desperately wheezing for air. Putting all her weight onto the grip, Isis drove the blade as deep as it would go and dragged it toward her, cutting a deep gouge into the strange wood. Dark gray ooze continued pouring out of the cut as more sparks showered down upon the group. The vine finally released its grip on Eris, causing both she and Alex to fall in a heap on the ground. Eris coughed harshly and gulped in air as she rolled onto her side, one hand rising to her throat. Alex carefully sat up, her eyes wide as she looked around.

Isis jumped out of the tree and as soon as her boots hit the ground, she felt a vine wrap tightly around her ankle. Before she could react, she was yanked off her feet and her face slammed into the soft wet ground as she was dragged backward into the murky forest. She clawed at the dirt, but was unable to get a proper grip. The deeper into the forest she was pulled, the lower the visibility. Branches, plants, and small stones scratched at her face as she sped past them and she could taste the damp earth on her tongue. Resorting to desperate measures, Isis threw her body to the side so she flipped onto her back. Reaching into her core, she held one hand out and focused everything in her on the root that was latched around her ankle. Suddenly, it felt like something yanked her to her feet and her momentum stopped. Her muscles burned as she continued to focus on holding the vine still, even as it continued trying to jerk back and break away from her hold. Dropping into a crouch, she pulled out her knife again and stabbed it deep into the tough wood. Sparks and gray ooze splashed up at her and she felt the hold gradually loosen as an ear splitting shriek sounded throughout the forest. It took a few strong kicks with her free leg, but Isis managed to break free from the vine's hold. She immediately dropped her hand and the vine cracked in the air like a whip before disappearing back into the foliage.

There was a loud snapping sound as another vine lashed out for her wrist, but this time, Isis was prepared. She twisted away from the plant, dropping into a crouch so she was out of the reach of the vine, relying mostly on her sense of smell and hearing to give her an idea of her surroundings. Behind her, she could hear the roots of another tree uncoiling and rising quietly from the ground. The entire forest seemed to be moving and the occasional flash of lightning revealed branches that looked like hundreds of snakes slithering above her. Isis coughed and ran the back of her hand across her face, cleaning off the blade of her knife on the ground before slipping it back into its scabbard. She cautiously rose back up and pressed her senses outward, searching for anything out of the ordinary. It was so dark that she had difficulty seeing any significant distance in front of her.

As she began moving forward, trying to avoid the vines that still reached for her, Isis suddenly heard a strange sound, an unsettling chortling. It was a sound that made all the hairs on the back of her neck stand straight up and she felt a tremor go through her hand. The call was answered by another, coming from her other side. There was only one creature that made that sound and it was one not even experiments would confront, especially not without a large team. Out of the corner of her eye, Isis caught a glimpse of glowing stormy gray eyes to her right. She swallowed and continued backing up, the eyes moving right along with her as the unseen creature followed her every step. Isis turned her head, meeting its gaze with her own. Her hands moved to hover over the pommels of her sais. The creature made a quiet whooping sound in response and its head began moving from side to side. The rain picked up even more, water streaming down her face and dripping into her eyes, plastering her hair to her skull. Another strange giggling bark came from behind her, but Isis didn't move her attention from the creature in front of her. They were pack animals and they were trying to surround her.

Moving gradually to the side, never taking her attention off the pair of eyes in front of her, Isis noted that she couldn't smell or hear the other women. That was a concern because it meant she had been dragged much further than she had originally thought. The glowing stormy gray eyes suddenly disappeared in the darkness and the scent vanished as well. The rustling behind her stopped as did the vocalizations. Isis continued backing away, her senses sharp for the predators and the vines, which still reached for her.

Turning to continue back the way she had come, Isis found herself face-to-face with glowing gray eyes and the massive jaws of an enormous werehyena and before she could even flinch, the animal pounced. She grunted when her back slammed into the cold wet ground, the full weight of the huge carnivore pressing down, threatening to suffocate her. Lighting briefly illuminated her surroundings again, revealing that the werehyena was bigger than a grizzly. Warm saliva splattered across her face as the huge yellow teeth snapped uncomfortably close to her head. Turning her face to the side as she pushed against its throat with her forearm, she quickly unsheathed one sai with her free hand and immediately drove it deeply into the rancid-smelling creature's glowing eye. It let out a scream of pain and jumped to the side, scratching its destroyed eye. Isis took the opportunity to get back to her feet and, when lightning lit up the sky again, she jumped on top of the beast, which immediately began thrashing around as it tried to throw her off. Clutching the creature tightly with her thighs, Isis tried to drive the sai into the back of its skull. The guardian silver easily sliced through flesh and muscle, but she couldn't get enough leverage to drive it through the thick bone. The animal continued making giggling yipping and whooping sounds as it tried to latch onto her leg with its powerful jaws. The lightning and thunder suddenly stopped, but the rain continued.

Switching tactics, Isis shifted her position and grabbed a fistful of the damp rough fur and flesh on the scruff of the neck. She wasted no time as she reached over the head and drove the sai deep into the creature's head, pushing the longest prong of the weapon deep into the werehyena's eye. A yellow fluid with a glue-like consistency sprayed out as she wiggled the prong, forcing it all the way back into the head until she found the weakest point of the skull. Letting go of the fur, she slammed the heel of her hand onto the pommel of the sai. The animal shuddered and keeled over, pinning one of her legs with its huge mass. Isis let out a grunt as she hit the muddy ground with a splash, once again finding herself under the weight of the werehyena. As she kicked at the creature, Isis took note of its size: it was at least double that of any werehyena she had ever heard or read about.

As she kicked at the carcass, Isis could hear a few other members of the pack calling to each other. They were getting closer, obviously unimpeded by the vines, impenetrable shadows, or the cold rain that was steadily falling. The corpse gradually melted into a more human form, the unnaturally pale flesh standing out even in the shadows. Isis finally got her leg free and backed away from it, staring at the misshapen form. The limbs were unnaturally elongated, as was the rest of the body. The snout hadn't melted back into a normal-looking human face, giving the creature the strange appearance of a chimera: half human and half monstrous animal. As she briefly studied it, Isis realized it would have been impossible for the creature to survive in its human form. It had probably never even been in that form before, which was a very disturbing thought.

The sound of some brush being trampled brought Isis

back to the present. Her eyes darted about the darkness that surrounded her, almost appearing as a solid mass, and she leaned away from a vine that lashed out at her. Around her, she could hear something sweeping through the brush and splashing through the wet ground, gradually closing in on her. Leaping over the corpse, Isis took off running into the shadows, intent on meeting up with the rest of her team. As she ran and slid, Isis reached up to the communication device that was still in her ear, pressing the button once. All around her, there was a whisper of leaves and branches snapping as an unseen pack pursued her. Every now and again, she would catch a glimpse of empty glowing white or gray eyes. Dropping to her knees, Isis slid under an enormous werehyena that sailed right over her, its claws nearly slicing her face, and disappeared somewhere amongst the trees. Leaping back up to her feet, Isis continued running through the writhing forest.

"Can anyone hear me?" she asked, waiting for a moment before switching the channel. "Respond if you can hear me."

When she received no response, Isis increased her pace and tore through the slithering trees. The icy rain continued pelting down and the branches of the trees kept reaching out, trying to latch onto her. Isis soon caught another scent that didn't belong, but pushed it to the back of her mind for the time being. The most important thing was to reach her teammates. They had no idea of the danger lurking in the large forest.

~~*~*~*

"I just had a marvelous idea: how about we get the hell out of here?"

Jade looked back at Eris' croaking voice, noticing the guardian wincing at the pain of speaking. *Here I thought we would have a bit of respite. Should have known,* the protector thought with a shake of her head. They had decided to risk using their head lanterns, since none of them were able to see two feet in front of them. The bright glow had a very limited radius, but it was better than nothing. Shae finished rubbing some cool salve from their small first aid kit on Eris' heavily bruised throat. Ducking out of the way of a vine that dropped down from above them, Shae moved over to where Jade was standing with her hands on her hips, looking in the direction Isis had been yanked. The younger protector shivered and rubbed her arms, obviously a little nervous about the situation.

"You and Alex take Eris back to the boat," Jade ordered, keeping her voice soft. "I'm going after Isis and we'll regroup on the beach then head back to the ship. We need to rethink our approach, maybe convince the elves to let us bring a couple more people ashore."

"The communication devices aren't working anymore," Alex spoke up from where she still stood near Eris, covering their backs. Jade and Shae looked over at her, watching as she gestured to her ear. Jade ran her hands over her face, scrubbing some of the rain from her features. They hadn't even been on the island that long and already things were going to shit.

"Eris, I swear to the guardians, if I find out you had anything to do with this," Jade warned as she looked over at the guardian, who was once again tugging at her head lantern. It had been like pulling teeth getting her to wear the damn thing, which she said made her look as though she belonged to the peasantry.

"Darling, if this had been my doing, do you *really* think I would have hung myself?" Eris rasped in annoyance.

"She has a point," Alex mentioned, smiling a little at the sour look Jade gave her. Eris turned her nose up and moved away from the direction where Isis had disappeared.

"My poor niece is probably dead. May the guardians have mercy on her spirit or memory or whatever, et cetera, et cetera," Eris said with a dismissive wave of her hand. "It would be wiser to stay in a group. But throughout history, protectors have proven time and again that they lack any kind of common sense, so I imagine you'll go running off after her and wind up hanging from one of these pretty trees. I, however, have no interest in dying here. So I'm going back to the ship and all of you can run off on a pointless endeavor."

Alex drew her handgun and fired at a vine that had been snaking toward Eris' ankle, causing the guardian to jump in surprise and nimbly step away from the tree. All around them, the forest was writhing. The wood creaked and the leaves rustled, which made a constant, eerie slithering sound. The sound was made worse by the fact that they couldn't see anything.

"Shae, Alex," Jade said, nodding toward their prisoner. Alex quickly moved to comply, moving over to where the guardian was standing with a hand on her hip, which was cocked to the side. Eris pursed her lips as she looked Alex up and down, making sure to shine her head lantern's light in the protector's eyes.

"Be careful," Shae whispered to Jade. The older protector looked over at her teammate, hearing the concern in her voice.

"You too," Jade said, lifting her chin in Eris' direction. The guardian was now looking around, squinting a little. Raising one hand up, she trailed her fingers through the air. Dropping her hand, Eris leaned back as she looked at something in the distance.

"No tricks, Eris," Jade warned before turning to Shae. "Go now. Before these vines are the death of all of us."

Shae quickly moved over to where Alex and Eris were standing. She tapped Alex's shoulder and Alex drew her gun, walking back in the direction they had come from. Jade turned and headed off in the opposite direction, following the claw marks in the mud.

As she walked deeper into the forest with only the small circle of light to see by, Jade could hear the creaking and slithering of all the branches and roots surrounding her. The rain began to let up a bit and Jade continued making her way through the darkness, her boots squishing in the mud. She had always loved walking in forests, having been born in one, but this one didn't feel welcoming. The longer she walked, the more Jade felt as though she were being slowly devoured.

Her head lantern flickered once, causing her insides to clench up for a nerve-wracking moment. Jade began to feel strange, as if she were moving through a dream. The humidity increased and the air felt incredibly heavy, as did her steps. Every so often, she would feel a vine brush against the back of her head or neck, almost a tender caress. Around her, the sounds started to echo and what little she could see took on a soft, hazy appearance.

Quiet whispering made Jade hesitate and she looked around, shining her head lantern about the shadows. She noticed a thin mist had formed over the ground, concealing her feet. Crouching down, Jade swept her hand through the mist so she could see the ground. Once she saw mud, she also noticed some large splotches of blood. Following the trail with her eyes as she continued sweeping the mist away, Jade noticed it led slightly away from the drag marks she had been tracking and more toward what looked like an open glade, which appeared to be a little less dark than the forest. It wasn't too far; she could keep her visual on the other track if she chose to investigate the blood. It would be nice to not have to worry about the grabbing vines that surrounded her in the forest. The whispering around her continued as she moved to follow the trail. *Isis, I swear, if you got yourself killed,* Jade thought as she drew her gun and pointed it in front of her.

She emerged into the glade and moved across the lush, bright green grass when a sudden beam of light on her face drew her attention to the right. Jade turned and froze in horror at the sight in front of her. A golden light shone behind a woman hanging from her wrists and ankles in the middle of a Y-shaped tree. Her limbs had been pulled uncomfortably far, nearly to the point of dislocation. She had been slit down the middle and her organs were in a glistening pile below her. Behind her, the vines looked like a giant web. The ones around her wrists and ankles continued tightening. They had burst through her chest and eyes, gradually turning her body into part of the tree and rendering her completely unrecognizable. Jade had seen a number of horrific things in her long years, but the sight before her almost surpassed all of them. Her stomach lurched and she felt vomit swell up in her throat. Jade forced herself to look at the body again, trying to figure out if it was Isis, but it proved to be an impossible task. Her feet felt cemented in place and she found she couldn't move, though Jade wasn't entirely sure she wanted to. She desperately wanted to shut her eyes, but found that she couldn't. After a while, there was a strange rustling behind her and she thought she heard a snarl, but she still couldn't move.

Suddenly Jade felt someone grab her arms and she was yanked to the ground. Something soared over her head, so close her hair was swept over her shoulder and coarse fur brushed against her cheek. Jade slammed into the wet grass with a grunt, the ache bringing her back to the present, and quickly pointed her gun at the mysterious person who had tackled her. She couldn't hide her surprise when she found herself face-to-face with Isis, completely unharmed. She was dripping wet and her short dark hair was plastered to her skull. *Guardians, I never thought I would be so relieved to see those glowing eyes,* Jade thought, deciding not to hassle her teammate about her not wearing her lantern. The experiment flipped back to her feet and quickly moved forward a few steps, placing herself in front of Jade.

Isis drew her own guns and fired a few shots, causing Jade to look over to what she was shooting at. She only caught a glimpse of mangy brown fur as whatever it was disappeared deeper into the shadows. Isis holstered her guns again, backing up a few steps. She turned back to Jade and the confusion must have shown on the older protector's face.

"What?" Isis asked, twisting to quickly look behind her and then looking back to the older protector. Jade opened her mouth to respond, but closed it again, unsure of how to answer. She still felt an overwhelming sense of relief at seeing Isis alive and unhurt. Her eyes wandered back to where the gruesome scene had been and saw nothing, not even the strange tree. The mist had vanished — if it had ever even been there — as had the strange gold light. Jade swallowed and looked back to Isis, who offered her a hand. Jade accepted it and allowed her teammate to help her up. She quickly started brushing some of the dirt and leaves off her clothing.

"I could have sworn," Jade began, but then shook her head. "Never mind."

Isis studied her for a moment and then looked back off in the distance. "We need to get back to the others. The woods are crawling with werehyenas."

Jade felt her eyes widen. "What? Werehyenas? But . . . that's not possible."

"These are mutations, at least double the size of a common werehyena. They can't survive in their human form, so they're permanently in beast form. At least until they're put down," Isis continued to explain, disregarding Jade's statement as she began to lead her teammate back the way the protector had come from. "Their eyes glow."

"Grenich," Jade said, unsurprised when Isis nodded once. "So Set probably used the dagger of Oriana to get to the Island of Avalon at some point. But why?"

"I don't know," Isis said as they continued making their way alongside the forest, keeping clear of the deadly vines, which occasionally lashed out at them. "I can't find any strategic benefit to this location, but there has to be one . . ."

Isis trailed off and suddenly stopped, tilting her head.

She looked back in the direction they had come from, then in front of them. Licking her lips, Isis looked around and fixed her attention on the forest.

"Isis, what's wrong?" Jade asked as Isis made her way over to a nearby tree. The experiment let out a growl as she lithely danced away from the roots that reached out for her. She moved back over to where Jade was standing.

"Do you hear humming?" she asked and Jade stared at her.

"Um," Jade hesitated, taking a moment to listen. She could hear the slithering and creaking from the trees, but little else. "No. I don't hear any kind of humming."

Isis kept looking off in the distance as she ran a hand over her face. "It's coming from that direction, as best I can tell."

"As best you can tell?"

"I . . . Something might be interfering with my senses," Isis confessed as she kept her attention forward, not meeting Jade's gaze. "My sense of distance and time is off, possibly direction too. It's . . . concerning."

Jade swallowed. "I think I may have hallucinated back there, before you tackled me."

Isis paused and looked over at the protector, putting her hand up to stop her. Jade looked at her green eyes, glowing luminously even in the light of the head lantern.

"I thought I saw a tree with a dead body in it, mutilated beyond recognition," Jade explained. "It was gone when I looked over to it again, after you shot at the werehyena."

"There's a strange pollen-like substance in the air," Isis mentioned, glancing to the side at the trees. "It's heaviest in the forest, which might account for your hallucination. I noticed it when I was trying to find a path around the trees. It's something artificially made, not a natural substance."

Jade nodded, still disturbed by the gruesome image she had seen. Fiddling with the compass in her pocket absent-mindedly, she reached up to her ear and tested the communication device. After trying to contact her teammates and the ship a couple times, Jade gave up and dropped her arm. Isis had moved a few feet away, looking across the open field; her attention fixed somewhere above them. Jade tried to follow her gaze and noticed a decent-sized hill a short distance away.

"We should try to get to higher ground," Isis mentioned. "Try to see the others, get a sense of direction. I don't know if we'll find our way to them otherwise."

"Actually, I think I have a better solution," Jade mentioned, pulling out the compass. Isis put her hands on her hips, one corner of her mouth twitching in what might have been a small half-smile.

"It points in the direction of the Leaves of Ivy and therefore right to Eris," Jade reminded her and Isis nodded in understanding.

"From what I've observed, the forest is acting like a kind of barrier or net," Isis explained. "It keeps intruders trapped inside, so it's very likely they're still in there somewhere. We need to find them before the werehyenas do. Afterward, we should consider finding higher ground in order to get an idea of where everything is, try contacting the ship again. If there is a Grenich presence on this island, escaping won't be easy."

"Okay. Do you think you'll be able to find your way back here?"

"I am not certain, but I think I will be able to," Isis replied with a small shrug. Jade rubbed the back of her neck and looked at the dark forest, uneasiness creeping into her mind. She pulled out the compass and looked at it, frowning.

The arrow was pointing away from the woods, indicating the other three had gone deeper into the island.

~~*~*~*

"This is completely different from when I was last

here."

Alex looked over at Eris, who had been strangely quiet since they had separated from Jade. They had been walking for about an hour by her estimate and they had yet to come upon the beach. None of their surroundings looked even remotely familiar, which was odd because Alex didn't think they had gotten that far before Eris had nearly been hung. The trees started growing closer together, making it darker and more difficult to navigate. It was beginning to feel claustrophobic. The ground was uneven, making for a very unsteady walk and they were frequently stumbling and slipping in the mud.

"That's not exactly breaking news," Shae replied, waving away an insect that was flitting about her face. "It was what? Hundreds of years ago? Things change nat —"

"How can you *possibly* be so dense?" Eris snapped irritably. "I'm not referring to new trees or rocks or any superficial change in the scenery. The entire place is different: the air, the atmosphere, the shadows, the whole bloody island. It's like a completely new environment."

Alex looked over to Shae, who seemed concerned as she kept glancing behind them, searching for any sign of their two teammates. It was still too dark to see anything outside of the range of their head lanterns. She and Alex had been taking turns covering each other's backs. Since setting foot on the island, Alex had been feeling uneasy. Something just wasn't right about the place and she wouldn't be surprised if her friends felt it as well. Isis certainly had been acting on edge since they had stepped on the island.

"Alex, shouldn't we be hearing water or something by now?" Shae asked, unbothered by Eris. Alex nodded, twisting around when she heard a twig snap somewhere nearby. Every now and again, she would hear an animal or bird moving around or catch a glimpse of something moving in the darkness.

"Have you damn fools gotten us lost?" Eris growled,

throwing her arms up in the air. "Unbelievable. I'm going to die, surrounded by the guardians' pets. That's just bloody perfect."

"Hey, Eris, you want to keep the chatter down to a minimum? You know, just in case there are unfriendlies out there?" Shae said, her patience starting to wear thin. The guardian raised her hands and moved away a few steps. She crossed her arms over her chest and began tapping her foot, looking off into the forest.

Alex motioned for Shae to come over as she pulled the map out of her pack. She looked out at the seemingly impenetrable shadows. It bothered her that she could see nothing, every direction looked exactly the same. They had enough provisions for a three-week journey, but they would run out of food and water eventually. Their situation was not ideal and could become even more difficult. Glancing at the map briefly, Alex looked up again and tried to get her bearings.

"Next time, Jade gets to babysit the petulant guardian convict," Shae muttered as she grabbed her canteen and unscrewed the top. She took a small swig before putting the cap back on and re-attaching it to her pack.

"Shae, I have no idea where we are," Alex whispered, using one knuckle to wipe some sweat from her brow. The rustling of the map seemed abnormally loud in their silent surroundings. Shae stared at her and Alex met her gaze briefly before looking back at the map.

"Please tell me you're not serious," Shae said, running a hand over her hair.

"Excuse me? Protectors?" Eris spoke from behind them, her tone condescendingly pleasant.

"I made sure to memorize some of the maps of this island and study some accounts of it from the Meadows library, because I knew how much of a hassle Eris would be. The fey are almost obsessively detailed when it comes to describing this island. According to their record keepers, there are quite a few markers on the land, giant rocks and oddly-shaped trees and the like, and we haven't passed any of them. I also haven't seen any of the chalk marks I made," Alex explained, ignoring Eris. "We've been retracing our steps, but we haven't passed a single tree with a chalk mark. Even if we had gotten turned around or left the path, which I'm certain we didn't, we should have passed something that would have told me where we are."

"Ladies? Whatever your names are?"

"So what does that mean? We're lost?" Shae asked, putting her hands on her hips. Alex bit her bottom lip as she looked in front of them again, tuning out Eris as she continued calling for the two protectors.

"We might be, but that's impossible," Alex answered, confused. "It just . . . it doesn't make any sense. I don't understand how —"

Eris' ear-piercing whistle interrupted her and both protectors turned to glare at her in annoyance. She gave a sarcastically innocent smile and pointed off into the shadowy forest.

"We seem to have company with very sharp teeth," she mentioned with her typical nonchalance. Alex looked in the direction the guardian pointed and felt her blood run cold. She swallowed and carefully folded the map, handing it over to Shae, who was also standing rigidly, her eyes wide in alarm. As she cautiously moved over to Eris, Alex heard a strange chortling start from the two sets of glowing gray eyes amongst the trees. The one creature didn't look too thrilled with Eris' head lantern shining directly at it.

They were enormous, larger than any animal Alex had ever encountered. There was the faint smell of disease in the air, decay and rot. It was not a scent that should have been on the Island of Avalon. Alex reached Eris' side and calmly grabbed her arm, pulling her back. Two pairs of large yellow fangs appeared under the glowing eyes. Their heads swayed side to side as they began chortling again.

"Eris, I need you to be completely honest with me,"

Alex began, feeling a tremor go down her spine. "Are you creating a hallucination? Or messing with our perception?"

"'Fraid not, sweetheart," Eris replied. "Those are most certainly *not* my doing."

A chorus of snarls traveled through the forest, moving in a wide circle around the three women. Both Shae and Alex looked around, shining their lanterns as they tried to get some idea of just how many creatures there were, which proved to be impossible.

"I think it's safe to assume they've got us boxed in," Shae observed dryly.

"What in the name of the guardians are these things? They stink worse than you lot," Eris said as she scrunched up her nose in disgust. One of the creatures bolted out from behind the trees, growling as it skidded to a halt just outside the circle of light, before slowly backing away again. Alex forced herself not to react, but she felt herself flinch. The beast was big enough to be almost eye-level with her. There was more muffled chattering around them, echoing throughout the suddenly silent forest. Alex had no idea exactly how many creatures surrounded them, but they were very obviously outnumbered.

"Eris, listen to me. I need you to stay behind me," Alex instructed, keeping her voice soft and calm, not taking her eyes off the massive animals in front of her. "Don't make any sudden movements and don't talk."

Eris rolled her eyes. "What are you on about? Aren't these your kin?"

The second creature bolted out from the side, again skidding to a halt just a few steps from the light. It snapped at the air, baring its enormous teeth. Alex could hear Shae switch the safety off her gun behind them. The creature began backing up slowly, but continued watching the three women, growling deep in its throat. It stopped just before the trees, lowering its head and continued growling. Alex heard rustling somewhere behind her and found herself wishing Isis were there. It seemed like the type of situation where an experiment could make the difference between life and death.

"Eris, for the love of everything. Stop. Talking," Alex hissed. "Those are wereanimals, hyenas judging by their calls. They aren't fond of shape shifters and even less fond of guardians."

"Well we have that in common," Eris whispered to Alex, though she stayed behind the protector as instructed. Alex reached down to her holster and immediately heard a yipping start to her right. Resting her hand on the firearm, she turned her head slightly.

"Shae, how's it looking behind us?" she asked as she started backing up.

"There might be a couple back here, but compared to up there? I'd wager it's the safer bet," Shae responded. "Alex, their eyes are glowing."

"I noticed. Okay, I suggest we remain calm and keep backing up until we lose our unwanted company. Don't use bullets unless you absolutely have to. Our ammo is going to have to last who knows how long," Alex said quietly as she continued backing up. Shae suddenly yelped and Alex twisted sharply just in time to see her teammate get dragged deeper into the forest, disappearing somewhere in the darkness.

The sound of a loud snarl brought her attention back to the werehyenas in front of her and she narrowly dodged the enormous animal that lunged at her. It fell to the muddy ground clumsily and rolled a little before coming to a stop, shaking its head as it got back to its feet. Alex quickly straightened up and grabbed Eris, shoving the guardian in front of her.

"Run!" she yelled. Eris didn't even hesitate as she sprinted off into the shadows, running straight ahead. There was a maniacal cacophony of chortles and giggles as the pack of werehyenas gave chase. Alex could hear them tearing through the plant life, sweeping through the forest with ease. She had no idea which direction they were heading in and could only hope they could outrun the creatures behind them, at least until they found a tall enough tree to climb.

Vines grabbed at the two women as they continued to run through the impenetrable darkness, which seemed like a solid mass surrounding them. They were stumbling and slipping on the uneven wet ground. They lacked the sturdy footing of the werehyenas, who were quickly closing in on them. A particularly sharp vine sliced open Alex's cheek, but she ignored it as she continued running.

Seeing a light out of the corner of her eye, Alex instinctively ran toward it and soon came upon Shae struggling to free herself from the vine, which had wrapped her arm tightly against a tree. She was covered in mud from being dragged through the forest and was thrashing about wildly as she tried to get loose.

"Eris!" Alex yelled, looking over her shoulder for the guardian. She swore loudly when Eris didn't respond. She couldn't see the wayward guardian anywhere and hoped she had enough sense to continue running away. Alex shook her head as she drew her knife and began sawing at the unnaturally tough bark.

"You need to go get her," Shae hissed as she continued yanking against the tight binding. The vine constricted even more causing her to suck in her breath.

"I'm not leaving you," Alex replied unbothered as she continued hacking at the vine, wishing she had a machete. The sound of werehyena chortles were getting closer and Alex heard a couple run down the path, likely chasing after the guardian. She ignored them for the time being as she finally slipped her knife into the vine. Sparks shot out and viscous gray goo sprayed out of the strange plant. The vine finally released its death-grip on Shae and Alex grabbed her teammate, pulling her over to a nearby ditch. The two women ducked down, switching off their head lanterns, hidden by the thick fronds of an enormous fern and unnaturally dark shadows. Small roots curled out of the ground, but strangely, didn't attempt to grab them.

They couldn't see anything, but they could hear everything around them, including the few werehyenas that ran past their hiding place. One of the massive animals suddenly slowed its pace to a jog and sniffed the air. Shae put her hand over her mouth and Alex carefully unholstered her gun, holding her breath when another werehyena paused next to the first one. The creatures licked their chops and started noisily sniffing the ground. One werehyena suddenly shook itself off and Shae winced as she was hit with some of the creature's spittle. The first werehyena growled and snapped at the second. Alex closed her eyes when the sudden movement of the first one splattered mud onto their faces. The second one whined and licked the jaws of the first. After a moment, they heard discordant chortling in the distance. Both stragglers took off running in the direction of the pack's call, whooping and howling in response.

Alex and Shae waited briefly, making sure the two wereanimals weren't coming back, before climbing out of their hiding place and switching on their head lanterns. They exchanged a look and Alex could see the concern in Shae's eyes. She too was worried about Jade and Isis, though Isis was definitely better equipped to deal with wereanimals than any of them.

"Come on. We need to find, Eris," Alex whispered, glancing again in the direction the werehyenas had disappeared. Shae nodded and she started to follow Alex, but winced in pain. Alex looked over at her when she heard the protector hiss softly.

"Are you okay?"

"I might have busted a couple of ribs when I was being pulled through the forest," Shae replied. "Probably sprained my wrist too."

Alex bit her lower lip, not sure what to do in this situation. They had only brought along a basic first aid kit and setting ribs was not something she knew how to do.

Why didn't I listen to Remington when he tried teaching me more advanced field medicine? If we ever get back, I'll never hear the end of it, Alex thought, remembering the many times the ancient trainer had tried to talk her into lessons. She had always been more interested in studying the lore of shape shifters and guardians as well as studying combat. Shae glanced at her and shook her head.

"I'll be fine. We can see to my injuries when we're out of the nightmare forest," she mentioned, moving past Alex with an affectionate shoulder nudge. Alex followed her as they began walking in the direction Eris had been headed. The trees soon gave way to a large open field, which was oddly lighter than the forest. There were massive werehyena tracks in the mud, bigger than anything Alex had ever encountered. A howling and giggling drew her attention to the right.

"Whoa," Shae suddenly said, pausing. She pointed at the ground when Alex looked at her questioningly. Alex looked to where she gestured and her eyes widened. The tracks became large grooves, as if the enormous animals had turned so sharply they had actually fallen. At first, Alex assumed Eris had changed her direction and the creatures had followed her. But as she looked up, she noticed two foot prints a short distance away, unmistakably humanoid. Looking back to the enormous tracks, Alex noticed some claw marks. The werehyenas had actually dug their claws in the ground in their rush to run away.

She looked over to Shae and shrugged. "We know she has some ability to affect perception. She probably cast an illusion or spell or something like that."

Shae nodded, but didn't look convinced. Alex moved forward, following the footprints that appeared in the circle of light. She could hear Shae behind her, covering their back. Alex considered switching positions, since Shae was injured, but as she opened her mouth to suggest it, something caught her eye and she froze. Shae collided with her and let out a quiet gasp of pain.

"Dammit, Alex, that —"

Shae stopped when she saw what had caused Alex to stop: a sidewalk. Alex felt her mouth drop open as she crouched down to examine the squares of concrete. Bright green grass grew up around the cement and fuzzy green moss grew between the cracks of each broad slab. There was a set of muddy footprints on the otherwise pristine concrete.

"That . . . that shouldn't be," Shae said, moving next to Alex and touching the concrete carefully with her boot. Alex shook her head, not believing her eyes.

"Let's just focus on finding Eris right now," she said carefully after a moment, nodding at the muddy footprints on the concrete. "It looks like she followed the sidewalk."

Shae just nodded and followed behind her teammate. They soon came upon an asphalt road, perfectly cared for and lined with bright streetlamps, and a few quaint little houses with picket fences. Alex was so baffled by the unusual sight that she almost walked into Eris, who was standing near a crosswalk, leaning against a streetlamp with her arms crossed over her chest.

"This definitely wasn't here last time," she mentioned, tilting her chin up. Alex and Shae looked across the asphalt road to the small town sprawled out before them. There were numerous humans going about their daily lives. The place was illuminated by the streetlamps all around them, which effectively banished the heavy inky shadows that had pervaded the forest. Eris looked up at one out of the corner of her eye, raising an arm and studying the guardian gleam in her flesh for a moment. She soon dropped her arm and turned her attention back to the strange sight.

"Well . . . this is unexpected," she commented with a laugh. It was one of the biggest understatements Alex had ever heard.

CHAPTER SEVEN

Jensen stood on the deck of the ship, looking across the calm waters to the dark outline of the Island of Avalon. He squinted, trying to make out the shore in the shadows. Night had fallen a little more than an hour ago and even the brightness of the moons couldn't pierce the shadows of the island. It was so dark that it almost resembled a black hole or a poor photoshop.

Around them, the air was filled with small sentient balls of lights, "star showers" as the elves called them. To Jensen, they looked similar to fireflies except they were spherical and there were a multitude of different colors. The lights floated in the air, illuminating the night around the ship.

The Four hadn't checked in and that didn't sit well with him, even though he had seen them get to shore safely. Glancing to the side, he noticed Radar was sitting on the floor, working with her tablet. He had asked her about the battery life and she had mumbled something about chargers before waving him away. The bright screen illuminated her face and her glowing brown eyes were darting over it. Steve was in the sleeping quarters with a selkie. It was his shift to sit by the radio and wait for the

175

Four to make contact.

"Good lord, Aldridge, do you ever switch off?"

Jensen twisted to look behind him where Sly, Alpha, and Nero were playing a card game. Sly glanced up from her cards, arching an eyebrow when she met Jensen's gaze. She was resting her long legs on the empty chair next to her, where Jensen had sat for a single hand.

"Can't a man enjoy the lovely Seelie Court weather and sights?" Jensen replied, mirroring her look. Sly shook her head, tapping her coffee cup when Alpha pulled out her ornate silver flask. Alpha smiled at her and poured some of whatever alcohol she had brought into Sly's coffee before bringing the flask to her own lips. Sly grinned and brought the steaming mug to her lips, sipping it carefully.

"I still say this would be more fun if we played the strip version," Nero groused good-naturedly. Both Alpha and Sly chuckled.

"You're just looking for an excuse to be nude, showoff," Sly pointed out.

"Sly, I have a body that looks like it was chiseled by the guardians. It is a *travesty* to keep it hidden," Nero said with mock haughtiness. "Tell them, Jensen."

"If I didn't know you, you would be completely insufferable," Alpha remarked, laying her cards face down, folding her arms in front of her and resting her head on them. "Ugh, why did I agree to this? I'm so bored and I miss my club."

Sly gave her a supportive pat on the back, putting her own cards down, and rising to her feet. She moved over to Jensen, who had turned his attention back to the island. He turned his face up to the rose-colored moon above them. Sly leaned down and crossed her arms on the rail, her gaze wandering across the water.

"You're not at all concerned for them?" Jensen asked softly.

Sly shrugged. "I'm not the type to be concerned. Jade's a big girl. She can take care of herself and she's been in much more hostile situations than this. Although, with the kind of trouble Blitz tends to attract, perhaps I should worry. If I were capable of such a thing."

"You refer to her by her alias?"

Sly chuckled as she straightened up and looked at Jensen. "Come now, Jensen. You aren't anywhere near as blind as the other protectors and you most certainly aren't naïve. The woman isn't firmly on the side of the angels. Oh, she may put on a good show for you protectors and the guardians, but I think we can both recognize that she does it merely for their peace of mind. Do you honestly think it was Isis who went to that island?"

Jensen shifted his weight a little and cleared his throat. Sly was right, as she frequently was. He knew Isis often shifted into the Blitz persona, usually for survival. The protectors had all seen it, frequently, though most of them ignored it or didn't acknowledge it. Jensen himself didn't care, but he did worry about how some of their older allies would react. Many were already uncomfortable with the experiments and Jet and Lilly's willingness to give them sanctuary. Looking up to the rigging, Jensen could barely see Jack on his high perch. The seven-series hadn't left the deck all day and his attention was always on the island. He was a silent sentry, still as stone.

"This is an easy mission, Jensen. Believe me, they won't all be like this," Sly said. "Take my advice and relax. Enjoy the brief sojourn because it's unlikely we'll have many more."

Jensen turned and watched as she walked back to the table, trailing her fingers across Alpha's shoulders. Alpha reached a hand up and Sly intertwined their fingers, pulling Alpha to her feet and leading the rebel leader to the sleeping quarters. Nero picked up a couple chairs and walked over to Jensen, setting one chair down behind him. In perfect unison, both men folded themselves into their chair and lifted their feet up to rest on the rail. For a moment, they sat in a comfortable silence as they frequently did when out on reconnaissance missions. The water babbled softly and the boat remained still and peaceful.

Nero pulled a nice black flask out of his pocket, offering it to Jensen, who took it gratefully. He held it under his nose, breathing in an oddly sweet scent, and took a small sip, raising his eyebrows as he looked back to his friend.

"Guardian liquor?" he asked as he handed the flask back to Nero. The man chuckled, holding the flask to his lips, taking a small swig and swallowing.

"I asked Passion to give me some of the good stuff, night before we left," he explained as he screwed the cap back on. "Something that would give me a buzz but not leave me blackout drunk. As usual, she delivered."

Nero closed his eyes and turned his face to the sky above them. "Guardians, what would we do without the woman?"

Jensen laughed softly. "Life would certainly be much duller."

Nero crossed his feet on the railing. "That's putting it lightly."

Nero cracked an eye open and studied Jensen, who was sitting back in his chair with his hands laced over his stomach, but his eyes were fixed on the island.

"Expecting smoke signals or something?"

"Or something," Jensen replied, rubbing his temple. "Apologies, my mind is wandering tonight. Too many thoughts vying for my attention."

"Seems to be your default mode," Nero commented, resting his hands behind his head. "Eris is probably just being Eris and they have their hands full with her. Isis versus the trickster of the Meadows. Damn, that has *got* to be interesting to watch. Shame we couldn't have tagged along."

Jensen made a noncommittal noise in response, fiddling with one of his cufflinks. Sighing deeply, he ran his hands over his face. Nero lifted his hand up and played with a couple of the floating lights, which weaved in and out between his fingers. Jensen kept his attention on the island, his gaze roaming over the beach.

"I think I'm going to turn in soon, get some shut-eye before my shift waiting at the radio," Nero commented, making no move to stand from his chair. Jensen glanced over at him, noticing he had closed his eyes. Nero was the sort who could sleep in the midst of a firefight and Jensen had always marveled at how almost nothing fazed the youngest Deverell.

"If I didn't know you, I'd suggest you do the same," Nero yawned. "But you almost never sleep when we're out on missions, even something like reconnaissance."

Jensen half-smiled and interlaced his fingers over his stomach again. "Must be all the assassination attempts over the years."

"Eh, you're old news, Aldridge. Assassins have probably moved on to the experiments by now. They would bring in a much higher bounty," Nero replied, causing Jensen to chuckle. He cracked an eye open and studied his friend, not moving from his relaxed position.

"I know it's ridiculous, but I can't help worrying about them," Jensen mentioned, his gaze once again on the island. "I don't like being on the sidelines, Nero."

Nero lowered his feet to the deck, sitting up. "I know. I'm worried about my brothers, even though I know I'm the one who gets into the most trouble, by far. I still worry about Isis on occasion, despite knowing she is more than capable of kicking practically everyone's ass in the known universe. It's natural to worry about our loved ones. Jensen?"

Jensen quickly got to his feet, moving closer to the railing and ignoring Nero's concerned questions. He could have sworn . . .

Waving away Nero's questions, he hurried up a couple steps to the base of the mast where Jack was still perched on a spar. The experiment had risen to his feet so that he stood at his full height, his attention also on the island. Before Jensen could call up to him, Jack dropped off the thick wooden spar and landed in a crouch in front of the protector.

"Did you see it?" Jensen asked as he followed the seven series to the front of the boat. A few selkies who had been working on the deck looked over at them as they passed by. Jack nodded distractedly, not even glancing at Nero when he approached them.

"Either of you want to explain what's going on?" Nero asked, looking between the two of them. Jensen opened his mouth to respond when Jack suddenly pointed toward the island.

"There," he exclaimed. Nero immediately went quiet as he looked to where Jack was pointing. Jensen stared at the small yellow light flickering near the top of what little could be seen of a mountain, a sense of dread creeping into his mind.

"It's not a natural light," Jack confirmed what Jensen had been thinking. "You probably can't see it, but there are a couple forms moving about up there. I can't make out who, or what, they are however."

Jensen glanced over at Nero, who looked like he might be sick. He ran a hand over his short hair, exchanging a look with Jensen.

"It appears the Island of Avalon isn't as uninhabited as the Seelie Court believes," Jack commented, his attention remaining on the dim glow. Jensen nodded distractedly, his attention not moving from the mountain, the only thing he could really see on the island. He suddenly had an unsettling feeling of being watched.

~~*~*~*

The humming became louder and more intense the further they traveled, following the compass directing them to the Leaves of Ivy. Jade didn't hear it, but it vibrated painfully within Isis' head and her hearing became noticeably duller. Soon, all she could hear was the strange hum, which meant another sense was impaired. She remained quiet, moving through the inky shadows, still unable to see through them. The Seelie Court's circadian rhythm was different from Earth's and the Meadow's and she was trying to adjust to it. The intensity of the darkness was unnatural, which caused her great concern. Glancing up, Isis noticed a metallic glint nearby, hidden in a tree. She stopped as she studied it, recognizing it as some sort of surveillance equipment. Looking around, Isis noticed the darkness was starting to thin a little. Now she was able to make out the shapes of the trees surrounding them. The vines had also stopped trying to grab them.

"Weird question: do you smell asphalt?" Jade suddenly asked from a few feet away. Isis turned her face away from the metallic object and quickened her pace, freezing once she passed the tree. The humming had abruptly stopped as had the discomfort it caused. Isis twisted, furrowing her brow as she looked back to the tree. Her eyes slowly traveled over the foliage, the sky, and the rest of her surroundings. Aside from the darkness not being as intense, nothing looked any different and she could suddenly hear a multitude of sounds again.

"I have been smelling asphalt since the glade," Isis replied, her eyes still roaming over the trees. "The humming stopped."

"You've been hearing humming?"

Isis ignored Jade as she moved back over to the tree and cautiously reached out her hand, holding it just past the trunk, watching as it was swallowed by the shadows. Her sensitive fingertips brushed through an imperceptible barrier of some sort and she could feel a strange vibration, similar to what she had been feeling in her head. Isis pulled out her switchblade and quickly carved a small slash in the tree, intending to investigate after they found the other three. *Preferably on my own,* she thought as she looked over her shoulder, watching Jade approach. She could read the uneasiness in the older shape shifter's every step, her eyes darting around their surroundings. Isis quickly closed the blade again, tucking it back in her belt and started heading deeper into the island.

"Is it just me or is it not so dark anymore?" Jade asked as she followed her teammate.

"You are not mistaken. Check the compass. Make sure we're headed in the right direction," Isis instructed as she continued following the scent of asphalt. She heard Jade open the compass behind her, checking their direction before snapping it shut again. As the two women continued walking, Jade stuck her hands in her pockets and blew a dark strand of hair out of her face. The weather was pleasantly warm and they saw no signs of the earlier storm.

"I swear, it feels like we stumbled into some kind of fairytale or alternate reality or something," Jade mentioned off-handedly and Isis shook her head.

"I can assure you we are still on the Island of Avalon in the Seelie Court," she responded and Jade rubbed her eyes in obvious frustration.

"Metaphorically, Isis. I wasn't speaking literally," Jade explained wearily. Isis kept her attention on the mountains in the distance, uninterested in the figurative language normals were so fond of. She was more concerned with potential hostiles that could be awaiting them. The wiser course of action would be to take their chances in the woods and find a way back to the ship. Protectors, however, didn't share her practicality and were much more driven by emotion than even they realized. Isis wanted to see what kind of enemy they were dealing with and was therefore willing to venture deeper into potentially hostile territory.

"Isis? Jade? Can you hear me?"

Isis slowed down and tilted her head at the garbled

sound of Shae's voice in her earpiece. It was barely audible through the static. "The communication devices are working again."

Jade had stopped in her tracks and was staring ahead of her. Isis moved forward to stand next to the older protector, her gaze traveling down the asphalt that lay before them. Twinkling street lamps ran along the winding sidewalk that traveled through the strangely normal-looking small town in front of them. Cookie-cutter houses lined both sides of the road, identical in every visible way. In the distance, there were more buildings clustered together and Isis theorized that was the town's center. Looking back to her teammate, she noticed that Jade's eyes were wider than usual and her mouth was partly open as she stared at what was undoubtedly an odd sight.

"This is Isis," Isis responded to Shae.

"Thank the guardians," Shae's relief was apparent. "You're not going to believe this —"

"We just walked into what looks like a town, human from the scent of it," Isis said, looking around. "I assume that's what you think I won't believe."

There was a pause and then Jade pressed the button in her earpiece, wincing at the crackling static. "Shae, are Alex and Eris with you?"

"They are," Shae answered. "We're in the diner downtown. It's about a half-hour walk from the edge of town."

"We'll meet you there. Alex, try to get in contact with the others on the ship."

Jade nodded to Isis, who slid her sunglasses over her eyes, and they made their way down the road, heading for the town. There was no one walking on the quiet streets and very few people on their porches, despite the weather being pleasant. The front porch lights were on in every house and there were signs of lights being on inside the dwellings as well. Isis noticed a woman with knitting on a front porch, rocking in a tall chair. She could feel Jade looking at her and knew the older protector was worried about how out of place her attire seemed. Most of her weapons were hidden, but the ones that weren't might cause any humans to react poorly.

"There are cameras on all the lamps," Jade muttered under her breath as they passed by a man reading a newspaper on his front porch in a simple porch swing. He didn't even glance up from whatever article he was reading as they passed by his house.

"I am aware," Isis responded as they continued on their way. A soft clunk behind them made Isis turn her attention back the way they had come. Nothing was out of place, except the porch swing where the man had been reading a newspaper was empty. The swing slowly moved back and forth, striking the house behind it. Her gaze traveled upwards, but she saw nothing. *This is very familiar,* she realized as her eyes continued to scan the house.

"Isis?"

She looked back to Jade and shook her head, gesturing that they should continue on. Jade watched her and she was obviously not thrilled with Isis' silence, but she continued to keep pace with her. Isis adjusted her speed and stride so that it wasn't too difficult.

A half-hour later, they walked into the more brightly lit downtown area, which resembled a ghost town. The few people they passed by didn't react to the two strangers. Isis wasn't reassured with the visible lack of reaction, or acknowledgment, from the people. In so small a town, there should have been at least a few second looks. Especially from humans, which so far was all they had encountered.

"There's the diner," Isis mentioned, tilting her chin up to where the diner was across the street. It looked like a typical place from the 50s and bright neon pink letters declared John & Jane's atop the roof. The outside was very simplistic and inside looked to be the same, but with a 50s flare. Isis noticed Eris, Shae, and Alex sitting in a booth next to the window. Shae noticed them and smiled, waving for them to come in. Looking behind her, Isis noted how simplistic the town was. *Too small to be a town,* she realized as she looked over to the mountains in the distance.

"Well, let's go in and see what they've been up to, figure out what to do next," Jade suggested wearily as she started across the street. Isis followed behind her and kept her eyes sharp for anything out of the ordinary, noting every anomaly she saw. Everything was a little too peaceful and quiet, a little too uniform.

They stepped into the clean diner, which was brightly lit and smelled heavenly. As Isis continued to follow Jade, she noticed a few servers moving around the different tables. A larger woman in a yellow blouse sat at an old-fashioned register and behind her there were a couple cooks working with food. The patrons were smiling and there was a quiet hum of conversation going throughout the place. Behind the counter, on a high shelf, an old radio was playing a jaunty oldies tune. Almost everything in the diner was in pastel shades, except for the booth cushions, which were a dark red. Looking down at the spotless black and white tiled floor, Isis took note of every sound and scent. She counted five people at the counter and six in the booths, not counting the three members of their group.

The layout was strangely familiar to her as were the scents, but she attributed that to her missions at Grenich. She had been in so many little establishments that they started to blend together after a while. Turning her attention to the three sitting at the table, she noticed Eris was happily devouring an enormous banana split. The guardian barely acknowledged them as she stuck her spoon in the scoop of bright pink ice cream, closing her eyes as she savored the cool dessert.

Jade slid into the booth next to Shae, who looked a little banged up. Bruises decorated her exposed arms, the darkest one being on her right wrist, and there were a few superficial scratches on her shoulders and face. Alex looked barely awake as she sat between Eris and the window, resting her head on her hand as she watched the guardian enjoy her ice cream. The protector also looked somewhat worse for wear and her exposed skin was streaked with dirt. Both she and Isis turned to look behind them when someone emerged from the bathrooms, a tall woman who rejoined her companion at the counter.

"Are you all okay?" Jade asked, turning her attention to Shae.

"Shae might have a sprained wrist and some bruised ribs; run-in with more vines," Alex reported and then gestured at her ear. "We managed to make some kind of contact with the ship, but the static is terrible. We could barely understand each other through the garbled mess. Not sure how much Steve understood, but I did try to explain the situation."

"I expected as much," Jade commented as she gently cradled Shae's wrist and carefully checked for any broken bones. Shae visibly winced at the older protector's ministrations, but didn't react otherwise. She looked up at Isis, who was standing silently next to the booth, arms crossed over her chest.

"Are you okay?" she asked and Isis turned her attention to her, noticing the concern in Shae's expression.

"My regenerative capabilities are still working and therefore healed what little damage I sustained in the forest," Isis responded, glancing at Eris when she plucked the cherry off the top of her large dessert and pulled the stem out. "Did you encounter any werehyenas?"

"Yeah," Alex answered, shuddering. "A lot of them. They're none too fond of Eris."

"Disgusting mutated beasts dislike me? My heart is breaking," Eris commented dryly, her voice still rough, and then tossed the cherry stem in her mouth. After a moment, she pulled it out again, a small knot in the center of the red stem. Putting it in one palm, she passed the other over it and the stem disappeared. Isis couldn't tell if she used magic or just sleight of hand. Eris turned her attention back to the ice cream, savoring another spoonful.

"Jade, there's something really weird going on," Shae said, wincing when Jade pressed on a particularly sensitive spot. She looked over at Alex, nodding, and Alex turned and gestured for the waitress. She was a rounder woman with a dark complexion and wore a fading yellow uniform with a small pink rose in her hair. When she spotted Alex, she smiled and held up a finger before turning back to the patrons at the counter.

"We asked about the population about five minutes ago, give or take. She told us it was around eighty-one," Shae said, her eyes gliding between Jade and Isis. Isis looked at Eris when the guardian twisted the spoon in her mouth and held it between her teeth. She observed the four women, not speaking. Her throat was noticeably bruised and Isis estimated the damage would take a few days to heal, perhaps a week.

The waitress finally moved over to their table, beaming at them and exposing a gap in her teeth. She pulled a pencil out from behind her ear and retrieved her notepad from a pocket in her apron, tapping the eraser on it. She looked over at Isis and didn't react to her luminous eyes at all. Isis looked over at Jade, who also noticed the unusual reaction. Very few humans had ever seen Isis' glowing eyes, but the ones who had, had an immediate and natural reaction. The ones who had heard the legend of Blitz had almost always fixated on the spooky glowing eyes when describing her. The server hadn't flinched or even done a double-take.

"Glad to see you're enjoying our famous triple scoop. Nothing better for a sore throat," the woman spoke in a chipper tone and glanced at the two who had just arrived, resting her pencil on the notepad. Eris pulled the spoon out of her mouth and smiled at the waitress.

"Martha, it is *heavenly*," Eris practically purred and scrunched her nose up, mimicking the waitress's smile.

The waitress giggled and covered her mouth with her hand. Isis raised an eyebrow and glanced down when she noticed a movement. Eris' bare foot slid out from beneath the table, gently brushing against Martha's shin. A soft purple light pulsed briefly beneath Eris' skin and her guardian shimmer looked like stars, as if a galaxy had been painted in her flesh. The server shivered a little and she let out a quiet sigh before turning her attention to the other women, glancing again at the two new arrivals.

"What can I get for you all? It's on the house, since you're new in town," she said, her voice losing none of its friendliness. Her dark green eyes sparkled as she looked expectantly between Jade and Isis, who kept staring at her and waiting for her to react. Martha continued tapping her pencil on her notepad, seemingly incapable of not moving.

"I was just telling my friend Jade here about how small this town is," Alex said with a polite smile. "Um, refresh my memory, about how many people live here?"

Martha giggled again. "Oh, there are exactly sixty-two people in town. Sixty-three next month, when Katie has her baby."

Jade stared at the waitress, her face not betraying any emotion. Isis twisted to look over her shoulder, something tugging at her mind. She heard Jade request a few more minutes and the waitress walked away, practically skipping.

"Maybe she misspoke earlier?" Jade suggested. "It's not that big a difference."

"Three times, in the space of about an hour?" Alex responded. "We have asked her three times and each time, the number of people noticeably drops by at least twenty."

"Four times," Eris suddenly spoke before tossing the cherry in her mouth, rolling it around a bit before biting into it. All four women looked at her and she smirked, chewing thoroughly and savoring every bite.

"What are you talking about?" Shae finally asked when Eris swallowed the fruit and dabbed at her mouth with a clean paper napkin. The guardian interlaced her fingers together, her eyes traveling between the shape shifters as a crafty smile split her lips.

"You actually asked four times, darling," she finally answered, holding up her index finger and circling it around. "This whole place is swimming in some sort of spell. Whatever magic is at work is also affecting you, but at a much slower rate than the humans."

Eris kept her index finger raised and a faint shimmering purple mist formed around it. She then slashed it down diagonally in a fast smooth motion. The air sparkled with a gold mist briefly, which twinkled before vanishing. Eris studied her hand, rubbing her thumb and index finger together as she examined the last remnants of the glittery gold substance. She made a face of disgust and shook her finger, ridding it of the mysterious substance. Looking next to her, Eris reached over and dunked her finger in Alex's full glass of water.

"Hey," Alex protested, raising her hands in irritation.

"Just as I thought, the Magic Orders," Eris said, ignoring Alex as she dried her finger with her napkin. "Amateur and sloppy, all looks, no substance. It needs an anchor and for a spell this complicated, there will be a number of anchors. So much hassle for such mediocre results. It's the magic version of a child's finger-painting."

"The Magic Orders declared neutrality in the war against Grenich," Alex stated, glancing over to Jade, who looked incredibly skeptical. Eris scoffed as she finished cleaning her finger and placed the napkin aside.

"Well, crude as this is, it doesn't strike me as particularly neutral," Eris responded as she looked back to Alex. "Members of the Magic Orders never struck me as stupid, but this suggests I may have to rethink that conclusion."

"And we should take your word for it, Eris? The last time I checked, you were notorious for taking away people's free-will," Jade mentioned.

"True, but if this were me, would I draw your attention

to it? And believe me, if I were interested in messing with primitives, I would start with you," Eris replied, unbothered. "Besides, my magic doesn't require anchors. I actually know what I'm doing and don't require training wheels."

"But how did you know it was magic? And how do you know we're affected?" Shae asked. Eris rolled her eyes over to her and picked up her spoon again, twirling it just over her ice cream.

"Sweetheart, magic is part of who I am. I am more sensitive to it than all the guardians, sensitive enough that I can actually see it and feel it. It's in the air, this place stinks of it," Eris paused and looked around. "You lot just see a quaint little diner, peculiar but still normal, filled with a bunch of humans. I see tendrils of gold flame everywhere, streaked with dark blue, looks a bit like an enormous spider web or a snowflake. The humans' heads are filled with it to the point where I can't see their faces. Gathers around all the senses, invades the mind so that they only perceive what some little enchantress or enchanter wants. It's a bit cruel, though undoubtedly entertaining. The mortals are like adorable marionettes, moving about when someone pulls their strings."

Eris shook her fingers until a translucent purple sparkling mist appeared around them again. Then she reached up, plucked at nothingness, and one of the humans sitting at the counter suddenly slapped the back of his neck, grumbling something under his breath.

Eris grinned and looked back to Shae, gesturing vaguely at her head. "It's not as apparent in you, just a teeny spot of gold and blue about the size of a small almond, but it's nestled right in your temple. Immortals tend to have stronger defenses, so it'll probably be gone within a few hours. Might make a couple of your memories hazy, but there won't be any lasting effects once you get off this island."

The guardian sat back and looked around the diner, her

gaze briefly resting on Isis, who was looking out the windows. Eris reached out and held her fingers just in front of Isis, her hand moving subtly up and down as if she were stroking the air. Noticing the movement, Isis glanced over at the guardian, studying the woman as she tried to figure out what she was doing.

"Hmm, that's rather interesting," Eris remarked, turning back to the others. "The spell seems to be repelled by my dear niece over here. I've never seen anything like it before. There's an actual halo of nothingness around her, like she's in a bubble."

The three women looked over to Isis, who ignored them as she continued looking around the diner. She was only half-listening to their conversation, her gaze drawn to the back of the diner. The lights flickered a couple times, but remained on and bright. Jade turned her attention to Alex again.

"We've got to get off this island, but I don't know how to get through that forest," she said quietly. Alex rubbed her upper lip and Eris turned back to her ice cream, using her spoon to play with the slowly melting mounds.

"I'm going to use the restroom," Isis spoke suddenly and turned away from the booth, making her way toward the back of the diner. She paused at the small hallway and glanced down both sides. Her eyes drifted over the signs distinguishing the men's from the women's rooms. Oddly, there was no scent from either door, nothing to mark them as restrooms.

"I want to start a bar fight!" Eris' sudden shout came from behind her, followed closely by the sound of her smacking the table with her fists. "Let's start a bar fight!"

Isis turned to the women's room and swallowed, listening closely to the other side of the door. It was silent, empty, so she pushed the door open and stepped inside. The bathroom was well lit and pristine, as though it had never been used before. On the far wall, there was a long row of windows with opaque glass. The one nearest to the sinks was open, letting in the pleasant night air. Outside, she heard a breeze rustle through the grass.

Isis crossed the clean bathroom and hopped up on the counter of sinks, resting her hands on the window ledge as she stared out into the night. A breeze swept through the grass again, brushing past her face. There was empty field as far as the eye could see, but in the distance, Isis could just make out the outline of an enormous structure. Squinting, Isis studied it as best she could. It resembled an old Gothic building, something like a hospital. The old structure looked oddly out of place, even in the strange setting. A tall fence surrounded it and there was no road or path leading up to it. After a moment, Isis hopped off the sink and turned away from the windows.

Moving over to the stalls, Isis looked around inside the first one. Stepping over to the next, she looked around again and frowned when she didn't see a trace of what she was looking for. Looking inside the next one, she paused when she spotted a tiny carving in the wall. Moving closer and studying it, Isis read what would appear to be chicken scratch to the untrained eye. Mouthing the translation to herself, her attention turned upwards. Isis counted the ceiling tiles then moved over to the toilet, cautiously stepping up on it. Using her fist, she gently tapped each tile until she found one that was a little looser than the others and pressed up on it, moving it off to the side. Isis hesitated and looked around, making sure she was still alone in the bathroom.

When she was satisfied that there was no one else around, Isis reached up into the ceiling and carefully felt around until her fingers brushed against plastic. She looked up at the shadowy empty space as she continued to feel around, trying to get some idea of what was in the hidden bag.

Five experiments stood on rickety stools, their heads in a noose, and her handler stood a few feet behind her. Isis stared at the taut ropes and tried to figure out the best approach. Her handler was expecting her to shoot with both hands, which she had to remember. Jack was standing at the end, his neck tightly in a rope, face blank like the others. If she missed, she would be labeled "malfunctioning" and likely put down. The stools were suddenly kicked out from beneath the experiments and Isis fired without a second thought. Once the experiments fell to the ground, she quickly tossed the gun to her other hand and fired, eliminating the threats who had kicked out the stools. A quick command from her handler and she had holstered the gun again.

A sudden weight slammed into Isis, sending her crashing into the wall behind her and falling in an undignified heap to the floor. She smashed her head on the stall next to her, causing stars to burst in her vision. Before she could recover from the fall, the animal was on top of her, its jaws around her forearm, which she barely managed to raise to protect her face. Isis found herself face-to-face with the glowing golden-green eyes of a large female jaguar. For a moment, the two stared at each other. Then the jaguar tightened her jaws, causing the bones in Isis' arm to creak ominously, threatening to break. Blood was already spurting out from where the jaguar's teeth had sunk deeply into her flesh. Isis couldn't smother the gasp as she struggled to find a better position. *Survival's going to cost a pound of flesh,* she thought in resignation.

Throwing herself to the side, she pulled the jaguar on top of her legs, which she had folded up to her chest. Gritting her teeth, Isis pushed with everything she had in her, sending the big cat sailing backwards and into the back wall. The animal tore out a massive hunk of her forearm and blood sprayed everywhere. Had she been a normal, blood loss would have been a concern and Isis could clearly see the stark white bones in the deep wound.

As quickly as she could, Isis scooted backwards, her eyes never moving from the stall. She slid in the massive amount of blood that spilled from her wounded arm, frequently falling to one elbow. Isis briefly glanced down at her arm, which was already sealing up. She turned back and barely managed to roll out of the way as the jaguar flew through the air, its claws extended. Isis immediately jumped to her feet and withdrew her sais, spinning them once to assure herself that her rapidly healing left arm could still hold a weapon.

The jaguar stared at her and the animal form began to gradually melt away. The fur disappeared, replaced by pale flesh. The face shrank back into its human form and the hair darkened, lengthening a little. The golden green eyes remained, but one blink turned them human again. Isis remained still, standing in the ready position as the other experiment gradually straightened up into a standing position, staring at her.

"You're not supposed to be here," the woman spoke slowly after a moment. "You're not . . . the seven series isn't part of this exercise."

"Last minute change in orders, I was sent to observe and report back any mistakes," Isis quickly came up with a plausible cover. The other woman still stood stiffly, looking at Isis, who realized her mistake. She was wearing black, the forbidden color at Grenich. Even when they were on missions, they couldn't wear it. Doing a quick mental check of her wounds, Isis was satisfied with the healing progress. They wouldn't hinder her.

Quickly running at the other experiment, Isis dodged under a well-aimed roundhouse kick and sliced her sai down the woman's arm. Blood sprayed out and splashed across the floor. Isis chambered her knee and lashed out with a strong front kick that sent the woman stumbling back. The woman withdrew a knife she had in a hidden sheath that was tucked in the back of her pants. She advanced a few steps and Isis took a step back, making sure she kept herself out of slashing range. Her opponent could take as much damage as she could and it was likely she could take even more. She had the advantage, so Isis had to play it moderately safe.

The other experiment lunged forward with a knee

strike, which Isis blocked with her own knee and was barely able to duck out of the way of the knife. She leaned back as the other experiment slashed at her throat. Spinning around, Isis attempted to stab her sai into the other woman's back, but a side kick sent her stumbling a couple steps back. Another slash caught her off guard and opened a large gash in her chest, spilling her blood across the floor. Isis stumbled back a few more steps, deflecting another strike with her sai and using a snap kick to knock her opponent away. She could feel her chest seal up, but it still stung.

"You're the traitor, the one called Blitz," the woman observed as she adjusted her grip on her knife. Isis lunged forward and tried to slice the woman's throat open with one sai. As she expected, the woman moved away from the strike, but Isis brought up the other sai and sliced the hand that held the knife. She then followed through with another side kick to the chest, which sent the other experiment sprawling.

Wasting no time, Isis kicked the knife out of her momentarily weakened grip. The other experiment quickly kicked the back of her legs, the strike sending Isis to her knees. Isis briefly abandoned her sais to grab the experiment's wrist, wrapping her powerful legs around the woman's throat and locking them. The woman began to thrash around, trying to break free of the hold. Isis held tight, patiently waiting for the struggles to stop. She felt the body beneath her begin to shift and immediately grabbed her abandoned sai. Without thinking, Isis sat up and plunged it straight through the woman's chest, piercing the heart and lungs.

The woman stared at the weapon in her chest for a moment, as did Isis. The experiment looked at her and Isis felt a brief hesitation. The struggles had long since ceased and the woman shuddered once as she fell back to the floor. Isis got up and retrieved her other sai, listening to the other's labored breathing slowly cease. Moving over to the body, Isis pulled her sai out of the body, staring at the bloody weapon. Death didn't bother her — though the complications that came with it were sometimes a headache — or it hadn't in the past. *I'm spending too much time around normals,* she thought as she shook her head. A knock on the door, caused her to immediately get in the ready position again, sais held up.

"Come on, I've got to fix my face," she heard Eris' voice on the other side of the door, followed by Alex telling her to settle down.

"Isis?" Alex's voice was slightly muffled behind the door. "Are you okay?"

Isis moved over to the door, unlocked it, and Eris sauntered in. Isis quickly yanked Alex inside when she paused, staring at her teammate. She could feel the protector's questioning gaze as she locked the door again.

"Whoa-oh-oh," Eris laughed gleefully as she looked around at the gruesome scene and clapped in delight. "Bravo! I would feel left out, seeing how I was the one who suggested the bar fight, but damn! I'm impressed. Kudos to you, Frosty."

Alex's eyes widened significantly as she stepped further into the bathroom, her mouth opening and closing a couple times as she noticed all the blood on the walls and floor. She turned back to Isis, staring at her expectantly.

"Uh oh, I think someone's in for a scolding," Eris remarked as she glanced over at the two shape shifters. "You've been a very naughty girl, spooky. Hey, other one, there's a body over here."

"A what?" Alex hissed, turning back to her teammate. Isis ignored her as she moved into the main part of the restroom, carefully stepping around the large pools of blood, and turning on the sinks. Eris raised an eyebrow as she pulled out a small pouch from an inner pocket in her shirt. She picked up a small tube, immediately turning her attention to her eyelashes.

Isis crouched by the body and began searching it,

swiftly emptying the pockets of anything useful, which wasn't much. Isis tossed Alex the cell phone over her shoulder and heard the protector catch it. Continuing to rifle through the pockets, Isis found a signal jammer and a couple bladed weapons along with her cover ID. There was also a strip of paper with coordinates, which she mouthed silently to herself. Moving over to the open window, Isis grabbed the ledge and pulled herself up, her gaze traveling out over the empty space. Dropping back to the ground, Isis looked over at the guardian and briefly considered arming Eris. Things would undoubtedly get dicey, probably very soon, but she decided it was too much of a risk. Eris' magic would have to suffice for the time being.

Moving back to the experiment, Isis dragged the body back into one of the empty stalls. Dropping her inside, Isis closed the stall door and knelt down, pulling out some small tools from a pouch on her belt.

"What . . . Isis, what the hell happened?" Alex asked.

"Bit obvious, isn't it? Your teammate got stabby," Eris chuckled as she continued focusing on her eyelashes. Alex glared at the guardian and moved further into the bathroom, stepping around the puddles of blood. She continued looking around at the blood splattered on the walls, moving over to the windows so she could look outside.

"We need to get off this island. As soon as possible," Isis stated as she manipulated the simplistic lock on the door. "Eris, you're going to take us to that box. No games."

Eris smirked at her in the mirror but didn't say anything as she turned her attention to applying eyeliner, carefully drawing around her eyes. Once Isis finished locking the stall door, she tucked the tools back into their pouch on her belt. Moving over to the stall she had been in originally, Isis stepped up onto the toilet again, reaching into the ceiling.

"That's not what I asked. What are you doing?" Alex said, obviously not thrilled with the evasive response. Isis pulled down the plastic bag, examining the silver gun inside as she stepped off the toilet and out of the stall. She opened the bag and pulled out the gun, quickly taking out the magazine. She sniffed the first bullet, cringing and turning away. The strong skunky smell was one she recognized though it wasn't something she had frequently encountered.

"Co-ag, they'll be using co-ag rounds," she muttered to herself as she began pulling the bullets out of the magazine. It wasn't the first time she was happy to have worn gloves. She wasn't sure of the potency of this particular concoction, but skin contact with it wasn't a risk she was interested in taking.

"Great, now she's talking to herself," Eris said from where she stood at the far sink.

"Hurry up, Eris," Alex snapped, turning her eyes back to Isis, putting her hands on her hips. "Isis, I really need some kind of explanation about this."

"No, you don't," Isis said sharply and Alex stared at her. It was rare for normals to get on her nerves, but their constant questioning at the most inconvenient times sometimes tried her patience. Isis turned her attention back to the magazine and continued removing the bullets. Alex sighed and looked around at all the blood, running a hand over her mouth.

"Bloody hell, you protectors have woe-is-me down to an art form," Eris muttered before opening her mouth so she could apply bright red lipstick. Isis looked over at her, curious about the faint scent of the makeup she was using. The subtlety was unique to the Meadows, but there was an interesting pleasantness to it. Isis moved across the floor and put the gun on the side of the sink, holding onto the bullets.

"She was probably a fairly new eight-series and she ambushed me, in jaguar form," Isis explained as she moved back to the empty stall, dropping the bullets in the toilet. "Judging from the relatively novice fighting and skill level, she was still in training. It means we're likely in a training field, a simulation of a potential real-world mission. A whole town? Chances are there are a number of experiments and there's a high-probability they're running a very elaborate exercise, a coup maybe."

"Fun, fun," Eris said, a wolfish smile splitting her lips. Isis flushed the toilet, watching as the bullets disappeared before leaving the stall.

"Co-ags are highly potent anti-coagulants created by Grenich. It can be used to coat bullets or blades. They interfere with an experiment's regenerative abilities and it thins the blood significantly, which leads to a high probability of bleeding out," Isis continued to explain as she moved back to the sink and picked up the gun. "You can counteract it with a shot of pure adrenaline, which will restart our rapid healing, but it's unlikely we could find pure adrenaline in this small town. Odds are there's not even an emergency room or hospital."

Isis easily disassembled the gun in seconds, removing some of the smaller bits of it and dumping them down the sink drain. Eris raised an eyebrow as she watched Isis' dexterous fingers work. Putting the gun back together, Isis put it back in the bag and replaced it in the ceiling.

"Chances are the handlers have already seen us, in which case there are a couple ways they will respond," Isis continued. "The most likely is the experiments will be given additional orders to target us, which will be challenging for me to deal with while protecting all of you."

"Isis, we're a team. If what you're saying is true, we will deal with it together," Alex interrupted, watching the experiment as she replaced the ceiling tile. Isis glanced at her teammate as she stepped off the toilet and exited the stall.

"Less likely is a salt the earth directive," Isis continued, looking over to where Eris was applying dark eyeshadow to her eyelids. "They wouldn't use experiments, more likely they'd deactivate the barrier and let the werehyenas eliminate the town, then send a cleaner team to put them down. It would be costly, but the benefits would be enough for some to seriously consider it. I have a couple ideas about how to counter such a strategy, but none that would be guaranteed to work and all would result in significant casualties, especially if you insist on trying to save the humans."

"Well, that's reassuring," Alex said, looking over her shoulder. Isis pointed at the window, directing her attention outside.

"There's what looks like a safe zone a short distance away from here, but we have to move now," Isis explained. "This diner is not a defensible location and it's likely under surveillance, as is the rest of the town."

Eris had put away her makeup and climbed up on the sink, looking out into the night. Raising her hand so her palm was facing the ceiling, she wiggled her fingers before making them into a claw shape. A small ball of translucent white light formed in her palm. Holding it before her face, she blew gently on it and the light shattered into multiple small lights, vanishing into the night, like dandelion spores.

"Well now that's interesting," Eris commented and Isis moved over to her, pulling herself up so she could see out the window again. The night looked the same, but the air felt a little charged.

"Sorry, dear, can't let you see behind the curtain," Eris said, her eyes never moving from the open window. "Hypothetically, if I were to lead you to the Box of Original Elements, I would suggest looking in the direction my creepy niece wants to bring us."

Alex moved over to the windows, glancing back at the door and hoping their luck would hold out. "Are you saying the box is in this supposed safe zone?"

"Ah-ah, now that would be telling. There's no fun in

just giving you the answer," Eris chided as she got off the sink. "I merely suggested it would be wise of you to start in that general direction."

"It's there," Isis answered as she let go of the ledge and dropped to the floor, ignoring the annoyed look Eris sent in her direction. She adjusted the gloves on her hands and looked around the bathroom.

The sudden sound of a faint voice caused Isis to turn toward the stall where she had hidden the body. She tilted her head slightly and craned her neck a little, trying to pick up any words. Both Alex and Eris stared at her, neither expecting the sudden change in behavior. Isis shook her head, knowing she wouldn't be able to decipher the words. Leaving the earpiece with the body would buy them some time.

"Her handler will soon become aware of the experiment's absence," Isis explained. "We probably have about an hour, maybe two. I suggest moving as fast, so you should retrieve the other two."

Alex stared at Isis, who looked expectantly at her. Eris stood off to the side, gathering up her makeup and slipping the pouch back into her inner pocket.

"What will happen to the people in the diner?" Alex asked and Isis held her gaze, considering the costs and benefits of telling her the truth. A plan had already started to form in her mind and she could adjust it, if the need arose.

"They were in contact with us, and with one of us being a high-value target, chances are they'll be tortured for information and then liquidated," Isis answered honestly. Alex massaged her forehead, closing her eyes and cursing under her breath.

"I assume you mean to rescue them," Isis commented, turning her attention to Eris. "Can you break the anchors?"

A huge smile split Eris' lips and she rubbed her flat palms together. "My dear, I thought you would never ask."

Isis held up a hand, indicating she wanted the guardian to hold off for a moment. Eris pouted, but a dark gray mist continued forming around her hands. Isis turned her attention to Alex.

"Will you please talk to Jade and Shae? We're going to go out the window in here, less surveillance and it will be easier to move a larger group unseen if we go through the grasses."

Alex looked at her for a moment, trying to get an idea of what her teammate was thinking. Isis held her gaze, remaining patient and keeping her expression impassive. Alex finally looked behind her, to the door.

"You're going to keep an eye on Eris, I'm assuming," she finally said and Isis nodded once. The protector turned and left the bathroom. Isis waited until the door closed fully before turning to where Eris was playing with the translucent gray mist she had built up between her hands. The guardian looked over at the shape shifter, a knowing smile playing on her lips.

"Can you keep the humans docile?" Isis asked softly. "Make sure they don't panic or react to the unusual things they'll undoubtedly see?"

The smile still played on Eris' lips as she bounced the gray light to her left hand. "Darling niece, are you requesting I take away the humans' freedom? But that would be wrong and a violation of their rights."

Isis stared at her, unamused. "You're fully aware that I don't care about black and white morality. We're here to do a job and the humans will make that difficult enough, but the protectors won't leave them behind. If they panic, it will make the situation even more difficult. I can only remedy so many complications."

"And you never know when a good living shield will come in handy," Eris pointed out, moving closer to Isis and walking so that she stood behind her. "Oh, I can make them do all kinds of things, teach them all sorts of useful tricks, turn them into docile little lambs."

Eris rested her chin on Isis' shoulder, whispering softly in her ear, "Just say the word."

Isis crossed her arms over her chest. "Numb them to the more panic-inducing parts of this situation, suppress what you can, and try to keep them from seeing too much. If it's in your power, make this seem like a dream."

"Hmm, you are an intriguing one, I'll give you that," Eris stated as she took a step back. "Lucky for you, I enjoy a challenge. Your wish is my command."

Isis watched the guardian as she moved over to the door and pulled it open, propping it ajar with her foot. A cool breeze drifted in from the window as Isis went back to the sinks, patiently waiting for the others to enter. She looked at her glowing green eyes in the mirror, silently sorting out different strategies in her mind.

CHAPTER EIGHT

Another grim day dawned in the Meadows. It was overcast, but whatever sunlight there was illuminated the overcrowded healing halls, where all the afflicted healers lay. Rain pattered gently on the windows, preventing heavy silences from falling. The afflicted healers from the lands of men had been moved to the halls of the Pearl Castle in the women's lands, since it was larger and it would be easier to pool their resources. The male healers had also felt that quarantine was a wise course of action.

Lilly sat beside one ailing woman's bed, embroidering. Amethyst and Eshmun found they were very limited in what they could do. They were trying to alleviate the healers' pain and discomfort as much as they could, but even that proved to be almost impossible. Lilly looked up from her embroidery to where the two head healers were sitting in a corner of the room, at a pair of small desks that had been pushed together. They were pouring over giant tomes, searching for any mention of the virus in the hopes of finding more effective treatments. Both had a desk lamp for even more light.

Across the aisle, messengers were changing the sheets of a bed. Another afflicted healer had passed away late the previous night, which had made the younger healers even more scared than they already were. The head healing guardians were having difficulty convincing the younger apprentices to work in the healing halls. Some of the male guardians weren't helping matters and questioned the wisdom of healers working in such close proximity to a virus that only affected them.

Lilly looked up when a plate holding a couple of large heavenly-smelling muffins were placed on the table holding her embroidery supplies. She smiled as Passion noisily dragged a chair next to her and took a seat, smiling at her old friend. Many of the guardians had looked over at Passion when they heard the echoing scrape of the chair's legs dragging across the floor, staring at her in irritation.

"Jet would never let me hear the end of it if I let you starve," she mentioned, ignoring the angry stares as she grabbed one of the muffins off the plate and leaned against the head of Lilly's chair. Lilly laughed softly as Passion began picking at the muffin, gratefully accepting a hunk the guardian offered her. She had volunteered to help in the healing wing when Ivy told her of the situation. Amethyst and Eshmun were grateful for any help they could get as they seemed to be perpetually short-handed. Lilly had been in the Meadows since the previous afternoon, trusting Remington to alert her should a situation arise on Earth that required her attention.

"Is your husband still trying to smooth things over at home?" Passion asked, popping a bit of muffin in her mouth as she looked over at Lilly. Lilly smiled a little and nodded, causing Passion to sigh. She laid her head on Lilly's shoulder, gazing across the healing wing.

"I recognize that look, my friend. Something's on your mind," Passion observed, glancing over to the door when Electra entered the room with Phoenix. They were both wearing old clothes, things they wouldn't mind getting dirty, and had their hair tied back. They were ready to start working in the healing wing. Lilly leaned back and rested her head against Passion's, momentarily forgetting her embroidery.

"Some of our allies have had understandable concerns about the experiments. This attack on the Meadows just seems to have stoked those fires," she responded, looking over to the door when Electra entered the room. "There has been talk of groups dedicated to keeping experiments in check through any means necessary. I fear for the safety of my family in a way that I haven't for a very long time."

"There are always rabble rousers," Passion mused. "You and Jet have weathered worse in the past. I have every faith that you will manage this as well. And besides, you have the blessings of the guardians. We may be infuriatingly hands off for most things, but neither Adonia nor Aneurin will desert you entirely. None of the High Council will."

Lilly smiled. "We're lucky to know you, Passion. Your friendship has always been a blessing to us both."

Passion chuckled as she picked up Lilly's embroidery, running her fingers over the colorful flowers. She sobered after a moment, sitting up and turning so that she was facing Lilly, her expression becoming serious but still kind. Somewhere nearby, a healer coughed and another moaned softly.

"Both of you have been good to me and my daughters. It is selfish of me, but I am glad Isis is with you. I feel as though you protect her as much as she protects you. The mansion . . . I've come to realize that it's really the best place for her after all she went through at Grenich," Passion said with a sad smile, glancing over to Electra when she approached the two women. "When she first came back, Electra and I talked about arguing for her to stay here in the Meadows."

"Aneurin never would have agreed to that," Electra mentioned, winking at Lilly. "No matter how persuasive Mom thinks she can be. With some members of the High Council, perhaps, but there are a few who are immune to her charms."

Passion playfully swatted at Electra, who nimbly danced out of the way. "My daughter wisely pointed out that perhaps the Meadows wasn't the best place for her to heal. I sometimes forget that our idea of serenity isn't monolithic. I don't think the guardian haven would be a very pleasant place for the experiments, not even Isis. It's much too quiet here. Hell, some days even I can't deal with it."

"Some days?" Electra asked, raising an eyebrow. Passion mirrored her expression with a devilish grin and Electra laughed, shaking her head as she turned her attention back to the healer she was looking over. Lilly chuckled at the banter between the two, enjoying their company.

"No, I don't think the experiments would fare well in a place like the Meadows," she agreed. "They need changes in scenery and things to do. I don't know if the guardians would be able to handle their presence. The mansion lost most of its kitchen staff due to Dane, who has a passion and enthusiasm for cooking."

Passion smiled as she pulled her hair back into a tight bun, securing it with a band she wore around her wrist, "Jet has mentioned him on occasion, though I'm not sure I've ever heard him referred to by his proper name before. Your husband has some impressively colorful names for him."

Lilly laughed and shook her head. "He is certainly an interesting character, very unlike the other experiments. I honestly don't know how Dane managed to survive so long in Grenich and still have some spark in him."

"Isis mentioned that he was born in Grenich," Electra said, crossing her arms over her chest as she leaned back against the footboard of the bed she was standing near. "Is he the only experiment you've worked with who was a lifer, so to speak?"

Lilly contemplated the question, shaking her head after

a moment. "No, Radar was also born in a Grenich facility. They're the only two who chose to stay and fight."

"Orion told me a little about the different ways shape shifters are recruited," Electra mentioned, looking over to a bed across the way when a male healer started tossing and turning.

"Electra has been doing quite a bit of research about the experiments," Passion explained, watching as her daughter went over to soothe the thrashing healer. "I should do similar, but I can't bring myself to speak to Orion yet."

Lilly looked over at her. "You are still angry with him?"

Passion nodded. "Before all this, I never had any reason to be. He was one of my closest friends, almost as close as Jet, and I mourned for many years after his death, or supposed death. I don't think I'll ever be able to forgive him for being in the shadows for so long. He nearly cost Isis her life and . . . I feel as though he is still not being entirely forthright with us. I think he knows more than what he tells and I fear that it will cost us dearly in the future."

Lilly bit her lower lip, concerned by Passion's words. She had long suspected the eldest Deverell was keeping things from them. Orion had always been a quiet man, but his silence and secretiveness was becoming a cause for concern.

The sudden sound of glass shattering brought both women's attention over to the bed across the aisle, where Electra had been attempting to comfort one of the younger healers. Lilly and Passion stared in horror at the scene that greeted their eyes.

The healer was sitting up in the bed, his posture rigid, and his hands wrapped tightly around Electra's throat. Blood was oozing out of his pores and eyes and nose, soaking through his light clothing and dripping on the bedding. The look in his eyes was feral as he continued throttling Electra, who was struggling and gasping for breath. She was scratching at his face in her attempt to get free, tearing his already thin skin, which was peeling off. Phoenix dashed across the healing wing, quickly getting to her friend's side. She started tugging frantically at the healer's arms, trying to pull him off Electra.

"You . . . You have sent them to their deaths," the healer spoke in a rough hiss. "You have released evil for a fool's errand."

Both Passion and Lilly rushed to help Electra, as did Amethyst and Eshmun. The two head healers struggled to pull back the arms of the unnaturally strong healer as Lilly and Passion helped Phoenix in her efforts to pry his fingers from Electra's throat. The younger guardian continued to try to get free of the man's grasp, gagging as she struggled to breathe. Blood was starting to drip down his stringy hair as his fingers tightened. His light blue eyes were wide and unblinking, rimmed with blood, a wild look in them. Amethyst muttered something to Eshmun, who nodded in response, and then she ran to the back of the room.

"Lenus, let go! You're killing her," Eshmun grunted through gritted teeth as he switched tactics and wrapped an arm around the sick guardian's neck, attempting to pull him back. Amethyst soon reappeared with a large syringe, which she plunged into one of the throbbing veins in the sick man's neck when Eshmun moved his arm out of the way. The effect was almost instantaneous as the man's grip loosened slightly, enough for Lilly and Passion to break his grasp. Electra fell to the floor and quickly scrambled back a few feet, coughing harshly and gasping as she tried to get her breath back. Lenus' blood was splattered all over her face and clothing, and bloody handprints colored her throat. Passion was at her side in an instant.

"The eyes in stone, they are always watching," Lenus mumbled before collapsing back, his body going into violent spasms. Bloody foam spewed out of his mouth like an erupting volcano, causing both Eshmun and Amethyst to curse as they set about trying to help him.

"The eyes in the stone are always watching, always watching," a strange chanting began to echo through the healing wing. Lilly and Phoenix both looked away from Electra and Passion, staring at the strange sight that greeted them. Every healer was sitting up in bed, their eyes forward and gazing at nothing; their lips were all that moved. Their skin looked even more papery in the dull light.

"The eyes in the stone, always watching," half the room spoke in unison, with the other half chiming in just a little later, creating a strange disjointed harmony. They spoke the same words over and over again.

"I'm not seeing things, am I?" Phoenix asked Lilly, her eyes not moving from the healers. Lilly shook her head in response and then the healers' heads all swiveled in their direction. They continued repeating the words.

Lilly moved out of the way as the few healers working in the wing moved to help their patients, though they were rather hesitant. She moved over to where Passion was kneeling on the floor next to her daughter, who was still gagging. Electra held her now sensitive throat; her dark green eyes were wide with concern as she looked around the healing wing. Lilly leaned down and placed a gentle hand on the young guardian's shoulder.

"Are you all right?" Lilly asked, concerned. Blood stained her own hands and dress from her struggles to help Electra, but she didn't pay them any mind. Electra looked up at her, nodding once after a moment and allowing Passion to help her to her feet. A healer approached them, offering Electra a towel to clean the blood off herself.

"The eyes in the stone are always watching, always watching," the eerie mantra continued throughout the healing wing. Blood was starting to drip down the faces and arms of some of the sicker healers, gathering in bright red pools on the clean linens.

"What is going on?" Electra let the soft question hang

in the air as she looked over to where the healers were working. Lilly exchanged a look with Passion and she could tell the guardian was just as uneasy by the man's disquieting words. She wanted to offer some words of comfort, but knew they would be empty.

It suddenly went quiet as the healers slowly laid back down in their beds, all closing their eyes and falling asleep. Lilly looked over at Passion again, who visibly swallowed and glanced over at her friend. She could see the same fear in Passion's eyes that she felt deep within her bones.

~~*~*~*

The darkness began to deepen again as they started traveling to the strange isolated building. Isis noticed the shadows crawling down the rough stones of the mountains, rapidly approaching the open field. She had chosen to take the form of a coyote in order to move through the soft grasses, which stretched far over their heads. Much of the vegetation in the Seelie Court grew much faster and taller than its counterpart on Earth, which proved to be beneficial.

Isis paused to sniff the ground and listen to the sounds in the air. They had been walking for close to two hours and as far as she could tell, they still had another hour or so to go. The humans weren't showing any signs of slowing down, though they did seem to be rather hazy. Eris' magic was frighteningly effective. She had cast a mirage to further conceal their movements. To them, it looked like a smoky black translucent mist, but according to Eris, anyone looking at them would just see a field of grass. Isis cast a glance back to where the guardian was sauntering alongside Jade, just behind Isis. Shae was in the middle of the group of humans and Alex was bringing up the rear.

In the distance, Isis could hear a crackling fire. A fairly large one, from the sounds of it and the faint traces of smoke she could smell in the air, which meant the anomaly, the empty diner, had been discovered. The feeling of a small hand on her flank made Isis glance back. The youngest member of their group, a young girl of no more than eight years of age, was watching her. The young girl was dressed in the same dull colors as everyone else, including a light blue hijab. She didn't seem to be attached to anyone at the diner — none of the patrons or staff did — which was quite unusual since diners tended to be places to socialize and interact. But most of the humans were merely acquaintances and only the staff seemed to be friends with each other. A soft rustling nearby drew Isis' attention to the left, but she saw nothing. Out of the corner of her eye, she glimpsed a light way up high. Turning her attention to the enormous mountain, she could make out the faintest yellow glow near the top. It was barely visible through the clouds that ringed the enormous peaks and she knew the normals would be unable to see it.

More rustling, this time to her right, caused Isis to start moving again, jogging quietly through the grass. The sweet smell of flora filled her nose and a breeze brushed through the field, sweeping down the tall grass. Isis glanced over her shoulder, making sure the humans remained in an orderly line. Jade was still glaring at Eris, who ignored her as she sighed loudly again and rolled her neck.

"Your face is going to freeze like that. Then you'll be even uglier than you already are. Hey, your face will match your soul," she remarked in a chipper tone. Isis let out a soft growl, warning them both to remain silent. Eris delighted in needling Jade, who mostly ignored her. However, when she realized the guardian was using her powers, it became a different story.

"Eris, I swear to the guardians, I am going to tell the High Council about this," Jade warned softly. Eris yawned and stretched her arms over her head, obviously unconcerned with the prospect. Isis turned around and moved over to where Jade was, and the older protector knelt down to her level.

"I'm going to scout ahead," she whispered softly. "Keep moving forward and you'll reach the place in about an hour. I suggest moving in a slight zig-zag, just to make sure you have no tails and it will make your trail not as easy to follow. I'll meet you at the fence surrounding whatever that building is."

Jade nodded and Isis turned, taking off through the grass. Ignoring the soft sweeping sounds and nocturnal animals, she kept her senses pressed outwards. She hadn't realized it back in the diner, due to her trying to figure out feasible strategies for survival, but this place was definitely familiar. Now that she was on her own, Isis was beginning to realize just how much she could recognize. There were no clear memories, nothing to explain what she had done on the island, but small details were beginning to jump out at her. Isis knew the grass had been kept shorter when she had been here.

Suddenly skidding to a halt, Isis paused before allowing her body to melt back into its normal human form. She looked around at the surrounding grasses, glancing up to the night sky, and then carefully knelt down and used her fingers to brush aside the loose soil. Under a small amount of dirt, there was a thin steel wire. Isis stood up, taking a couple large steps back before kneeling on the ground again. Brushing her hands around her, she found she was encircled by the wire, which appeared to reach in all directions. Carefully standing again, she looked over her shoulder and glimpsed the shadow of a nearby tree. A flash of bright yellow caught her eye and in one fluid motion, Isis had spun around and drew her sais.

There was nothing but grass. Isis swallowed and started making her way in the direction of the enormous building. After a while, she finally came to a rusty chain-link fence that towered over her. Nasty spirals of barbed wire sat atop it and old broken flood lights stared down at her. Isis took a small ball bearing out of a pouch on her belt and gently tossed it at the fence, unsurprised when it bounced harmlessly off. Preferring to be safe, Isis stepped forward and gently tapped the fence with her boot. Upon receiving no shock, she turned, retrieved the ball bearing, and started walking along the fence. Isis could faintly hear the quiet murmurs of a conversation just ahead and wondered if normals were at all capable of being silent for a measurable amount of time.

She soon came upon the group, faintly impressed to find they had all fifteen humans with them. The humans milled about and didn't seem interested in anything. Only the young girl showed any sign of curiosity or liveliness and Isis wondered if she might have some resistance to guardian magic. She was sitting in a patch of grass, playing with some pale blue flowers. Eris was leaning casually against a brick pillar that used to hold a spotlight, watching the young girl with something resembling amusement.

"Don't lie to me, Eris. Take your spell off these humans and do it now," Jade hissed at the guardian.

"Okay, one: that would be incredibly stupid and most assuredly ill-advised. I may not know much about humans, but I do know how skittish they are about anything they deem abnormal," Eris responded, glancing at her nails. "Two, your comrade over there requested I make them into docile little lambs to begin with. Not my fault you two aren't on the same page. For what it's worth, she's the smarter of you both, which isn't saying much. She's letting you protectors call the shots, which is how we wound up saddled with all this baggage in the first place."

The three other women turned when Eris tilted her chin in Isis' direction. Shae turned back at Eris' last statement and Isis could almost picture her eyes narrowing at the guardians. Out of the other three, Shae was by far the most protective of the seven series. Isis ignored them as she approached Jade, her senses still sharp for anything out of the ordinary.

"Isis is a protector, same as us," Shae stated with a ferocity that wasn't typical of her. Eris stared at her and laughed softly, her light blue eyes twinkling with delight.

"I do believe you're the only one who genuinely believes that. Your naiveté is just adorable, little Miss Feel Good," Eris cooed as she crossed her arms over her chest, scrunching up her nose as she smiled at the protector.

Jade turned her full attention to Isis, her expression was one of disappointment. "You can't just take away humans' free will to make things easier. That's a violation of their rights and goes against everything we believe, everything we fight for."

"That is your morality and it is not feasible in our current circumstances. You can practice it when we get back to the world where you have the advantage, but right now you don't. As a protector, you never would have left the humans behind, so I had to adjust our strategy and that included making the humans as docile as possible. You want them to have a chance at surviving this? Then let me do what I was made to do," Isis responded, turning to look over at Jade. "Believe me, protector, your morality is a luxury and it's one that you can't afford in the present circumstances."

Eris clapped softly in approval. "At least one of you is a realist."

"It is *really* quiet," Alex suddenly observed, looking around at their surroundings. Her hand was resting on the holster she wore on her hip. A few of the humans looked over in her direction, but none spoke. Some were studying Isis, unsure what to make of the odd woman. Isis disregarded them as she approached Alex, squinting at the night. The inky darkness had stopped advancing and now just cloaked the mountains. Isis didn't think that would last for very long and wanted to get inside the building before the darkness started moving again.

"We should be prepared for the nights being longer than we're used to," she mentioned, moving past Eris as she made her way to the gate.

"It's padlocked," Shae mentioned from where she stood nearby. Isis pulled out a couple thin tools from her belt and made quick work of the lock. A soft whispering through the grass drew her attention back to the field. Isis swallowed as she looked at the imposing Victorian-style building lurking in the shadows, which she was almost certain was a hospital. It wasn't dilapidated, but it hadn't been occupied in quite a while either. The windows were all grimy and vines had stretched over the walls, almost consuming the building. The grass was tall and there were a few trees dotting the property, all twisted and writhing. The trees were similar to the ones in the forest, with none of the brightness and whimsy of the Seelie Court. Isis swallowed and turned away from the gates, tucking her tools back into her belt.

As she moved a few feet away, she turned her attention to the sky, noticing that it became somewhat lighter in the distance. Looking over to Jade, she caught her attention and motioned for her to come nearer.

"Isis, should we take any precautions?" Shae asked.

"Don't enter that building without me," Isis replied, "Other than that, inside the gates should be neutral ground, for the time being."

"Alex, keep an eye on Eris," Jade ordered as she walked over to where Isis was standing. For a moment, the two women stood in silence, both looking up at the sky.

"I've seen coups before, Isis. They generally aren't this quiet," Jade commented. Isis looked over at her.

"I've instigated coups before, some are quiet. Those are often the most effective ones," Isis remarked. "Of course, normals have a very different vocabulary and some of your definitions are not what I'm used to."

Jade rubbed her forehead and Isis blinked a couple times, wondering if the older protector was going to stop fixating on the humans. She needed her teammates to be sharp and on their guard, as the situation wasn't going to get any safer or easier. Jade looked over at her and sighed softly, thinking over her words.

"Look, this might be the right play, maybe the only one. But . . . sometimes I worry that you genuinely don't distinguish between right and wrong," she said truthfully. Isis allowed herself a subtle half-smile, more for Jade's benefit than her own. For their many faults, normals could be quite endearing at times.

"Jade, I have lived with protectors long enough to understand your morality, what you term right and wrong. But your rigid insistence on such things is why your people don't have very long lifespans. You must adapt at times," Isis said, looking back to the sky. "I try to respect your values and morals, but in a situation like this, it is impossible."

Jade rubbed the back of her neck. "What did you want to tell me?"

Isis knelt down on one knee and brushed her hand over the soil, uncovering another steel wire. Jade crouched to get a closer look at the wire, reaching out to touch it. Isis quickly grasped her wrist, shaking her head once.

"This is a very old experiment trick," she explained. "It was only used by a few series and they referred to it as a spider's web, if memory serves. It's a highly sensitive material, manufactured at Grenich, and it is aptly named: step on it and a vibration travels down the entire length. There's usually a center to the web, a place where every thread meets, and whoever is watching that would be alerted to someone's approach. Damn things are nearly impossible to avoid, especially if they're laid by someone with experience."

Jade stared at Isis, not thrilled with the new information. "If we were already blown when we entered the —"

"You misunderstand. Whatever other experiments are in town will be using modern technology and surveillance equipment. I have never used a spider web and, as far as I know, Coop or Shocker haven't either and they are much older than I am," Isis interrupted, rising to her feet and looking back toward the enormous hospital building. "Apparently experiments have practiced, or at least been stationed, in this place for quite some time. It is not outside the realm of possibility that there might be some still here, perhaps hiding."

"And that's why you don't want anyone entering that building without you," Jade finished and Isis nodded in response. "Just for my peace of mind: if it's an earlier series, you will be able to help us handle them, right?"

Isis gave a small shrug. "While most early lines are destroyed when newer products are designed, there are still a few that have their uses. I know of at least two series that have been manufactured since the beginning of the Corporation and there are likely a few more that I wasn't aware of. Depending on their purpose, a seven series likely wouldn't fare well in a one-on-one battle with some of them, not with their vast experience."

"That's not reassuring," Jade remarked under her breath, following as Isis turned and started moving toward the gates.

"It's not meant to be. Reassurances are pointless."

Jade looked up at the sky and shook her head, an expression Isis was used to. "Do you have any plans as to how we're going to get off this island?"

"First, we need to find the Box of Original Elements. I anticipate that taking the better part of the night," Isis began to explain as they stepped through the gates and onto the winding dirt road that led up to the building. "As strange as it may sound, moving during the day is our best bet. The werehyenas may be able to move in the daylight, but it reduces their speed and strength slightly. Wereanimals also don't see as well in the day as they do in the night. Guardian legends of old suggest they have a severe ultraviolet light allergy, but Grenich may have been able to breed that out of the mutations. They are still incredibly nocturnal though, so daylight will be our ally. I haven't figured out how to get past the woods yet. We need to find or construct some kind of Faraday cage, one that can block magic as well as electricity."

"Right, sounds easy enough."

"I assure you, it will be incredibly difficult, if not outright impossible."

"Guardians, give me strength," Jade grumbled under her breath and Isis looked over at her, curious.

"I don't think most guardians can hear you. Perhaps Hecate, but I don't believe she would be listening currently," Isis stated, looking around at their surroundings. The darkness seemed to be deepening again, but only slightly. There was something very odd about the Island of Avalon and Isis didn't like it at all.

Turning her attention back to her teammate, Isis noticed the look Jade was giving her, which told her she had missed something when she responded to her. Likely more figurative language. *Normals can be so utterly confusing,* Isis thought as they continued walking.

~~*~*~*

"What the hell is going on over there?"

Jensen glanced over at Nero, who stood next to him on the deck. The sky was starting to lighten and soon the sun would start to rise, but a cloak of shadow remained ringed around the whole island. Jensen's gaze drifted up to the peak of the mountain where the barely visible light remained, as it had throughout the night. It was rather unsettling, for such a small thing.

Jensen leaned down and gripped the ship's railing, concern filling his every thought as he stared at the unnatural shadow hanging over most of the island, resembling a solid mass of nothingness. Radar was still working on her tablet below deck. In the middle of the night, she had woken Jensen up, her glowing brown eyes alight with excitement. She had found a network, the source of which was somewhere on the island. It was encrypted, but Radar was certain she would be able to crack it and get in. Then she would probably be able to access the security Alex had mentioned when she briefly made contact.

Jensen wished he had been more awake to share in her excitement, but she didn't seem to mind when he waved her off and turned over to go back to sleep. When he had woken up, she had been hard at work, her fingers dancing over the tablet screen with lightning speed. *I hope she's made progress,* Jensen thought as he tried to see through the shadows that concealed the island.

"What kind of necromancer bullshit is this? Fuck, is there going to be a zombie horde?" Nero continued to grumble. Jensen looked around the ship, noticing Sly a few feet away. She was sitting on the set of steps, looking at the island with a thoughtful expression. Jack was beneath the shrouds of the topmast, keeping a sharp lookout on top. *Or he might have climbed up to the crow's nest again,* Jensen thought, remembering that the seven series moved about frequently between his various perches.

"Excuse me, sir?" Jensen turned, noticing the selkie standing next to him and peering over the side. "Begging your pardon, but did you hear a tapping just now?"

Jensen shook his head. "No, I'm afraid I didn't. Just the normal sounds of the water."

"Could've sworn I heard a tapping," the selkie responded, grabbing the railing and leaning over, peering down at the ship's side. After a moment, they straightened up and shrugged, wandering off to work on some other task. Jensen watched them leave before moving over to the side, glancing down at the dark blue water.

"I got in!"

Jensen looked over at the sound of Radar's excited voice. She bolted onto the deck of the ship, skidding to an abrupt halt when she noticed the darkness covering the island. After staring at the unusual sight for a moment, the E-series shook her head and turned her attention back to the shape shifters on the deck. Jensen and Nero both moved over to her, as did Sly who looked intrigued.

"I figured out a way to hop into a network on the island without being noticed and the signal is incredibly strong," Radar said as she spiritedly began to explain in increasingly technical terms what she had done. Jensen often wondered if even a computer scientist could understand half of what the E-series said. But judging from her unusually animated manner, Jensen assumed it was good news.

"Radar, sweetheart, you're dealing with a group of luddites at the moment," Sly interrupted her excited explanation. "Just give us the important bits."

"Right, of course," Radar said, still half-smiling, shaking her head as she re-focused on the screen and tapped a few things. "Okay, I just started looking, so no news on the Four. However, there is a town on that island, covered in surveillance like they said, and it is *crawling* with what looks like eight-series. Chances are Blitz has led them to a temporary safe hideout, somewhere just outside of town. She'll look for a place away from the security cameras, a place to lay low until she can figure out their next move."

Radar paused briefly, glancing up and over Jensen's shoulder. Jensen twisted slightly and almost jumped when he noticed Jack standing right next to him, his pulse jumping up slightly. *Never going to get used to that,* he thought with a shake of his head. Jack moved around to stand next to Radar and look over her shoulder, his attention fixed on the screen. Somewhere above them, a bird let out a loud cry.

Radar, who had turned her eyes back to the screen, suddenly froze. Her dark glowing eyes widened significantly and she dropped her tablet. It was the first time Jensen had ever seen an experiment show blatant fear. Even Jack looked frightened as he caught the tablet and stared at the image on the screen. He carefully handed the tablet back to Radar and then ran a hand over his mouth.

"Um, guys," Nero said, looking up when he noticed the elves approaching. "Clue the rest of us in because your expressions aren't exactly comforting."

"What's going on?" Maeve asked.

Jack looked over at the protectors and swallowed, hesitating and then gesturing for Radar to show them the image on the screen. She glanced at him, questioningly, and then turned the screen so the protectors could see. The three protectors and two elves leaned in, studying the image. It was surprisingly clear, showing an elaborate room with well-dressed people standing around and mingling with each other. It looked like a high society gala. Jensen noticed two impeccably dressed men standing off to the side, watching the room, occasionally talking to each other. Then he saw them: off to the side, but still near the nicely dressed men. Two figures he remembered from countless debriefings.

"Tracy and Nick Chance," Jensen whispered, trepidation invading his mind. Nero looked as though he would be sick, and Sly kept her expression impassive. The elves looked at the shape shifters, unsure what made them so uneasy.

"We'll explain later," Nero mumbled softly, squinting at the screen and then pointing to the two men. "Jack, who are they?"

Jack scrubbed a hand over his short hair, exchanging another look with Radar before turning his gaze to Nero. "Those are the sons of Set and Pyra, Vincent and Vladimir. I believe normals would refer to them as the face of the Grenich Corporation. It's their job to keep investors happy, make sure their covers hold up, and a lot of other busywork. They're also incredibly powerful necromancers, second only to their father."

"If they're here, it means all these people are likely very important investors," Radar added, pointing at the large gathering on the screen. "That means this probably isn't just a training field, it's also used for demonstrations. That means live rounds, probably unlimited ammunition. Investors do enjoy fireworks and high body counts."

"Bet you're regretting not taking it easy when I told you, huh Aldridge?" Sly commented with a half-grin. The elves looked horrified at the experiments' words and Jensen could understand why. Closing his eyes briefly, Jensen inhaled the clean sea air, considering what they should do. He opened his eyes again and looked over at Nero, nodding toward the elves.

"Nero, why don't you explain to our generous hosts about the Grenich situation? Brainstorm some precautions we can take," he suggested before turning to Sly. "Sly, could you wake up Steve and Alpha, and catch them up on everything?"

Sly half smiled, raising an eyebrow, and turned to the door to the cabin while Nero quickly brought the elves off to the side, smiling in his affable manner and putting his silver tongue to good use. Jensen almost rolled his eyes when the youngest Deverell immediately started flirting with both elves. He moved closer to the experiments, making sure to respect their personal space. Both Radar and Jack were looking at the screen again. Radar had one hand over her mouth.

"I need you both to be completely forthright: how bad is this?" Jensen asked softly. Both Jack and Radar looked up, studying him with luminous eyes. Radar bit her lower lip, looking briefly at Jack before turning the screen around again, and tapping on one of the minimized windows.

"They're able to watch the activities on the island from a number of places, including a balcony, which is the light we're seeing near the peak of the mountain. There will be viewing spaces throughout the mountain range, some closer to the ground. And there's also a screen room in the main area, right there. I'm counting at least twenty monitors, and cameras covering every square inch of that town."

"You have to understand, these demonstrations are meant to satisfy investors. They're like sport," Jack added. "The better the kills, the more carnage, the more skills demonstrated, the more entertained the investors are likely to be. When the investors are happy, they are more likely to open their wallets, to borrow one of your metaphors."

"Okay, but surely every experiment has been in these demonstrations," Jensen mentioned, putting his hands on his hips and closing his eyes when a thought came to him. "Demonstrations, how chaotic do they get?"

"From what I've heard, they generally tend to be a bloodbath," Radar mentioned. "The E-series were never used in the demonstrations, except for the defective ones. Defective experiments are often used as high-value targets."

Jack seemed to be following Jensen's train of thought. "This sort of situation would appeal to Eris, the discord of it all."

"Not to mention all the bad blood there is between necromancers and guardians," Jensen pointed out, scratching the back of his head. "Is there any way you can get word to the Four? I doubt the elves will allow us to go to the island, so they may have to get extra creative on this one."

"I'll keep trying to make contact with them and I'll keep an eye on this situation," Radar said, raising her tablet a little. "They don't know I can see them. It's a small advantage, but it's an advantage nonetheless."

She turned and hurried back to the cabin room, disappearing through the door as Steve and Alpha were walking out. Steve looked over at Jensen and spread his hands, his tired eyes clearly asking what the hell was going on. Jensen shrugged in response, mirroring Steve's spread hands. He turned back to Jack. The experiment's luminous brown eyes stood out even in the grayness of the early morning hours.

"Based on what I've seen of Grenich, I assume it's not outside the realm of possibility that they'll attack the ship," Jensen said, looking out across the dark water. Jack was quiet for a moment, his attention going back to the mountain.

"You are correct," Jack affirmed quietly, looking back to Jensen. "You should know that Set's sons don't have the same amount of restraint as their father. It makes them sloppy at times, but no less dangerous."

Jensen studied the seven series as he turned his body to face the mountain. He looked back to Jensen after a moment.

"From what I have observed, the general strategy of the protectors is based partly on the assumption that Set wants to retrieve the Key potentials. I know the doctor, Orion, has long believed that Set is consumed by his need to possess the Key. When dealing with Set, it's not a bad strategy or an inaccurate assumption," Jack paused and turned his attention back to the mountain. "But his desire is not shared by all necromancers. Milo has told me that his sons and grandsons aren't as concerned with the prophecy, neither are many of the other necromancers. Chances are they view Isis and me as malfunctioning experiments and would sooner put us down than capture us, make examples of us."

Jensen swallowed, following Jack's gaze up to where the dim gold light was. It was difficult to see as the sky got lighter. "If we get word to the Four, warn them about this, do you think Isis would know that?"

Jack dropped his shoulders, considering his answer. "I'm not certain, but I think she would. Isis frequently knows more than I do when it comes to Grenich matters. Milo tells us both the same things, gives us the same information; what little he still manages to find."

Jensen nodded, feeling somewhat reassured.

Experiments were blunt and they never lied. If Jack believed Isis would be all right, than it was likely she would be. She did have a knack for surviving and beating seemingly insurmountable odds.

"Well then, we should probably focus on how to get ready for whatever they might throw at us," Jensen said with a small smile, nodding over at the elves. "Maybe do some damage control with our hosts. I have a feeling the Seelie Court will have some words for Jet and Lilly when this is over."

Jack nodded and followed Jensen when he made his way across the deck to where Sly and Alpha were talking with a group of selkies.

~~*~*~*

Isis cautiously moved across the peeling floor, her sharp eyes piercing through the shadows. The faint scent of antiseptic was barely detectible in the dusty stale air. There was a heavy silence that pervaded the entire space. It was completely dark inside. Behind her, she could hear Jade instructing the still hazy humans how to barricade the doors and windows. They were looking everywhere but at the protector, which seemed to entertain Eris. Jade was keeping her head lantern aimed at where the humans were working, so it would be easier to see. All three of her teammates had their head lanterns on again and Isis wasn't sure that was wise. Any kind of light would make for an ideal target in darkness.

Isis looked over to her left when Alex approached her, quietly looking across the empty space. The building had been fairly gutted, but Isis was sure there were still a few useful tools to be found in the halls. Abandoned hospitals could be treasure troves if one knew what to look for. A layer of dust clung to every surface and cobwebs were abundant. Isis faintly heard Shae curse and glanced over to the protector, who was flailing her hands about wildly, trying to brush away the enormous cobweb she had walked into.

"I'm going to look around," Isis mentioned under her breath. Alex nodded and gestured at Shae. Shae walked over, brushing away the dust and cobwebs that stubbornly clung to her hair and clothes. Isis moved over to the stairway, running her fingers over the closest web, and then rubbing her fingers together. *Strange, it's thicker and stickier than spider webs typically are,* she thought as she brushed her fingers off on the floor. Turning her eyes up the staircase, Isis squinted as she scanned the shadows of the upper levels.

"We'll secure the space down here, you two should do a quick sweep of the upper levels. Meet back here in an hour," Alex said to Shae, glancing over her shoulder when Isis approached them again. Shae nodded in understanding, but Isis didn't look away from the empty space surrounding them.

"Isis?"

Isis turned her attention to Shae when she said her name, noticing the concern on her and Alex's faces. She nodded once to show her understanding before turning and moving to where the group was still barricading the front door. Eris was sitting cross-legged on a dusty desktop, but perked up when Shae and Isis passed by. Quickly rising to her feet, she started to follow the two women.

"Eris, you stay where I can see you," Jade ordered firmly and Eris pouted.

"But the humans are so *boring*," she moaned.

"I don't object to her accompanying us," Isis said as she continued on her way to the long stairway behind the main desk. Eris looked over at Jade, a triumphant smirk playing on her lips, and the protector shook her head.

"Fine, I could use a break. But if she steps out of line, feel free to use whatever methods you want," Jade called over her shoulder, mumbling under her breath, "Since we've already disregarded everyone else's rights."

Isis glanced at the older protector, wondering how long she would dwell on that. Knowing normals, it would be an unreasonable length of time. *It probably would have been wiser to lie and then leave the humans where they were,* she thought before jogging up the stairs to the next floor. It was as quiet and dusty as the others, cloaked in shadows. Old wallpaper was peeling off the walls; some of it already lay on the floor. Out of the corner of her eye, Isis could see glimpses of Jade's head lantern below them.

"Lots of cobwebs," Shae whispered and shuddered. Isis glanced over at her, noticing Eris just over her shoulder. The guardian was practically skipping as she looked about curiously. She wasn't wearing her head lantern, refusing to mess up her hair any more. Shae's lantern seemed to provide enough light to prevent the guardian from complaining.

"I haven't observed any symptoms that would suggest you suffered from arachnophobia," Isis replied as they continued making their way down the hall. It got progressively darker, the further they traveled.

"I don't," Shae replied, pausing when Isis stopped abruptly. "What's wrong?"

"This is not an effective method, too time consuming," Isis replied as she looked around. "You and Eris should go the opposite way. We can meet back at the stairwell."

Shae looked at Isis skeptically. "You know I trust your judgment, but splitting up doesn't seem like the wisest move right now."

"Which is why I suggested you and Eris sweep the opposite way," Isis said, looking over to the guardian. "She's not trustworthy, but she will act in her own self-interest. At the moment, your enemies are hers. If she wants to survive, she needs us."

"Unfortunately, the creepy critter speaks true," Eris put in reluctantly. Shae looked over at Eris and then at Isis, biting her lower lip.

"I don't like the idea of you not having anyone to watch your back," she confessed.

"I can assure you, I have been in significantly more dangerous situations, sometimes on my own," Isis said. "While it's not preferable, it is doable. I will be fine on my own and I promise that I will finish the sweep quickly."

Shae's shoulders dropped as she looked at her teammate and Isis could tell she didn't like the idea of separating, which was expected. Shae didn't like solo work in situations that had a lot of uncertainty. It was understandable, especially for a normal, but sometimes it was unavoidable. After a moment, Shae nodded and gestured for Eris to move in the opposite direction. The guardian turned with a little hop in her step and started off into the murky shadows.

Isis turned back to the dark hallway before her, noticing all the open doors to the numerous rooms. It was classic Victorian style architecture: a sprawling brick building with towering windows. Normals would likely term it spooky, but Isis had seen so much grandiose and intimidating architecture that it was rather ordinary. Everything was overwhelmingly gray, though she imagined it had been white at some point. Glancing up at the ceiling, she noticed modern lighting fixtures, which told her the building had been used not that long ago. Running her fingers over the smooth walls, Isis glanced inside one room when she noticed the tattered misty curtains drift up as though a light breeze snuck in. All the glass was intact . . .

"I won't ask you to help me escape. I couldn't ask you to take that kind of risk. But you know," she paused when a couple blank faced people passed by them. "You know the head of this place is dangerous. I just . . . I need you to help me get a message to someone."

The man looked up from their game of chess and she briefly met his gaze before looking out the window, the sunlight warming her face. The man bit his bottom lip, tugging a little at the collar of his pristine uniform, obviously hesitant to respond. She was wearing a loose gown, tan in color, as was almost everyone else in the enormous room.

"Look, just keep your head down and you'll be fine, okay?"

She let out a bitter bark of laughter, looking behind her when the door opened and a pair of orderlies entered, almost as blank faced as the other people in the room. Looking back to the man sitting across from her, she leaned forward, her dark green eyes intense.

"Get away from this place and for the love of everything, don't approach me if I ever return. I won't be . . . me anymore," she warned and then slumped back in her chair. The orderlies paused at the chair and, when she didn't react, they grabbed each of her arms, hauling her to her feet.

"I'm afraid we didn't have a chance to finish our game. My apologies," she said with a polite smile. The orderlies turned her around and pushed her in front of them, leading her out of the room. The bright sun beamed down through the window, illuminating the plain white room and making it shine.

Isis blinked and shook her head, turning sharply to look down the empty hallway. A wet feeling on her face caused her to reach up and brush a hand over her cheek, beneath her eye. She was surprised to find her eyes had teared up. The dust in the air must have irritated them. *I should have worn my sunglasses,* she thought. Rubbing her fingers together, Isis looked up again, her gaze traveling over the grimy walls.

She noticed an old cobweb further down the hall. Moving with her usual quiet stealth, she made her way down the hall to the webbing. Brushing it lightly with her fingers, she felt the odd sticky substance, tracing a strand that went down the wall. Realizing that it went further down and around a corner, Isis followed it and wound up in a large open space, which looked frighteningly reminiscent to the memory or vision she had experienced. There were a few empty chairs spread out around the floor and a table that had been flipped over. Cards from various decks were messily spread out across the floor. Another smaller table was off to the side, a chessboard set up and waiting for players.

Isis swallowed and entered the room, her eyes traveling over every square inch of the space, searching for anything out of the ordinary. Dim gray light spilled in through the windows on the far side of the room, casting the space in an eerie glow. Heavy silence pervaded the room, adding to the creepy atmosphere. Taking a few more steps inside the room, Isis felt a mild discomfort. This was another place that was familiar, though she didn't know when she had ever been here. She stiffened up when she heard a faint scratching from somewhere in the shadows. Isis waited patiently, her eyes scanning the area as she waited for any further sounds. Swallowing thickly, she suddenly spun around and looked at the blank wall behind her.

It was a plain white wall, nothing out of the ordinary, but Isis remembered it had once been splattered in blood. And she remembered standing in the exact same spot, holding a gun. A gun she had recently fired, her first kill as a seven series. Like most of her early Grenich training, she couldn't remember anything clearly. It was just fragmented bits and pieces, nothing concrete. It was a memory that was only just out of reach, maddeningly so. She could practically feel it brush against her fingertips . . .

Suddenly, a merciless strong kick to her lower back sent her careening forward. Isis quickly tucked her head and used her forward momentum to roll, springing to her feet almost instantly. She yanked her sais out from their scabbards, spinning to face her attacker. The faint glow of light glinted off the guardian silver blades.

Behind her stood a young woman with six arms and her brown eyes glowed brightly in the murky shadows of the room. What little flesh showed was light brown and she wore dark clothing, which fit tightly and had obviously been altered for her. Her long black hair was tied back in a tight bun, not a strand of it out of place. The mysterious woman stood in a ready position, her glowing eyes looking Isis up and down quickly. Isis spun her sais and slid them back into their scabbards, holding her hands out in front of her.

"I do not want to fight you," she spoke calmly and quietly, gesturing to their surroundings. "This place hasn't been used in years, it's outside the simulation, which means you're no longer active. So you must be a target, same as I am. If we ally with each other, we can get out of here."

The woman narrowed her eyes at Isis, suspicion apparent in her expression. She suddenly reached to the side and grabbed the nearest chair in reaching distance, throwing it at Isis. Isis sidestepped the hurled projectile, but was instantly tackled by the mysterious woman and thrown to the ground.

CHAPTER NINE

Sly sauntered along the deck of the ship, watching as the selkies went about their business. They were really a talented crew and certainly the best mariners Sly had ever met. Most of the time, they took no notice of their passengers, but a few would smile politely at her and Alpha. They were also quite entertained by Nero, who had always been rather friendly and outgoing. Sly knew how to manipulate people, but Nero genuinely liked others. It was . . . cute.

Sly jogged up the steps to the bow of the ship, leaning over the side to admire the fine mermaid carving that adorned the front. After a moment, she turned her attention back to the vast open expanse of water that stretched out in front of them. Closing her eyes, she inhaled the sweet clean morning air. Sly wondered if the Seelie Court would allow a shape shifter to vacation in their lands, a notion that she wasn't entirely averse to. Aside from the interesting cultures within the Court, there was also an abundance of flawless jewels and the air was so clean. The complete lack of humans was also a major selling point.

"You would be bored after a day, mon chéri."

Sly laughed and ran her fingers through her dark hair, opening her eyes to find Alpha standing a few feet away from her. The rebel leader approached and rested her elbow on the side, facing Sly.

"When did you become French?" Sly asked with a slight grin. Alpha smiled her usual crooked smile and looked off across the water for a moment.

"I would've thought this morning would answer that question," she teased, reaching out and brushing some of Sly's smooth hair behind her ear. "I know that look. You're restless and want a change of scenery, but I don't think this world is the answer to that."

"No?" Sly looked out over the waters again, shrugging half-heartedly. "Might be a nice vacation. No humans, no protectors, no Grenich presence."

"No Jade, no me," Alpha added to Sly's list. "We both have responsibilities that bind us to Earth. Jade would never leave the protectors in a time of need and I could never leave the Rebel Lair or the rebels. And, as much as you declare otherwise, I don't think you could run from a fight. Grenich is messing with people you care about, that's not the kind of thing you have ever been able to let slide. It's one of the many things I love about you."

Alpha pushed off the side and stood again. "I'm going to check on the breakfast situation, make sure Steve hasn't completely fucked it up. That man could start a kitchen fire trying to hard boil an egg."

Sly laughed and watched as her lover descended the short stairway, sashaying her hips for Sly. Alpha did enjoy being a tease on occasion and she had a delightfully playful streak, which Sly had always found incredibly attractive. A soft tapping drew Sly's attention back to the waters and she looked for the source of the noise, carefully leaning over the port side. Behind her, she heard the loud calls of birds, quite a number of them from the sound of it. A pleasant breeze swept over the calm waters, whipping up Sly's hair. The shape shifter closed her eyes and lifted her face to the sky again, allowing the tension to leave her body.

The sudden sound of a grunt followed by a loud thud drew her attention back to the deck and she turned to find Jack straddling a strange man. He grasped the man's wrists, fighting for control of the knife the stranger held. The stranger's eyes glowed bright blue. He was much bigger than Jack, though the other experiment was holding his own. Sly froze for a moment, unsure what to do, when Jack turned his luminous brown eyes up to Sly.

"We're under attack, warn the others," he ordered between gritted teeth before refocusing on the mysterious man. Lifting him up and slamming him to the deck a couple times, Jack desperately tried to get his grip to loosen. The man suddenly threw his weight to the side, rolling over with Jack and winding up on top of him. Sly snapped out of her state of shock and ran forward, aiming a kick at the large man's head. He dodged and lashed out with his knife, nearly cutting Sly's leg. The momentary distraction allowed Jack to throw the man off him and flip back to his feet. The seven series charged at the attacking experiment again.

A sudden loud bell clanging drew Sly's attention across the boat to the stern, where one of the selkies was wildly ringing a bell near the wheel of the ship. They quickly leaped away from the bell when a second mysterious man sliced at them with a knife. The selkie jumped away from another slash and disappeared from Sly's view.

Quickly hurrying down the short stairway, Sly started to move across the deck and skidded to a halt, narrowly avoiding being tackled by another man. The man rolled forward, rose to his feet and jumped back, hitting Sly with a back kick that slammed her into the side of the ship. Sly fell to her knees with a gasp, stunned by the force behind the kick. The man turned to face her and when she saw the glowing gray eyes, Sly felt the blood freeze in her veins. Swallowing, she staggered back to her feet as the man drew a large combat dagger from a scabbard at his waist and began to approach her. *Well, this isn't good,* Sly thought as she held her hands in fists protectively in front of her, preparing to go down fighting.

Just before the man could advance on her, the end of a staff struck the back of his head with a satisfying *thwack*. The man spun to face his attacker and was promptly struck across the face with the same staff. His legs were swept out from under him and the mysterious man crashed to the ground, revealing Radar standing behind him. Smashing the staff down on the hand holding the knife, the young experiment got his grip to loosen and swiftly kicked the knife over toward Sly, who lunged forward and grabbed it. The mysterious man lashed out with a strong kick that struck Radar in the side, sending her stumbling away a few steps, and then flipped to his feet. He lunged at Radar and grabbed hold of her staff. She promptly raised her knee, burying it in his gut and slamming her head into his mouth. Releasing the staff with one hand, Radar struck with the back of her fist, knocking the man away from her.

Knowing Radar would be able to handle herself, Sly tucked the knife in her belt and quickly ran across the deck, diving through the door leading to the kitchen area and captain's quarters. She could hear the clanging of pots and pans. *How the fuck did so many manage to get on board without us knowing,* she thought as she skidded to halt in the kitchen. Steve slammed a pot on the hand of a mysterious woman and used another to strike her across the face before sliding under the counter, popping up on the other side.

The mysterious woman growled as she spun around, her broken jaw resetting instantly. Her glowing green eyes briefly darted over to Sly, but turned back to Steve. Sly looked to the side where Alpha was struggling with another mysterious man, one whose eyes weren't glowing. At least, Sly thought he was a man: his skin was dark blue and streaked with neon green; his flesh was unlike humans, more resembling tough leather; and his eyes were an unnatural gold color, like coins. Two sharpened incisors poked out just under his upper lip.

He roughly shoved Alpha away from him and she lost her balance, sitting down hard on the floor with a quiet yelp. Sly instantly reached to the side and grabbed a heavy iron skillet. As the man took a menacing step toward Alpha, Sly ran forward and swung the skillet with all her strength. It made a sickening cracking noise as it connected with the strange man's head and he dropped like a stone. Sly moved forward and slammed the heavy skillet down on the man's head a few more times, florescent green liquid spraying up every time she brought it down.

When she was satisfied the creature wouldn't get up again, Sly threw the skillet off to the side and helped Alpha to her feet, keeping the experiment Steve was still fighting off in her peripheral vision. Suddenly, Radar appeared in the doorway, staff in hand. The woman looked over to her and bared her teeth, reaching over and grabbing a large chef's knife, which she hurled at Radar. The young experiment used her staff to bat the projectile away. The mysterious woman briefly turned back to Steve, grabbing a nearby plate and hurling it at him. The protector was barely able to duck out of the way.

"Jack's holding the deck with the selkies and our escorts, but Jensen and Nero may require assistance. We were separated when the attack began. They sent me to help you, though I advised against it," Radar reported, her eyes traveling to the strange blue and green creature. The moment of distraction proved a poor decision as the mysterious woman launched herself over the counter and at Radar, tackling the young experiment to the ground. Steve instantly moved forward and grabbed the collar of her uniform, hauling her up and Alpha moved to grab her other arm. The woman quickly kicked Alpha directly in her diaphragm, knocking the wind out of her. She then spun in

Steve's grasp and punched him in the stomach. When he doubled over, she grabbed his shoulders and slammed her knee into his face. A powerful side kick to his midsection knocked him flat on his back.

Radar got back up and jumped onto the woman's back, her staff pressed tightly against her throat so the woman couldn't breathe. Her hands flew up to the staff and she stumbled backwards, slamming Radar into a wall. Radar grunted but held tightly to the staff, keeping the pressure firm against the woman's throat.

"I can handle her. Go help the others," she commanded, wrapping her legs around the woman as she slammed her into the wall again. Sly only hesitated briefly before moving to Alpha and helping her up, pulling her out the door. As they ran the short way to the staircase, they heard the loud cries of birds. Sly and Alpha exchanged a look, knowing they were thinking the exact same thing. Alpha swallowed and followed as Sly tore up the stairs.

The selkies were fierce and were holding their own admirably, but the experiments were clearly the superior fighters. Sly could see a few fallen selkies around the deck, which was splattered with blood here and there. A loud *thunk* brought Sly's attention to the starboard side, where a heavy grappling hook had landed, catching on the side of the ship. A selkie darted past Sly, brandishing a pair of impressive looking small axes. The selkie slammed the blade of one axe down on the rope attached to the grappling hook, slicing through it, and Sly heard a splash. The selkie put the axes back in their belt and pulled themself up on the side, grabbing a hold of the rigging, and swiftly scaled the ropes to the top under the top mast, helping another crewmember who was already fighting a couple experiments up there.

Alpha pushed Sly forward, reminding her of their task. Sly shook her head and started running through the deck, dodging out of the way of experiments and selkies and weapons. A few experiments in bird form dived at them, shifting right before they landed on the deck, forcing Alpha and Sly to weave and dodge as they moved through the ship. Around them, the air was alive with the sound of steel meeting steel and every now and again, a scream. As they got closer to the open door leading to the sleeping area, Sly noticed two sets of glowing eyes in the shadowy hallway and instinctively hid behind a wall, pushing Alpha behind her. A moment later a bullet slammed into the frame, sending splinters of wood flying.

"Well that's fucking perfect," Alpha grumbled. "Don't suppose you thought to arm yourself before coming out for some fresh air?"

Sly shook her head, thanking her lucky stars that most experiments were only using blades. "We were only allowed to bring a few pistols. The Seelie Court isn't too crazy about Earth weapons, no honor in their opinion. And, unfortunately, said pistols are in the bunks. Hopefully those two had enough common sense to make use of them or just toss them out of the porthole so they won't be used against us."

Both women turned when they felt a rush of air and saw a blur of color sweep by them followed by a splash. They glanced up to where Keane was standing on the edge of the boat, holding a rope in his hand, smiling triumphantly and looking like something from the cover of a crappy romance novel. Sly put her palms together and dipped her head in what she hoped was a sign of gratitude. Keane nodded once in response and jumped down, approaching them. Sly turned her attention back to the doorway, listening to the sound of two bodies slamming against a door. Those experiments were going to get into the sleeping area soon and Sly didn't know the situation in there. It was possible there were even more experiments inside and who knew what kind of shape the two protectors were in? Sly bit her lip as she tried to think of any kind of plan.

"Don't suppose you have any ideas about how to get past the two gorillas," Alpha yelled over the melee, her attention focused on the chaos surrounding them.

"Aside from rushing them, which is an overall horrible plan," Sly replied, glancing over her shoulder when she felt a gentle but insistent tapping on her arm. Keane removed a shield from the wall they were standing against, holding it in front of him and then ducking behind it, poking his head up again. It was black and decorated with gold, obviously selkie judging from the detailed seals etched on the front.

"I don't know. I doubt that's bulletproof — huh," Sly paused, running her hand over the smooth metal of the shield. Knocking on it, she studied the material, which was much sturdier than she had thought. Looking back to Keane, she mimed a gun and then looked at him questioningly. He clenched his teeth and shrugged, resting the shield against his chest as he mimed firing an arrow with a bow.

"Well, I suppose we don't have much of a choice," Sly said, reluctantly, looking around at the brutal fight surrounding them. "Why do I have to have a goddamn sense of honor? I swear to the guardians . . ."

There was a loud shattering sound, followed by a gunshot and then a moment later another shot and a grunt. Sly frowned and carefully peered around the corner.

Two strange people in dark clothing were making quick work of the large experiments. They moved just as fast as the other two, maybe even faster, easily dodging kicks and punches while landing their own. They were wearing hoodies with the hoods up but from what Sly could see, it was a man and a woman. The woman leapt up and wrapped her legs over the broad shoulders of the man she was fighting, and then slammed her elbow down on his head. He crashed to the ground and she landed in a graceful crouch, looking over to the younger man.

He had disarmed and shot his opponent and was

holding the gun pointed at the still body. Turning to the woman, he moved over to her and fired a round in the head of the man she had just downed. Both turned to the door and raised their legs, kicking it open. The two strangers disappeared inside the bunk room. Sly didn't wait to see what would happen next as she ran into the hall, dashing to the room.

The woman leapt onto the back of a larger man who was strangling Nero with a garrote. Her hood fell back, revealing a head of long black hair, which was tightly tied back, and light brown skin. Drawing a knife from the scabbard at her waist, the woman buried it in the throat of the man. When she yanked it out, a geyser of blood sprayed out of the wound and the man threw Nero away from him. The protector crashed to the ground, rolling across the floor and smashing into the nearest wall. He groaned and held one arm, his face contorted with pain. There was a bright red ring around his neck that Sly could see even from where she stood.

Sly was tackled to the floor by a sturdier woman and she was unsurprised when she looked up into a pair of glowing blue eyes. As she struggled with the woman, she could see the man who had been attacking Nero had now focused his fury on the mysterious woman. She slashed at him with her knife, but the wounds healed as quickly as she inflicted them. The man grabbed her arm, landed a few punches to her face, and then tossed her across the room as though she were a doll. The mysterious woman smashed into the wall and let out a gasp, the knife skittering from her loosened grip. Instantly flipping back to her feet, the woman kicked one of the cots at the man. He shoved it away, tossing it as though it weighed nothing, but the momentary distraction allowed the woman to slide across the floor to where her knife was, partly hidden under another cot. Grabbing the weapon, she readjusted her grip on it and got into a defensive stance, her glowing brown eyes fixed on her opponent.

Sly turned her attention to the experiment on top of her and struggled to throw her off. It felt as though the experiment was built of solid granite and Sly was sure the woman was probably all muscle. The experiment snarled as she lifted Sly up a couple times and slammed her to the ground, attempting to wrap her hands around the smaller woman's neck. Sly decided it was in her best interest to focus on not letting her opponent throttle her. The experiment suddenly twisted slightly and kicked behind her, knocking Alpha to the ground.

"Fuck these fucking experiments," Sly could barely hear Alpha's breathless annoyed declaration over the sounds of fighting. She was struggling to keep the woman's strong hands away from her throat. Her sharp nails managed to rake the side of Sly's neck, causing her to gasp. A sudden shot and Sly found herself splattered with blood and brain matter. The experiment slumped on top of her, hot blood spilling all over the shape shifter, and Sly quickly pushed the body off her, grunting at the effort it took. She sat up, panting, and looked in the direction the shot had come from.

The strange man, who had a very young look to him, was standing with his gun pointed in her direction. Sly glanced down at the body, stunned at the young man's marksmanship: he had shot the other experiment straight through her temple. It was an impressive shot, one that even Sly wasn't sure she would be able to make.

"Shit," Sly grumbled when she spotted Jensen sitting on the floor a short distance away. He was holding his shoulder tightly, blood leaking through his fingers. His face was tight with pain and she could see he had taken a few other hits. As she moved to help him, the mysterious young man suddenly pointed the gun at her and she stopped, studying him. He was wearing plain charcoal-colored clothing, including the loose-fitting hoodie. He had dark slightly wavy hair, cut short. His eyes were large and wide, almost bugging out of his head. They were a greenish brown color and they were glowing. *Of course he's an experiment,* Sly thought with no small amount of irritation.

"Seven series?" Sly asked and the young man just continued to stare at her. Sly glanced over to where the woman was still fighting with the other experiment, who wasn't going down. The man in front of her began to move to the side, keeping the gun trained on her. Sly looked back to the mysterious woman, who had punched the massive experiment in the crotch and then darted around him so that she was behind him again. Leaping up onto his back, the woman searched out the base of his skull and drove her knife straight down. The man shuddered and then toppled forward, bringing the woman down with him. The woman was panting as she got to her feet, her glowing dark brown eyes darting around the room.

Sly heard two sharp clicks, one behind her and one to the side. Before she could even react, the mysterious woman ran forward and placed herself in front of the mysterious young man, arms stretched out to the side to better protect him from the other shape shifters.

"No, please, wait! We're friendlies, we want to help," she cried out, desperation tinging her voice, and Sly looked behind her. Alpha, who must have been helping Nero, had retrieved one of the pistols in the room. She now stood behind Sly, holding the gun trained on the younger experiment. Glancing over to Jensen, Sly noticed he had retrieved another one, which he was pointing at the man. His other hand still held his bleeding shoulder and his intense gaze, filled with pain and anger, was focused on the man threatening his friend. Sly pushed herself to her feet, gesturing for Alpha to lower the gun. She sent a warning glare in Jensen's direction as she carefully approached the two experiments, both of whom watched her.

"Look, we don't really have time for niceties," she began. "And we don't have much time to chat, seeing as how there's a hostile takeover going on overhead. Now, we all seem to share a common enemy. So how about you two help us deal with that and then we can have a nice chit-chat about whatever it is you're doing here. Sound fair?"

The woman glanced over her shoulder to the man, nodding once. He lowered his gun slowly, but still stared at Sly with suspicion.

"Before we head out into the chaos, what should we call you?" Sly asked. The woman swallowed thickly and lowered her arms as she got into a more comfortable stance.

"We . . . never really had names. But I've been calling myself Mia and he's Rami," she answered carefully, following Sly over to the door.

"I'm Sly and the lady behind me is Alpha. Alpha, my dear, would you mind hanging back and protecting the boys? Make sure they don't do anything too stupid and or get themselves killed?" Sly asked. Alpha rolled her eyes but grinned.

"I guess, but you'll owe me," she responded, handing Sly the pistol she held. "I'll grab Jensen's. He's not in any shape to use it, much as he'd like us to think otherwise."

"Jensen!" Nero yelled and ran across the floor, sliding to his friend's side and pulling him down into his arms, despite the wounded protector's protestations. "Don't you die on me, man!"

"I'm not going to die, would you . . . for fuck's sake, Nero, I'm not hurt that badly," Jensen grumbled, yelping at the pressure Nero put on his wounded shoulder. Both Mia and Rami stared at the two, obviously quite confused, while Sly just shook her head.

"I will avenge you, my friend, this I swear!" Nero continued overdramatically, barely able to smother his laughter. Jensen punched him in the arm with his good hand, causing the youngest Deverell to cringe and gasp in pain.

"Don't mind those two. They're idiots," Sly said to the two puzzled experiments as she turned to face them again. "Sounds like the fight isn't going our way. Shall we?"

Rami stepped past Sly and disappeared in the hall, followed closely by Mia. Sly made note of the baggy hoodies they both wore, something she had never seen on experiments. Arching an eyebrow, Sly followed them out into the pandemonium.

~~*~*~*

Isis was thrown again and slid across the slick tiles, winding up near the railing overlooking the main area downstairs. Dust displaced by her fall filled her nose and made her cough harshly. The strange experiment leapt at her and Isis pulled her knees up to her chest, sticking her feet into the woman's stomach, and sending her sailing over her head. She hit the floor hard and a cloud of dust billowed up around her. Isis quickly scrambled to her feet, barely having a chance to prepare herself before the woman lunged at her again. The woman bared her teeth, grabbing Isis' shoulders, and slammed her knee into her stomach. Isis raised her arms up between the woman's, quickly breaking her grasp, and kicked her away. The woman, undeterred, moved forward again, sweeping her leg out in a powerful roundhouse kick. Isis dodged to the side, forcing the woman to spin around to keep the seven series in her line of sight. Isis' eyes widened when she spotted Eris and Shae coming around the corner.

"Hey!" Shae yelled, moving forward to help her teammate.

Without thinking, Isis charged the other experiment, their bodies slamming against the dusty wooden railing. The rotting wood instantly gave way under their weight and the two women plummeted through the air. A desk on the floor below broke their fall, bits of broken railing scattering across its surface around them. Isis heard something snap in her hip, the breath leaving her body in a rush. She bounced off the desk, falling to the ground.

Isis lay still and swallowed, feeling the various internal wounds and broken bones fix themselves. There were delicate specks of dust drifting about in the air, which had been kicked up from the fall. She cringed in pain, trying to get her breathing back under control. Adrenaline was still pulsing through her system in dangerous quantities. This experiment was a capable fighter and Isis knew she was probably going to have to make use of her guardian abilities, something she preferred to do only in dire situations.

"Aren't cats supposed to land on their feet?" she heard Eris' bored voice overhead. A rustling sound on the other side of the desk made her roll to her side, pushing herself to her feet in a crouched position. Out of the corner of her eye, she saw a movement and held out a hand, gesturing for Jade to keep the humans back. As quickly as she was able to, Isis pushed off the floor and jumped up onto the desktop. A sudden shot from above followed by a bullet piercing the desk between her feet caused her to backflip off the desk and she heard Eris let out a soft cry of surprise. Isis drew her gun before her feet even touched the ground and pointed it in the direction the shot had come from.

"Put it down, seven series," a calm dulcet voice came from somewhere overhead. "You're good, as are we."

Isis squinted as she tried to see through the darkness that cloaked the third floor. After a moment, a few pairs of glowing eyes appeared. Within seconds, her mind rushed through every single strategy and possible outcome, almost all of which resulted in casualties on both sides. Isis quietly switched the safety back on her firearm and carefully straightened up to her full height. The mysterious woman sprang up from behind the desk and Isis instantly crouched down in a ready position, prepared for whatever attack the other experiment would try.

"Jo, at ease," the voice overhead commanded and the woman almost instantly relaxed her stance. Isis very cautiously straightened up again, her eyes not moving from the other woman.

"Isis, care to clue us in?" Jade's soft voice hissed from over in the shadows. There was a quiet whooshing sound and a woman with dark tan skin descended from one of the upper levels on a cloud-colored rope, landing lightly on the desktop. She was on the smaller side, but her luminous brown eyes told Isis she was just as formidable as Jo and likely more so. The woman reached behind her with two of her six arms and unhooked the glistening rope, which ascended up into the shadows again. She hopped off the desk and approached Isis, studying her intently for a moment. She then leaned back a little, her gaze traveling over Isis' head, and she crossed all six arms.

"Do you know who we are?" the woman asked, turning her attention to the dark room off to the side.

"I don't know who you are individually, but you are obviously part of the A-series," Isis responded, watching the short woman. She didn't like how close the other experiment was getting to Jade's position, especially when she didn't know their intentions. The woman nodded and turned her glowing gaze up the stairs, looking to where Shae and Eris still stood, dumbfounded.

"Good, then we both have a general idea of the other's abilities," the woman observed, turning her glowing gaze back to Isis. "Based on the sudden flurry of activity in the mountain, including the increased number of hunters, I assume you must be an intruder?"

Isis raised an eyebrow, falling silent for a moment. "And all of you are likely target practice, hence you holing up in here."

The woman nodded and approached Isis again, the very portrait of calm and collected. "The normals have a popular saying: the enemy of my enemy is my friend. Do you believe there's any truth in it?"

Isis looked over her shoulder, noticing that Jo had crept closer and was now studying Isis. The look in her eyes was one of scrutiny, obviously measuring her up. Looking back to the shorter woman in front of her, Isis briefly considered her options.

"We sent out two scouts to investigate how you got to this island. They haven't reported back yet, but I expect them to at any moment. I am quite curious how you managed to get here, especially with normals in tow," the woman continued and Isis swallowed, adjusting her stance slightly. The A-series were known to be crafty and they were incredibly gifted tacticians. The group on the boat could be in real peril and might need backup. Isis looked behind her when Jade cautiously stepped out from the shadows of the neighboring room. The lead woman craned her neck a little, watching Jade briefly before looking back to Isis.

"It is not a hostile action and they have been given specific orders not to harm any non-Grenich persons," the woman assured her, putting four of her arms behind her back. "We desire a way off this island. Hiding is not an effective long-term strategy. Sooner or later, the necromancers will allow new products to breach the perimeter. This island isn't endless and there are only so many places we can find shelter. We don't have the numbers or the power to challenge them. We need to leave if we want to survive."

Isis was silent as she studied the woman's face, searching for any signs of deception. She didn't know her angle and there had to be one.

Suddenly, the young girl in the hijab ran out from the side room and leapt into the shorter woman's arms, causing Isis to stiffen slightly. Next to her, Jade started forward, but Isis held out a hand, signaling for her to stay back. The woman lifted the young girl off the ground, allowing her to perch comfortably on two of her arms. Behind the woman, Jo smiled very faintly as she looked at the girl.

"Hello, Noor," she whispered to the girl, resting her forehead against the human's. "How are you this evening?"

The girl smiled and made some signs with her hand before wrapping her arms around the woman's neck in an embrace. The woman looked back at Isis, who looked over at Jade. Jade met her gaze, obviously confused. Isis shrugged and shook her head before turning her attention back to the woman.

"Do you have a name?"

"Reva," the woman answered, setting the girl down. The girl instantly ran to the other experiment, Jo, and wrapped her small arms around her legs. Jo glared playfully at the girl, who perfectly mirrored her expression.

"How many in your group?" Isis asked, glancing up to the floor where the glowing eyes had been.

"Originally there were over a hundred of us on this island. Recently it was down to forty-five and now there are only nineteen left, seventeen here and the two scouts we sent out," Reva answered, one pair of her arms crossing over her chest. "All A-series."

Isis looked to the stairway when Shae started to descend the steps, followed by Eris, who looked intrigued by the two women. Isis watched as the guardian pursed her lips together and sauntered over to the desk, resting her weight against it. Jo looked over at her, narrowing her eyes, which seemed to amuse Eris.

"I assume you're the ones who laid the spider web," Isis mentioned, looking back to Reva. "A rudimentary method of surveillance, but effective. It's quite impressive in size, from what little I saw."

"We have to work with what little we have. Noor here has been a great help to us," Reva mentioned, nodding over her shoulder to the girl. "She's not as affected by Grenich influences due to her youth and children can move around unseen."

"They're also not very high value targets," Isis added, impressed with the ingenuity of the A-series. She could already predict her teammates' disapproval though. Normals tended to be very protective of youth in her experience.

"Isn't that dangerous?" Jade asked. "For her?"

Reva glanced at her and then back to Isis, ignoring the protector. "There are stories about 7-series who work with normals and we had heard one of the laboratories was destroyed a few years ago by experiments. Are you one of the escapees?"

Isis met Reva's gaze. "I need to have a word with my team. Bring your group down here and then we can talk about getting off this island."

Isis moved back toward Jade — never taking her attention off Reva — and gestured for her and Shae to follow her into the other room. Eris meandered after them, staying in the opening of the large room, resting her back against the wall. Isis looked over to where the humans were sitting on the ground, concealed in the shadows. Alex was standing next to them, her gun drawn and pointed at the floor. At the sight of her teammates, she let out a breath and re-holstered the weapon.

"I don't even know if I want to ask," Jade commented, scrubbing her forehead and glancing to Alex. "We're dealing with experiments who have six arms, fully functional from what I saw, and one mopped the floor with Isis. I'm betting the others can too."

"I don't believe my hitting things cleaned any surfaces. If anything, the scuffle displaced a lot of dust. Or are you speaking of her fighting ability, in which I concur that the struggle did not go in my favor."

The three women stared at Isis with different expressions ranging from exasperation to puzzlement. Isis hesitated, unsure what they expected of her. The normals expectations were so fickle and something she could never entirely predict. Behind her, Isis could faintly hear the other A-series landing softly on the desk and some hurriedly descending the stairs.

"The A-series, or the Arachnid Series, are one of the original experimentation lines that I told you about, Jade. They have always been extremely useful, very hardy, and are among the most valuable experiments. However, they cannot be created from the usual Grenich methods. Most of their features, the multiple arms for example, are genetic traits left over from early experimentations, so they're the only experiments who aren't sterilized. The Corporation doesn't mass produce the line — it would be impossible to do so — which is part of why they're so valuable. Another problem the Corporation has always had with the A-series is that it's harder to wipe their memories. They're unlike most other experiments and I'd guess their manner is actually closer to normals than experiments. At least, from the limited experience I have with them."

"Question: can they produce silk?" Eris asked before turning to look at the A-series whistling sharply and drawing their attention. "Hey, any of you odd critters produce silk? Because I could use some new clothes."

"Enough, Eris. Start refreshing your memory about the whereabouts of that box. We're going to get it once we're done here," Jade snapped at her before turning back to Isis. "If they're so valuable, then why are they here?"

Isis shrugged. "This group must be defective somehow. It doesn't mean they're useless. Quite the contrary: we may have just stumbled upon a makeshift army who can get us off this island."

"But how?" Alex asked quietly, leaning forward slightly. "Even if Eris leads us directly to the box, there's still a town full of experiments to worry about. And past that, we have the impossible to navigate forest full of werehyenas between us and the ship."

"Not to mention how are we going to ferry humans and more experiments to the ship?" Shae added, looking between her teammates.

"I need you and Alex to try calling the ship, to give them a status report. Keep an eye on the humans and each other. Remain in sight of each other at all times," Isis ordered and then looked to Jade. "You and I are going to talk to the A-series."

Jade nodded and the group split up again, all focused on completing their assigned tasks. Isis could feel Jade glancing at her as they moved over to where the large group of A-series waited. Most of them were sitting on the steps and their eyes widened as Isis passed by. Reva was leaning against the desk with Jo standing nearby. A younger black woman was kneeling on the floor, communicating something to Noor, who was beaming.

"She was at the diner in town," Isis mentioned, nodding to the little girl. "I didn't see any parent or other adult with her."

"Noor was placed here with her parents originally, but they disappeared a few months ago, likely transferred or liquidated," Reva replied, glancing over at the young girl before looking back to Isis. "She's technically an orphan by the normal's definition. She stays here mostly, with us. Sometimes she wanders into town, normally for food or on a supply run."

Isis looked behind Reva at the other A-series on the steps. "You're aware we're in the Seelie Court. This is the Island of Avalon, a sacred land to the fey, so you're technically trespassers. You could not have known anyone would stumble upon this place, as that is unlikely to the point of being impossible, but you obviously weren't planning on staying in this place, waiting for your death."

Reva looked at Isis, a smile dancing across her lips briefly. "No, we had no intention of lingering like sitting ducks, to borrow a phrase from the normals."

Isis nodded, looking around at all the A-series. "A group this size isn't easy to move, even if they're all experiments, especially not through a barrier like the forest. You must have some means of transportation."

Reva bit her bottom lip, looking between Jade and Isis. She looked to the young black woman, who was playing with Noor. The woman met her eyes and Reva nodded for her to come over to the small group.

"Gem will show you our exit strategy," Reva said. "Perhaps you can help us with the complications we can't seem to remedy."

Isis raised an eyebrow at that and looked over at Jade, who appeared rather concerned at that last bit of information. Even though Jade didn't have as much experience with experiments as Orion, she had enough to know that they rarely showed uncertainty. Isis held up a hand to indicate she needed a moment before turning and going to the open area where Eris, Alex, and Shae were with the humans. The humans were all lounging on dusty couches and chairs, unconcerned with whatever was going on around them. Eris was standing against the wall, fiddling with the Leaves of Ivy, clearly bored. Alex was in a corner, testing her earpiece, and Shae was standing near the window, her attention on the night, what little could be seen through the drawn curtains.

"We're going to look at a possible method of transportation," Isis stated, drawing the attention of the protectors and the guardian. "We should be back within a few minutes. If you are able to contact the ship, tell them there might be a couple A-series on board and they're not hostile. Don't respond with aggression."

"Yeah, I'm having trouble getting through," Alex remarked.

"I might be able to help with that," a quiet voice spoke up from behind Isis. She turned and noticed a tall, dark-skinned man standing a few feet away from her. He held four of his arms behind his back and two at his side, a normal stance for an A-series. They spent so much time concealing their extra limbs that it frequently became a habit.

"The E-series you brought with you patched into the

network I created, which was really quite impressive," the man explained. "They were able to boost the signal of your communication devices. We didn't know if you were friendly or not, so I have been interrupting it. I'll go up now and readjust it, free up the signal, and you'll be able to contact your ship."

Isis nodded and the man quickly left, disappearing somewhere in the darkness. She looked back to the room once more and then turned to where Gem was standing near Jade. Isis noticed she was wearing a lot of shades of brownish red, including a jacket that concealed her four extra arms. All the A-series were wearing clothing that they had obviously adjusted to suit their needs.

Isis approached Gem and followed the A-series to the back of the building. She glanced over her shoulder, making sure Jade was behind her. The older protector moved to follow but paused at the stairway, where most of the remaining A-series were standing or sitting, most looking unsure. Isis stopped and watched her teammate as she studied the group and then the two women standing off to the side. It was one of the first times Isis had ever seen Jade look genuinely upset.

"We're going to do whatever we can to get you out of here," she promised the group of A-series. They looked at her and Isis could read the puzzlement in some of their expressions. She imagined it was an expression she frequently wore, but for the first time, Isis thought she understood Jade's feelings and her statement. The older protector had seen people do terrible things in her long life. As a protector, Jade had an innate need to try to fix things and seek justice, even when it was a futile pursuit.

The protector quickly moved over to where Isis and Gem were waiting, exchanging a look with the 7-series.

"I'm sorry, we can —"

"Don't apologize when it is unnecessary," Isis interrupted her, turning to follow Gem. "It's probably one of the first times a normal has spoken to them as if they were equals."

Jade was obviously surprised by Isis' response, but continued to follow Gem down a long dusty hallway toward the back of the building. They had kept the hallways bare, like the rest of the hospital, and Isis doubted they even used any electricity. Such prudence was likely a large part of how they went undetected and unbothered for so long.

Gem suddenly turned sharply to the left and led them to a door. The experiment paused and pulled a chain from around her neck, which held a few keys and a flashdrive. After unlocking the door and pushing it open, she led the two women into a space that served as a garage. It was mostly empty except for one massive vehicle that was covered in a large tarp.

"I present our potential exit strategy," Gem said as she pulled the large tarp off of the vehicle, revealing a dark green bus. *Haverford Psychiatric Hospital* was written in neat white block letters on the side. Isis and Jade looked at each other before approaching the bus.

"Does it run?" Jade asked, looking over at Gem. The young woman nodded and ran a hand over the bus, affectionately.

"I rebuilt the engine myself," Gem explained, putting her hands on her hips. "We could probably squeeze everyone on board, but the problem is how to get past the net. Once we go into that forest, our sense of direction is going to be skewed. Aside from that, we also have the huge pack of werehyenas to contend with. Their claws and teeth will tear right through this."

Right when Gem finished speaking, an idea dawned in Isis' mind. She looked over at Jade and knew that she had thought of the same thing. Jade looked reluctant, shaking her head, and Isis shrugged, knowing it was their only option. The protector closed her eyes and let out her breath quietly, rubbing her eyes.

"Actually, we might be able to help with that," Jade

mentioned, turning to face Gem.

~~*~*~*

Eris studied one of the humans, a woman with a disgustingly soft pastel pink sweater tied about her shoulders. She had blonde hair, held back with a light pink headband, which complimented the rest of her nauseatingly light colored clothing. Out of all the humans, she was the only one who stood out but Eris couldn't figure out exactly why. It was bothering her: the woman was . . . off in some intangible way. Eris had been watching her the entire time and she acted just like all the other humans: disinterested, almost stoned. Like the other humans, she never looked directly at anything, but she appeared much more interested in their surroundings than the others.

Eris approached Shae by the window and cleared her throat, waiting until Shae looked over at her. "If you have handcuffs or anything that can used as such, might I suggest putting them on the lady in pale colors?"

Shae glanced over Eris' shoulder, where the guardian indicated. "The soccer mom? Eris, are you serious?"

"Listen, protector, something is *not* right about that woman. I don't think my spell took," Eris insisted. Shae rubbed her eyes, obviously not convinced.

"What makes you say that? Can you tell me exactly why she's so unusual? Because from what I've seen, she's acting just like all the other humans."

Eris bit the inside of her cheek. "Look, she's just really creepy."

"Most suburbanites are," Shae replied. "We just don't go slapping cuffs on them. Hang out by Alex or me if you're so scared. We'll protect you from the dangerous Capri-wearing monster."

Eris rolled her eyes as she moved away from Shae and looked over to where the other protector was still talking with the ship. From what little Eris had overheard, it sounded as though the ship had been attacked. The experiments were quite useful and it seemed like the necromancers knew what they were doing. Eris couldn't help but admire their dedication and thinking process. It was a tad sloppy, but they had built quite an impressive army.

"Yeah, Jade and Isis are looking at an exit strategy right now. Eris has yet to show us to the box though. No idea how long that's going to take."

"Maybe she'd be more inclined to help if you quit talking about her as if she weren't in the room," Eris called over her shoulder tauntingly. She heard Alex pause and smiled as she imagined what sort of amusing expression the protector was making behind her back.

"Eris, with your attitude, how have there not been attempts on your life?" Shae asked without any malice. Out of all the protectors, she was definitely the least cold to the guardian. Eris could tell she was one of those annoying sorts who just liked everyone for no damn reason. She and the youngest Deverell had that in common. It was repulsive.

"Many have tried, but I'm just too talented," Eris replied as she rested a hand on the back of her neck, closing her eyes and putting her head back. She wondered how long the other two would be. She was bored and wanted to play or do something entertaining. How long she planned on having them chase their tails was something Eris hadn't decided yet. Letting the healers rot was an appealing notion; it meant the guardians wouldn't be at their sharpest, which meant she might be able to run. Being in a cage was dreadfully dull and it had been quite some time since she had wandered Earth . . .

Still, she had yet to figure out a way off the blasted island. Appearing wasn't an option with the powerful electrical fields the necromancers had set up, which had been reinforced with a strange magic that Eris had never encountered before. Besides, guardians of magic would be able to trace her if she Appeared too much. She had made that mistake the first time she escaped and didn't intend on making it again. Eris growled to herself, realizing she would probably have to give up the box. *Well, at least I can have a bit of fun first,* she thought with a subtle smirk.

Opening her eyes, Eris looked again to where the humans were milling about. Eris had already decided she wouldn't miss a single one of them — primitive creatures. Her eyes wandered over to the couch and settled on the strange woman in the pale colors again. Moving a few steps closer to get a better look at the odd human, Eris' eyes widened when she finally realized what was different about the woman: she could clearly see her face, no trace of the magic affecting the other humans. There was a halo of nothingness around her, similar to the one around Isis!

Taking a few large steps back, Eris turned her head to yell for one of the protectors. An unexpectedly strong hand suddenly clamped down over her mouth, spun her around, and before Eris could react, she felt a sharp blade dragged over her throat from one ear to the other. Blood sprayed all over her face and the surrounding wall. Eris attempted to gasp in surprise and pain, but found she couldn't. It felt like she was drowning as she opened her mouth and gurgled, trying desperately to breathe. Her knees gave way and she felt herself plummeting to the ground, her vision swiftly going black.

The last thing Eris was aware of was a distant scream, a thumping sound, and glass shattering, followed by someone running.

CHAPTER TEN

Isis stood by the doorway, watching Jade converse with Gem about traveling specifics and possible strategies. She was leaning against the wall, one foot resting on the plaster. A sudden scream inside the building made Isis go rigid, whipping her head around to turn her attention to the open door. *Will the damn normals ever follow simple instructions? I specifically told them to keep an eye on the group and each other,* she thought as she dashed up the two steps and into the building. Tearing through the hallways, she entered the large room just in time to see a woman in light clothing jump through a gap in the barricade and through the window, the shattering sound echoing in the night. Out of the corner of her eye, Isis saw Alex on the ground, tightly holding Eris' throat, which was gushing dark crimson blood. Shae was on the ground near the barricade, holding her head, blood leaking through her fingers.

Running forward, Isis cleanly sailed through the broken window and landed on the dark ground outside, rolling forward and springing to her feet. She quickly drew her gun and pointed it at the woman's retreating form, firing once. The woman dodged, glancing over her shoulder as she continued running away. Isis glanced to the side when three A-series ran out from the main entranceway. The seven-series gestured in the direction the woman had run, shaking her flat hand twice to indicate they should go after her.

As the A-series gave chase, Isis ran back inside the building, moving swiftly through the space as she hurried to the room where the protectors were with the other normals. She fell to her knees and slid across the floor to Alex's side. Jade was kneeling on the other side of the fallen guardian, cursing under her breath as she tried to help stem the flow of blood.

"She's bleeding out," Alex said as she kept pressure on the gushing wound. "Fuck, I can't stop the bleeding!"

"Jade, make sure Shae is okay. I can handle this," Isis muttered, quickly unsheathing her sai. Jade looked at her briefly but hurried across the room to where Shae was still gripping her head, softly moaning in pain.

"Isis, her pulse is getting weaker," Alex said worriedly. Isis ignored her as she plunged the longest prong of the sai straight through her palm, piercing through flesh and muscle. When she pulled it out, she immediately laid her bleeding hand flat on the gaping wound in Eris' throat. Closing her eyes, she imagined the damage and focused on repairing it. She could feel soft lavender light on her face, warming it slightly even as the rest of her body started to feel cold. Suddenly, it felt like some giant unseen hand reached up through the earth and tightly gripped her middle, squeezing as it pulled her deep into some chasm of nothingness. Isis gritted her teeth against the sensation and kept her focus on the guardian. The pressure became constrictive, wrapping all around her and cutting off her breath. Her hearing became dull and all sound seemed to stop, as if she had been transported into the vacuum of space.

Dizziness and lightheadedness washed over her, making Isis feel as though she would pass out. She kept her hand resting on the guardian's throat and felt the pulsing blood lessen, gradually stopping. Somehow, she could feel the internal damage lessening, repairing, and then Isis felt the skin start to knit together beneath her still bleeding palm. Eris' erratic heartbeat gradually started getting stronger. Isis swallowed as her body started to tremble all over, wondering if she would be able to hold onto consciousness much longer.

Eris suddenly arched her back and inhaled deeply, coughing and gagging. One hand flew up to her throat, shoving Isis' palm away.

"What the bloody hell do you think you're doing, you damn fool?" Eris coughed, feeling her throat anxiously. "That was fucking stupid! Where is that damn monster? I'm going to rip her apart and throw the bloody chunks of her to the feral beasts out in those forests!"

Isis slumped down and backed up, resting her back against the nearest wall, trying to quell the nauseous feeling. She could hear Alex's concerned voice asking after her, putting a supportive hand on her shoulder, and Isis swallowed thickly, waving her off. Even the small movement took a monumental amount of effort and caused her arm to ache. Closing her eyes, Isis leaned her head against the wall behind her, which was currently the only thing keeping her upright.

"If I have a scar, I'll have all of your damn heads on a silver platter. Where the bloody hell is a mirror?" Eris demanded as she got to her feet and stormed off down the hall like a petulant teenager. Through the faint ringing in her ears, Isis could hear Jade snap at Eris, who continued demanding a mirror. The faint scent of strawberries told her Shae was approaching.

"Jesus, Isis, what happened? You're white as milk." The concern in Shae's voice was clear. Isis swallowed again and grimaced, keeping her eyes closed. She felt completely drained and briefly wondered how long it would take her to recover her strength. Even after healing Jensen, Isis hadn't felt so . . . depleted.

"We have a problem."

Isis cracked an eye open at Reva's voice. The stern-looking A-series stood nearby, holding a small walkie-talkie in one hand. Isis raised her eyebrows, not trusting her voice at the moment. Reva clipped the walkie-talkie onto her belt.

"They think she was a 9-series," Reva reported, putting her two main arms on her hips and tucking the others behind her back. "And she disappeared in the tall grass, possibly through a hidden door into the mountains. We suspect there are a few around the town and at least one in the field. They're still searching, but it is unlikely they'll find anything. The newer series can move like phantoms in this place. They're almost impossible to track."

Isis nodded and did a mental check of her body, debating whether or not she wanted to attempt standing up at the moment. Curling one leg up at the knee, she quickly decided she needed to rest another few minutes after her leg started shaking violently.

"I'm covered in blood! My shirt is ruined! This is *completely* unacceptable!" Eris continued grousing loudly. Isis swallowed, preparing to speak.

"We will need to move as soon as possible," Isis mumbled, placing a hand over her eyes. "She will report back to —"

"Isis, Nick Chance and Tracy are here," Alex whispered to her and Isis opened her eyes, which widened significantly. She looked over at her teammate, dread creeping into the edges of her aching head. Alex looked just as concerned as she shifted her weight.

"Radar was able to hack into some security feeds. Apparently Set's sons are also here," she reported quietly. "She said to tell you that this place is being used for demonstrations, which I thought we knew."

Isis shook her head and immediately regretted it. "No, I assumed this was a training field or simulation. If it's used for demonstrations it means live rounds and if Set's sons are here, I would venture to guess they're entertaining important investors. All the more reason we need to leave right now. There's no way we can handle that amount of firepower."

Using the wall behind her, Isis struggled to her feet. Even after she had gotten up, she still needed to lean against the wall to stay upright. It felt oddly warm, like the rest of the room. Glancing around, Isis noticed that there was a change in the room's temperature.

"Where is Eris?" Isis asked, coughing quietly. "We need her assistance with the exit strategy."

"Hey Eris, have you finished your temper tantrum yet?" Jade called out sweetly from where she was standing in the doorway leading to the hall, her eyes on where Isis assumed the guardian was.

"Fuck off, Jade," Eris' irritated shout filtered clearly through Isis' ears, which had thankfully stopped ringing. After a moment, the guardian re-entered the room, scrubbing at her hands and face with a hand towel, both of which were now clean of blood. Walking across the room, she moved over to where she had tossed her small bag. Opening the top flap, Eris grumbled as she yanked out a new shirt and tossed it onto the head of a human sitting nearby. Fiddling with the buttons of the shirt she was wearing, which still glistened with wet blood, Eris yanked it off over her head and threw it to the side, unbothered by the presence of others in the room. Grabbing her clean shirt, she pulled it on, pulling her hair out from the collar and straightening the shirt, smoothing it. She then turned her attention to Isis, studying her for a moment before scoffing and shaking her head.

"You are such a daft idiot, definitely take after the shape shifter side of your lineage," she grumbled, turning to Jade. "You might want to get that one some water or something with electrolytes. She did something completely fucking stupid. It would probably be wise for her to regain some strength and energy before we attempt any further idiocy."

"What's wrong with her?" Alex asked, reaching out and steadying Isis when she began to tilt slightly. Isis grabbed her arm, holding on much tighter than she intended. Eris raised an eyebrow as she retrieved the towel she had been scrubbing her hands with, looking back to Isis.

"Something that I've only read about," she answered, turning her attention back to her hands, scrubbing at them even more as she made a face of disgust.

Eris threw the towel over at one of the humans, shaking her hands and reaching toward Isis. The woman instinctively leaned back, swatting Eris' hands away even as she almost fell over. The guardian gave her a look of utter irritation.

"Really?" Eris said coldly. "Relax, I want to see how much damage you did to yourself. Since you had some idea of what to do, I imagine you've done this before."

Isis swallowed and lowered her arm, allowing Eris to rest her fingertips against her temples. Eris closed her eyes and pleasant warmth emanated from the soft pads of her fingers as she whispered quiet words under her breath. After a moment, Eris opened her eyes, lowered her hands, and stepped away from Isis, shaking her head.

"Brilliant work there, sweetheart," she scolded. "Do you have *any* idea how long it's going to take for you to recover? You're basically useless to us now."

"Eris, quit being melodramatic," Jade warned, glancing over to where the A-series were on the other side of the wall.

Eris rolled her eyes over to the protector. "I can assure you, I'm not being dramatic in the slightest. Hell, I'm surprised she can actually still breathe by herself."

Isis raised an eyebrow and let go of Alex's arm, standing defiantly. "We don't have time for this. Eris, you can alter the magic of others, correct?"

Eris massaged her brow, squeezing her eyes shut. "Darling, I know your brain is jelly at the moment, but you're going to have to be a tad more specific. There are many —"

"Necromancer magic woven into technology," Isis clarified, closing her eyes and controlling her breathing in an attempt to stop the room from spinning. Opening her eyes and looking to Eris again, she noticed the curiosity sparkling in her light blue eyes.

"We're going to be taking a bus through the forest, so we'll need concealment as well as a way to get through or protect ourselves from the effects of that net," Isis continued, leaning against the wall again. Speaking allowed her to focus on something other than how worn out she felt. It was one of the first times she had so greatly underestimated the cost of an action.

"Huh," Eris said, poking the inside of her cheek with her tongue, half-smiling. "You'll definitely need a deflection charm. If the oddballs have some kind of pouches, smallish in size and heat proof, I'll need about six to ten, depending on the size of the bus. Shielding will be a piece of cake, been doing that practically since I took my first steps, but deflecting? That's much more complicated and it's going to require some creativity."

"You're going to start working on that, once you show Alex and me to the Box of Original Elements," Isis stated, taking a cautious step forward. Her gait was noticeably less graceful than it usually was, but she felt steadier. Steady enough to attempt walking, at least, and that was all Isis was concerned with at the moment. Isis glanced over to where Reva was standing in the entryway, watching them closely.

Turning her attention back to Eris, who was looking at her with her usual smirk, Isis swallowed and straightened her back. "You owe me your life and now I'm calling on the trickster's code."

Eris' mouth dropped open and she looked genuinely shocked at the statement. Alex and Shae exchanged a look of confusion, obviously having no idea what Isis was referencing. Jade looked intrigued as she crossed her arms over her chest, a small half-smile playing across her lips.

"I beg your pardon?" Eris asked, squinting at Isis.

"I could have let you die. I didn't. You owe me a life debt and I'm collecting on that," Isis explained confidently. "All I ask is that you bring us to where you hid the Box of Original Elements. Do that and we will be even."

Eris was quiet for a moment, a half-smile dancing across her lips. "Trickster's code. You act as though it is an official decree."

"If it were, you would not be concerned with it nor would you follow it," Isis pointed out. "It's a matter of honor, something most normals value."

Eris looked a little impressed as she nodded once. "Very well. I will do as you ask, even though I don't owe you as much as you assume. A life debt would require us to be equals."

Outside, Isis heard thunder in the distance and dropped her head. She had felt the drop in barometric pressure and predicted that a storm was approaching. It was the last thing they needed at the moment, but it seemed as though it was one more thing they would have to deal with. Isis knew it wasn't solely bad luck. The necromancers were going to make the situation as difficult as possible and she wasn't entirely certain she would be able to counter everything they threw at her, especially after expending practically all her energy.

"I would recommend we start enacting a plan and soon," Reva spoke up from the entryway. "It's only a matter of time before this space is discovered and we don't have the resources or numbers to endure a siege."

~~*~*~*

Sly sat in a chair in the sleeping quarters, slowly sipping her oddly sweet coffee as she watched the two experiments across from her on the floor. Around the space, the dim lights flickered, barely keeping the night shadows at bay. Both Mia and Rami had their hands bound behind their backs with zip ties, a safety precaution, and sat cross-legged on the floor. Sly knew zip ties were a laughable safety measure, one any experiment could get out of in a split second, but Sly didn't really want to get into a whole drawn-out lesson about experiments especially since the Seelie Court was likely already more than a little angry with them. Mia and Rami were being cooperative, so Sly decided to humor their hosts.

Behind her, Steve was helping Maeve stitch up the deep wound in Jensen's shoulder. There would be no permanent damage, but it was definitely going to leave a scar. The protector was gritting his teeth in pain as the needle pulled his flesh back together. Alpha was sitting next to Sly, gazing suspiciously at the two experiments across from them. Nero was sitting on a cot nearby, studying the two new experiments with fascination. Keane was dozing in his hammock in a shadowy corner, completely worn out from the tough battle. After he and Maeve had stitched up the few wounds they had received during the fight, Keane had flopped into his hammock and had been there ever since. The elves didn't sleep on cots and so had set up hammocks, something they obviously had experience doing.

Radar was sitting at the desk, fiddling with Jensen's phone. Every now and again, they would hear a quiet click as she adjusted her magnifying eyeglasses. Jack was standing in front of the closed door, silently observing all the occupants. It had taken most of the afternoon to fight off the experiments, who Mia said were 8-series, and the entire crew was exhausted. Maeve had spoken with the captain, who wasn't happy to have lost close to a fourth of her crew in the fight. Since sunset, they had been standing on the deck holding a private memorial for the fallen. The passengers had been instructed to stay off the deck until they were retrieved by a selkie. Sly wasn't thrilled with that, but wasn't in a position to argue it.

Setting her coffee cup on the ground, Sly retrieved a switchblade from her pocket and opened it. Approaching the experiments, she walked behind them and cut the zip ties off, ignoring the few protests around her. Retracting the blade, Sly walked around to face them. Mia encircled her wrist with the fingers of her opposite hand, looking over at Sly and watching her curiously. Rami also watched the strange woman, though he looked much more suspicious than his partner. His gaze traveled all around the dark room, pausing on each occupant. When his gaze fell on Jack, his eyes widened slightly and he stared at the experiment for a moment before turning his gaze back to Sly.

"So our group on the island who found your hideout, told us the A-series has a few extra limbs," Sly mentioned as she picked up her mug, sipping her coffee and looking pointedly at their unexpected guests. Mia and Rami exchanged a look that the shape shifter couldn't read. Outside it was a quiet evening; just the sounds of the waves and the soft mournful songs of the selkies. Even though it was a language Sly didn't understand, the sadness was palpable. Each note seemed to claw at the heart and even Alpha shifted uncomfortably every now and again.

Mia looked back to Sly and swallowed, unzipping her hoodie, which was still stained with various colors of blood from the battle. She paused, her eyes briefly turning back to Sly before she fully removed the hoodie to reveal a tighter shirt underneath. There were two long slits down the side of the shirt and Sly felt her eyes widen significantly when four extra arms hesitantly slid out from the slits, two on each side. Rami crossed his arms, making no move to take off his hoodie, but his eyes occasionally traveled over to Jack.

"Oh my god, that is fucking awesome!" Nero exclaimed as he sat straight up on the cot, his wide eyes lighting up with awe. Both Mia and Rami looked over at his sudden declaration. Nero went over to Jensen and started swatting his arm to make him look, ignoring Jensen's shout of pain. Sly heard Keane turn over in his sleep and she looked over to Radar, who was still focused on the phone. Looking behind her, she noticed Steve staring at the two experiments, open-mouthed.

"Dude, dude, can you shake my hands?" Nero asked as he moved closer to Mia, mindful of her personal space. She stared at him, unsure what to make of the giddy protector, and her eyes slid over to Sly, who was reclining back in her chair.

"Oh right, you don't like touch. Sorry," Nero apologized as he looked around the room, snapping his fingers when he thought of something. He ran back to his bed and grabbed a deck of cards. Alpha was staring at him in disbelief and a little embarrassment while Sly just rubbed her forehead and did her best to ignore his eagerness.

"I assume all your arms are functional," Sly mentioned, looking up again and studying each limb. Mia nodded and brushed a strand of hair behind her ear.

"Yes," Mia responded simply as Nero returned, almost tripping over his own feet in his enthusiasm. He held out the deck of cards, waggling it slightly.

"Okay, can you catch this and then toss it between your hands?" he asked, still beaming from ear to ear, practically bouncing on his heels.

"Nero, are you high?" Alpha asked in exasperation. Mia glanced over to Rami, who was looking over at Jack again. She turned to Nero and held out her left hand, nodding. Gently, Nero tossed the deck underhand and Mia caught it, half smiling as she tossed it from hand to hand, first going up and then going down. Nero began swatting at both Sly and Alpha in excitement, much to their annoyance. Mia finally tossed the deck back to him and he caught it, laughing in amazement.

"Ma'am, may I just say that you are so freaking cool? Did everyone see that?" Nero asked, looking around at all the other shape shifters.

"What about you?" Sly asked, ignoring Nero and nodding to Rami. "Do you speak?"

"I speak when it's required," Rami replied in a soft even voice. He was much more aloof than Mia and obviously not thrilled with the situation. His glowing brown eyes fixed on Sly and she smiled as she stared right back, unbothered by him.

"Ooh, you've got pluck," she teased, pausing to sip her coffee again. "Not something a lot of experiments demonstrate — at least not so openly, not in my experience. Since we aren't in any particular rush at the moment, now is as good a time as any to ask: what the hell do you want exactly?"

Mia looked over at Rami, who narrowed his eyes at Sly. She merely smiled back pleasantly at him. Strangely enough, Sly found that she invoked the suspicion of many experiments. *Must be doing something right,* she thought as she took another sip of coffee.

"For over a year, we've been looking to get off the island. It is no longer safe, not after Blitz's rebellion, and we are running out of hiding places," Mia began after a moment. "There was an unusual amount of eight series activity over the past few days and a new pack of werehyenas was released into the forest. This suggested the Corporation was preparing for something big, likely a demonstration. We were sent to the shore to investigate and at first, we saw nothing out of the ordinary, aside from your ship arriving. Then yesterday, we spotted an abnormal number of birds. We tracked them to the shoreline and saw them circling your ship. Last night, a few shifted and took to the water, essentially boxing you in.

"There wasn't time to go back to the base for back-up, so we shifted into birds and joined in the fight," Mia paused and looked over at Jack, then to Sly again. "There are rumors circling, stories among the newer series. We've heard rumors of a group of experiments that have allied with normals to fight against the Grenich Corporation. There have been whispers about a woman they call the Bane of Grenich. We thought they were just rumors, but we haven't seen any seven-series in quite some time. Grenich isn't known for stopping production on profitable lines, not without good reason."

Mia paused, looking over at Rami and then shaking her head to get a strand of hair out of her face. She turned her gaze to Jack.

"You don't fight like any seven-series I've ever seen," she mentioned. "It's what made me, what made us, start to wonder . . . Are the stories true? Is Blitz real?"

Sly hid her smile behind her mug and glanced to Alpha, who appeared to be intrigued by the question. She looked over her shoulder when she heard a soft scuffing sound. Jensen had wandered over, one hand holding his heavily bandaged shoulder. Turning her attention back to the two A-series, Sly bit the inside of her cheek, debating how much she should tell them. Before she could decide, Jack stepped forward so that he stood at her side.

"Yes, it's true. Blitz is on the island with three others," he said. "My name is Jack, another seven-series and one of her allies. The woman over there is Radar, an E-series. We work with a doctor who was part of one of the original rebellions against the Corporation, as well as a few other experiments."

Sly glared at him and opened her mouth to tell him to quiet down when Mia and Rami suddenly sat straight up. They shifted their position rapidly, quickly getting to one knee with their heads bowed. Sly froze and Alpha raised her hands slightly in surprise, looking between the two experiments.

"Whoa," Nero and Jensen said quietly behind them.

"Um, what are you doing?" Sly asked. The two A-series

were definitely the strangest experiments she had encountered, which was really saying something. If it hadn't been for their glowing eyes and the way they fought, Sly might not even have believed or identified them to be experiments.

"We wish to join your cause," Mia and Rami spoke solemnly in unison. "We pledge our lives and abilities to the service of you and your allies. By our life, by our death, whatever you require, if it is in our power to give, it will be yours."

Sly stared at them, not quite believing her eyes or ears. It had been decades since she had heard or seen a sworn oath, especially since they were so archaic. Not even the guardians used them anymore, relying more on official treaties and the like. Sly turned back to look at Jensen and Nero, who looked as confused as she felt. Nero met her gaze and mouthed, *"An oath of loyalty?"* Sly raised an eyebrow and spread her hands in a way that said, *"Well obviously."*

"Yeah, okay, that's great," Sly began as she turned back to the two experiments. She looked over at Jack, who was staring at the two A-series.

"The normals believe in free will and equal rights," he explained quietly. "You needn't bow and swearing allegiances aren't required. If you ally with us, you are both free shape shifters."

Mia and Rami looked up at Jack, quizzically. Rami slowly got to his feet after a moment, followed by Mia. The woman bit her bottom lip and massaged the side of her throat with her left hand, her eyes turning toward one of the small portholes in the room. The dark sky was dappled in a rainbow of colors from the different stars and the bright half-moons.

"If we are truly free, may I request your aid in helping our group?" she asked him. "They are trapped on the island. There is a Grenich net on the forest, which makes it impossible to navigate. We were able to do so after stealing some equipment from two handlers we managed to ambush. The others will not be so lucky, security will have been heightened."

"Wait, if you can't navigate that forest, that means our team is also trapped on the island," Jensen mentioned, unable to hide the worry in his voice. Sly looked over to Nero, who was standing near Steve, both of them concerned.

"None of you can set foot on sacred ground," Maeve mentioned tiredly from where she was cleaning up the first aid supplies. She appeared almost apologetic as the shape shifters looked over at her. The fading light highlighted the streaks of blue and purple in her dark hair as she stood up again. Around them, the lamps in the sleeping area flickered briefly.

"The fey are very strict about their traditions, which must be respected even if you don't agree with them," she continued. Nero and Jensen exchanged a look, which Sly didn't miss. Rolling her eyes up to the ceiling and shaking her head, she debated using the handcuffs she had brought. The last thing she needed was two men acting impulsively, something younger male protectors were notorious for. What she wouldn't give for her lover to be on board: Jade had always been better at handling male protectors.

"Normals would be useless in this situation," Rami put in, looking over at Radar. "There's synthetic pollen in the air that heightens the effects of the net on normals, causing them to hallucinate. Humans are most affected, but would also affect shape shifters. It was left over from when the island was a holding station for pre-experiments."

Jensen moved over to where Maeve was, followed closely by Nero and Sly. The elf finished putting the supplies away and turned to face them, pulling herself up to her full height, her hair gleaming in the dim lighting. A low mournful wail sounded from outside, causing Maeve to look over her shoulder to the porthole.

"Maeve, please," Jensen began respectfully. "Grenich has defiled a land considered sacred to your people for who knows how long and they will continue spilling blood if they go unchallenged. Is that truly preferable to allowing a few more people on that island?"

Maeve looked at him with her bright eyes. "Two wrongs do not make a right, Mr. Aldridge. I will not allow you to escalate a war on that island. It is not even my call: I am merely here to make sure the wishes of my rulers are respected."

Jensen scowled and turned away from the elf, stalking over to where Radar was still working on his phone. Sly smiled politely at Maeve, who looked rather concerned, and followed after Jensen, her smile instantly dropping once she turned away from the elf. She had a feeling the protector was going to do something stupid and she intended to stop him. Nero followed on her heels. Glancing over to the side, Sly noticed Jack talking to Rami and Mia. The two A-series appeared to be much more comfortable with him, which didn't surprise Sly at all.

"If we wait for a while, we can take one of the rowing boats," Jensen muttered under his breath, glancing over at Radar. Alpha, who was leaning her weight on the other side of the desk with her arms crossed over her chest, scoffed and shook her head.

"Protector men, you're all so goddamn rash and entitled," Alpha grumbled, not even bothering to look at Jensen. "I don't think Jet sent us here to cause an interdimensional incident."

"We can be back before the elves even know we're gone," Jensen replied curtly and Alpha narrowed her eyes at him, straightening up so that she stood at her full height. Sly put a hand on her hip and rubbed her eyes with her free hand. *Here it comes,* she thought.

"Aldridge, I swear to the guardians, if you disrespect the laws of your allies, I will rescind the treaty I have with

Jet and you protectors can fight Grenich all by your goddamn selves," Alpha warned, her dark eyes flashing.

"Okay, that's enough. Both of you," Sly quickly interjected, raising a hand to prevent the argument from escalating. "Just stop. I'm stuck on a ship and I just barely survived an attack by living weapons. I'm tired, I'm sore, I'm hungry, and the last thing I want to deal with at the moment is you two bickering like children. At the risk of sounding cliché, we have much bigger things to worry about."

"I don't think any of you were listening when they mentioned the synthetic pollen in the apparently impossible to navigate forest," Radar chimed in, raising her goggles up to rest on her head. She turned her glowing brown eyes to Jensen and handed back his phone.

"You should be able to contact the mansion now. I can talk to Shocker and instruct him how to connect with my tablet. Jet and Lilly will be able to see what we do," Radar explained as she looked around at the shape shifters. "And going to that island would cause more problems than it would solve. You wouldn't have any kind of advantage and believe me, as normals, you would need one to take on a single experiment, let alone a large group of them."

"She has a point, Aldridge," Sly nodded, tilting her chin at Jensen's shoulder. He gave her a sarcastic smile, obviously not appreciating the blow to his ego.

"Well we can't just sit in here and do nothing," Nero mentioned, putting his hands on his hips. "They have no back up and that island is crawling with necromancers and experiments, both of whom are heavily armed."

Sly glanced over at Nero and rubbed her chin, thinking. "We're in communication, right? We can act as their eyes, give them a heads up if it looks like anything's going sideways. Radar, how does the security system look in the mountain?"

Radar picked up her tablet and swiped a few apps on the screen, pulling up an image. "Well, it's fairly straightforward but it's still incredibly strong. It's not a system that can be breeched through guerilla warfare or hacking. If I work at it, I might be able to activate a lockdown. It would keep the investors and necromancers trapped for a window of time, might be worthwhile if the Four are going to try to move a large group."

Sly ran a hand over her hair, patting the back of her head as her mind raced. They couldn't afford any more casualties, not if they wanted to keep the Seelie Court as allies. Sly didn't really care about alliances, but she did want to leave the place in one piece. That was easier to do if they were on friendly terms.

"Mia, how many are in your group?" Sly asked, glancing over to the A-series.

"There were twenty-seven when we left, but if there's an active demonstration, the experiments might have started picking us off," Mia answered, rubbing her palms together.

Looking back to Jensen, Sly was unsurprised to see he had already started dialing the mansion. He nodded to Sly, indicating the phone worked. He turned away and wandered off, keeping the phone close to his ear.

"OK kiddos, we're going to help kick some necromancer ass and hopefully retrieve your friends," Sly said, winking at Mia. The A-series stared at her, perplexed. She had tucked her four extra arms away, as had Rami. The latter had even pulled his hoodie back on, though he hadn't zipped it up. Sticking his two free hands into the pockets in the front of the jacket, he glanced over at Radar and then at Jack.

There was a solid knock on the door to the sleeping quarters, causing both Rami and Mia to immediately get into identical rigid ready stances. Sly shook her head, remembering what a pain experiments could be. Especially the ones who didn't have much experience with normals or the world at large. Maeve quickly crossed the room and answered the door, revealing a selkie.

"The service has concluded. You may move about freely," they reported, tears still glistening in their eyes. When Maeve nodded her understanding, the selkie turned and left. Sly moved over to Jack and he turned when he heard her approach.

"Be straight with me: what are the chances of Grenich launching another attack on this ship?" Sly asked, holding his glowing brown gaze.

"They almost certainly will," Jack replied. "They know we're at a disadvantage and they can attack us on two fronts. I have some value, but killing any of our allies would be a win for them."

Sly glanced over at Rami and Mia, who didn't seem in a hurry to leave the sleeping quarters. *Jade, darling, I really hope you're almost done on that island because we are in need of backup,* Sly thought as she followed the others out of the sleeping quarters. If there was going to be any kind of battle, she didn't intend to fight on an empty stomach.

~~*~*~*

Jet glanced up from his laptop to where Lilly sat at the desk, her eyes watching the screen of the monitor. She was currently listening to Jet's sister Raven's report of yet more unrest among protectors. Also on the line were some other operatives, all in different countries. Most of them had a less than pleasant encounter with experiments while in the field. Jet almost wished he could send Orion and Roan into the field, since they seemed to have more experience with this shit.

"Lilly, I appreciate that you and Jet are in a tough position, really I do," the deep voice of Gabriel — one of the operatives who mostly worked in the Baltic countries — came through clearly. "But you have no idea of the type of slaughter that's left in their wake. They're worse than assassins and even separatists. I lost two good informants just this past week. We need to be allowed to put them down if the situation warrants it."

"You'd have us completely turn against everything the protectors have always stood for?" Lilly asked, subtly raising an eyebrow. Jet heard a scoff from one of the operatives. Raising his eyes, he stared out the towering window at the beautiful day outside. What he wouldn't give to be able to go for a walk.

"We have killed separatists before and assassins," another operative, Nelly, pointed out. She was the daughter of one of the Monroes' allies, a newer agent but surprisingly good for her age, albeit a little reckless.

"Only when the lives of innocents have been in immediate danger," Lilly was quick to point out. "We cannot just resort to the tactics of assassins when it suits us."

Jet heard his phone vibrate on the small table behind him. Reaching behind him, Jet grabbed the phone, recognizing Jensen's number. Looking over to Lilly, he caught her eye, mouthing, *"Do you have this covered?"* Lilly smiled in response and nodded once.

Quickly standing up, Jet left the study and quietly closed the door behind him, answering the phone as he started moving down the hall. He could smell some kind of bread or pastry in the air, indicating Dane was in the kitchen as usual.

"Jensen?"

"Having an E-series comes in handy," Jensen's remarkably clear voice responded and Jet smiled. He could hear the grin in his tone, something he didn't hear nearly enough.

"So it would appear. How are things going?" Jet asked as he moved over to the stairs, glancing up to the second floor. He noticed Coop sitting in between the balusters, reading a book. Jet moved over to the staircase and took a seat, reclining on the stairs. In the kitchen, he heard Dane curse softly, likely reacting to something going wrong with a recipe. Jet knew they would hear all about it at some point.

"Yeah, not great. Grenich has apparently been using the Island of Avalon for demonstrations," Jensen reported, the lightness vanishing from his tone almost instantly. Jet's smile gradually disappeared from his face and he swallowed.

"But that's . . . how is that even possible?" Jet asked, not believing his ears.

"It's," Jensen paused and sighed. "It's a very long story, Jet. One I will be happy to relate in full once we get back, but we've got a bit of a time-sensitive situation at the moment. Shocker wouldn't happen to be hanging around, would he?"

"Actually, he is. Dane was having an issue with a mixer and refuses to deal with normals," Jet said, trying to keep the irritation out of his voice. He leaned back and opened his mouth to call out for Shocker, but stopped when Coop landed lightly on the tiled floor a short distance from the staircase.

"You want Shocker?" the experiment asked and Jet nodded. The L-series turned and moved toward the kitchen. Jet watched him leave, no longer fazed by most of the experiment's quirks and abilities. *Good lord, this is my life now,* he thought, almost chuckling.

"He'll be here shortly. What are you going to have him do?" Jet asked curiously.

"Radar says she can patch the mansion into the security feeds she managed to hack into here so that you and Lilly can see what we do," Jensen explained. Jet raised his eyebrows, impressed with Radar's prowess.

An hour later, Jet and Orion were watching Shocker in the security room as he fiddled with a mess of wires. Every now and again, he would grumble, usually when something sparked. Jet winced every time he saw a spark of electricity, keeping the fire extinguisher in his field of vision. In Shocker's ear was a Bluetooth device, which allowed him to work with both hands. Remington was next to him, an open toolbox nearby. The old trainer would hand the experiment whatever tool he barked out, unbothered by the younger man's sharp tone.

"Damn newer experiments, think they know every fuckin' thing," Shocker groused, wincing when a wire sparked near his face. "Yes, I heard you! I'm doing it! Calm your tits!"

"You swear you don't know about this demonstration place?" Jet asked Orion as Shocker continued working with the wires. Orion had his arms crossed over his chest and he stared straight ahead at the dark security monitors. Upon hearing the question, Orion raised his eyebrows and shook his head once.

"I knew they existed, but I was never able to find any of their locations," he replied, one finger tapping on his upper arm. "As I've explained multiple times, employees weren't privy to information that didn't directly affect them. Roan knows a bit more about the training fields, simulations, and demonstrations, but even he doesn't know their exact locations."

"Or so he tells you," Jet remarked and Orion let out a bitter laugh.

"Believe me, Jet, no one distrusts my brother more than I, but I know how he thinks and how he operates. Keeping that information from me wouldn't serve any purpose," Orion explained, glancing over at Jet. "As much as I don't trust Roan, he and I both share a common goal: the destruction of Grenich and Set."

"The enemy of your enemy," Jet said skeptically and Orion raised a brow, turning his attention back to the blank screens.

"It is nowhere near that simple," he said in his cryptic manner. Jet opened his mouth to inquire further but Shocker got to his feet and turned on the screens. The experiment sat down at a computer in front of the screens, nodding as he followed Radar's instructions, his fingers flying over the keys. Remington pressed the button that made the screens flicker to life, revealing static. The door to the surveillance room opened and Lilly walked in, glancing up at the screens as she approached Jet. He wrapped an arm around her waist and she did the same, smiling up at him.

"And that ought to do it," Shocker said as he pressed one last button and leaned back. Half the screens blinked to life, showing a place Jet had never seen before. He squinted as he studied the strange scenes of the eerily empty town.

"Well that's a bit unsettling," he stated as he moved closer. Shocker suddenly bolted up to his feet, nearly tripping over the chair as he moved back, cursing under his breath. His glowing silver eyes were wide as they fixed on one screen and all the color drained from his face. Remington was studying the different screens.

"Shocker, are you all right?" Lilly asked softly, moving toward the experiment, her eyes briefly traveling to the screen. Shocker glanced at her as he yanked the Bluetooth out of his ear, tossing it to the desk.

"Fuck this," he grumbled as he turned and all but ran out of the room. He nearly collided with Dane, who sauntered into the room, drying his hands with a towel. The dark-haired experiment glanced briefly after Shocker, his glowing eyes traveling to the screens as he moved further inside.

Jet looked over to Orion, opening his mouth to ask him what that was about. The question froze in his throat when he saw how tightly Orion was gripping the chair. His arms shook almost imperceptibly with the intensity of his white-knuckled grasp. Jet looked over at Remington, who looked just as confused as he felt.

"Well that explains Shocker's mad dash," Dane commented, his eyes never moving from the screen as he moved closer, gently tapping one screen with his knuckle. Jet turned his attention to where Dane was indicating and felt his heart stop in his chest.

The screen showed a number of people mingling in a large room, sipping what looked to be champagne. It looked like some kind of high-society ball: the women were wearing exquisite gowns and the men were dressed in suits and tuxedos. Off to the side were two stern-looking men, their eyes studying the crowd. One of them said something, drawing the other's attention. The other smiled, shook his head, and sipped his drink.

Jet's eyes were drawn to the two who stood near the two stern-looking men, obviously acting as bodyguards. The man and woman were dressed just as nicely as the others in the room, only a little less extravagant. He hadn't met either one in person, but Jet had seen them on security footage many times before. The man, blond with aquiline features and dark symbols painted around his eyes, was the one he remembered most vividly. The face was seared in his mind from the little footage they had of the massacre at the Rebel Lair. It was this man he had instructed Isis to put down if the opportunity arose, something he was still hoping she would do. If he didn't do it first, that was.

Looking back to Lilly, Jet noticed the tears welling up in her dark blue eyes but also the fury. She looked at him, her mouth becoming a tight straight line. He moved over to her and wrapped his arms around her, gently kissing her as he looked back to the picture on the screen. Dane glanced at them before turning his attention back to the screen.

"If they've brought Nick Chance along, means they want a pretty spectacular bloodbath," Dane mentioned, his eyes never moving from the screen. "Last time I saw him, he was flaying me from head to toe. Thought Blitz took care of him, though I do sometimes wonder if the Sadist of Grenich can be killed."

Jet looked over to Orion again, noticing how the man looked almost green. The eldest Deverell looked like he was going to be sick and suddenly, Jet felt pity for the man who had once been his greatest ally. A tremor went through him and Orion dropped his head down, closing his eyes. Taking a deep breath, he turned around to face Jet.

"Dane's right. If Chance is there, they probably want him to drum up even more chaos. He has a reputation for going into active demonstrations to make things even bloodier, if the show isn't entertaining enough for the investors."

Dane picked up the Bluetooth Shocker had abandoned and placed it in his own ear. "Radar, do you have any control of the cameras?"

Jet looked over at Orion. "What have we sent the Four into?"

Orion opened his mouth to respond but closed it again, his expression not even slightly reassuring. Jet looked over at Remington, who approached the small group. Crossing his arms over his chest, he glanced between Jet and Lilly. Behind them, Dane continued to quietly converse with Radar.

"I have every faith in the Four to get out of this situation on their own," Remington began thoughtfully. "However, according to Jensen, they're not on their own."

Jet nodded, looking over to Lilly, "We have to contact Titania and Oberon immediately. I have no idea how to go about convincing them to let humans and strange experiments in their lands, much less how to go about asking them to open their gate to Earth."

Lilly's eyes brightened. "Tell them we'll blindfold the rescuees. At the very least it will prevent strangers from seeing any of the Seelie Court."

Jet nodded. "That's wise and it certainly addresses a major concern. I'm not sure if it will be enough to convince them to help us though. The Fey are notoriously unpredictable with their decisions."

"Sorry to barge in," a quiet voice came from over by the door. All the shape shifters in the room turned to see Declan standing in the doorway with his hands behind his back. His light blue eyes were intensely serious and he swallowed, as if he were choosing his words. The young protector didn't even glance in Dane's direction, keeping his attention on his parents.

"Uh, there are a couple members of the High Council here. They request a word with Mother and Father in the library," he explained softly, his eyes drifting over to Remington and Orion.

"Did they say what it's in regards to? Has the situation in the Meadows gotten worse?" Lilly asked, puzzled. Declan shook his head and lifted his shoulders.

"They only said to summon you to the library," he replied as if the words felt odd in his mouth. Jet rolled his eyes and put a hand to his face, briefly massaging his brow. The use of the word 'summon' told him at least one was a guardian man and likely an old-fashioned one. The only time Declan used terms like that was when specifically instructed to. Jet nodded, glancing at Lilly before looking back to Declan.

"We'll be right up," he said before turning his attention back to Dane, who was still watching the screen. "Dane, could I impose upon you to watch the situation and look for anything out of the ordinary? Or just anything that raises any red flags?"

Dane reclined back in the chair, putting his feet up on the desk, and gave a dismissive wave of his hand in response. Jet raised his eyebrows, surprised Dane hadn't protested, and he turned back to the other two protectors in the room.

"Orion, I want you to go to the Meadows. Let Passion and Electra know what's going on. Something tells me we're going to need their help in the near future. Lilly or I will meet you there. We need to have another chat with Roan."

Orion nodded and quickly left the room. Jet next turned to Remington, tilting his head in Dane's direction. Remington nodded once and turned his focus back to the screens. Jet then turned to Lilly, offering his elbow and they left the room together, heading for the library.

CHAPTER ELEVEN

"Who do you think is here?" Jet asked softly as they moved through the brightly lit hallway. Lilly smiled and rested her head against Jet's shoulder, soothing his anxiety with her nearness. Her bare feet were silent as she walked across the cool tiles.

"I would imagine Adonia and Aneurin," she guessed, placing her other hand on his elbow. "They seem the most likely."

Jet nodded, hoping his wife was right. Those two he was the most accustomed to and even though Aneurin could be infuriating, Jet at least knew how he thought.

When they reached the library, Jet couldn't hide his surprise when he saw Artemis and Aneurin in the grand room. Artemis was gazing out one of the tall windows and Aneurin was sitting on the chaise lounge, picking at it with a look of mild disgust. Jet exchanged a look with Lilly before clearing his throat loudly. Aneurin raised his eyes to the two protectors and Artemis turned from the window. Her arms were crossed at her chest, the long sleeves of her dress draping down, almost resembling wings. The dark blue of the dress enhanced her soft features and Jet could see the concern in her clear blue eyes.

"Ah Jet and Lilly. Good to finally see you," Aneurin greeted, getting to his feet, and smiling in an unusual jovial, welcoming tone. Jet fought the urge to raise an eyebrow at the overly congenial manner, instead smiling diplomatically. Aneurin approached and shook Jet's hand before turning to Lilly, gently taking her hand and kissing the back of it. Lilly smiled politely and dipped into a slight curtsy, as was customary. Jet turned his gaze to Artemis, incredibly suspicious of Aneurin's attitude. Whenever the head male guardian went out of his way to be so pleasant, it usually meant he had made a decision that Jet would not be happy with.

"How goes the mission?" Aneurin asked. If Jet didn't know better, he could swear there was a note of anxiety in his tone.

"I would think you would know more than we do," Jet half-lied, sticking his hands in his pockets. "The Meadows is more connected to the Seelie Court than Earth is. I was hoping you might have some news."

Aneurin grit his teeth exaggeratedly, the smile never fading from his eyes. "Unfortunately we do. Hecate has brought some news of a rather . . . disconcerting nature to the attention of the High Council."

Well shit, Jet thought as he focused on Aneurin, keeping his expression neutral. He wasn't sure how the guardian would react to the necromancers' presence in the Seelie Court, but it probably wouldn't be a good response. The male guardian looked over at Artemis, who merely watched them.

"It would appear the necromancers have taken up residence of a sort on the Island of Avalon. I don't know how Set managed this, but he did," Aneurin continued, his tone still light. "As you know, the Seelie Court and her people are considered allies of the guardians. This violation of their consecrated land cannot go unanswered."

Aneurin paused, running a finger over the back of a chair and then rubbing his thumb and finger together. Jet raised his eyebrows, waiting for the guardian to continue. He chanced a glance over at Artemis, who still stood by the window. Her mouth was set in a tight line and her expression betrayed nothing. Looking to Lilly, she watched Aneurin and turned her eyes to Jet, questioningly. Jet shrugged, still unsure how Aneurin planned to respond to the situation.

"Also we cannot leave a guardian in such peril," Aneurin continued. "Though Eris is a prisoner, she is also a guardian, as you are aware."

Jet felt his eyes widen as he turned his attention back to Artemis. He swallowed as he attempted to come up with something to say.

"Aneurin, surely you are not going to recall Eris after only a day," Lilly interjected, stepping forward. "What about all the healers? They will die without Betha's Tears."

"As tragic as the loss shall be, shedding more guardian blood is not a solution," Aneurin continued. "We have a duty, first to our people and next to our allies. More healers can be trained and we shall do all in our power to minimize the impact on Earth until then."

"So in order to avoid shedding guardian blood, you're willing to let that many healers die? Are they not also guardians?" Jet pointed out and Aneurin looked over at him. "Aside from that, if the necromancers really are on that island, then they are in close proximity to the Box of Original Elements. Surely we don't want them to get their hands on it?"

"The necromancers can do nothing with the Original Elements. It would be useless to them, even if they could find it. Knowing Eris, that's probably impossible," Aneurin responded with a dismissive wave of his hand. Jet licked his lips, feeling tension settle in his shoulders. Both his father and Remington had often warned him about the futility of trying to reason with the more old fashioned guardians. Jet never really appreciated those warnings until he had been named leader of the protectors.

"If you recall Eris, the Four will stay out there to finish the mission. They won't come back until that box is found. Protectors don't abandon people in need; it goes against everything we stand for."

"Mmmm, are we counting young Isis as a protector?" Aneurin asked innocently, glancing over at Artemis, who shook her head in warning. Jet turned his attention to Artemis, hoping she would see reason.

"She lives among protectors, works and fights alongside them, and she is loyal to Lilly and me. So yes, I believe she qualifies as a protector. Are you just planning on letting them fend for themselves?" Jet asked Artemis, struggling to keep his tone even. "Passion is *really* not going to appreciate that."

Artemis swallowed, thinking over her response. "The High Council has decided to grant the Four another day to find the box. After that, they are to return to the ship and come home. The water guardians are going to submerge the Island of Avalon for several decades, until we can be certain the Grenich threat has been eliminated."

"You can't do that!" Jet shouted in protest, looking between the two guardians, who were startled by his outburst. He looked over to Lilly, who was staring wide-eyed at Artemis. She met her husband's gaze and nodded hurriedly, indicating that he should explain the situation.

"Look, Aneurin," Jet began, keeping his tone calm and level. "We made contact with the Four, just now. Radar's been able to hack into a security system and we know there are some necromancers on the Island of Avalon. We don't know much, but apparently the island is being used as a kind of testing ground for new experiments. Jensen says that the Four have a group of civilians with them, innocent humans and a few shape shifters. They need some more time, just a couple more days."

Aneurin looked back at Artemis and she met his gaze, holding out a hand with her palm up. She looked almost pleading and Jet knew she was likely on their side. Artemis was a stickler for the rules, but she tended to side with the protectors' judgement. The male guardian turned his attention back to Jet and Lilly, rubbing the back of his neck. It was one of those rare times the man looked genuinely uncomfortable.

"Other shape shifters? Don't you mean a group of experiments? More living weapons?" Aneurin asked. "We also know about the situation in the Seelie Court and I hope you understand why we cannot allow more experiments into Earth. If we had the time to screen them, perhaps it would be a different story, but we don't have the time. The threat of Grenich is too great and we cannot act rashly."

"You can't act rashly? You're talking about submerging an entire island, thereby killing everyone on it. You don't think that's rash? How can you even begin to justify that?" Jet couldn't believe what he was hearing. The guardians were infuriatingly hands-off at times, but what they were considering was slaughter. Jet turned his eyes to Lilly and she looked as horrified as he felt.

"If we're going to fight Grenich, we need to use our methods," Aneurin explained. "The Seelie Court has no protectors. They have no defense against the necromancers, not without our help. The guardians cannot have a constant presence in their lands, so we must be more aggressive in our response to this invasion."

Jet turned and approached Artemis, putting his palms together, not bothering to conceal his desperation. "Artemis, please, I beg of you. Don't let the High Council do this. Please, give the Four a few more days. That's all they need."

"The man who killed your son and daughter is on that island," Aneurin commented and Jet spun around, his eyes narrowing as he pointed at the male guardian. A red haze fell over his vision and for a moment, he felt capable of throttling Aneurin.

"Don't. Don't you dare try that," he warned, iciness

creeping into his voice. The male guardian adjusted his tunic and tapped his thumbs together lightly. Behind him, Lilly stood stone still, fury glistening in her dark blue eyes.

"I apologize, I meant no offense. But surely you want the man to pay for his crimes? Don't Brindy and Devlin deserve justice?" Aneurin asked calmly. Jet let out a short bark of laughter, rubbing his eyes and shaking his head. He almost didn't believe his ears. There were times when he wondered how in the hell his ancestors managed to tolerate the guardians for so many years. As much respect as Jet had for them, as much as he loved some of them, the High Council was exasperating more often than not.

"How little all of you must think of us," Lilly spoke softly from behind him, "To think that our personal grief would be such that we would see the loss of innocent lives as justice."

"The decision has been made," Aneurin said, resorting back to his regular dismissive manner. "Eris shall be recalled later tonight. The Four have twenty-four hours to vacate the island, alone, and then it will be submerged."

He disappeared in a flash of brilliant gold light, not giving Jet a chance to respond. The protector looked over at Lilly, who was resting a hand on top of her head, looking as though she was going to be sick. Jet turned his gaze to where Artemis still stood by the window and moved to stand across from her. She turned to face him, her arms crossed over her chest.

"You know this is wrong, Artemis," Jet whispered, glancing at Lilly.

"It is unfortunate and tragic, but we must protect our allies. We are almost certainly going to need them in the near future," Artemis replied softly, looking over toward the open door of the library. Jet bit the inside of his cheek and rubbed his chin, keeping Lilly's gaze. Her mouth was set in a tight line and she raised her chin up slightly.

"Artemis, I cannot in good conscience tell the Four to leave a group of innocent humans and shape shifters on an island the guardians plan on destroying. I don't believe any of them would willingly leave knowing all that I do," Jet said softly, looking back to the guardian. "It goes against everything the protectors have always fought for. Everything the guardians trained us for."

Artemis swallowed and dropped her gaze to her feet briefly, studying her dark blue shoes. Jet put his hands on his hips and walked a few steps away, shaking his head. His mind raced as he tried to figure out a solution to the situation. He didn't want to violate the fey's sacred ground, but he couldn't stand by and watch the guardians submerge the island while there were still people on it.

"I cannot go against the wishes of the High Council," Artemis began carefully, drawing Jet's attention back to her, her eyebrows knitting together. "I cannot remind you that my daughter has a reputation for finding ways around rules, if not outright breaking them. And it would likely be frowned upon if I were to suggest you meet with Roan, just to see if he would be able to offer any kind of helpful advice. I know it would be completely unethical for one of the apprentices to arrange a meeting with Titania tomorrow morning in Vespera and Hecate's hall."

Artemis looked at Jet, raising one eyebrow very subtly even as her expression remained unreadable. The protector stared at her for a moment, his mouth opening and closing a couple times as he tried to form words. Glancing back at Lilly, he could see a spark of hope in his wife's dark blue eyes.

"Jet," Artemis drew his attention back to her. "I might be able to buy them a couple extra hours, but that's it. You have to work with the little time you have. Tread carefully."

Jet nodded in understanding. "Thank you, Artemis."

Artemis offered him a small smile and nodded toward Lilly before disappearing in a flash of silver light. Once she was gone, Jet crossed the room and passed by Lilly.

"Do you think the Four are up to this?" Lilly asked

softly as they moved out of the library and back down the hall. Jet glanced up to the stairway, noticing Coop perched on the stairs. His bright blue eyes were fixed on the ground below, though he did glance in Lilly and Jet's direction when they stepped into the main hall.

"They're going to have to be," Jet responded darkly.

~~*~*~*

Isis looked off into the night, uneasy about the continued darkness. Even if the Seelie Court were on a different circadian rhythm, the night had to end at some point. It only got darker, which just didn't make any sense. Glancing up at the sky, she noticed how the stars and moon were hidden by the deepening shadows. The darkness had gradually increased and it was almost as dark as it had been in the forest. Isis couldn't sense any bodies of water, no scent or sound. Behind her, she could hear the scraping of shovels in dirt and the subtle scent of damp earth tickled her sensitive nose. The Seelie Court dirt had a strangely sweet scent, almost fruity. She shifted her weight, testing her balance to make sure it was normal. Once they had emerged into the fresh air, Isis found her strength had returned much faster and she lost the sluggish feeling that had been affecting her in the old hospital.

"Dig faster, you fools."

Isis turned around at Eris' disinterested voice, noticing the guardian playing with a small ring of cloudy purple light woven around her fingers. She was up in a tree, stretched out on one of the twisted branches. Below her, Alex and one of the A-series, a man with pale hair, were digging in the dirt. It had been over three hours and this was the fourth hole they had to dig. Eris would conveniently forget and then remember the location of the box. She was still playing games and being a nuisance, as they had expected.

"It's getting darker," Isis mentioned from where she

stood, squinting in the night. She estimated it would be a few more hours before she was at full strength. *Hopefully,* she thought as she started to move in a wide half-circle around the small group, her eyes piercing the thick shadows. As much as she didn't like to admit it, she was vulnerable at the moment. Chances were the necromancers would notice it and use it to their advantage.

There was something tugging at her mind, but Isis was too focused on keeping watch. She could feel something moving about in the darkness, circling them, likely scoping them out. In her ear, Radar would occasionally update her on the goings on in the party in the observation area. The experiments had started sweeping through the town, putting down their assigned targets. It was only a matter of time before they turned their attention to the old hospital. Every now and again, Isis would hear a shot in the distance. The A-series would stiffen each time, indicating he heard it as well. It had been some time since Radar had come in and Isis hoped there hadn't been another attack on the boat . . .

Isis suddenly whipped her head to the right, drawing her gun and firing a single shot. There was a flash of movement and what felt like a wrecking ball slammed into her body, knocking her flat on the hard ground. Isis gasped and drew her sai, slashing at whatever held her on the ground, successfully knocking it off her. She immediately rolled to the side and got into a crouch, adjusting her grip on the sai. There were glowing gray eyes in front of her, but Isis couldn't make out anything else in the darkness. She straightened up, as did the eyes, and then lunged at it. As she struck out, she felt a large hand tightly latch onto her arm and toss her over a broad back, throwing her to the hard ground once again. Isis rolled away when she heard the foot speeding down toward her head. Leaping to her feet, Isis ran at her attacker again and leapt up, locking her thighs around the neck. Using her forward momentum, she threw the experiment to the dirt and plunged her sai in the back of where she assumed the head was. Yanking her weapon free, Isis didn't check to see if her assailant was dead. She ran toward the other three, whistling sharply.

"Isis?" Alex asked, looking over in her teammate's direction. Isis noticed a nearly invisible glint of glass in the hills behind them and picked up her speed. The pale-haired A-series suddenly tackled Alex to the ground, covering her as a bullet struck the pile of dirt from the hole they'd been digging. Alex's hand suddenly reached out of the hole and grabbed the lantern, which was quickly extinguished. Eris immediately jumped out of the tree, hiding behind the trunk. Isis finally reached them and slammed into the tree next to Eris, carefully peering out from the other side of the trunk.

"Bloody protectors," the guardian grumbled, rotating her wrist a couple times. Isis glanced over at her, noticing an odd shadowy mist growing around her hand. Once it was about the size of a large cantaloupe, Eris leaned back and tossed it into the air. It formed a dome, which promptly encircled them. Isis looked around, puzzled by how it was a little lighter inside the shield.

"You can come out now, pups," Eris said as she and Isis approached the hole. Alex was brushing the dirt off her hands as the A-series hopped out of the hole, looking around for any sign of the shooter. Alex climbed up after him, looking around with her hand resting on her sidearm.

"Save your rounds," Isis said quietly.

Isis looked through the wall of the dome, which shimmered like waves of heat. She could just make out a few forms in the dark, quickly descending from the mountain. Glancing behind them, she spotted two more shapes approaching from the vast field.

"Okay, kiddos, this lovely shield is both sight-proof and soundproof, however it is not bulletproof or stab-proof. I suggest we get a move on and head back inside, find better cover. Somewhere with less crossfire, somewhere a bit more defensible," Eris mentioned from the center of the small group, squinting as she looked around. "You just had to extinguish our one source of light, didn't you? I can't see a bloody thing."

"I can," Isis said simply as she started toward where the hospital was, her senses sharp for any enemies lurking about. "Is your magic scent-proof?"

"That it is," Eris replied. Isis looked over to the pale-haired man, who had soft blue eyes. His extra arms were concealed by a dark blue and silver shirt.

"Can you watch our backs?" Isis asked and the man nodded in response. Isis gestured to Alex. "Put your hand on her shoulder, just to keep your speed in check."

The man looked over at Alex suspiciously, but quickly turned his back to Isis and rested two of his hands on Alex's shoulder. The protector drew her gun and pointed it at the ground, meeting Isis' gaze and nodding that she was ready. Isis checked to make sure Eris was ready to move. The guardian was looking up at the dome, squinting a little.

"Well now, that's quite interesting," she muttered under her breath as Isis motioned for them to start moving. They moved at a quick pace, but still cautiously.

"What is?" Alex asked, her eyes darting from one side to the other as she kept her focus on the inky night. The A-series was watching their back, his eyes never moving from the space behind them.

"Well, it's not something non-magic wielders would be able to appreciate," Eris remarked, gesturing vaguely toward the translucent black fog that concealed them. "You see the gold shimmering around the edges there?"

Isis risked glancing upward, almost instantly spotting the barely visible gold shimmer Eris was referencing. It hugged the curve of the dome, as if it had latched onto the smoky magic the guardian used to conceal them. Alex also looked up, but the A-series kept his attention focused on the night. He pulled an impressive-looking knife from a sheath he wore about his waist, tightly holding the grip.

"Yeah, kind of," Alex answered and Eris smirked.

"That, my dear protector, is another magic spell. It's trying to pierce through mine — so amateur," Eris scoffed, kicking a small stone out of her path.

"Shit," Isis mumbled, rubbing her forehead when she realized what she had been missing. It had been an incredibly foolish oversight, one she likely wouldn't have made had she been in any other setting. She could feel Alex looking over at her, but continued moving forward.

"It has been quite some time since I have been in a training field or simulation," Isis began, noticing the enormous outline of the hospital. "I had forgotten that the necromancers control all aspects of the setting, including the length of days and nights."

"And the weather," the A-series added, as Isis ran a hand over her short hair. It had been a foolish oversight and one that would undoubtedly cost them. The wind suddenly picked up and swept through the trees, rattling the leaves.

"Are you saying the sun might not rise?" Alex asked, almost having to shout over the howling wind. Isis instinctively ducked when the sky was split by lightning. A short time later, a crash of thunder shook the ground beneath their feet.

"That is a possibility," Isis responded, glancing up. "It's certainly a strategy I would make use of if it were available to me."

As they reached the back entrance of the hospital, Isis pounded loudly on the heavy door with the side of her fist. It gradually creaked open and Isis gestured for the other three to go through. The A-series swiftly bolted inside, followed closely by Alex. Eris was just about to saunter inside when a glass bottle suddenly shattered against the wall near them, flame spreading across the stone. Isis shoved Eris inside and then followed close behind, turning to help Jo pull the door closed again. Jo quickly pulled the impressive wooden bolt across the door before twisting the deadbolt. She raised her eyebrows at Isis, obviously unimpressed with the 7-series' close call. Isis gave a small shrug and moved past her, heading for the large main room.

"We have a problem," Jade said as Isis and Alex stepped into the room. She nodded over her shoulder, indicating she wanted Isis to follow. The 7-series quickly did, matching Jade's pace as her teammate led her over to the main desk. A young A-series with a dark complexion was sitting in front of a computer screen. Reva stood behind him and Shae stood next to her. She glanced up when the three women approached. Isis paused, unused to seeing Shae without a smile. It was odd, but expected in the situation. Shae gestured at the screen.

"Evan here helped us connect to the ship while you were out there," she explained. "We've managed to get Radar on screen using some technological wizardry."

"It's really not that complicated. Once I was able to speak with the E-series, she was able to construct a rudimentary video call," Evan mentioned, turning to start explaining but his shoulders dropped when he realized that none of them would be able to understand. Isis slid over the desk, peering down at the laptop Evan had opened. She noticed Radar on screen along with Sly, Jensen, and Nero. There were two experiments standing in the background whom she didn't recognize. She heard Jade pull herself over the desk and lean down next to her. Alex stayed on the other side of the desk, resting her elbows on the dusty surface.

"Your scouts?" Isis asked, pointing at the two strange experiments in the background. She heard another crash outside, at the back of the building, and twisted to look behind her. Shae also glanced behind, but turned her attention back to the screen.

"Mia and Rami," Reva responded with a nod. "They mean you no harm."

Reva approached Isis, who turned to look at her. "Please forgive us. We had no idea you were the Bane of Grenich, who some call Blitz."

Isis' eyebrows knitted together and she stared at the A-series. "What?"

"You're one of the 7-series who rebelled against Grenich, the one who destroyed one of the main laboratories," Reva explained. "It's why there has been a dramatic increase in demonstrations. It's the first time we have ever seen the necromancers act rashly."

"Apparently, you've got fans and quite a reputation," Shae put in, amusement creeping into her voice. Isis stared at her, squinting in confusion. She had absolutely no idea what they were talking about. Glancing down, she noticed Evan staring at her in a way that could be considered awe.

"News about the destruction of the laboratory spread fast," Evan explained, looking away almost bashfully. "We were hoping to join your cause once we found a way off this island."

Isis closed her eyes and shook her head, already having too much on her plate. She still felt a little drained and didn't have anywhere near the energy needed to come up with some kind of cover story or response. If experiments were spreading rumor and gossip, it could potentially be advantageous and she would have to talk to Orion about it if she managed to get off the Island of Avalon. Isis could hear Eris chuckling in amusement, obviously entertained by the whole situation.

"Seems as though there is a revolutionary in the family. The High Council will be *so* pleased," the guardian said, putting a hand over her mouth as she giggled.

"Okay, well, as interesting as that is," Jade mercifully interrupted whatever else the A-series were going to say. "I mentioned bad news. Radar managed to get in contact with the mansion."

She gestured at the screen and Sly quickly knelt down next to Radar. "Hello, ladies. Well, as usual, the guardians have decided to get involved and, in doing so, are going to completely fuck everything up. As is guardian tradition."

"I'm almost scared to ask," Alex commented as Isis sat on the desk and dropped her face into her hands. The last thing she needed was more people getting involved.

"They're recalling Eris and you four as well. You have twenty-four hours to vacate the island and then the water guardians are going to submerge it to rid it of the pesky Grenich presence," Sly explained and Isis could hear her tapping on the desktop with a finger. "You're to return alone, no guests."

"Typical," Eris sighed from where she stood and Isis looked over at her. "Oh well. It's been . . . something. I'm going to have to shower for the next decade to scrub the stink of fish and disgusting animals out of my beautiful clothes. Best of luck staying alive."

Isis looked over at Reva and noticed the puzzled expression that spread across her face. She put her feet on the ground, turning her attention to Eris. The guardian moved over to the steps, draping herself on the stairwell. A sly grin was spreading across her face, but there was something in her eyes. An odd hesitance, almost as if the news wasn't something that pleased her entirely. Resting a hand on the pommel of her sai, Isis bit the inside of her cheek.

"However, there is a bit of a silver lining," Sly continued. "As I've told your new experiment friends — after young Shae finished having a conniption fit — the protectors are stupidly noble and honorable, which is why they have such short lifespans, as Isis frequently points out. They're not the type to leave anyone behind. Jet's going to talk with Titania and hopefully get the door to Earth opened, so your merry band can go on through. The fey will likely want the mortals to be blindfolded, so be prepared to do that. Unfortunately, you only have twenty-four hours to get your group to the boat and away from that island, so I hope you've made some progress finding that box."

"Apparently the guardians are content to just leave the healers to die," Jade explained, running her fingers through her hair. "Also, we have another problem."

Reva cleared her throat. "As you know, Grenich often uses a failsafe in training fields with live targets and rounds. This one is no different. Every single human on this island has a small implant imbedded in their inner elbow, in the bone. It's a metal capsule filled with a strong neurotoxin and it will burst if it crosses any of the barriers."

Isis spun around to face her, her eyes narrowing. "And you're only mentioning this *now*?"

"We weren't entirely sure who you were," Reva stated. "I was waiting for word from the scouts."

Isis shook her head and moved to stand in front of the computer, leaning down so that she was eye-level with Sly. Jensen moved closer, his brow furrowing in concern.

"Ah, there's the notorious troublemaker herself," Sly greeted, squinting as she studied Isis' face. "You feeling okay? You're not looking so great."

"The necromancers have control of this island. They control the day and night cycles. We're not going to see daylight, not while the experiments are still active," Isis explained. "It's going to be difficult to keep track of time and it's going to be even more difficult to extract this entire group in such a short window of time."

"Sorry, my dear. I'm afraid we're still bound by Seelie Court laws," Sly mentioned, exchanging a look with Jensen. Isis shook her head.

"More boots on the ground would just complicate things," she responded. "Is there any chance the guardians would give us an extension? Even if it's only a day or two?"

"Doubtful, knowing how bullheaded the High Council is," Sly said, apologetically. "In fact, if you could get your living weapon self back to this ship as soon as possible, it

301

would be most appreciated. We're dealing with some experiment shenanigans on our end too. Some . . . well, Mia tells us they were 8-series, attacked the ship. Lost quite a few selkies; poor bastards had no experience fighting experiments."

"Jensen got stabbed," Nero put in, leaning over Sly. "He almost died, Isis."

Jade rolled her eyes and Shae snickered softly. Isis studied Jensen on the screen, searching for any sign of how wounded he was. He didn't appear to have almost died, though he was a little paler than was normal. It wasn't the first time she wished they had brought a guardian healer with them.

"He's over-exaggerating, Isis. It's a shoulder wound and I've had significantly worse in the past," Jensen argued, shooting a glare at Nero. "The experiments seem to be in agreement that another attack is pretty much imminent."

Isis nodded and ran a hand over her face, trying to figure out if four experiments would be enough to hold off another attack. The protectors were good fighters, but they would definitely need experiments if they wanted to fight off an assault. The sons of Set were known to be natural strategists. His grandsons tended to be hot-headed and impulsive, but his sons were calm and calculating. Something shattered against the front door and Isis twisted to look behind her. Why weren't they using live ammunition? That was somewhat peculiar.

"I agree with the experiments: if the sons of Set are here, they'll keep attacking until they sink the ship," she said after a moment, looking back to the screen. "I'll do my best to get there as soon as I can."

Isis straightened up and slid back over the desk, hopping down on the other side. She turned her attention back to Reva, whose glowing brown eyes stood out in the gloom surrounding them.

"Do you and the others know how to safely extract the

implant?" Isis asked.

"We do. Took out Noor's some time ago," Reva answered, crossing all her arms over her torso. "It'll take some time, but it can be done."

"Eris' spell is still at work, so they likely won't feel whatever you do. Pick the best ones suited to the task and get to work. Doing it simultaneously will prevent the necromancers from catching on," Isis instructed. "The rest of the A-series need to start gathering whatever weapons you have and putting them on the bus. You're going to move out in an hour."

Isis strode over to the stairway, grabbed Eris' upper arm and dragged her to the back of the hospital. She ignored the guardian's annoyed protestations as she peered into each small patient room, shoving the woman into an empty one with a sufficiently barricaded window and shutting the door behind them. Twisting the lock, Isis turned to face Eris.

"Are we finally going to play rough?" Eris asked, raising an eyebrow. In one smooth motion, Isis withdrew one of her sais, spinning it once. Eris' eyebrows raised a little, but she still didn't show any signs of fear.

"Why Isis, I do believe I may have finally gotten under your skin," she said as Isis crossed the small space and yanked Eris' arm out, ignoring the guardian's yelp of surprise. With a single stroke, she severed the Leaves of Ivy. Eris' eyes widened significantly and her mouth dropped open as she watched the guardian charm fall to the ground. Isis kicked the severed bracelet beneath the empty bed, spinning her sai and sliding it back into its scabbard.

"What the bloody fuck do you think you're doing?" Eris snapped, shoving Isis. "You had no damn right! I am going to make your pitiful existence a living —"

"Freedom," Isis stated calmly, looking over at Eris, unbothered by her fury. "That's what you want, correct? More than anything else? You've been looking for a way to escape from the moment you were taken out of your cell."

Eris opened her mouth and closed it again, staring at Isis, mystified. Isis crossed her arms over her chest, waiting for the guardian to speak. It was quiet except for the occasional shattering of glass or quiet whoosh of fire from outside. Eris looked at her suspiciously as she put her hands on her hips, cocking one hip slightly.

"What of it?"

"I can give it to you," Isis said, pausing briefly when she heard footsteps move past the closed door. "But not without a significant price."

Eris raised an eyebrow. "Come on. You're willing to turn traitor for a useless relic? Either you've completely lost your bloody mind —"

"Oh I never said that was the only thing," Isis interrupted, her glowing green eyes rising to meet Eris' gaze. The trickster went silent, pursing her lips, obviously intrigued. Isis turned back to the door, running her fingers over the ancient peeling paint.

"I cannot promise your safety or that you will survive," Isis continued, not turning around. "You need to be sure: is freedom worth any cost, even your life?"

Eris was quiet a moment and when Isis turned back to her, she noticed the thoughtful expression on the guardian's face. Holding up a palm, a ball of cloudy white mist appeared and illuminated the women in the room. Eris tossed it up to the ceiling, where it acted as a lamp. She looked back to Isis, a half-smirk dancing across her ruby red lips.

"What is it you want me to do?" Eris asked.

"The first thing you're going to do is put a spell on the bus. Make sure it can move through the town, invisible to enemy eyes. You'll work under the observation of the others. How long is the spell on the humans going to last?"

"As long as they're on the same world as me," Eris replied, her eyes lighting up. "Do you need me to make an adjustment?"

Isis nodded. "And you need to do it without the others noticing, after the A-series have finished removing the failsafe. Also, cast an illusion to make it look like you're still wearing the Leaves of Ivy."

Eris looked down to her upper arm, where the charm had once been, and passed her other hand over the flesh. Once it passed over, a perfect replica of the charm appeared on her arm. Eris looked back to Isis and smiled. Putting her hands on her hips, Isis thought about the plan once more. It was definitely going to be risky, but she was fairly confident she could pull it off.

"So what's the plan?" Eris asked, unable to conceal her curiosity. Isis pursed her lips briefly, figuring out exactly how much she needed to tell the guardian. After a moment, she started to explain her plan, making sure to be as clear as possible. Eris' eyes sparkled with delight and her smile grew. By the time Isis finished, Eris was practically clapping her hands in excitement.

"You're absolutely mad, you do realize that right?" she asked when Isis finished explaining. Isis stared at her, puzzled.

"I can assure you, I'm quite sane by most standards," Isis replied, looking over her shoulder. "We don't have much time, so get to work."

"Out of curiosity, where are you going to be while I'm working on the bus?" Eris asked.

"I have a few errands to run," Isis replied, purposefully being vague. She had been working on a number of ideas and backup plans since they left the Meadows. The one she was currently focusing on was the one most likely to work, so long as not too many people knew about it. It would probably result in the most severe consequences, but Isis would deal with that if it came to pass.

Opening the door, Isis stepped out into the hall and heard Eris follow her. There was the muffled sound of glass shattering against the wall of the enormous stone building. The 8-series were going to launch an assault on the building and, chances were, the sons of Set would soon send Nick Chance out to cause even more bloodshed. While Isis was sure she could fare reasonably well against another experiment, she was less sure she would be able to fight a necromancer for any extended amount of time. She noticed Gem standing a few feet away, near the garage door. Her glowing brown eyes were wide as she looked around the enormous hallway, obviously unsure of what to do.

Isis turned to Eris. "Wait for my signal and then meet me at the rendezvous point."

Eris smiled and dipped her head once before turning and hurrying toward the garage. She passed a smaller A-series on the way and crooked her finger at him, indicating that he should follow her. The man glanced over at Isis and then followed the guardian into the murky gloom of the garage. Isis approached the other A-series and Gem turned to her, her glowing brown eyes meeting Isis' green gaze. She looked quite young and Isis couldn't help but wonder how old she was.

"Do you have any explosives? Preferably the kind that can be wired to a remote trigger?" Isis asked her softly. Gem looked at her and nodded.

"There's some on the second level."

"I need you to gather all of it and put it in a duffle, along with everything else I'll need to construct a bomb. And I'm going to need a few grenades," Isis instructed, keeping her eyes on the young experiment. "Is the bus the only vehicle on this island?"

Gem shook her head. "There's also a motorcycle in the garage, one of our group lifted it during a sweep some time ago. I need to check the fuel, but it still runs. Why? Do you need someone to act as a distraction?"

"No, I'll be doing that," Isis replied. "Bring the duffle to the front desk. And I'll need some cover to get away, so if there are any A-series who can lay down cover fire, it would be most appreciated."

As she moved into the hall leading to the front part of the hospital, she could hear a soft conversation continuing in front of her. The A-series were moving into the front room where the humans were, Reva instructing them to use the utmost care.

"Someone needs to go watch Eris as she puts the concealing spell on the bus," Isis mentioned and Alex quickly moved toward the garage. Making her way over to the desk, Isis replaced her earpiece and switched it on.

"Can you hear me?" she asked and there was a slight echo from the computer.

"Loud and clear," Nero's voice responded. Isis switched off the earpiece again.

"We've got a small group of 8-series who currently have us pinned down," she explained, looking around at the shape shifters still in the front area. "We'll be slaughtered if we attempt to escape right now. They'll mow us down before we even reach the property's gates, even if we're in a bus, and they're going to try to smoke us out. Thankfully, experiments can be fairly predictable and we tend to keep a store of tools in our safe houses."

"By tools, I assume you mean weapons?" Jade asked as she massaged her forehead.

"Some weapons, some explosives. Really anything that can be of use in adverse situations," Isis stated, putting her hands on her hips. "We need a distraction of some sort, so I'm going to blow up a few of the posts that are keeping the werehyenas out."

Jade snorted and dragged her hands over her face. "Guardians, I *really* wish I were surprised or shocked, but I'm not."

Isis ignored her as she started to double-check all the weapons she had on her. "Wereanimals can't be controlled. They will attack any living thing, including experiments and necromancers. That's why Set doesn't deploy them on missions and why experiments don't work with them. They're highly dangerous and uncontrollable animals."

"It would definitely provide a good distraction," Evan mentioned, scratching the back of his head. "The 8-series would have a hell of a time trying to put down a pack that large. Normal ammunition won't affect them; couldn't pierce their hides."

"They'll be using co-ag rounds and likely blades coated in co-ag. I'm not sure what kind of effect they'll have on wereanimals," Isis pointed out, unconcerned, and Evan swallowed, whistling softly.

"Well, we know what kind of effect those'll have on us," he mentioned quietly. Isis glanced over at him, noticing he was massaging the back of his neck, a sign of nervousness. Co-ags tended to have that effect on experiments.

"Isis, please tell me you aren't planning to go out in that madness by yourself," Shae said quietly, watching as Isis holstered a firearm. "You said it yourself, you'll be killed. There's too many and what about the necromancers?"

"I move faster on my own and I've been modified for this exact sort of situation," Isis replied with a dismissive wave of her hand. "I'll stay in communication with the ship. They'll be able to warn me if the 8-series or necromancers lay any sort of trap. I'll meet up with you on the beach as soon as I can."

Jade and Shae exchanged a look, obviously not thrilled with the plan. Isis had noticed protectors didn't like splitting up, which was generally a very wise idea. However, there were times when it was unavoidable. The situation they were in was one such time.

"Look, that unnatural darkness outside? It's a double-edged sword: it may inhibit our vision, but it does theirs too. I can use that to my benefit," Isis tried to reassure them.

"But how are you going to get past them?" Jade asked.

Isis looked up to the second floor where she heard Gem scampering around. She could smell the faint hint of blood as the other A-series started extracting the failsafe from the humans' arms.

"A couple A-series are going to be on the roof," Isis said. "They'll be able to draw their attention away from me for a short time. If they can make it look like they're trying to defend the location, the 8-series will focus on them. Experiments will almost always focus first on a more aggressive combatant. It's hard to ignore someone shooting at you. The A-series also have a motorcycle and I'll use that to slip past them."

Isis turned sharply at the sound of glass shattering and splintering wood. What looked like a spear had been thrust through one of the barriers. Isis ignored it for the time being, knowing it would take them a while to break down the barriers. Right now, they were just trying to intimidate them and get them to act impulsively. The sound of another Molotov cocktail shattering against the side of the hospital was heard outside and Isis could see the flickering warm glow of fire out of the corner of her eye. Fire would be the more pressing concern, especially if they had flames made by Pyra.

Pressing the button in her ear, Isis turned to the side. "Radar, think you can control what the necromancers see?"

"I can try," Radar sounded incredibly unsure. Isis knew it was a long shot, but it didn't hurt to ask. She was more determined than ever to get off the island.

"I can give you a hand if you need it," Evan told Radar from where he still sat in front of the computer, turning his gaze to Isis. "I'm not as good as an E-series, but I'm not useless."

Isis nodded in agreement as she adjusted the gloves on her hands, looking up when Gem came running down the stairs. The young A-series had a fairly large duffle slung over one shoulder, which she carefully placed on the front desk, nodding to Isis.

"Okay, when you see a tower of flame in the distance, you floor the accelerator and head for the beach. Don't look back and don't stop, not for any reason. You're only going to have a very small window to get to the beach," Isis stated as she moved across the floor to the desk, opening the duffle. There were a number of wires and blocks of C4, probably enough to take out two or three of the electrical posts, more than enough to take care of the barrier. Pulling the zipper closed again, Isis slung the bag over her shoulder.

"Have we just completely given up on the Box of Original Elements?" Jade asked.

"There's no time," Isis replied, turning her attention to Gem. "Get two or three A-series to the roof. You're going to draw the 8-series away from the garage and keep their attention off me so I can get off the property. Use grenades, bullets, anything that will draw their attention."

Gem nodded and moved to carry out Isis' orders. Isis turned back to the other two, who were watching her. She could see tears gathering in Shae's eyes and Jade looked fairly resigned. Another Molotov cocktail shattered against the side of the building and Isis could hear the faint roar of the spreading flame. While the barricades were steady, they wouldn't hold forever. The smell of chemicals invaded her sense of smell and Isis turned her head away from the windows, moving off toward the garage.

She heard a quiet scuffing sound and turned just in time to have Shae wrap her arms around her in a tight hug. She nuzzled her face against her neck and Isis put an arm around her, a response she found most normals responded to positively. She forced her body to relax and lose some of the tension she often experienced when someone touched her.

"Don't you dare do anything stupid, OK?" Shae whispered, her voice shaking a little. "Don't go and get yourself killed, all right?"

"That's not my plan or intention," Isis replied, unsure why Shae was so upset. They had been on dangerous missions before. It was their job.

"Isis, stay in contact and please exercise caution out there," Jade said sternly, though Isis could read the concern in her gaze. She nodded and carefully extracted herself from Shae's embrace.

"I have been in more dangerous conditions," Isis attempted to be reassuring. "You are the ones who are going to have to navigate through the worst of it. Truthfully, you have the more difficult and dangerous job. Please be careful."

Shae smiled a little and nodded, stepping aside to let Isis pass by. Looking to Jade one last time and getting a nod from the older protector, Isis turned and made her way down the hall to the garage. When she reached the door, she heard a sound similar to the whoosh of a strong wind.

Pushing the door open, Isis spotted Alex standing a good distance away from the bus along with a few A-series, who were watching the vehicle, curiously. Isis turned her eyes to the bus and spotted Eris inside it. Crossing the distance, Isis peered through one of the windows and studied the guardian. She was using a nail gun to attach something inside, her dark hair pulled back from her face. A few strands had fallen loose, framing her face. Her lips were moving as she spoke words under her breath and nailed another small object to the bus. There was a brief shimmer of translucent black mist. Eris moved to the center of the bus where the emergency hatch was open and got up on one of the seats, pulling herself out.

"Be with you in a moment, petal," she said without looking at Isis. "Might want to take a few steps back."

Isis complied, turning to approach Alex and nodded over her shoulder, indicating she wanted her teammate to follow her. Alex looked over at Eris, who was chanting in a soft melodic language. A glow formed around her hands and began to creep up her arms, swirling in a mist.

"As soon as Eris is done with the concealment spell, I'm going to have her cast a smaller one on the bike over there," Isis tilted her chin up to the corner of the garage where there was a dark-colored tarp thrown over a motorcycle. "Jade and Shae will fill you in on the rest, but I'm going to create a distraction so all of you can get out without being slaughtered."

Alex opened her mouth to speak but stopped when a large bottle struck near one of the windows in the garage, orange flame licking at the glass. She cringed, obviously not liking how aggressive the experiments were getting. Isis adjusted her gloves again before putting her hands on her hips.

"Sure you can outrun them?" Alex asked with a skeptical raised eyebrow.

"On a bike, hidden by a concealment spell?" Isis replied, shrugging as she continued looking toward the windows. "Shouldn't be a problem. It's more navigating a way off the island that concerns me. Keep your wits about you. Even with the distraction, the experiments are cunning and a few will likely hang back. They'll be armed and they won't take prisoners."

"Is that your way of wishing me luck?" Alex responded, a hint of humor in her voice. Isis noticed most of her mannerisms were similar to Remington, including the dry wit.

Before she could respond, there was a rush of wind and a crackling sound, like fireworks fading after the loud bang. Alex and Isis looked over to the bus, noticing a cloud of sparkling translucent black mist coated it, shimmering even in the shadows of the garage.

Eris hopped down to the front of the bus and then to the ground, brushing her hands together and smiling as she admired her work. "That, my furry four-legged critters, is how you do real magic. She's ready to go."

"Feel up to doing one more?" Isis asked and Eris

looked over at her.

"As long as it's smaller than that monstrosity," she responded, following Isis over to the bike. Isis pulled the tarp off it, ignoring the plume of dust and dirt that came with it. Eris waved her hand in front of her face, coughing lightly.

"Darling, you could at least make it a challenge," she commented. "I assume you want to be hidden as well?"

Isis nodded and watched Eris get to work.

CHAPTER TWELVE

Roan was jolted awake by a loud pounding on the glass wall of his cell. He squinted and grimaced, raising a hand to shield his eyes from the incredibly bright light. For a moment, he felt disoriented and tried to clear the cobwebs from his mind. It wasn't often that he was able to sleep peacefully or for very long. The previous night had been one of those exceedingly rare times and he was more than a little annoyed at having it interrupted. Judging from the amount of light, it was mid-morning and he would not have minded sleeping until the late afternoon.

"Wake up, Roan!"

Roan turned his head to the side, still holding a hand up to shield his eyes, surprised at the unusually demanding voice. "Passion?"

Using his free hand to rub his eyes, Roan blinked a few times to clear his vision as he sat up and looked at the glass, dumbfounded. Passion stood in front of the cell, looking as disheveled as he had ever seen her. Her hair was messily tied back from her face and it looked as though she hadn't slept in days. She was wearing an apron over her dress, which was smeared with blood. Her bright eyes were blue and they were blazing with anger, but for the first time it didn't seem to be directed entirely at him. Despite how angry she looked, Roan was happy to see her. He hadn't heard anything about her since the Changing of Seasons ceremony.

Orion stood beside her, looking tired as he always did. Whenever he saw him, Roan couldn't help but wonder if his older brother ever got any sleep. In his hands, he held a tablet and the glow from the screen made the rings under his eyes stand out even more. Roan immediately wrapped his blanket around his waist and moved over to the privacy screen where his clothes were hanging. He had a feeling something had gone very wrong and it would probably take some time to sort through.

"What happened?" Roan asked as he quickly pulled on his pants. His voice was still rough with sleep.

"Did you know Grenich had a presence in the Seelie Court?" Orion asked, raising his voice just enough that Roan could hear him. Roan stepped out from behind the screen, his long fingers quickly doing up the buttons on his shirt.

"Um, hmm," he wracked his mind, turning his head slightly as he moved over to the glass. "Yes and no. There has been, or there was, a processing facility there for quite a while. I don't know if it would still be operational. They move those damn things so frequently, it's hard to keep track of them. I know it was also used as a training field, one of the less brutal ones if memory serves correctly. Orion, you probably have much more up to date information than I do."

Orion shook his head. "I've been so preoccupied with freeing experiments that I didn't pay much attention to the various training areas. They're difficult to get any information on, especially without an inside source."

Roan looked over at Passion. "They're impossible to infiltrate. Going to one is basically a suicide mission unless you're a full-blooded necromancer or have an invitation from Set's inner circle. Not even Milo was able to gain access to one."

"The Four are currently trapped in an active demonstration on the Island of Avalon," Orion mentioned quietly and Roan felt his eyes widen significantly as he whipped his gaze back to his brother. He took a few steps to the side so that he was standing directly in front of his older brother, who was still looking down at the screen.

"You mean to tell me the Four, including Isis, are in a death trap?" Roan asked, feeling anger rise in his chest as he smacked the glass loudly, drawing Orion's attention away from the tablet. "Why do you always do this? Why do you always come to me when you've gotten yourself, and usually others, in the absolute worst situation imaginable? I'm very curious about what sort of damn bullheadedness led to this particular predicament."

"As much as I'd love to give you a play-by-play," Orion began, contempt dripping from every word as he glared at his brother. "You are a prisoner, one who happens to have some decent information. Right now, we need to know if you were privy to any ways out of a training demonstration. Or maybe you helped design a few. God knows that wouldn't be out of character for you."

Roan narrowed his eyes and started to grind his teeth, struggling to control his temper. It wasn't the first time he had wanted to wrap his hands around his older brother's neck and throttle the life out of him. He swallowed and licked his lips as he turned his attention back to Passion. Knowing that it wouldn't be productive to talk to his brother when they were both frustrated and angry, Roan figured it was wiser to address Passion. The guardian raised an eyebrow and looked at him, waiting for him to speak.

"I know you're angry with me and I know that is entirely my fault. But if you want my help, I'm going to need some information and not just the vagaries my elder brother is so fond of speaking in. Apparently even when his own niece is in mortal peril," Roan said without looking at Orion, though he could almost feel the glare his brother leveled at him. Passion was quiet for a moment, her eyes narrowing as she looked at him. Glancing once at Orion, Passion let out her breath through her nose and turned back to Roan.

"They went there to retrieve the Box of Original Elements. The High Council granted Eris a temporary release —" Passion began, crossing her arms over her chest.

"Eris? Your sister, Eris? A guardian who has the ability to alter perception, who can control the will of others and who has no qualms using said abilities?" Roan asked, his voice steadily rising in volume as he looked back to Orion. "You let them take a guardian who thrives on chaos to a goddamn island that's controlled by Set? Have you *completely* lost whatever lingering shreds of sanity you had?"

"Okay, you know what," Orion handed the tablet to Passion and faced his brother, his blue eyes blazing. "I will not be lectured by a goddamn assassin whose answer to everything is murder — as shown by the body count to his name, which is longer than almost all the serial killers in history put together!"

"Funny, that certainly doesn't stop you from coming to me for advice whenever it damn well suits you. Advice which you typically end up ignoring anyway," Roan shot back, clenching his fists. "And if we're talking the moral high ground versus the gutter, you are right next to me in the shit, brother."

"Excuse me, Deverells —" Passion attempted to interject and rolled her eyes when they didn't even glance at her. She looked back down to the screen, mumbling something under her breath as she tapped on a window.

"And exactly how did your warped brain come to that conclusion?" Orion asked, inches from the glass.

"You worked at Grenich almost as long as I did, you ass! You treated how many wounded bodies, how many mangled experiments? Tell me, Orion, how many shape shifters did you send to be tormented by Set and the handlers? How many did you unknowingly torture with Grenich concoctions? I'd venture to guess it rivalled my own. I put my targets down quickly and humanely. Can you claim the same?"

Orion's nostrils flared and he clenched his shaking fists at his side. "At least I never killed innocent people and I never enjoyed suffering. My work was never about death."

Roan scoffed and shook his head. "At least my work was honest. And I never enjoyed it, it was a job."

"That's why you always look like a junkie after a fix whenever the opportunity to cause more suffering and death presents itself. But then again, why should I expect any different from an unrepentant assassin," Orion spat the words as if they left a bad taste in his mouth. Roan thought he heard someone clear their throat, but he disregarded it. This argument had been a long time coming, too long, and he wasn't going to back down from it.

"Boys," Passion tried again, her eyes on the screen.

"Unrepentant? Yes, that's exactly why I've helped you all these years, going so far as to save your life a few times in the past. I have repeatedly risked my life for you," Roan said, his face gradually turning bright red as his anger got more intense. He had finally had it with his brother's hypocrisy. "I'd do so again, in a heartbeat, if given a chance. You know I would die for you and our brothers without a second thought!"

"But apparently that selflessness didn't extend to my wife!" Orion snapped.

"Christ almighty, how many goddamn times do I have to tell you!? She was going to kill you! You saw the goddamn gun! The only reason why you, not to mention Ace, are still alive is because by some fucking miracle I managed to get to your personal office before you did!" Roan shouted, causing Orion to jolt slightly. Roan could feel his heart pounding in his chest, but he didn't give a damn. Orion had been guilt tripping him for decades and Roan was done with it. He had allowed his older brother to be petty and bitter, but now he was starting to endanger others with his thirst for vengeance and he either didn't realize it or didn't care. It had been foolish to allow Orion to keep it up for this long.

Orion opened his mouth to respond but was interrupted by a sharp whistle, followed by an annoyed voice saying, "Oi, idiots! Can we save the bickering for later? You know, when there aren't shape shifters in mortal peril?"

Both Orion and Roan turned their attention to where Passion was holding the tablet, now facing them. The screen showed the meeting room of the mansion, where Jet and Lilly were sitting with a speaker phone in the middle of the table. Remington sat a little further away from the screen. Across from the protectors sat a woman in an elegant purple gown, which sparkled slightly in the daylight. The woman's dark hair was twisted and braided in a fancy way that made it resemble a butterfly, which had probably taken hours to achieve. Her ears were larger and pointed, much more dramatically than an elf's from what Roan had read. Even if he hadn't known the difference in ears between elf and fey, the large feathered wings, green with hints of shimmering purple, were a giveaway. *Fey nobility, judging from the getup,* Roan thought as he ran a hand over his face.

"Well, that outburst certainly answered a few questions I had," Jet grumbled. Roan glanced over at Passion, who looked nothing short of furious. Lilly, Jet, and Remington also didn't look pleased about the Deverells' behavior. The fey woman was unbothered as she drummed her nails on the table. Roan couldn't help but feel a hint of embarrassment, not liking that people had seen him angry. He and his older brother had always had the uncanny ability to get into arguments at the most inappropriate times, even in their youth.

"You see what I've had to deal with? For *years*," Milo's irritated voice filtered through the speaker. Orion stepped away from the glass, moving to stand against the opposite wall, not looking at his brother.

"I apologize, Queen Titania," Jet spoke apologetically to the fey across from him. "The Deverells have more information on Grenich than most and they are usually able to take part in civilized conversations."

"Is the blond man in the dungeons?" Titania asked, remarkably disinterested. Jet massaged his brow and Roan almost chuckled at the protector's obvious vexation.

"Yes, he is a prisoner of the guardians," Lilly answered truthfully.

"Wonderful," Titania replied, looking as if she didn't want to be there.

Roan leaned his shoulder against the clean glass, looking at the screen. "A warning would have been nice, Jet. But I imagine circumstances didn't allow for one."

"You would be correct in that assumption," Jet confirmed.

"They're attempting to negotiate with the Seelie Court to open the door to Earth," Passion added. "The Four have found some survivors, both humans and experiments. Neither of them is welcome in the Meadows, nor would they be granted passage through the palace of the fey."

Roan looked between her and the faces on the screen. "So . . . leave them there? Grenich tends to treat its humans fairly well. They have to in order to keep up the façade of the simulation. They are training for field experience."

All the protectors stared at him, horrified. Titania merely folded her arms on the table, quietly observing all of them. Orion shook his head and mumbled something under his breath about that being typical.

"The prisoner seems to be infinitely more practical than all of you," the fey finally spoke. "You cannot have a war without casualties. It is naïve to believe otherwise."

"He doesn't have all the facts," Passion pointed out quickly, turning her attention back to Roan. "The guardians are going to submerge the island in twenty-six hours. They have granted the Four twenty-four hours to evacuate the island, that's all the time they have to escape. And they're not going to leave the survivors behind. The High Council won't change their minds. Roan, that clock is ticking and they're running out of time."

Roan looked over at Orion, smirking grimly. "If only it were that simple, right brother?"

Orion shook his head and dropped his gaze, rubbing his eyes. Roan now understood why his brother was easier to rile up than normal.

"We've been trying to explain to Titania about the threat Grenich poses," Lilly began.

"And my husband and I fully trust the guardians' ability to take care of this problem," Titania interrupted. "Order your people to evacuate the island. If they choose to stay that is their choice."

"Do you really think submerging a single island is going to rid your lands of Grenich?" Orion asked, attempting to cover the testiness in his tone. The fey woman looked over at him, raising a single elegant brow.

"Normals are so delightfully innocent," Milo commented. "It would be adorable if it didn't contribute to the problem."

"Set has found some profitability in the Seelie Court," Roan put in. "He has a way into your lands and he is not going to leave, certainly not without a fight. He probably already has spies planted in your courts. My lady, believe me when I say, you're not going to be rid of the necromancers anytime soon."

"That's impossible. The Seelie Court has always been loyal to my family," Titania replied, but there was a hesitance to her tone. Roan glanced at his brother before looking to the fey again.

"So you know the names of every single person in your world? You trust every single person who works for you? There's not even a slim chance that some fey noble or guard has some beef with you or the king?" Roan pressed. "There's not even the slightest possibility someone in your world would betray you?"

"Queen Titania, we have seen Grenich methods firsthand and how ruthless they are," Remington spoke softly. "Please trust Jet and Lilly when they tell you not to underestimate Set. That is a grave and fatal mistake."

Titania looked unsure as she turned her gaze to Jet and Lilly. She laid her hands out in front of her. "My lands still bear the scars of the War of the Meadows. If Chaos were to declare war again, I do not know if any of the worlds would survive that."

"There are two shape shifters, one on the Island of Avalon and one on the ship, who could be our only chance should that happen," Lilly said gently.

"If you are speaking of the guardian prophecy about the Key, would it not be more prudent to make sure the Key never falls into Set's hands or ours?" Titania pointed out. Roan noticed Passion's grip tighten around the tablet. He met her gaze and shook his head once. She licked her lips and stayed quiet, but didn't look happy about it.

"Allowing the protectors to save a group of innocents seems like a charitable act, one that would likely help restore a tarnished reputation," Orion suddenly spoke, scratching his chin. "Seems like a good legacy."

The fey woman's eyes widened briefly as she looked back to the screen. Roan rolled his eyes over to his brother, half-smiling. Orion did have his moments and was quite clever when the situation called for it.

"Plus, it would likely be a blow to the Corporation's reputation. Might weaken them a bit," Milo mused. "If nothing else, it would dissuade the more powerful necromancers from popping into your world."

"And I would owe you a favor," Passion stated

suddenly, drawing everyone's attention to her. "A favor from a guardian is a valuable thing to have, as I'm sure you know."

Titania leaned back in her seat, a thoughtful expression on her face. She was quiet for a moment, obviously thinking over the proposition.

"The humans must be blindfolded before they get on the ship and the blindfold must remain on until the door to the Seelie Court is concealed again," Titania spoke authoritatively. "And our earlier condition still stands: none but that small group may set foot on the sacred island. And should the Seelie Court ever have need, if Grenich ever attacks us, then we expect the aid of the guardians, shape shifters, and all their allies."

"Obviously," Lilly said. "That is why we renewed all the alliances of old."

"I expect that favor to be fulfilled whenever we request it," Titania continued and Roan immediately looked over at Passion. That had been a rash thing to offer and he wasn't sure it was the wisest decision. The Deverells had a history with the Seelie Court as did a few protector families and the fey were notoriously shady. They really only looked out for other fey and the trafficking scandal hadn't come as a surprise to anyone who had regular dealings with them. Roan couldn't help but feel sympathy for the other races who lived in the Seelie Court and who inevitably got swept up in the fey's shenanigans.

"Wouldn't have offered if I thought otherwise," Passion responded.

"Very well. I shall send word to the gatekeepers and they shall open the door for your people," Titania spoke firmly, holding herself like the queen she was. Roan struggled not to roll his eyes; he wasn't a huge fan of monarchies or royalty.

"And if we could keep this between us, it would be much appreciated," Jet added as an afterthought. Roan noticed his older brother suppress a cringe, which he understood. Jet was a good leader, but he frequently found his hands tied by the High Council. Titania raised an eyebrow as she looked over at him, obviously suspicious of the statement.

"We'll let you lot sort out any further details," Passion interrupted as she turned her attention back to the screen. "I apologize for leaving so abruptly, but I am needed back in the healing wings."

Roan watched as they said their goodbyes and then Passion exited out of the conversation, shutting down the tablet. She let out a long breath through her nose as she held the tablet between her crossed arms, focusing on the ground for a moment. Turning her attention to the two Deverells, she glared at them and Roan could see the fury blazing in her eyes. Around them, the bright morning light seemed to intensify a little. Roan swallowed and held his hands behind his back, regretting letting his temper get the better of him.

"Children, both of you, little boys who are constantly at each other's throats," Passion began in a low dangerous voice. "Your childish bickering could have very easily cost us the lives of the Four just now, not to mention the innocent people they're trying to get off that godforsaken island. They need our assistance and you let your tempers get the better of you."

Orion opened his mouth to speak, but Passion held up a hand. "Don't. There is no justification for your behavior. You have some damn nerve calling yourself a protector, Orion. I have half a mind to throw you into that empty cell next to your brother, but that would be an unfair burden on the guards. And you," Passion turned her gaze to Roan, who stood silently. "You're just as much to blame as your brother so wipe that smirk off your face. You claim you want to atone for your past, all the pain and suffering you willingly caused, and then you pull that shit? It has always been the same with you two: Orion pushes your buttons, you lash out, he reacts or vice versa and round and round it goes."

Passion roughly shoved the tablet at Orion, causing him to stumble back a couple steps. Orion cleared his throat and hung his head, looking like a chastised boy. Passion ran her fingers through her hair, interlacing her fingers at the base of her neck. She closed her eyes briefly and lifted her face up to the clean morning light and the air that drifted in through the open barred windows across from the cell. Opening her eyes again and dropping her arms, Passion looked back to the two men.

"I know you're both keeping things from the protectors and by extension, the guardians. I'm not a fool, neither are Jet and Lilly. At this point, I really don't have the time or energy to even begin to try unraveling your motivations, but I recommend taking a good long look at your strategy and your endgame, because you're not winning many allies at the moment," Passion said, shaking her head. "If we were relying solely on you two, I would fear this war already lost."

"The only secrets we keep are for the protection of others," Orion mumbled. Passion turned her gaze over to him, studying him for a moment.

"You should be more worried about fighting Grenich and the necromancers. It's a battle we can't win if we continue fighting amongst ourselves," Passion replied, a distinct coolness to her voice. "Sort out your shit and do it when we're not in the middle of important negotiations. Do you understand me?"

"Yes, Passion," the two brothers answered simultaneously. Passion nodded and gestured for Orion to follow her. Orion glanced over at his brother and Roan gave him a warning look. The former assassin watched as his brother followed the guardian out of the dungeons. Pressing his palms together, Roan paced around his cell with his fingertips pressed against his lips. No outsider had ever escaped a demonstration alive. If anyone could, it would likely be Isis or Jack. But with a group of normals?

Roan wasn't sure if even an experiment could manage that.

~~*~*~*

Jade peered up to where the A-series lookouts were standing with impressive sniper rifles, trying her best not to check in with Isis. It had been two hours since she had made her swift escape from the hospital grounds. She had checked in a half-hour ago to let them know she had managed to reach the town unscathed, but needed to maintain radio silence while she set up the explosives.

Hearing some shuffling behind her, Jade turned to see Shae leading a small group of humans over to Alex, who was standing near the open bus door. Though she hated to admit it, Isis' plan to have Eris temporarily alter the perception of the humans had been a wise decision. It made things infinitely easier, especially since the A-series didn't bother to conceal their glowing eyes and several of them didn't even try to hide their extra arms. Moving across the dusty ground, Jade approached the bus and glanced up to where Gem sat in the driver's seat. Her feet rested on the dashboard and she was fiddling with her nails. Her glowing brown eyes would occasionally turn to watch the humans board the bus.

"You worried about Isis?" Shae asked as she helped an elderly woman board. A younger A-series took the woman's gnarled hand and led her to a seat.

"Kind of," Jade replied, looking behind her at their gloomy surroundings. "It's really quiet. The 8-series seem to have disappeared and that just doesn't sit well with me. When have we ever seen experiments retreat?"

"Didn't Eris put a concealment spell on the motorcycle?" Shae pointed out, drawing Alex's attention to her. The other woman bit her bottom lip and checked off another name as a younger man stepped up on the bus.

"When has Eris ever done something without a catch?" Jade replied, looking over to where the guardian was fiddling with some old tools. She had been unusually quiet and well-behaved since Isis left. Jade was beginning to get very suspicious.

"Not to be too alarmist: but I have noticed some evidence that suggests experiments are less susceptible to Eris' abilities than normals are," Alex mentioned, ticking another name on the sheet in front of her.

Jade stared at her. "You're just telling us this now?"

"Just figured it out now," Alex said, almost apologetically as she shrugged. "I've been a little distracted by everything else that's going on."

Jade massaged her forehead. "Well, that's one more wrench thrown into our already substandard plan."

"That was the last group of humans," Shae mentioned, putting a hand on her hip and rubbing the side of her throat. "Just need to get the A-series on board."

Jade looked over to where Reva was standing with her back against the wall. "Reva, the normals are all on board. Time to get the rest of your group on the bus."

Reva nodded and moved back into the hospital to collect the few A-series who were gathering last minute supplies. Jade had been impressed with how many weapons the experiments had managed to acquire and cobble together in their time at the hospital. The A-series who were in the garage quickly moved to the bus and got into the vehicle.

A small, insistent tugging at her pants drew Jade's attention down to her left side. Noor was standing beside her and her young face reflected concern, her large brown eyes shining as she looked up at Jade. She gestured with a small hand, pointing toward the doors and then using both hands to sign something.

"She is worried about the other one," Jo mentioned from behind Jade as she moved over to the bus. "She doesn't think your teammate is coming back."

Jade crouched down so that she was eye-level with Noor, smiling reassuringly. "Don't worry, sweetie. Isis has been in scarier situations than this. She'll be fine and we'll meet up with her at the shoreline, you'll see."

"Attention, citizens of Westerville," a booming happy voice sounded over the P.A. system, causing the three protectors to exchange a look. "There is some rather concerning adverse weather headed our way."

There was a pause and soft snickering was heard over the dusty system, disturbing the cobwebs wrapped around the old speaker. Jade moved over to the large garage door, peering out into the night. A few dim flames were still dying down from the Molotov cocktails, but it was silent. She could just make out the gate in the distance and it was the first time she noticed the speakers mounted on top of the brick posts. *They're probably scattered throughout the town,* she realized. Looking behind her, she saw Reva lead the last few A-series out of the hospital and to the bus. She met Jade's gaze and nodded, waving to the small group to board the large vehicle.

"I'm sorry. I can't keep up the charade. It's an insult to your intelligence," the same friendly male voice continued. "This is directed to our protector visitors. Welcome. My name is Vincent Carver and I wish we were face-to-face. I am a huge admirer of yours."

Jade watched as the last experiments got on the bus and noticed Noor was trembling, looking terrified. The young girl wrapped her arms around Jo's leg and buried her face. Jo also seemed to be incredibly unsettled as she wrapped two of her arms around Noor, her attention fixed on the old speaker. Jade whistled softly, drawing the A-series' attention, and jerked her head toward the bus. Jo quickly lifted Noor into her arms and ran up the steps, disappearing inside the vehicle. Reva followed close behind her, calling to the two lookouts, who promptly leapt down from their perches, belaying down the ropes attached to the harnesses they wore, and made their way to the bus. After they disappeared inside, Jade gestured to Alex and Shae to get on board and started making her way to the large vehicle.

"Now, my brother and I do our best to be good hosts. So hopefully you've enjoyed your stay so far," Vincent's voice continued. "We have a proposition for you, Jade."

Jade paused and looked up at the ceiling toward the speaker. As she was looking, the lights snapped on and the sudden brightness nearly blinded her. Quickly raising her hand, Jade shielded her eyes from the painful white light as she kept her attention on the speaker, assuming there was a camera near it that she couldn't see.

"Ah that's better. Where was I? Oh yes, it seems as though you would like to leave and we're fully prepared to let you. In fact, we're willing to ensure safe passage to you and all the new friends you've made," Vincent continued on. "As a show of good faith, we've recalled the 8-series and they're under orders to stand down until commanded otherwise. I know they can be a tad bit . . . overzealous, which is probably quite upsetting and frightening."

Jade raised an eyebrow and called out, "And exactly what do you want in exchange for your generosity?"

"Ah, you are a clever one. You do have something in your possession that's worth all the lives on this island: the seven series, 7-299. You, or anyone really, deliver her to us and we promise to vacate the Island of Avalon immediately. Your group can leave unscathed. It's a fair trade," the voice explained matter-of-factly. "Isn't that right, 7-299? You know the sons of Set are men of their word. We don't care about the normals or the defectives and we don't have the same bloodlust as our guards. This doesn't have to get bloody. To borrow a phrase from the normals: the ball's in your court."

Jade pursed her lips, her attention drawn to where Eris was still fiddling with tools. The guardian seemed completely unconcerned with what was happening, which really didn't surprise Jade. Her earpiece suddenly crackled to life.

"He's right: if you wanted to trade me for safe passage,

you could," Isis said quietly. "I could buy you enough time to get off this island unscathed."

Jade swallowed and looked at the full bus, noticing Shae and Alex standing at the windows. Shae was shaking her head and Alex was watching her, waiting for her to respond. Jade nodded once to them and pressed a button on her earpiece.

"Isis, listen to me: burn these assholes to the ground," Jade ordered, moving quickly over to Eris. She reached out a hand to grab the guardian and almost fell forward when the image exploded into thousands of small circles of gray light. Her eyes widened as she spun around, looking for the guardian. There was no sign of her.

"Goddam —" Jade started to yell when suddenly, there was a loud bang and a roar. The ground beneath her feet shook and Jade stumbled a bit, struggling to keep her balance and stay upright. Gritting her teeth, she ran back to the bus and bounded up the steps.

"Drive," she yelled to Gem as she slammed her hand on the button to close the doors. In the rear of the bus, Alex quickly closed the back door and made sure it was tightly latched. As the bus began to move forward, clipping the doors that slowly swung open in front of them, Jade pressed the button on her earpiece again.

"Whoever's listening, we're on the move but I lost Eris. If you still have access to the security cams, try to find her and let Isis know if you see her," Jade ordered, sitting down next to a human and switching the channel in her earpiece. "Isis, Eris is making an escape attempt. If you see her, do your best to incapacitate her, but under no circumstances is she to get off this island free."

Alex looked over at her teammate, obviously surprised at the order. Jade ignored her as she looked out the windshield, watching as the wind picked up and swept through the grass. It was so murky, she couldn't see anything. Looking to the front of the bus, she noticed the headlights barely pierced the darkness before them, which resembled a solid wall, and Jade hoped the superior sight of experiments would be enough to get them through their perilous journey.

The sudden sound of a scrambling on the side followed by scratching on the top of the bus drew the protectors' eyes upwards. Jo promptly stood out of her seat and pulled out her sidearm, firing a few shots into the roof of the bus. Jade jolted when she glimpsed a shadow drop down on the opposite side of the bus. Jo crouched down low, her bright glowing brown eyes traveling up and down the length of the bus.

"Well, this is definitely going to be a wild ride," Shae mentioned dryly from the seat behind Jade. The older protector pulled out her own sidearm, glancing at the human sitting next to her. She quickly stood up and moved to the front of the bus, whistling sharply to draw everyone's attention to her.

"Okay, things are about to get a lot tougher. So if you're a shape shifter, arm yourself and plant yourself at a window seat. The human you're sitting nearest to is now your responsibility. Keep them safe, protect them from whatever we encounter. As of now, you're officially a protector, right up until we get aboard our ship. We've got limited rounds, so do your best to conserve your bullets," she ordered. "If you're a human, sit in an aisle seat and keep your head down."

The humans moved almost robotically as they shifted over to the aisle seats and bent low, almost hugging their knees. Jade bit her lower lip as she moved over to a window seat, wincing when another massive explosion shattered the quiet and a plume of bright orange flame rose into the sky some distance away.

"Well, we're definitely going to have a story to tell," Shae commented from behind her. "If we make it out of this alive that is."

"Come on, Shae. Don't lose that wide-eyed optimism we love," Jade grumbled, though she offered her teammate a small smile. Shae snorted and shook her head, checking to make sure she still had her knife on her belt. Jade silently exhaled and turned her eyes out to the impenetrable shadows outside. Every now and again she would catch a glimpse of a pair of glowing eyes in the gloom. She hoped that Eris' spell would hold up, at least until they reached the beach.

The sound of bullets hitting the side and shattering glass drew Jade's attention to the opposite side of the bus. Alex let out a cry of pain and fell back, hitting the floor of the bus hard. Jade immediately went to her teammate's side as an A-series quickly scrambled over the seats to the vacated window. Alex looked annoyed as she sat in the aisle, breathing through her nose and cursing under her breath. She turned her eyes to Jade, who quickly crouched down next to her. The older protector had to check her balance when the bus hit a particularly large stone and rocked to the side.

Jade peeled Alex's hand away from where it was pressed against her bleeding shoulder, checking her back too. "Looks like it went clean through. Fairly certain you'll live."

The two winced and ducked their heads when more bullets hit the bus, both looking across the aisle when Shae cursed loudly. Jade glanced toward the rear when she heard a whistle, noticing an A-series at the back, the younger man with pale hair. He tossed her the first aid kit before returning to his position.

"I guess I was right about experiments being less susceptible to Eris' magic," Alex pointed out with a small smile, grimacing in pain. Jade snickered and shook her head as she sorted through the first aid kit. Only Alex would be pleased about being wounded if it proved a hypothesis or theory.

"Glad to see your sense of humor is still intact," Jade commented, cleaning out the wound. Alex hissed and winced in pain, but remained still as Jade did what she could. A sudden grunt drew their attention to the A-series with the pale hair a few rows back. His face was contorted in pain. Jo quickly moved to help him, ignoring the shattered window and glass sprayed everywhere.

"They're using co-ag rounds," she called out. Jade and Alex exchanged a look, both hoping Isis was doing better than they were. Alex pressed the button on her earpiece.

"Isis, if you can hear me, the experiments are using co-ag rounds. Be careful," she reported before pressing the button again and switching the channel. "Radar, keep your eyes peeled for Isis as well. If the ship is attacked again, they might be using the same ammunition."

"Noted," Radar's voice responded. Alex grimaced as she put a hand on the seat she was leaning against, peering up at the nearest window. Jade put a hand on her shoulder, gently pushing her back down as she shook her head.

"You stay down," Jade warned, looking toward the windows. "We may need you the closer we get to the beach. I have a feeling things are only going to get more dicey."

Alex sighed and nodded, looking over to where the A-series was still on the ground. He was bleeding quite heavily from his side even as Jo finished binding his wound.

~~*~*~*

"Whoa!" Nero's loud exclamation drew Sly and Jensen's attention to where he was standing at the bow. Jensen turned his attention back toward the stern where Mia and Rami were standing silently. Jack was perched in the crow's nest and the selkies were standing around, all heavily armed. The elves were sharpening their swords and knives on the steps leading up to the stern of the ship. Alpha was standing watch on the port side of the ship while Sly remained at the starboard. There was a distinct uneasiness felt by everyone on the ship, which permeated the air and reflected in their rigid stances.

The night had been silent until an enormous explosion on the island shattered the quiet. They had seen a pillar of flame in the distance, which made Jensen's heart skip a few beats. Both he and Sly had been trying to get in touch with Isis without success. Radar couldn't find her on the video feeds she had access to, though she thought she had glimpsed her on one of the feeds in the necromancers' ballroom.

"Well, at least the fire is a good sign for once," Sly mentioned as she checked her pistol. "Blitz is *very* good at blowing shit up. I rather like that about her."

Jensen felt his phone vibrate in the inner pocket of his vest and he quickly pulled it out, thankful to have something else to focus on.

"Jensen, we've been able to negotiate for the Seelie Court to open their door to Earth," Lilly's voice explained hurriedly. "But the humans have to be blindfolded before they get on the ship and the blindfolds must remain on until the door to the Seelie Court is concealed again."

"Thank you, Lilly," Jensen said, looking over to Sly and giving her a thumbs up. She looked indifferent as she turned her attention back to the pistol, turning her gaze briefly out into the night. Jensen said goodbye before hanging up, slipping the sleek silver phone back into his inner pocket.

"Good news?" Nero called from the bow.

"Mostly," Jensen answered. "We have a way to Earth. It's just a matter of reaching it."

"Ah, we've gotten through much worse," Nero responded, playfully nudging a selkie who was standing near him. Jensen smiled and laughed softly, wishing he had his friend's optimism. Their earpieces crackled to life.

"I'm seeing disturbances in the water both in the north and south," Jack's calm voice filtered clearly through the small communication devices. "No visual on what is causing it, but it would be prudent to remain on your guard."

Jensen swallowed and looked over to Sly, who raised her eyebrows a bit but didn't react otherwise. She was remarkably unfazed, even for Sly. A cool wind swept through the ship, brushing over Jensen's face. It was refreshing in the otherwise humid night.

Noticing Radar sitting on her own in front of the door that led to the sleeping quarters, Jensen wandered over to her and sat down nearby, careful to remain outside her personal space. She was looking at the screen, as she had been for most of the day.

"You know, it would be okay if you took a break," Jensen said quietly. "I'm sure Jack wouldn't mind watching the feeds for a bit."

"This is the job I'm best suited for," Radar replied without looking up from the screen. Jensen couldn't help but smile as he put his head back against the wood behind them and closed his eyes. He hated waiting, especially before an expected attack. He never knew what to do with himself and the tension that built up in his shoulders often made him ache.

"Do a lot of surveillance work at Grenich?" Jensen asked, opening his eyes and looking over at Radar. She nodded, tapping at a picture on the screen and moving it so that it was in the center before enlarging it a little. Jensen turned his gaze back up to the stars overhead. The sky sparkled with a rainbow of colors, practically every star a different shade. The Seelie Court nights were truly a sight to behold and Jensen didn't think he would ever grow tired of the vibrant colors in the world.

"What is she . . . ?"

Jensen turned his attention back to Radar, noticing her squinting at the screen and holding it closer to her face. She rubbed the bottom of her chin and mumbled something under her breath. Jensen straightened up and craned his neck, trying to see what had her attention.

"Radar, what's going on? Is something wrong?"

Radar opened her mouth to respond, but closed it again as she studied the screen closer. Her glowing brown eyes suddenly widened significantly and her grip tightened on the tablet.

"What is she *doing*?" she asked to herself, tapping the middle screen to enlarge it. Jensen caught Sly's eyes and gestured for her to come over, which the shape shifter promptly did. She slid her pistol in its holster and stood in front of the two shape shifters, her hands on her hips as she looked to them expectantly.

"Okay, what has gone to shit now?" Sly asked, drawing Radar's attention to her. The E-series quickly got to her feet and turned so that Sly and Jensen could see the screen. Both of them watched as Isis grappled with an incredibly tall man. They were both tackled by a large werehyena and Jensen couldn't help but wince. The force with which they hit the ground made his ribs ache. Isis squirmed out from beneath the enormous wereanimal and sprinted away, sliding under some kind of blade that swept out from a shadowy corner. There was chaos all around her and multiple fires had already broken out. The nice little town was no more. It more resembled a hellish underworld with monsters prowling throughout the streets.

"I don't have a visual on the bus, but Blitz keeps turning up on every security feed in the town," Radar explained, running a hand over her short hair. "She's intentionally placing herself in the middle of the cameras and I don't understand why. If I can see her, so can anyone else who's watching, which means Set's sons have almost certainly seen her."

Jensen watched the screen, tilting it a little for a better view. Isis dispatched an 8-series with her usual frightening ease, her sais slashing and stabbing with precision. Once the body fell, Isis turned around and her eyes fixed on the camera. Her chest was rising and falling steadily, a little faster than was usual but it was probably due to the adrenaline. Spinning the sais expertly and with ease so that

336

she held one across her body and the other pointed toward her hip, Isis continued to stare at the camera. Then, she dropped her arms to her sides, turned, and continued walking down the road.

"She wants them to see her," Jensen murmured, barely loud enough to be heard. Sly watched the screen, pursing her lips and raising an eyebrow. Jensen met her gaze and stuck his hands in his pockets.

"What do you think? Is she trying to lure or distract?" Sly asked. Jensen shook his head and gave a small shrug. Whatever she was trying to do, it was thought out and had some purpose.

"Set's sons will not act impulsively," Radar mentioned. "If she's trying to lure them out, this won't work."

"No, they don't strike me as the type to do their own dirty work," Sly agreed. "They'd likely send out their guards."

Radar's eyes widened again and she stared at Sly. "But . . . that's very unwise. They'll tear her apart."

Sly smiled and was about to respond when a sudden loud bang, followed by a bright pink light, exploded over their heads. Both Sly and Jensen turned their attention to the sky, staring as another enormous firework, a bright green one with red inside, exploded over their ship and dissolved into a shower of sparks.

"What. The. Fuck," Sly yelled over another firework. Jensen looked over to Alpha, who met his gaze and spread her hands, obviously having no idea what the hell was going on.

"Don't suppose there's any chance this is a celebration of our victory," Nero called over to them, amused. Jensen looked around at the selkies and elves, who were staring up at the sky, all looking puzzled and some of the younger selkies appeared rather unnerved.

"It's a distraction!" Jensen yelled. "Keep your eyes out over the waters!"

"Dammit!" Sly followed him as he climbed up to where

the captain stood. Suddenly, the boat violently rocked to the side as something smashed into it underwater.

"If that's a wereshark, I fucking quit!" Alpha yelled over to them. Both Jensen and Sly gripped the sides of the ship as it rocked again. Jensen's stomach flipped, unused to being on the water for so long. He had never really been great on the water — it was more his late sister's department.

"What the hell is going on?" Steve yelled up to them as he emerged from the sleeping quarters with a selkie. The selkie quickly ran to the stern of the ship, reaching an empty space between other selkies.

"They're probably trying to provoke us into using our weapons," Jensen replied, before calling out, "Stay calm and nobody go in the water for the time being. If something attacks, use your blades. Bullets are a last resort until instructed otherwise."

"Never hurts to be too careful, right Aldridge?" Sly quipped with a teasing smile, tightly gripping the side when another collision rocked the ship. She looked less than thrilled with movement, but obviously had better sea legs than Jensen.

"In my experience," Jensen replied, cautiously peering over the side to try and catch a glimpse of whatever was hitting the ship. The sound and light from the fireworks continued roaring in the night, but the light wasn't strong enough to illuminate the dark waters below. Another violent crash caused Jensen to fall to his knees and he gasped when he put weight on his wounded shoulder, which was throbbing.

"If this continues, I'm going to have to haul anchors and position the ship further back," the captain warned, clutching the wheel when the boat rocked back and forth again.

"We can't leave without our people," Jensen argued.

"We won't be much good to them if the ship sinks," the captain replied tersely. Jensen gritted his teeth, steadying himself. He opened his mouth to argue when he heard Steve shout his name. Stumbling over to the rail that overlooked the deck, doing his best to protect his injured shoulder, Jensen's eyes scanned the deck until he saw the protector on the stern. He was helping two other selkies fight off a larger man with glowing gray eyes, who was trying to drag a third selkie off the edge.

Jensen cursed under his breath and started to make his way down the steps, Sly close on his heels, warning him against doing something stupid. Another crash sent them careening forward, landing heavily on their hands and knees. Jensen nearly passed out from the sharp pain that shot through him. *Note to self, don't do that,* he thought as he blinked a few times to clear his vision. More light filled the sky and illuminated the deck. Jensen was starting to find his feet again when a form darted past him.

Looking up again, Jensen felt horror fill his being when he saw Rami take a running leap at the man, tackling him over the railing and over the edge of the ship. He heard Mia yell out the experiment's name and Jensen quickly scrambled to his feet, running to where the experiment had gone over. He desperately sought out any sign of the A-series, focusing on the ripples of water. Next to him, Keane slid to a halt at the railing, his own eyes scanning the ripples in the waves. Jensen looked over at the elf after a moment and the elf met his eyes, shaking his head mournfully.

Another violent crash caused Jensen to lose his footing and sit down hard on the deck. The selkie whom Rami had saved offered him their hand, which he gratefully accepted. He looked over at Nero and Steve, both of whom looked shocked.

"Oh fuck," Steve suddenly said, pointing off into the distance. Jensen looked to where Steve was pointing. He felt his stomach sink when he spotted an enormous ship, at least twice the size of the one they were on, heading straight for them. A flag with the symbol of Grenich was fluttering in the sky at the top of the ship, illuminated by another large firework. It looked much more modern than the ship they were on and Jensen was relieved to see there weren't any visible cannons on the ship. It was a small comfort, but he would take what he could get under the circumstances. Running a hand over his mouth, he stared at the ship and prayed that the Four would hurry up. Jensen was fairly certain they were in desperate need of backup soon.

CHAPTER THIRTEEN

Isis ran down the street, buildings becoming a blur as she bolted past them. The acrid smell of smoke and burning materials invaded her nose, almost choking her. The strap from the mostly empty drawstring bag crossed her chest, occasionally bumping against her hip as she kept running. The 8-series had started burning whatever they could to keep the werehyenas at bay. The werehyenas had charged a lot more aggressively, which resulted in far more pandemonium than Isis had originally anticipated. Spotting a sturdy lamppost nearby, Isis ran and grabbed hold of it, swinging her body around so the tops of her feet smashed into the head of a werehyena. The animal howled as it was sent sprawling, shaking its head. Isis pulled out her sais and slashed open the creature's throat before burying the longest prong of the sai in the werehyena's eye. Quickly changing her direction, Isis ran back toward the center of town. Her eyes were sharp as she continued to look for any sign of Nick Chance or Tracy. Vincent and Vladimir were too careful and would never venture out into a live demonstration, especially not when it resembled a warzone. However, they would likely send at least one guard out for her. She was just too tempting to let escape.

Ducking into a small space between shops, Isis took a minute to catch her breath. Glancing out into the street, she could hear gunfire close by and could faintly smell a few handlers in the vicinity. They would hang back until the experiments had cleared the streets, but she needed to keep track of them as well. Isis had been running and fighting for a long time, three hours to her estimate. Swallowing, she figured she had at least another hour and a half before she had to make a mad dash for the rendezvous point at the shoreline. She was saving her bullets for that last run, since she was unsure how many werehyenas would be lurking in the forest. Conserving bullets was the wisest strategy.

Her gaze was drawn to a peculiar wooden box, which looked strangely out of place, across the street in the doorway of one of the shops. It was larger, very ordinary looking, and there were two thick straps running around it. The plain box was completely innocuous except for the crest burned into the wood above the iron latch: the seal of the royal line of guardians. The wood seemed to glisten, even in the dim firelight, and Isis could sense an aura of power about it. A nearby fire created heat shimmers, which gave the box an even more ethereal appearance.

"The Box of Original Elements," a familiar voice behind her purred. Isis turned and let out a gasp when she felt the sharp blade of a knife slide between her ribs, just under her heart and lungs. The tip of the knife struck one of her lower ribs and Isis couldn't help but whimper softly. Eris gripped the back of her neck and leaned in close, pressing the knife up to the hilt.

"Thanks for the escape, dear niece. It is *most* appreciated," she whispered, kissing her ear before mercilessly shoving her off the blade. Isis fell backward, panting for air as she tried to get her bearings back and not fall on the medium-sized duffle she still carried. In the back of her mind, she noticed the wound wasn't healing as fast as it should have, which meant the blade had been coated in something. That would certainly make for some complications.

"You're not free yet," Isis warned, pushing herself up to her elbows, ignoring the ache that raced through her. Eris looked over to the woman, disinterested, and shrugged as she continued studying the bloody blade. She snapped her fingers and Isis turned her attention back to the box, which disappeared in a flash of gray and purple mist.

"Minor details, petal," Eris replied, using her knife to gesture around at the chaos that surrounded them. "Might want to worry about yourself. It seems these creatures are attracted to blood, guardian and shape shifter blood in particular. I imagine you're quite the appetizing little morsel. Ta."

With that, Eris sauntered off down the dark street, vanishing in a flash of bright silver light. Isis groaned and rolled onto her side, clumsily pushing herself to her feet. Her hand drifted over to her wound, pressing against it and she closed her eyes briefly. Blood loss could potentially become a hindrance, especially if she didn't find a way to bind it. Moving as fast as she could, Isis moved into the space between the buildings, finding an alley behind them. In the distance, she could see fireworks and figured that was likely where the ship was and therefore the direction she needed to move toward. Isis passed by a window, which exploded outwards and caused her to wince and duck her head, flames licking the space overhead. Isis paused when she reached a small gap between buildings, pressing her back against a brick wall and cautiously peering around the corner. A pair of werehyenas were eating an eight-series they had managed to catch. Isis swallowed and began to cautiously step out, keeping her senses sharp. Carnivores wouldn't leave a fresh kill, not even if they were wereanimals.

A sudden shot caused her to quickly duck back behind the safety of the wall. She heard one of the werehyenas chortle before another shot rang out. Peering out from behind the wall again, Isis noticed the two werehyenas were lying dead in the street. Closing her eyes, Isis pressed her senses outwards. The electric barrier that had prevented the werehyenas from entering the town was completely destroyed, which meant appearing a short distance wouldn't be too much trouble. Since she was now fighting with a disadvantage, Isis decided it was a worthwhile risk. Closing her eyes, she concentrated on the glade she and Jade had come across when escaping the woods. She felt inner warmth fill her and a bright light enveloped her followed by the familiar soft sound similar to glass breaking.

When she opened her eyes again, Isis was standing in the center of the glade. She let out a breath of relief, grimacing at the ache in her wound. The sound of a gun hammer being cocked made her spin around and she found herself looking down the barrel of Tracy's gun. The Grenich enforcer smirked and clicked her tongue at Isis.

"Tsk, tsk, tsk. So close," she said with mock sympathy. As she opened her mouth to say something else, Isis immediately dropped to the ground and swept her leg out, hooking her foot around Tracy's ankles and knocking her flat on her back. Scrambling over to her, Isis grabbed hold of her wrist and slammed it to the ground, fighting to loosen her grip on the gun. Tracy let out a growl and punched Isis right in her wounded side. Isis' vision went momentarily white. Tracy threw her weight to the side, winding up straddled on top of Isis. She squeezed the wounded experiment's sides with her thighs and Isis thrashed about wildly as she tried to get free. Every small movement was agonizing, but she refused to die at the Grenich enforcer's hands. Tracy fired near her ear, the high-pitched ringing sound making her wince.

Left with few options, Isis curled up a little and latched onto the back of Tracy's hand with her teeth, biting down hard. The Grenich enforcer screamed and squeezed tighter with her thighs, but Isis held fast and ripped a sizeable chunk of flesh off the back of Tracy's hand. She spit it out and threw her weight to the side, still fighting for control of the gun. Tracy suddenly brought her legs to her chest and kicked Isis off her. Isis slammed to the ground a few feet away but quickly got to her feet and drew her own gun as Tracy stood up. Each woman held their gun trained between the other's eyes and Tracy started chuckling, shaking her head. Isis focused on remaining still, doing her best not to waver on her feet.

"Oh 7-299, even when you're wounded, you *are* good for sparring, I'll give you that," she complimented. Isis squinted as she tried to read the woman across from her. *If she had a kill order, she would have done it already,* she realized. Tracy raised an eyebrow, obviously reading the experiment's thoughts. Isis swallowed, trying to clear her mind. A quiet breeze drifted over them, brushing up Tracy's short blonde hair.

Another firework split the sky in the distance as the two women remained locked in a standoff. Tracy watched Isis, patiently, baring her teeth as a smile grew on her face. Isis swallowed and kept her gun aimed at the enforcer. There was a sudden rustling sound and out of the corner of her eye, Isis thought she saw a shadow. Tracy immediately turned to look behind her, which was exactly what Isis had been hoping she'd do. Holstering her weapon, Isis ran forward and leapt up, putting all her strength into her elbow as she slammed it into Tracy's face. The force behind the blow knocked the woman flat on her back and momentarily stunned her. Isis pressed the advantage as she slammed her foot down on the woman's wrist and twisted it, grinding the small bones under her boot. Leaning her weight on the foot, she quickly grabbed Tracy's gun from her loosened grip and hurled it into the forest, where it disappeared amongst the dark trees. A small but still solid weight landed on Isis' back, causing her to stumble forward a few steps with a cry of pain. Tracy wrapped an arm around Isis' throat, attempting to cut off her air.

"Do you know what your problem is, 7-299?" Tracy whispered, her lips pressed against Isis' ear, her arm tightening around the experiment's neck. "You are ungrateful. Lord Set has given you a great gift, favored you, unleashed your true potential; he made you powerful and strong. And this is how you repay him: throwing a temper tantrum, like a child. You see, love, that is the difference between you and me. You chose to fight against what you really are and I chose to embrace it. That is why I am stronger and why I shall always win."

"You are wrong," Isis got out from behind gritted teeth. "That is why you will lose."

Isis threw her body forward into a somersault, slamming Tracy's back into the solid ground, causing the revenant to grunt in pain. Scrambling out from the momentarily loosened grip, Isis quickly got to her feet again.

She barely had a chance to catch her breath before Tracy struck at her with a cross punch. Latching onto her wrist and spinning into the smaller woman, Isis slammed her elbow into the revenant's temple. Spinning, Isis kicked Tracy in the chest, knocking her away. She leapt into an aerial cartwheel, her feet striking Tracy in the face and forcing her back even further, making her sit down hard on the ground. Isis took a few large steps back, putting a good distance between the revenant and herself. She could feel the warm wet blood pouring from her wound and did her best to ignore it, though she knew it was making her fighting somewhat sloppier.

The enforcer slowly got to her feet and touched a finger to her bloodied lip, rubbing the tips of her fingers together. She turned furious eyes onto the experiment standing a few feet away. Isis knew she wasn't going to be able to stay upright for much longer. Tracy almost certainly knew this and it explained her nonchalant approach to the struggle.

Another firework exploded in the sky, showering multicolored sparks and the smoky scent filled the air. Isis reached behind her back to where the small drawstring bag was and slid her hands inside it. She swallowed as she focused on keeping her mind completely blank, watching the dangerous woman's every move. Somewhere in the woods, she heard the wheezing of the bus's brakes. Her fingers brushed over two guardian glass bottles, as she searched out the object she was looking for.

"You are going back to Grenich, seven series," Tracy spoke soothingly, as though talking to a spooked wild horse. "If I have to drag your half-dead carcass back to a laboratory myself, you *will* go back."

Isis shook her head, her hands finally finding the spherical objects she had been seeking. "You greatly overestimate your abilities."

Yanking her hands out of the bag and flipping the switches to arm them, Isis hurled two spherical grenades at the revenant's face before turning on the balls of her feet and dashing for the woods. She heard the grenades explode, but paid it no heed as she ran through the reaching vines and branches. One sharp vine slashed her face as she darted past it, cutting open her cheek. The sweet earthy scent of the forest invaded her nose and she could barely detect the synthetic pollen anymore. Occasionally, Isis would slip and slide in the slick mud, but she kept pushing forward.

Glancing over her shoulder, Isis looked for any sign of Tracy, but saw nothing other than the unnaturally dark shadows. She couldn't even see a glimpse of the clearing anymore, just a wall of blackness. Pausing briefly, shrouded by the shadows, she reached back into the bag for the last items in there: two sturdy bottles filled with a glowing liquid. Carefully removing one bottle, Isis glanced around to make sure she was alone. The liquid was so bright it illuminated a large circle around Isis with a soft turquoise glow. Pulling the large cork out of the top, she set it on the ground and unzipped her catsuit, stripping it down to her waist, gritting her teeth at the pain from her wound. Carefully dipping her pinky finger in the glowing liquid — which felt more silky than wet — Isis pulled her finger out and stared in shock. The substance enhanced the subtle gleam in her flesh, making it shimmer and shine as though it were made of diamonds. Looking around, she noticed the menacing trees and vines were actually recoiling from the light.

Isis took a few breaths before massaging the strange substance around and inside the deep wound. It didn't burn or even hurt, which was unexpected. Instead, soothing warmth spread through the wound, which slowly started to knit together. It would take a while and she would still need a shot of adrenaline, but at least blood loss was no longer a concern for the time being.

Isis quickly pulled her catsuit on and zipped it up before securing the cork back on the top of the bottle, looking around at the dark woods that surrounded her. The liquid was so bright that it created an aura around her, which was probably going to be a beacon to the necromancers and werehyenas alike. Shoving the bottles back inside the drawstring bag, she secured it over her shoulder and continued on her way, brushing a hand against her stinging cheek. Isis moved at a brisk pace and could soon smell the faint scents of oil and gasoline in the air. The bus was nearby, but that wasn't all. There was another fainter scent on the air, one she had been hoping to detect for a while.

It was the scent of the ocean.

She could hear waves in the distance and the trees had thinned out somewhat. Without the barrier running around the forest, it was much easier to navigate. Isis started running toward the smell of the bus, but froze when there was a loud explosion and the unmistakable flickering light of a fire. The smell of burning fur and flesh suddenly invaded her nose.

~~*~*~*

Jade gritted her teeth when she heard the explosion. She and the surviving passengers from the bus were hiding behind some large boulders. The bus had been great cover when driving past the town, though they had lost two A-series to the snipers. Once they reached the living forest, they had run into a problem in the form of two extremely determined werehyenas. They had torn a huge hole in the side of the bus and nearly yanked another A-series from within. While the group had been able to deter them a little with bullets, they hadn't been able to get rid of them entirely. That was when Gem mentioned she had kept some C4 and could rig the bus to explode. Jo and Reva sliced their palms open a few times, spreading their blood around to lure the werehyenas while Gem rigged up the explosives and the protectors herded the newly blindfolded humans off the bus. Once they were all a safe distance away, Gem pulled out the remote and closed her eyes, tilting her head a little as she listened. After a short time, she pressed the button and the explosion echoed throughout the forest.

"Jade!" Alex called out and pointed in front of her. Jade turned to look where her teammate was indicating and felt a rush of relief wash over her. There was sand, beautiful tan sand, a short distance away from them. She could hear the soft lapping of water, even with all the other chaos. They had actually done it: they had gotten clear of the deadly forest and now they just had to ferry everyone to the ship. Jade looked back to Alex and Shae, both of whom looked utterly exhausted but hopeful.

"Okay, we can fit about six in the boat, so we'll have to do at least three trips. I need two A-series who are strong rowers and we need to do this as fast as possible. We don't have very much time," Jade explained, looking back into the woods when she heard a suspicious bird call. "Two shape shifters taking the form of a whale or dolphin or any kind of fast sea creature would also be beneficial. The humans need the boat, but the rest of us can shift into birds."

"We can cover the rest of you as you make for the ship," Shae added. "Ammo's running pretty low, so we'll do our best to make it last."

Jade cautiously raised her head to look over the boulder. She could see smoke and flames nearby, but she didn't see any trace of the werehyenas. Turning back to the group, she gestured for them to start moving to the beach. The A-series formed a tight circle around the humans along with the protectors. Jade started leading them toward the water, keeping her senses sharp for any unwanted company. The thundering and sizzling of fireworks got clearer as they approached the beach.

When her boots hit the soft sand, Jade immediately looked out at the ship. She pressed a button in her earpiece, pausing when she saw another ship, a more modern one, some distance away. Squinting, Jade noticed an unusual flag when a silver firework exploded, illuminating the scene on the water.

"Sly? Radar? Anyone there?" Jade asked.

"Jade! Everyone, I've got Jade on the com!" Nero's eager voice filtered through her earpiece, followed closely by a string of curses and strange popping noises. Jade gritted her teeth when she noticed how far the water was traveling over the sands. It had almost reached the boat, which they had pulled quite far inland. Glancing over her shoulder, Jade gestured for two A-series to go secure the boat and they promptly moved to comply.

"Everything okay?" Jade asked, checking her gun as she turned her attention back to the woods behind her. The rest of the A-series were already helping the first group of humans into the boat. She noticed Jo trying to get Noor into the boat, but the young girl kept climbing back out. A strong wind swept over the beach and through the trees, brushing through everyone's hair. Looking up to the sky, Jade noticed it was becoming gray. It would be dawn soon and she could practically hear the ominous ticking of a clock.

"Uh, that's a negative. Grenich appears to have pulled out *a lot* of stops," Nero answered, cursing as the popping sounded again. "They've got fucking drones and something's hitting the bottom of the boat. We're currently getting hit on all sides."

"Hang on," Jade called over to the A-series before turning her attention back to the earpiece. "Nero, do you think you guys can fight them off just for a bit, give the humans a window to get on the ship?"

"Maybe if we had more experiments. We've pretty much spent all our bullets," Nero replied. "I hate to say it, but we're basically sitting ducks right now."

Jade bit her bottom lip and put her hands on her hips. Noticing movement out of the corner of her eye, Jade spun around and drew her gun. Immense relief settled over her when she saw Isis walking down the shoreline toward them. It was quickly replaced by confusion when Jade noticed that Isis seemed to be glistening more than usual. That was . . . strange.

"Isis!" Shae called out and Isis looked up. Shae ran over to meet her and Jade followed close behind. Isis paused when they both reached her, her gaze traveling out to the ship.

"Don't suppose you managed to find Eris," Jade mentioned and Isis nodded.

"She caught me by surprise, managed to stab me," Isis said, pulling the strap of drawstring bag over her head. "One of the drawbacks of using blades is that you have to be in close quarters to your opponent."

Before Jade could ask after her well-being, Isis opened the bag at her side, revealing two glass bottles filled with a glowing turquoise liquid with specks of silver. The light from the liquid was so bright it illuminated all their faces. Jade's mouth dropped open as she carefully took the bag from Isis, examining the bottles in stunned silence.

"It works," Isis commented, her gaze straying back to the water. "My healing ability is hampered, so I tested it. It didn't heal the internal damage, which it wouldn't since it is guardian magic, but it did seal it."

"Betha's Tears," Shae breathed, unable to conceal her awe. Neither shape shifter had seen anything quite so beautiful before. Isis nodded as she moved past them, her eyes not moving from the enormous ship in the distance. Crossing her arms over her chest, she bit the inside of her cheek and tapped one finger on her upper arm.

"Isis, we've got to get out of here," Jade said as she pulled the strap of the bag over her own shoulder. "But the ship's being attacked — drones according to Nero and something is hitting them below too. We can't transport our guests under such heavy fire and we're running out of time. The sky's already starting to lighten."

Isis turned sharply, raising her hands, and Jade followed her gaze to where Noor was tugging at one of her legs. The young girl looked up at the seven-series with bright brown eyes, smiling happily. They had been having trouble getting her to keep the blindfold on. She wrapped her arms around Isis' legs, hugging her tightly. Isis stared at her, obviously unsure what to do in the situation. Jade looked over to the trees when she heard rustling and a familiar eerie chortling. Isis looked back toward the trees, her glowing green eyes scanning the shadows. Taking a few steps forward, the sand not even crunching under her light gait, Isis stared at the darkness in front of her face. Jade hung back, watching her teammate. Looking around at the open shoreline, she thought about what they were facing. Of all the places Jade had expected to die, the Seelie Court had certainly not been one of them. Then again, she had never really thought she would ever find herself in the Seelie Court in the first place. *My life really is strange,* she realized with a rueful smile.

"What do you think? Is it time to think of a last stand?" Jade asked, drawing Isis' attention back to her. Isis turned to her teammate, studying her for a moment, before looking past her to the opposing vessel.

"Normals, you're always too eager to die," she muttered as she stepped past Jade. "Get the humans into the boat, start ferrying them to the ship. Send a few A-series ahead to take care of the underwater attack, four or five should suffice."

The sand near them suddenly exploded, shooting straight up in the air and creating a wall. Both Isis and Jade took a step back with Shae letting out a yelp of surprise. Isis dropped her shoulders and rolled her neck, circling her arms to loosen her muscles. The water started churning and the waves became more violent, splashing at their legs.

"They're going to try using whatever they can against us. They're in control here, which gives them a significant advantage over us," Isis mentioned, lifting her chin up toward the group at the small rowboat. "Once the guardians start submerging the island, it's only going to make things more difficult. If we want to escape, we need to start moving."

"Wait, where are you going?" Jade asked, glancing to the trees when she heard rustling. The fireworks had been drowning out most of the noise, but now it seemed like every little sound was magnified to impossible levels. She was on high-alert and any sound could be a potential attack.

"I'm going to take care of the most pressing issue," Isis mentioned, nodding toward the other ship as she gently pushed Noor away from her. Jade opened her mouth to protest but Isis crouched down and swiftly began shifting into a different form. Her neck elongated and shrunk, black feathers sliding over and replacing the clothing she wore. Her eyes became round and glowing brown. Within seconds, a raven stood in front of Jade. Shaking her head once, Isis quickly spread her wings and took off, disappearing in the night sky. Looking over to the young girl, Jade couldn't help but smile at the look of amazement on Noor's face as she stared at the sky where the raven had been.

"You know, her impulsiveness is *really* starting to wear thin," Shae commented dryly.

"It has been wearing thin for quite some time, but at least she usually has some idea of what she's doing," Jade mentioned, turning when she heard a snarl. She felt her heart start to hammer when she spotted a pair of glowing gray eyes in the darkness behind them. Reaching over and grabbing Shae's arm, Jade motioned over to the boat and looked pointedly at Noor. Shae swallowed and crouched down in front of Noor, occasionally glancing over in the direction of the forest.

"Honey, I need you to listen to me and do exactly what I say: run for the boat and don't look back, okay? Not for any reason," Shae whispered. Jade stayed in front of them, her hand drifting over to the firearm in the holster on her hip. It would take at least two rounds to put the thing down, if she hit her mark both times. Wereanimals were difficult targets on account of how fast they moved.

"Go now," Shae whispered as she stood up. Jade heard the girl's soft footsteps in the sand and the werehyena lunged out from the shadows. Both Jade and Shae drew their guns at the same time and fired.

~~*~*~*

"Father is not going to be happy about this," Vincent observed in a sing-song voice. Vladimir ignored him as he observed the flaming wreckage of what had once been a fairly well-set up training field. It wasn't quite as impressive as some of the cities their mother had razed, but it was still decent. It would have been much more enjoyable had it not been one of their more lucrative demonstration locations. Their guests hadn't been overly impressed with the demonstration, until the werehyenas had breached the town and the bloodbath began. Vladimir couldn't help but admire the seven-series: it had been a rather dangerous risk she had taken, but it had been effective. He was starting to understand his father's obsession with that particular female.

"We have other locations," Vladimir finally answered with a shrug as he kicked at some flaming debris. He was wearing a bulletproof vest over his expensive silk shirt and a heavy helmet sat on his head. It was a sweltering night and the fire wasn't helping matters. He just wanted to do a last check of the damages and then go home. The paperwork was going to be a nightmare and Vladimir wanted to get a head start on it. That way he might have at least a tiny chance at actually having some downtime over the weekend.

"Sir," an eight-series approached, sidestepping the bullet-riddled corpse of a werehyena. "We've received word that they're still on the beach. Most of the werehyenas have been put down but there are seven or eight still in the forest. Do you want them put down?"

"No, let the defectives take care of the werehyenas. With any luck, the two groups will kill each other. Has Chance sunk the ship yet?"

The eight series shook his head. "No, the selkies and shape shifters are proving to be capable fighters."

"He's making excuses so that he can fuck around even more, like the goddamn child he is. Tell Tracy to get him under control. We don't have all night," Vladimir ordered, irritation creeping into his voice. He was sick and tired of Chance's antics, as were his parents. The man was impossible to control and driven almost purely by sadism. The attack on the laboratory had made him even worse as now he felt he had something to prove. The eight-series nodded, bowed his head, and then moved away to carry out his orders.

Vladimir glared at his younger brother when he chuckled. "I don't see what you find so entertaining. Chance is entirely your fault seeing as you're the one who has never been able to keep it in your pants."

"Cattiness doesn't suit you, brother," Vincent replied dismissively, unbothered as he kept looking at the screen of his phone. He was wearing the same body armor as Vladimir and appeared unconcerned with the destruction surrounding them. He nodded over to a bar across the street, slipping the phone back into his pocket. Vladimir looked to where his brother gestured, squinting when he saw the lights were on. The handlers had already evacuated the few survivors, moving them to a debriefing center. All the buildings were empty, or they should have been. Vincent approached him, standing just behind his brother.

"We appear to have a visitor waiting for us, according to the surveillance cameras that are still working," Vincent explained and Vladimir could hear the smile in his voice. His brother had always been the more accommodating host and better in social situations. Vladimir preferred to remain silent and observe, which actually complimented his brother's strengths. They worked well together, which was why their father had made them the faces of the Corporation.

"Think we should go say hello?" Vladimir asked, turning his head a little.

"Oh yes," Vincent answered, putting a hand on his older brother's shoulder when he reached for his gun. "None of that, brother. We have the advantage, no need to act aggressively right off the bat."

Vladimir gave his brother an annoyed look, but dropped his hand away from the gun. He didn't like going into situations unarmed, but it was sometimes necessary. The two crossed the street and Vladimir carefully pulled open the door. Vincent followed him inside the bar.

The colorful jukebox was blasting some sort of classic rock, which sounded like noise to Vladimir. The lights were all on, revealing the surprisingly clean and well-kept space. Stretched out across the polished mahogany bar on her stomach, was a dark-haired guardian woman. Her skin glistened even in the artificial light and her light blue eyes sparkled with mischief. She wore slacks and a nice dark blue top, not a dress like guardian women typically wore. Her features had a girlishness about them, though the way she held herself suggested she was older than she appeared, probably much older than either of them. A smile, sharp as a knife, split her ruby red lips in a faintly menacing way. Dark eyeshadow made her light blue irises stand out even more and her black hair was tied back tightly, not a strand out of place. Her legs were held behind her, swaying slowly back and forth. Her long fingers loosely traced the thin edge of a martini glass in front of her, which held a bright pink drink, a Cosmopolitan from the looks of it.

Vladimir's eyes were drawn to the ancient-looking wooden box that sat on a pair of bar stools next to her. There was a very appealing aura about it, a sense that it contained some sort of power. Vladimir glanced at the woman, who was watching him and his brother with a raised eyebrow. She almost appeared to be daring them to approach the box, even as she continued running her fingers around the glass. Vladimir took a step forward and the guardian woman swept her arm out, causing the unused bar stools to slide across the floor and form a barrier between the two men and her. The woman grabbed her glass and tossed the Cosmopolitan in an arc, causing them both to jump at the sound of shattering glass.

"Ah, ah," the woman warned, with a menacing smile. "Didn't mummy ever teach you boys not to touch another's things? It's very rude and I detest rudeness, almost as much as I do entitled brats."

Vladimir gritted his teeth, a red haze settling over his vision. He would have drawn his gun if Vincent hadn't raised his hand, warning his brother to keep a cool head.

"Forgive him, my lady. My brother has never been good when it comes to etiquette," Vincent said, laying on the charm. "I am Vincent Carver and this is my elder brother, Vladimir. I must admit, I didn't expect to find a guardian here. It's quite dangerous out there, especially for a daughter of the Meadows."

The woman laughed with a roll of her eyes, obviously amused. "Are you trying to frighten me, child? Save it for your guinea pigs and underlings."

"I merely meant that —"

"Carver, bit on the nose isn't it? Rather uncreative, I expected more from the big scary necromancer so feared by guardians and protectors alike," the woman continued, looking them up and down. "Though, just meeting the two of you has shown that creating things isn't his strong suit."

The woman dropped her long legs off the edge of the bar, swinging up into a sitting position. She gestured toward the bar stools that stood in front of the two men. The brothers exchanged a look and Vincent cautiously sat down. Vladimir looked back to the woman, who smiled at him in a disconcerting way, before taking a seat. The stools were suddenly dragged forward and the two men found themselves sitting at the bar with Vincent nearest to the strange woman.

"I wish to be taken to your sire, for I have important matters to discuss with him," the guardian practically purred as she ran the backs of her fingers down Vincent's face. "And as you can plainly see, I come bearing gifts."

Vladimir frowned when he thought he saw her fingers shimmer. Some kind of guardian trickery, he realized as he reached over and grabbed the woman's arm. She turned her icy blue eyes to him, unbothered by his touch. Suddenly, the world seemed to melt away and Vladimir stared at the woman's face. He wondered how he hadn't noticed how beautiful she was when they first entered, how perfect. All he wanted to do was make her happy, fulfill her every desire. The world continued to fall away and he realized that she was the only thing that mattered. Spending one minute in her presence was all anyone could ever want and they had been in her presence for several.

"There's a good boy," she whispered when he released her arm, stunned that he had the gall to lay hands on her perfect flesh. "I'm afraid I have been a little rude and do beg your forgiveness. It has been some time since I have been free and able to interact with others. I am Eris, rightful queen of the humans, breaker of minds, dreaded by the guardians and shape shifters alike. I was chained, but now I am free again and I wish to ally with Set and Pyra. I offer the Box of Original Elements as a token of friendship."

Vladimir smiled at the gloriousness of Eris, a thrill of excitement racing through him. She was truly a goddess. They needed another goddess on their side, a strong one like their mother. Vincent also couldn't take his eyes off of her, enthralled by the vision of beauty and power before him. Eris smiled as she looked between them.

"Get on one knee," she commanded and they quickly scrambled off their seats, dropping to one knee in front of her. Vladimir didn't even really feel the shard of glass that dug into his knee or the stinging alcohol that soaked through his pants.

"I overheard a little bird talking about a possible turncoat in the Meadows," Eris mentioned off-handedly, steepling her hands beneath her chin and tapping her index fingers together.

"Father has several contacts in the Meadows," Vincent quickly offered.

"He has one on the High Council," Vladimir added, not about to be outdone by his younger brother. Eris clapped happily as she looked back to them, obviously pleased by their response. Vladimir felt even lighter and thought he might actually float. Eris leaned over to the bar, grabbing a knife she had laid there. She pressed the tip of it to her index finger, her perfect eyes turning back to the two kneeling men.

"That's very good. Oh, we're going to have so much fun together," Eris said, waving the knife around to point at each of them. "Now, you're both going to be good little boys and take me to Daddy, right?"

Vincent and Vladimir both nodded eagerly. Eris nodded over her shoulder toward the box and Vladimir scrambled to his feet, hurrying over to grab it. The guardian gestured for them to lead the way

"But my lady," Vincent said as he climbed to his feet. "We're not done here. The protectors are getting away."

Eris rolled her eyes, obviously not pleased with the response. "Then have your pets take care of it. Is your presence absolutely necessary?"

"Vincent, we were leaving anyway. We can send the handlers back to gather up the remaining eight-series. We still have a few hours before this island is submerged," Vladimir said, shifting the box so that he had a better grip. "Lady Eris wants an audience with Father."

Vincent stared at him and then at Eris, who stuck out her bottom lip in a pout, his shoulders dropping in defeat. He smiled at Eris and nodded.

"You're right, brother. This way, my lady," he said as he offered Eris his elbow, which she gratefully took. Vladimir followed behind them as they left the bar.

~~*~*~*

Isis landed on top of one of the large sails, just under the crow's nest. Her feathers quickly retracted as her normal skin and clothes reformed. She returned to her human form within a matter of seconds. The dark color had protected her from most eyes, but now she was in the heart of a hostile location. Pressing a button in her earpiece, Isis carefully positioned herself so she was as hidden as she could be.

"Radar, if there's any surveillance on this ship, I need

you to hack into it," she whispered, squinting as she tried to catch a glimpse of any crew. It was odd that she hadn't seen anyone on a ship so large. She soon realized why: the deck was filled with a number of drones, all equipped with guns. This was a launch pad for them, one that probably didn't need a living crew on board. That didn't mean there wouldn't be guards, or possibly even Nick Chance.

A firework exploded in the sky, frighteningly close to the ship. Isis instinctively ducked and looked over to where the firework had been. The Tears of Betha had healed her somewhat, but the deep wound still pained her. She definitely needed a shot of adrenaline to restore her regenerative abilities. Checking her balance when a strong wind swept over her, Isis turned her gaze out into the night, looking for anything out of the ordinary.

"On it," Radar's voice responded. "Blitz, you should know . . . we had some casualties, including Rami."

Isis furrowed her brow. "Okay?"

"It is very upsetting to the normals," Radar explained, obviously feeling confused.

"Everything is upsetting to the normals. There's not much we can do about that," Isis replied. She spread her arms and dropped down to the deck, landing silently. She was moving almost the instant she landed, crossing the deck to where the mechanical planes stretched out in front of her. Approaching the closest drone, Isis crouched down to study it. It was definitely meant to be controlled from a different location. Her head jerked up when she heard a soft whooshing and her glowing eyes widened when she spotted one of the sleek drones hovering in the air. Thinking fast and moving faster, Isis dove out of the path of bullets that sprayed at her.

"Radar, I need this ship to be offline and I need that to happen now," Isis said as she dashed away from the pursuing drone. Bullets pierced dangerously close to her and Isis made a beeline for the door that would lead to a more sheltered location. Yanking it open, she moved inside and shut it behind her. Not waiting to see if the drone would continue firing, Isis moved down the cramped hall. Overhead, unnaturally bright lights flickered and buzzed, and she soon noticed a door at the end of the long hall that was ajar. The door was painted yellow and labeled "Bridge."

Drawing her sais, Isis paused at the door and did a mental check of herself to make sure she would be able to fight. When she was satisfied that she was fit enough to face an opponent, she put her shoulder against the door and shoved it open.

Rami jerked around and stared at her, wide eyed, while she held her sais ready. He was soaked and a sopping wet hoodie had been tossed carelessly in the empty seat where a captain would normally sit. Their glowing eyes met and for a moment, they just stared at each other, taken off guard.

"I was told you were dead," Isis mentioned, noticing he was staring at something at her throat. She knew it was likely the charm she wore and spun her sais a few times before returning them to the sheaths she wore about her waist. Looking back to him expectantly, Isis waited for him to respond. Rami shook his head as if to clear it and looked back to her face.

"Shifted into a shark, swam over here and then shifted into a bird, flew up to the deck," he explained, scrubbing his hand through his wet hair roughly, frustrated. "I thought I might be able to figure something out, but Grenich technology is above my skill level. I couldn't even disable the drones."

Isis approached him, glancing briefly to the windows in the front of the room. "What was your plan?"

Rami picked up a flashdrive. "While we were hiding, a couple A-series developed some viruses. They're pretty basic, but we have been able to disrupt some of the systems on the island before. Of course, that led Grenich to develop better firewalls. But we all keep a couple viruses on hand, just in case."

Rami bent down and picked up his shoe off the floor, tossing it to Isis, who caught it. She raised an eyebrow as she examined the sneaker. It was an ordinary cross trainer, but the tongue had been altered to be a hidden pouch, one that could hold a small flashdrive. Raising an eyebrow, Isis ran her hand over the shoe, checking for other hidden pockets. She had seen women hide flashdrives and other useful tools in wedge heels before, but hadn't considered using sneakers for such purposes.

"Impressive," Isis complimented, looking back to him, and Rami smiled a little, ducking his chin down, shyly. She glanced over her shoulder when she thought she heard a door open. Turning back to the bank of computers Rami stood in front of, Isis approached him and looked at the few screens that were on. Technology wasn't her thing either, outside of the occasional data retrieval mission.

"Radar, did you hear all that?" Isis asked.

"Loud and clear, also got a visual on you," the hacker's voice replied. "I've got control of most of the security feeds on the ship, but it's going to take a bit more work to actually gain control of the ship itself. I'm rather interested in the virus the A-series mentioned. I might be able to do something with it, given some time."

"I need the two of you to focus on getting the fleet of drones grounded. I'll figure out what to do about the ship," Isis instructed, looking about their shadowy surroundings again. "I've been on similar vessels and I think I remember enough to disable it. I'm going to give my earpiece to Rami so you can talk him through whatever you need."

Removing the com, Isis handed it to Rami who quickly put it in his own ear. She nodded once at him and he swallowed, obviously out of his element, but turned to the screens. Isis moved past him, drawing her sais again when she reached the door. Stepping out into the narrow hallway, she spun the sleek silver blades a few times. The weight felt good in her hands and the motion soothed her. Turning her head a little, she listened to the faint mechanical sounds emanating from deep inside the ship.

Moving toward the sounds, Isis headed for below deck and the engine room. The pasty bluish white walls blurred together and she peered around a corner, which led to an enormous opening. There should have been some sort of door, but instead there were only dark curtains. Moving to the odd fabric, which felt like stiff plastic, Isis stepped onto a mesh walkway and into a sweltering open space. The entire area was lit with a sickly yellowish green glow and the loud whirring of machinery drowned out all other sounds. Steam occasionally gasped out from pipes in various places. The air was heavy with humidity and she knew she would likely start sweating soon. The walls seemed to be a dark yellow color and glistened with moisture, making everything look as though it were coated with a thin layer of slime.

Walking silently around the mesh walkway that encircled the space, Isis studied the base of a massive transmitter. Moving over to the railing, she leaned her weight against it and looked down to the bottom level of the ship. Sand coated the ground, which made the hair stand up on the back of her neck. The golden sand glistened even in the dim lighting and the sand itself smelled faintly of bleach and the desert. Looking up to the night sky, Isis could just make out a subtle shimmer: a curtain façade, from the outside it would appear as solid ground but it was similar to a two-way mirror. Someone could have been watching and the person on deck would not have known.

Sheathing her sais again, Isis jumped up on the railing, spread her arms, and stepped off. Air rushed past her ears as she dropped to the ground, landing weightlessly in a crouch. Her fingers were buried in the warm soft sand, which felt strangely pleasant. Isis straightened up again, brushing the sand off her hands, her senses alert for anything out of the ordinary. There were three doors at the far end of the ship, all a strange muted yellow color with streaks of white or tan. Isis approached a wall, running her gloved hand over the damp rough surface. Pulling her hand away, strings of goo clung to her palm like mucus. Isis rubbed her fingers together and examined the slimy substance. Sniffing it, she made a face of disgust as the unmistakable stench of rot invaded her sensitive nostrils.

Her attention next turned to the trio of doors and she cautiously approached them, standing in a position that allowed her to look at all three of them. Her hands hovered over her sais, itching to draw the weapons. Moving over to the door on her left, Isis wrapped her hand around the knob and attempted to turn it. The door was locked so she moved on to the next one. After finding all three doors locked, Isis moved back to the wall and walked along it, her eyes searching for a small latch or panel. It would be hidden, but she would see it.

Isis paused when she noticed a ridge that was out of place, swallowing as she reached for it. The sound of a door opening brought her attention back to the three doors.

One slowly swung shut, locking with a soft click that only an experiment's ears could hear over the whir of machinery.

~~*~*~*

Jensen threw himself to the deck as another drone swept overhead, showering the surface with bullets. He noticed Nero pressing himself against the side of the ship a few feet away, looking to his friend with a worried expression. The smell of damp wood invaded Jensen's nose as he kept his head down until the sleek flying machine passed by. Once it was out of sight, Nero ran over to his friend, helping him to his feet. Looking back to the graying sky, Jensen winced at the pain in his shoulder, gently holding it as it protested any movement.

The selkies had brought out impressive shields, which were remarkably effective at shielding them from the deadly projectiles. Every time a drone swept in, they would form a wall over their heads. The attacks under the boat had been gradually lessening and Jensen hoped that it was on account of the A-series, rather than the prelude to some new horror.

"Does Chaos have no sense of honor?" Maeve called over to them and Jensen almost laughed at the question. The elves apparently still believed in honor, how he wished that were a reality. He cringed and instinctively ducked when a firework exploded over head.

"From our limited experience, he does what it takes to win," Nero shouted in response, pausing to fire a few rounds at the circling drone, smiling when he managed to hit a window. "This is par for the course for the Grenich Corporation. We should all thank our lucky stars that he hasn't unleashed a swarm of experiments to go with it."

"We got incoming!" Sly yelled from the port side. "First group of humans on boat. We're going to need some serious cover over here."

Alpha started directing the selkies where to stand and they were quick to comply, while Jensen and Nero moved to provide cover fire. Jensen looked over to where Jack and Radar were standing. Radar was hurriedly putting something together as Jack and Steve stood guard, both watching the sky intently. Jensen motioned to Keane to take his spot protecting the selkies, which the elf quickly did. Jensen ran up the steps to where the two experiments were.

"What's going on?" Jensen asked Steve, yelling to be heard over the gunfire.

"Radar's going to try and lasso the drone, I think," Steve explained, not taking his eyes off the menacing craft. He winced when it fired at the selkies again, who sought shelter under their shields. Bullets sparked off the colorful surfaces, clanging loudly as they struck. Jensen stared at him and then looked back to the experiments. Radar tossed a length of thick rope to Jack and then turned back to working on another coiled pile of the rough material.

"Radar, isn't bringing that thing closer the last thing we want to do?" Jensen asked, watching as Jack did a quick check of the rope he held.

"Well, there is the possibility of it exploding, but I don't think that likely," Radar answered, unconcerned. Jensen exchanged an incredulous look with Steve, who swallowed.

"Not what I meant," Jensen said and Radar turned her glowing brown eyes up to him. A green firework exploded over them, illuminating her briefly.

"That's a newer Grenich model, the AI is more advanced. This group right now is the third that has assaulted our ship. They return to that ship over there when they run out of ammunition and it sets off the next group of two or three. If I can catch one before it runs out of bullets, I can put in a flashdrive with a nasty virus on it. If I control it, I can probably gain control of the rest of the fleet."

"She can send it back with her own programming, which Rami can use to take that ship offline. Hopefully that will cripple it long enough to allow us a window to escape," Jack added, nodding to Radar. She straightened up, spinning the lasso a couple times to get a feel for the rope. The loop first spun in lazy circles with a soft swishing sound and Radar gradually increased the speed until Jensen had to take a step back.

"Wait, hold on a tick," Jensen said, holding up his hand. "Rami's alive?"

"Later," Jack replied as he and Radar turned and headed for the deck. Jensen shrugged as he moved over to the railing, noticing the boat had almost reached the ship and the drone was still attacking the selkies. One selkie reached out and yanked Nero under the safety of a shield, narrowly saving him from a bullet. Next to him, Jensen saw Steve wince in his peripheral vision as bullets continued to rain down on the shields. The two protectors watched as the experiments stood across from each other, circling their loop of rope. Radar threw first as the drone swooped past and the noose slid cleanly over the sleek form of the drone. A firm jerk of the rope tightened the noose and the drone banked to the side. As Radar fought to keep her grip, Jack hurled his rope and looped it around the drone.

Both experiments held firmly to their rope, holding the drone as it pulled sharply and banked against the ropes. Radar exchanged a look with Jack and nodded. Adjusting their grip, the experiments began to drag the machine to the ground. Once it was close enough, Radar stepped on the rope and Jack moved to stand on his rope as well.

"One minute, thirty seconds," Jack yelled as Radar quickly got to work. The selkies cautiously peered out from under the shields. Even Alpha glanced over to the experiments as she continued to help Sly get the blindfolded humans on board, who were strangely compliant and unbothered by the violence surrounding them. Jensen couldn't help but marvel at how quickly Radar managed to get a steel plate off the drone and withdraw the chip, replacing it with another chip from the silver chain she wore around her throat. Once she had finished, Radar made quick work of the lassos, yanking them off the drone.

"Jensen, Steve! We need your help! Quit gawking!" Sly shouted to them, irritation apparent in her voice. Jensen and Steve quickly hurried to the steps, running down them and moving to help with the blindfolded humans. Jensen noticed a six-armed woman with impressive biceps hanging off the side of the ship, helping the humans climb over the rail and onto the deck. Her glowing brown eyes indicated she was an experiment, but like Mia, she had long hair. The A-series were definitely a very different sort of experiment than they were accustomed to.

"Steve, get them to the sleeping quarters," Jensen ordered as he helped a heavyset woman climb over the railing. A young petite girl in a light blue hijab followed close behind her. She had a thin white cloth over her eyes, one she could obviously see through, and she smiled up at Jensen, waving. He smiled back and gripped her under the arms, effortlessly lifting her over the rail and putting her on the ground.

"I think she likes you, Aldridge," Sly teased, starting in surprise when the girl almost instantly wrapped her arms around Sly's legs.

"I think you're mistaken, Sly," Jensen replied smartly and Sly rolled her eyes. He looked behind him as Steve and Nero started leading the humans to the safety of the sleeping quarters. The A-series woman was about to descend, pausing only at Sly's behest.

"How many more?"

"One more boat of humans, then the rest of us will be able to swim over," the woman replied, her tone flat. "The werehyenas are about to swarm the beach, not sure how your team is faring against them."

Sly took a step back and the woman dropped back down to the dark churning water with barely any splash. Jensen squinted, just barely able to make out the flashes of gunshots on the beach in the distance. He put his hands on his hips, looking around at the selkies and the blood on the deck.

"Back, back, back," he heard Radar shout hurriedly and turned to watch Jack and her jump away from the drone. It rose unsteadily into the air as Radar pulled out her tablet, looking down to the screen again. Her fingers were a blur as they flew over the screen, rapidly typing in commands. The drone hovered over the ship, its guns still aimed at the selkies' shields. For a moment, everyone held their breath.

Suddenly the drone rose higher and flew straight over their heads, banking hard as it switched direction. It was a steel gray colored blur as it tore past the ship. Everyone watched it anxiously, except for Radar who continued looking at the screen. Jensen quickly hurried toward the tail of the ship, praying to the guardians for a miracle.

"Okay, it should take a few minutes to spread the virus and then I'll have control of them," Radar explained, shrugging. "Or it won't work and then we'll have a problem. At the very least, Rami now has another virus that I can do more with."

Jensen looked around the deck, noticing Keane kneeling over Maeve nearby. The elf had been wounded in the attack and she grimaced as Keane set about binding her leg. One of her hands tightly gripped his shoulder and her green eyes traveled up to Jensen, who offered her a sympathetic smile.

"We need help over here!" one of the selkies suddenly yelled out and Jensen hurried over to where the voice had originated. Jack was already kneeling on the ground, his back obstructing Jensen's view of the wounded individual.

"Oh god," he muttered under his breath when he saw it was Mia.

CHAPTER FOURTEEN

Dane sat with his feet up on the desk in the surveillance room, twirling one of his chopsticks around his fingers. A plate of half-eaten sushi — the remainder of his lunch — sat near him. His glowing brown eyes were focused entirely on the screen in the table in front of him. The light from it, as well as the two other larger screens in front of him, was the only thing penetrating the darkness of the room. Turning his face toward the ceiling, Dane let the quiet in the room wash over him.

His attention snapped to the side when there was a quiet knock on the door followed by the knob turning. Dane wondered if it was Coop or Remington poking their head in for a status update, as they would sometimes do. The experiment spent most of his time alone in the security room, a job he had volunteered for. He didn't sleep, didn't get tired, and preferred to be left alone, so he was a perfect candidate for the long hours needed for this type of surveillance. He was relieved of his watch in the afternoon and early evening, which allowed him to continue cooking and baking to his heart's content. Though he had been unusually extroverted for most of his life, Dane was still trying to get back to a point where he could be around people for extended amounts of time again, even those he knew. His experience with Nick Chance had left him more scarred than he cared to admit.

Dane raised his eyebrows when a guardian woman poked her head in and looked around. Her eyes fell on him and she offered him a slight watery smile, surprise reflected in her expression. There was something incredibly familiar about her, and it only took the seven series a moment to figure it out. Dane spun his chopstick and pointed it at her.

"Passion, right?" he asked and she nodded. "Yeah, took me a minute to place a name with the face. I recognized you from my period of infirmary when I was first brought here."

"Ah," she said, glancing at the screens for a moment before looking to him again. "I must admit my surprise. The few times I saw you, you were rather groggy and barely awake."

"I believe you normals refer to it as being at death's door," Dane stated, as he tapped his temple with the chopstick. "Body was broken, mind was still sharp."

He picked up some sushi and popped it in his mouth, chewing slowly as he watched her. Her body language suggested she felt unsure, which wasn't typical of her. At least, from what little Dane had observed. He grasped another sushi and turned his attention back to the screen, waiting for her to speak. There were currently only three screens on and Dane was focused on the one in the table he was sitting at, which was the most interesting. Isis, or Blitz, or whatever the hell she was calling herself, was examining a wall but kept glancing over her shoulder. There was something in that area with her, judging from her body language. Dane thought he had noticed a few peculiarities, but they could be attributed to the quality of the footage.

"I could leave if you prefer to be alone," Passion offered, gesturing behind her. Dane couldn't help but snort, turning his attention back to her. Normals were adorably transparent. Using his foot, he pushed out the empty chair next to him, nodding at it.

"Fair warning, things tend to get rather dicey when Blitz is involved," he cautioned, keeping his attention on the screens. "I have never met anyone, experiment or normal, who was quite as skilled at finding trouble as she is. It's like a superpower or something."

Passion was quiet as she sat next to him, studying him for a moment before quietly observing, "I think you're unlike any other experiment I've met."

Dane offered the plate of sushi, which Passion looked at before delicately picking out one with cucumber and seaweed. Dane smiled at the surprise in her eyes when she took a cautious bite of it. He did enjoy when people liked his culinary creations, especially the ones that required a lot of time and effort. He had spent most of the previous evening preparing the sushi, which proved to be one of those rare dishes he couldn't get just right no matter what he did. There always seemed to be some small aspect missing.

"Well, my lady, I'm fairly certain most protectors say similar things about you," Dane pointed out as he leaned back in the swivel chair. Passion leaned forward so that she rested on her elbows, smiling at him and helping herself to another pre-offered sushi.

"Fair enough," she conceded, going quiet for a moment as she chewed and swallowed the sushi. "How are things going?"

Dane paused, raising an eyebrow as he placed the dish down again. "Do you want the truth or a lie?"

Passion bit her lower lip and craned her neck, attempting to see the screen on his other side. Dane leaned back and put his feet back up on the desktop, watching the guardian as she rolled around to his other side and looked at the screen in the table. For a moment, she watched the fuzzy gray picture in silence, her fingers resting on the edge of the screen as the light from it illuminated her face. He had been quite surprised when she didn't turn on the lights upon entering, something most normals did instinctively, particularly when an experiment was present. Brighter lights tended to make their glowing eyes less intimidating or it made it easier to focus on other things.

Dane turned his attention to the two large screens in front of them, further into the room. On one, he saw the fidgety young A-series who Radar had mentioned was called Rami. Squinting, Dane studied his movements closely, watching as he paused and spoke into the com. He had noticed the young A-series was hesitating more often than was typical for an experiment. There was more uncertainty in his actions than was usual.

"I think I've figured out why that A-series was labeled defective," Dane mentioned as he folded his arms over his chest, drawing Passion's attention over to him. He tilted his head up at the screen he was observing, directing her attention to it.

"The A-series are a rather unusual line, both in behavior and appearance," Dane explained, glancing over at the screen Passion had been watching. "They're one of the types most vulnerable to mutations and abnormalities. Shape shifters are a very hardy species; we've got to be. For the most part, we're less likely to have the sort of psychological disorders humans suffer from. As you know, Grenich does a lot of alterations of our brains. Unfortunately, no matter how talented or experienced or careful you are, altering the brain, whether through magic or old fashioned means, is a risky endeavor. There are always going to be side effects. Every now and again, it results in an experiment who is neurodivergent in some way. The more severe ones are euthanized, obviously."

Dane pointed at the screen. "He has been checking in with Radar more frequently than an experiment normally would and he is more easily distracted, also seems to have a bit of trouble staying still. My guess? He has attention deficit disorder. In fact, I would bet all the A-series on that island have some sort of psychological disorder. The Corporation tends to assemble their fodder in groups with similar defects."

"He slaughters shape shifters for having treatable disorders?" Passion asked, horror apparent in her voice and expression. Dane shrugged, nonchalant as he leaned back in his chair.

"If you're not perfect, you're not worth the investment," Dane answered in his typical detached way. "No investor would be interested in faulty weapons, but if you put them in a simulation or demonstration, you might at least make some small profit on them."

Passion was quiet for a moment. Dane glanced over at her when he heard a sniffle, noticing her swiping at her eyes. Craning his neck, he tried to get a better look at her face, even as she turned away from him.

"Are you crying?" he finally asked, confused, and the guardian shook her head, using both hands to scrub at her eyes.

"I'm . . . I'm very sorry that you had to go through that," she said softly, clearing her throat as she looked up at the ceiling briefly, tears sparkling in her eyes. "That all of you had to go through that. The guardians should have realized what was happening and done something. We should be doing more now."

Dane looked around the room, wishing that Coop were with him. Coop was better at handling normals and their emotions. Searching for something to help him deal with the situation, Dane looked at his hands and then at Passion, who still wasn't looking at him. Normals seemed to like physical contact, he knew, maybe that was a good thing to try. Clearing his throat uncomfortably, Dane leaned forward and patted her shoulder with the flat of his palm, a little rougher than he intended, causing her to jolt in surprise.

"Um, there, there," Dane spoke in what he hoped was

a comforting tone. Passion stared at him, apparently confused. *Where the hell is Coop when I need him? I'm not good with this shit and I've probably just made it worse,* Dane thought with no small amount of irritation. He coughed quietly and removed his hand, sliding it back into his pocket.

"My apologies. Reassuring people is not something that comes easy to experiments, especially not to the seven series," he explained by way of apology. Passion smiled at him and held out her hand, which he stared at for a moment. Slowly, with no small amount of caution, Dane put his hand in hers. Tilting his head, he studied her hand, which shimmered faintly even in the dim light of the room. He wondered how it was possible that he had forgotten how pleasantly warm and soft flesh was.

"Thank you," Passion said, quietly, genuine gratitude in her voice. She gently squeezed his hand and he looked up into her eyes. Tears sparkled in her soft green eyes, but he could also see confidence and affection.

The moment was interrupted when the door was roughly thrown open and the lights were suddenly switched on, bathing the room in a harsh florescent glow, causing Dane to cringe at the assault on his sensitive eyes. He turned to look over his shoulder, noticing a male guardian standing in the doorway. The man was practically trembling in anger, which was reflected on his face. *Guardians are apparently unable to conceal any emotion,* Dane thought as he spun around fully to face the guardian.

"Hello, can I help —?"

"Do not speak to me, creature," the guardian snapped at him, his blue eyes flashing.

"Oh-kay," Dane replied, looking back to the screens and doing his best not to cringe. He wasn't sure what he had done to get on the guardian's bad side and he didn't care enough to try figuring it out.

"Merrick, you don't have to be rude," Passion said testily. The male guardian stormed over to her and whipped something at her, causing her to fumble with the small object. Out of the corner of his eye, Dane saw that it was some kind of chain or bracelet and there were charms that resembled leaves around it. He kept his attention on the screen in the desk, not interested in getting involved in guardian skirmishes.

"I take it from your silence that you recognize that," the male guardian, Merrick, continued shouting.

"It's the Leaves of Ivy," Passion replied, tossing the small chain onto the desk. "So you've recalled Eris and left the Four on their own, I assume."

"No, that *traitor*," the guardian spit the word with venom, "severed the Leaves with one of her weapons. The trickster is now loose upon the world again."

Wow, Blitz really is determined to alienate every last ally she has. Unsurprising, Dane thought as he rubbed his eyes before looking back to the screen. Blitz had finally found the panel she was looking for and removed it. She was currently fiddling with whatever circuits and wires she had found. Dane had a feeling he knew what she was doing, but with Blitz, he found it difficult to predict her actions. He leaned closer to the screen when he noticed a flutter of what looked like some kind of cloth. She definitely wasn't alone in that massive space. As he watched, he noticed a glint of something near the corner of the screen, a blade of some sort. Yet the strange form hung back and didn't approach Blitz. Dane stroked his bottom lip as he tried to figure out what the thing was and what it was doing.

"The Council has had enough of these games and this flagrant disregard for the laws of the guardians. Once she returns, she's going directly into the cell next to the assassin, where she should have been in the first place."

Passion shot to her feet, the chair wheeling backwards and crashing into the wall. "You lay one finger on Isis and I will end you!"

"Passion!"

Dane looked to the side, noticing a pair of regal-looking guardians standing in the open doorway. Neither looked particularly happy. He could smell Jet nearby as well and he leaned back in his chair, resting his hands behind his head and interlacing his fingers. *So much for peace and quiet,* Dane thought as he looked back to the screen on the desk, tuning out the argument taking place behind him. It was fairly easy to figure out that most of the older guardians disliked Passion, which was mutual on her part. Isis seemed to be their newest battle ground, something she would likely find a way to work to her advantage. Dane squinted, noticing a shadow creeping in from the corner of the screen, moving slowly toward Isis, darting behind machinery every time she looked over her shoulder. Picking up the earpiece, he switched it on but hesitated. *Come on, Blitz. This is espionage 101. You know there's something behind you,* Dane thought, biting his lower lip. Spinning around in his chair, he watched the arguing guardians. Standing from his seat and putting the earpiece in his own ear, he moved around to the front of the desk and crossed his arms over his chest.

"Radar, are you there?"

"I'm busy, Dane," the E-series terse reply came through and Dane almost smiled. All the E-series were so tetchy.

"Well, you're going to want to adjust your strategy a little or speed it up," Dane said. "Blitz isn't alone on that ship or at least she won't be for much longer. You should probably find some way to alert — uh oh."

Dane froze when Set's face suddenly filled the screen he was looking at, as well as all the others. The necromancer half-smiled, shaking his head and waggling his index finger in a chastising manner. His eyes suddenly turned so that they locked on Dane and for a moment, the experiment wondered if he could actually see through the screen. Dane swallowed and his hand instinctively drifted down to where he carried a concealed side arm, barely aware that the arguing guardians had gone silent. He didn't often experience fear, but a sinking sense of terror settled over his mind. The screens suddenly all went black and Dane looked around at all the empty glass, his mouth dropping partly open. There was a moment of stunned silence in the surveillance room.

"Well that's not good," Dane mentioned.

~~*~*~*

Isis went rigid when the ship was suddenly plunged into darkness; so thick she could barely see through it. The hairs on the back of her neck were standing on end as she tried to see through the impenetrable shadows. They couldn't have knocked out the power that quickly; it wouldn't have been that easy. Isis swallowed as she cautiously began to retrace her steps, keeping one hand on the wall. Before the lights had gone out, she had sensed something else was in the engine room, but it kept itself well-concealed. Her original intention had been to deal with it when she finished with her task. However, once the lights had gone out, whatever it was started moving around more. She could hear soft footsteps in the sand a few feet away, which made her uneasy. Tilting her head, she listened closely. Something was breathing nearby, in the opposite direction. Multiple somethings, actually. There was a strange scent in the air, one that was gradually becoming more pronounced, an odd scent that was similar to the chemical smell of insecticides.

Before Isis had a chance to ponder it further, her hand brushed against the rough material of a robe. With only a split second to react, she arched backwards and narrowly avoided the blunt weapon, a mace or hammer of some sort, that swept over her face. Isis kicked forward, striking at her opponent's knee and successfully knocking them to one leg. She immediately lunged forward and struck the face with her knee, feeling something give under the strike. Before she could react, a pair of clawed hands grabbed her back and threw her across the room. She struck the solid mass of a pipe and felt the air rush out of her body as she fell to the ground and into the sand. Trying to catch her breath, she inhaled sand and coughed harshly at the gritty feeling that invaded her mouth.

Hearing some type of blade being drawn, Isis flipped back to her feet and yanked out her sais. Spinning the weapons a couple times, she relied on her hearing to tell her where the threat was located. She didn't have to wait long for an attack as a curved blade swept through the air close to her stomach, nearly gutting her. Isis immediately struck out with her sais, stabbing and slicing at her opponent. It wasn't human — she could tell from how easily it moved — but it wasn't an experiment either. Isis drew first blood, which had that same strange chemical smell. Lunging forward, Isis attempted to drive her sais into her opponent's chest. Sparks flew from the clashing metal as both strokes were successfully blocked and she was shoved backward. Isis stumbled back a couple steps, nearly losing her footing in the slippery sand, and was barely able to block the next stroke of the short curved blade. Chambering her knee, she lashed out with her foot, forcing her opponent to the ground with a powerful kick.

Pressing her advantage, Isis quickly thrust the sharp prongs of her sais straight through her opponent and blood sprayed up in her face, stinging her eyes. She wasn't even given a chance to get to her feet before another weapon slapped the ground near her hand. Letting out a growl, she rolled away from the next strike. Flipping back to her feet, Isis used her sais to push the blade away from her and backed away from its wielder. Judging from the reach of the weapon, she guessed it was some kind of spear. There was a new scent in the air, one that made her cringe: co-ag, the blade was coated in it.

Just then, the backup power came on, bathing the room in a dim red glow. Isis spun her sais so that the middle prong was pressed against her inner arm. When she saw the man illuminated by the eerie blood-colored glow, she forced herself not to react. A grin slowly spread across his face and his bright white teeth practically glowed in the dim lighting.

Nick Chance spun the spear a couple times across his body, the air whooshing as the weapon cut through it. He was bare-chested and sweat glistened on his flesh. She could just barely make out the male symbols painted around his bright eyes. His expression resembled that of a ravenous animal that had just spotted fresh meat. However, he was exhibiting a kind of restraint Isis had never seen in him before. Chance's greatest weakness had always been his temper and impulsiveness. If he had learned self-control, it meant he was even more dangerous than before.

Isis spun her sais so the middle prong was pointing toward the ground again. The comforting weight of her weapons helped her remember to be patient.

"Well, well, well," Chance began in a quiet voice. "We meet again, 7-series."

Isis quirked an eyebrow but didn't respond. She knew she had to keep her wits about her for this fight, but she really wanted to kill Chance. It was an odd feeling, but she didn't want this man to hurt anyone else she knew. Isis rationalized that it was because she needed as many allies as she could get to fight against the Grenich empire.

"I did happen to catch the tail end of your little squabble with Tracy and it was fucking hilarious," the Grenich man chuckled, amused. "If I had a nickel for every time I wanted to throw explosives at her. You lived my dream, 7-299. Kudos to you."

Pointing his spear at the ground, he drew a half circle in the sand and Isis dropped into a ready position, the points of both sais aimed at Nick Chance.

"It's a shame to have to put down one as talented as you, but unfortunately, orders are orders," Chance spoke as if he were talking to himself. "En garde, 7-series."

Without any warning, he swept the blade up, sending a

spray of sand directly at Isis' face and eyes. She had anticipated the move and turned her face away, protecting her eyes from the gritty particles, which hit the side of her neck. Quickly whipping back around, Isis was barely able to block the follow-up strike with her sais. A spark flew out from where the blades met. Isis adjusted her footing as she held the blade away from her with the sais. She could see Chance's arms quivering with the exertion it took to push against her, but he still wore an expression of amusement.

"Very good, 7-series," Nick Chance complimented, his grin growing. Isis gritted her teeth and kicked him in the stomach, knocking him backward. She took a few steps back, glancing around for anything she could use to gain an advantage over him. Chance quickly found his footing, spinning the spear around in a two-handed grasp.

"I can't help but wonder why you're not using your gun," Isis mentioned as Chance advanced on her. She continued walking backward, relying on her hearing to tell her where she was. There was a dark space just past the large machinery; dark enough to give her a significant advantage over Chance.

"Because I'm not going to grant you a quick death," Chance replied, following her as she continued to back up toward the loud machinery. "No, no, no, 7-299, I intend to make you suffer for quite some time before I put you down."

Chance lunged at her, thrusting the blade straight at Isis' throat. Isis parried the thrust and ducked away from the spear. Chance pushed his advantage, moving forward again and forcing Isis back. The experiment struggled to stay out of the path of the sharp blade, spinning and dodging, ducking behind the various structures in the mostly open space. Chance glared at her with an expression of pure malice and swung the base of the spear, managing to sweep it under her legs, knocking Isis onto her back. Isis cringed when her head struck the floor, but quickly rolled away from the blade of the spear, narrowly avoiding being skewered. The gritty sand on the ground dug into her palms and stuck to her hair. Isis grabbed a fistful and hurled it at Chance, who let out a yell and backed up a few steps.

Isis quickly flipped to her feet and moved back even further, spinning her sais. She caught a glimpse of a pair of robed figures standing on the other end of the ship, near the mysterious doors. The gleam of their weapons shone even in the dim red light. Out of the corner of her eye, Isis noticed a rapidly blinking light in a corner. It was blinking in a specific pattern, and almost against her will, she turned around to get a better look at it. Suddenly, the walls of the ship became hazy, beginning to shimmer in and out of existence. Isis blinked, her eyes slowly closing and when she opened them again, she was standing in the middle of a desert of golden sand.

She spun around and dropped into a crouch, her sais held at the ready. Her other senses told her she was still on the ship, but her eyes saw nothing but desert. The dry air was hot, making it somewhat difficult to breathe. She was still wearing her catsuit, but all her other weapons were gone. Isis' eyes widened as she looked around, trying to make sense of her surroundings. She knew she was in danger, but didn't know how to get out of this strange place. Suddenly, a castle exploded out of the ground beside her, showering her in sand. It sped toward the harsh sky above her, blotting out the blinding sun and casting her in shadow.

"Seven series, come home. There are endless possibilities to what you could become, what you could help us achieve," a masculine voice spoke in a gentle tone. Isis swallowed as the heat started to intensify. Feeling a little dizzy, she closed her eyes and tried to locate the enemies she knew were surrounding her.

A sharp pain in her lower back brought her to her knees with a gasp. It was followed by a strange warm wetness crawling down her skin.

"It's done, let's go," she faintly heard a strange echoing voice, which she couldn't place. It sounded odd . . . not any species she had ever encountered before, none that she could remember. Isis swallowed and raised a suddenly empty hand to the wetness. When she looked at her palm, Isis saw it was coated in bright red blood, which glistened in the sun.

"Choose the wrong side and you choose death," the voice continued. A strange whispering came to her on the wind, soft and almost silent.

"Starlight and iron runs through your veins, daughter of the Meadows and Earth," the voice spoke with a steely edge. "Now get up. Get up and fight."

"You can end this, all of it, before it gets worse," the masculine voice continued, unaware of the other voice that whispered in her ear. "Seven series, you do not want to go to war with me. You don't have the numbers. Jet and Lilly are good rulers, great for the protectors. Do you really wish to cause their downfall?"

Wake up, wake up, Isis thought as she closed her eyes. She could feel the blinking light on her face, could hear the sand crunching under foot. Opening her eyes, Isis felt disappointment when she saw she was still surrounded by the sea of golden sand. Turning her eyes to the castle, she could hear a growling laugh deep within it. Carefully putting one foot under her, she ignored the way her leg shook. Her head was spinning, but she rose to her full height and forced herself to remain steady.

"I'm no fool so do not insult my intelligence," she spoke calmly to the disembodied voice. "Even if I were to return to the Corporation of my own volition, you aren't known to be forgiving. There is no scenario where I walk away with my life. You created the experiments to destroy the guardians and take over the Meadows. That means you would still go after the protectors and therefore would wipe out the Monroe family as well as their allies."

A deep rumbling laugh echoed all around her. "Clever thing, you are. I do miss you, 7-299. It is truly a shame that you insist on acting against your best interest. Killing you will be like shattering a mosaic."

Isis kept quiet, trying to remain steady and figure out what to do. Her mind was spinning with the conflicting messages coming from her senses. She could feel the gentle motion of the water beneath the ship, could feel the heaviness of the humidity in the air. Yet the heat of the desert also felt real on her flesh as did the sand that was carried in the occasional wind. Her eyes ached from the brightness of the sun, causing her vision to swim.

"You know, you did unintentionally bring me a gift," the disembodied voice took on an almost taunting quality. "You brought along a Deverell and the last Aldridge, a man I've been trying to find for years now. I suppose I should thank you for —"

There was a sudden shattering sound and Isis fell to her knees in the gritty sand, finding herself once again on the massive ship. Around her, there was the faint sound of people exchanging gunfire, but it sounded very far away. Her vision was hazy, as if she were looking through frosted glass, and everything sounded muffled. Isis shook her head, trying to get her senses to work properly. Blinking rapidly to clear her head, Isis could see shapes at the edges of her vision. Somewhere behind her a door closed and she took a few deep breaths before forcing herself to rise to her feet.

Isis barely had a chance to get her bearings before dodging a curved blade. The blade slammed into a pipe, causing steam to burst out, and Isis lunged at her attacker, grabbing the robes of the strange reptilian-looking creature; a follower judging from the pasty color of the skin. She slammed its triangular face into the boiling hot pipes that ran along the wall, using the opportunity to look around and get a rough estimate of how many hostiles there were. The creature shrieked and thrashed around, its burning flesh smoking and melting. Isis leaned back a little, avoiding the creature's wildly swinging talons. Yanking the dagger out of its belt, Isis dragged the blade across the creature's throat. Yellow blood spewed everywhere and she tossed the carcass away from her, making a face of disgust.

"Blitz, look out!"

Isis didn't even glance at Rami, knowing she was still surrounded by followers. Dodging out of the way of another curved blade, she quickly retrieved her sais and slashed at the attacking creature. As she took him down, she risked a quick glance around the engine room for Nick Chance or the strange figures who had accompanied him. There was no sign of them, which was to be expected.

Ignoring the sound of gunshots from Rami, she clashed blades with a follower who lunged at her with a hiss. His forked dark blue tongue shot out of his lipless mouth, tasting the air, and Isis lashed out with her sai, severing it. The creature let out a wet hissing noise as its tongue fell to the sand. It swung at her again and Isis parried the blow, noticing the dull red lights blinking. Their time was running out and they needed to get off the ship.

Blue sparks flew off the blades almost every time they met. Blocking one blow with her sais, Isis lashed out with a powerful roundhouse kick and felt a few of the creature's ribs give way under her foot. Lunging forward and sweeping her weapons in a wide controlled arc, she cut its throat open as well. Dashing for the steps, Isis wove around the followers who swarmed about her. It was a small pack, no more than twenty by her estimate, and therefore easy to fight off. One grabbed her arm tightly and she spun toward it, burying the longest prong of her sai in the creature's exposed temple. Kicking the body off her weapon, she shoved another follower away from her and jumped onto the stairs, running up them two at a time. The metal rattled as the followers pursued. Rami fired a few times, keeping the creatures at bay as she ran toward him. Grabbing Rami, Isis dragged him to the large opening and shoved him through the strange curtains. The two experiments dashed down the narrow hallway, ignoring the hissing shrieks of the creatures pursuing them. The pale bluish white walls were a blur as they continued their dash to freedom.

Finally, they reached the door leading out onto the deck. Rami grabbed the heavy handwheel and dragged the door open, letting in the fresh night air. He went through and into the night, Isis following on his heels. Pivoting on the balls of her feet, Isis pulled the heavy door closed, trapping the forked slimy tongue of a follower in the process. Spinning the handwheel, Isis nodded toward the deck.

"The virus is spreading in the AI, should keep the drones grounded for an hour or two, at least," Rami reported hurriedly as they moved away from the door. "Were you able to start the self-destruct sequence?"

Isis nodded, wincing when she felt a sharp pain in her lower back that caused her to stumble. Feeling the damp area, she fought the urge to gasp at the sting and looked at her hand.

"You're hurt," Rami stated when he noticed the red coating her palm. Isis ignored him and looked around the deck, briefly sniffing the air. *It would probably be wisest to Appear on the other ship, but I don't know if I can risk the energy,* Isis thought as she rubbed the side of her neck. The cool air felt good on her skin and she moved over to the side of the ship, looking down into the dark churning waters below. They had to get away from the island before the guardians arrived. Sinking the island would undoubtedly affect the currents and she wasn't sure even the selkies could navigate them.

"You're not healing and I smell the co-ag concoction. You could bleed out," Rami spoke from a few feet behind her. Isis cast a suspicious eye toward the fleet of drones and noted the sky was still graying. The sun would start to rise soon. The fireworks had at least stopped, but Isis could hear flapping wings. Rami moved over to stand next to her, opening his mouth to ask a question, when an enormous cloud, steel blue in color, shot straight up into the sky. Both Isis and Rami cringed at the cacophony of screeching from the enormous colony of bats and Rami covered his ears as they crouched down instinctively.

Without thinking, Isis grabbed Rami and yanked him close to her, shutting her eyes and focusing. The familiar muted sound similar to breaking glass filled her ears.

~~*~*~*

Jade allowed Sly to help pull her on board, half-listening to what she was saying. The humans and the A-series were all safely on board. Running a hand through her wet hair, Jade's attention was drawn to the enormous ship that was a short distance away. It was barely visible through the moving cloud that encircled it.

Turning, she watched as Jack and Alpha helped Shae and Alex on board. The A-series were all standing off to the side, obviously unsure what to do or where to go. Jade looked over her shoulder when Shae ran over to the bow of the ship, moving to stand next to the selkies.

"Oh, you're welcome, Shae. I'm fine, thanks for asking," Sly said sarcastically, without any malice. She turned her attention back to Jade, a half-smile playing on her lips as she looked the other woman up and down.

"The wounded are in the sleeping quarters," Sly reported, glancing over to Alpha as she started leading Alex toward the door. "Looks like all three of you should probably head there."

Jade turned her eyes to her lover, who looked pointedly to where she had her hand tightly pressed over her ribs. The werehyenas had made up for their low numbers with brutality and all three of them had taken their fair share of wounds. Blood was oozing out of a deep wound in Jade's side where the claws of a particularly large beast had caught her.

"It's fine, I'll bind it the next chance I get," Jade said with a dismissive wave of her free hand. "Any word from Isis?"

Sly opened her mouth to respond when an enormous explosion suddenly lit up the sky. Both Jade and Sly cringed at the bright light as an enormous red fireball engulfed the huge Grenich ship. All the selkies winced and some even ducked down. The water began to churn violently and their ship bobbed in the strong waves. A wave of heat swept over the ship and the aftershock knocked the vessel back a short distance, causing it to pull against its anchors.

"Get down!" Shae yelled, pulling the nearby selkies to the deck.

"Down, down, down!" Jensen, who had been standing at the bow, ran down the steps and across the deck, gesturing for the selkies to get down. He reached Keane, patted his shoulder, and gestured for the elf to get down on the deck.

"What in the name of the guardians —?" Jade began to ask, but then she heard an odd noise. It was a strange screeching, a piercing sound. Looking out over the water, she soon spotted a mass heading toward their ship. A rainbow of glowing circles was splattered throughout the mass and Jade's eyes widened when she realized what it was. She and Sly quickly ducked down as the enormous cloud of bats engulfed the ship. Most of them shifted into their human form as soon as they reached the ship, landing with a soft thump on the deck. Jade immediately spun away from a large man who attempted to grab her hair, striking his neck with the side of her hand in a powerful chop. He spun and backhanded her, which sent her sprawling and she tasted blood from her newly split lip. Suddenly Radar leapt over her, tackling the other experiment, allowing Jade to get back to her feet. Not wasting a minute, Jade ran to where Alex was standing, ready to fight.

"You're wounded, my friend," Jade yelled over the melee, resting a hand on her friend's good shoulder. "I need you to stay with the humans and the other wounded, protect them while we try to get this situation under control."

Alex didn't look happy, not wanting to leave her friends and teammates on their own. "If you get yourself killed, I won't forgive you, Jade."

Jade laughed and nodded. "Go on."

Alex turned and ran for the door leading to the sleeping quarters, narrowly dodging around experiments, who were attacking anything that moved. Jade didn't let out her breath until the door shut behind Alex. Glancing over her shoulder, she saw Sly struggling with a woman who held two blades. Before Jade could move to help her, one of the A-series grabbed the attacking experiment's arms with two of her own. Using two of her other arms, she disarmed the experiment and buried her own knives into her chest. The A-series then spun into a high spin kick, striking another experiment in the face, knocking them down.

Jade heard Reva shout an order to the other A-series and they jumped into the fray, fighting viciously against the attacking experiments. There was an almost instantaneous change in the mood of the fight. The A-series were remarkable as they threw themselves in front of selkie and shape shifter, fighting at first with their bare hands and soon with the weapons they took off their enemies. Not wasting a moment, Jade also continued battling the experiments who swarmed over the ship. Every time one fell, it seemed like two others took its place. Jade was soon slick with sweat and annoyed at the experiments continually targeting her wounded side.

"Gotta say, your new allies certainly come in handy," Sly jested as she fought near Jade.

"Only you would make a pun in the face of certain death," Jade laughed as she tossed an experiment over her hip. The experiment kicked up, catching the protector in her chest and dropping her to her knees. Looking up, Jade noticed Jensen a few feet away, fighting off two experiments. He was so focused on them that he didn't notice the third man sneaking up behind him. Jade tried to yell a warning but found she didn't have the breath. Awkwardly climbing to her feet, she stumbled forward, knowing she wouldn't reach him in time.

A shadow ran past her and grabbed the experiment from behind, spinning him around and holding him in joint-lock. Jade wasn't surprised to see her missing teammate, Isis. Her green eyes were blazing in the night and with a simple jerk, she had snapped the experiment's arm. The man fell to his knees with a yell and she promptly kicked him in the face, knocking him to his back. Smoothly drawing her sai and dropping to her knee, she buried the weapon in his skull. Yanking the sai free, Isis grabbed the knife the experiment had dropped. Hurling the blade up at the sails, Isis managed to hit another experiment, who plummeted to the deck and took out two more attacking experiments. She didn't even watch as she took off running at another experiment. Jade felt her jaw drop open as she watched Isis run past him, latch onto the collar of his uniform with one hand and leap into the air, twisting her body around and yanking the experiment to the deck of the ship.

"Damn!" Nero's impressed declaration was barely audible over the sound of clashing metal and fighting. Isis was moving faster than most could see, deflecting multiple blows and striking with her own weapons. She had her sais out and the shining silver blades flashed in the still dark night.

Hearing a shot behind her, Jade looked to the stern and saw Rami standing on a railing. He ducked when a bat sailed dangerously close to his head but almost instantly resumed firing at the attacking experiments. His glowing eyes were intensely focused and he held his four extra arms behind his back. Leaning forward, he kicked back at an experiment who was attempting to sneak up behind him. Rami spun around and jumped down, disappearing from Jade's sight.

Looking around the deck, she noticed the selkies seemed to be reinvigorated by the A-series fighting fiercely beside them. Jade couldn't help but notice how well the two groups fought together. *Wonder if the Seelie Court would consider letting them stay,* she thought, leaning away from a punch. The experiment leapt up and caught her in the chest with a strong kick, sending her sprawling. Jade rolled away when he attempted to stomp on her head and kicked out, catching him behind the knee. As he crashed down, she quickly climbed to her feet. The experiment was back up before her and lunged at her with a large knife. Jade grabbed his wrists and kept the blade away from her body. He forced her backwards so that she hit the side of the ship with a grunt.

"You are acting irrationally, 7-299. You can't protect any of them," she heard an experiment hiss nearby and noticed Isis was struggling with an attacker who had her pinned against the side of the ship. "You can't win this fight."

Isis let go of the weapon they were struggling over and used her now free hand to backhand her attacker as hard as she could, the echoing smack sounding over the fighting. The experiment suddenly spun Isis around and threw her to the deck of the ship and then lunged to finish off the job. Isis stuck out her feet, catching the experiment in the stomach, and used her forward momentum to send her sailing overhead. The woman slammed into another experiment, who had been fighting with a selkie. Isis quickly dropped her sai and yanked the gun out of her thigh holster, turning onto her stomach and firing two shots, taking care of both attackers. Glancing at the gun,

Isis stuck it back into the holster and pressed her forehead to the wooden deck. Reaching next to her and grabbing the sai, she slowly pushed herself back to her feet. Jade frowned when she noticed Isis's foot slip as the experiment struggled to stand. That was weird. Isis never faltered and she didn't fatigue either. Something was wrong.

Jade attempted to push her attacker away, but he leaned against her more, almost sending her over the side and into the ocean below. The experiment was blank faced and it was frightening to her. Jade was used to fighting opponents who loathed her, ones who showed some sort of expression or emotion. Fighting an experiment was like fighting a machine, one programmed to do one thing: kill.

The experiment suddenly went rigid and a tremor went through his body, his glowing eyes suddenly losing focus. His body slowly sank to the deck, revealing Isis standing behind him, holding a bloody sai. She glanced at Jade as she threw the blood off her weapon and then looked back to the fight. Jade noticed something glistening on the woman's back and only had to guess what it was. The catsuit was undamaged, but that didn't mean it hadn't been.

"You're wounded," Jade yelled over the intense fighting that surrounded them. Isis didn't pay her any heed as she ran forward and scaled one of the tall sails.

"Jade, I don't know how much longer we can keep this up!" Alpha warned from nearby. Jade looked over to where she was fighting alongside Shae. Shae was covered in mud and grime; her movements weren't as quick as they normally were. Both of them had been worn out and wounded from the battle with the werehyenas. Chancing a glance to the door leading to the sleeping quarters, Jade could see Keane and Steve were protecting it along with a couple selkies, but even they appeared weary. Looking around, it became clear to Jade that the experiments were purposely holding back, making their opponents expend their energy. Alpha was right, they wouldn't be able to hold them off for much longer.

Jade bit her bottom lip as she looked around her. She ducked under the blade of a short sword, leaping backward as another experiment attacked her. Jo noticed and jumped at the experiment, throwing him to the ground and stepping in front of the protector.

Both women jumped when there was a loud crashing sound near the center of the ship. The experiments also hesitated, but soon continued fighting. Jade stepped out from behind Jo and stared at the scene that greeted her.

Isis was trading kicks and strikes with an experiment who was significantly larger than her. When he attempted to skewer her with a short blade, Isis latched onto his wrist and proceeded to land an impressive amount of body shots, sending him stumbling back after she released his arm. She ran forward and drove her knee into his stomach then spun under the sharp blade that had been meant to decapitate her. Isis let out a growl as she attempted to bury her sai in the back of his neck, but was blocked. Another experiment tried to grab her, but she spun away and then leapt into a spinning kick that took the second experiment down. Running forward, she punched the large experiment in the groin and then aimed a kick at his knee, bringing him down to one leg. When he put a hand down to push himself up, Isis threw the sai in her right hand, piercing it and pinning him to the deck of the ship. Grabbing a fistful of his short hair, she pressed the point of the other sai against his jugular.

"Stand down or I drive this straight through his throat, into the brainstem!" Isis shouted and the reaction was instantaneous. The experiments stopped fighting and looked over to the woman standing in the center of the ship. Her green eyes were like fire in the fading night, glowing brighter than any of the other experiments. The selkies all turned their eyes to the shape shifters, and experiments, very obviously confused by the sudden halt in fighting. Jade looked around, catching Nero's eyes, which were wider than she had ever seen. He looked back at her and nodded, agreeing that he would follow whatever play she wanted to try.

"That's the disadvantage of using a strategy that requires a significant number of men: you need someone to command them," Isis stated, her voice loud enough for the attacking experiments to hear, her eyes never moving from the experiment she held. "I'd guess you have a handler on the other end of the com I see in your ear, probably one who's reporting to some high ranking underling."

The experiment stared at her, not responding or reacting, and she pulled his head back even farther. His eyes fell on the necklace she wore and Jade could swear she saw his lip curl up in a sneer. Isis pressed the point even more against his throat, drawing a little blood. Jade looked around at the other experiments, wondering why they weren't attacking. She had never seen a battle stopped so suddenly. Orion had always inferred that when an experiment was fighting, they wouldn't stop until they or their opponent was dead.

"You recognize me. Good, it means you know my value to your leader. I'm guessing your troop does as well. Your handler definitely will," Isis hissed. "If your handler is listening, recall these experiments or two Key potentials will shoot themselves in the head and wind up at the bottom of the Seelie Court ocean. And then the third possibility will eliminate himself in a way that ensures he can't ever be resurrected. You have two choices: call this fight a draw and leave the Seelie Court forever or keep fighting and be the reason your leader loses his precious Key. You have exactly one minute to decide."

Jade turned her gaze to Jack when he moved over to the side of the ship, resting one hand on the railing. Isis briefly met his gaze and he nodded once, hopping up onto the railing and drawing his gun, placing it under his chin.

For a while, there was nothing but silence. Suddenly, Isis let go of the experiment and ran to the side of the ship, leaping up on the railing. Easily finding her balance, she turned to look at the experiment who had been about to stand up, but hesitated. She drew her own gun and mirrored Jack's position and Jade could swear there was a glint of defiance in her teammate's eyes. *Never realized how much I missed that,* Jade thought, glancing over her shoulder when Sly approached. Her lover looked genuinely impressed.

"Isis! Don't!" Jensen yelled from nearby. The only thing that prevented him from interfering was Nero holding him back. Steve was similarly holding Shae's arm and she did not look happy at all. When she looked over at Jade, the older protector shook her head, warning her not to intervene. Jade could hear her heart pounding in her ears and her hands were twitching as she struggled not to react. Isis was good at reading situations and could usually work them to their advantage. However, this was a dicey one and one wrong move could very well result in disaster. They were already down a guardian, Jade didn't even want to think about what the consequences would be if this went sideways. There was a tense silence that permeated the deck, stretching on for what seemed like an eternity.

"Fall back," the large experiment suddenly called out. "Lower your weapons. We're being recalled."

He removed the sai from his hand, studying it for a moment, his eyes flickering back to Isis. He threw the weapon down and it stuck in the deck, his blood still sliding down the sleek silver blade. Isis watched his every move from where she stood on the railing, her gun still pressed under her chin. The experiments started shifting back into bats, taking flight and disappearing into the gradually fading night. It looked as though they were headed back to the island, which Jade had expected. There wasn't really anywhere else for them to go.

"My handler has a message from Set," the large

experiment called over to Isis. "He wishes to know if you have shown your allies the flashdrive he gave you."

Jade looked over to Isis, who didn't react to the question. The experiment shifted into a large bat and flew off into the night. Isis and Jack didn't move until every last bat had disappeared. Jack hopped off his perch first, looking around at the carnage still on the ship. This time, there were more experiment bodies than selkies, but they had lost at least three more A-series. Jade noticed a movement out of the corner of her eye and when she looked up, she noticed a few younger selkies were moving around the ship to relight the lanterns that had gone out during the battle.

"Isis!"

Jade turned around when she heard Shae's worried shout, noticing that the teammate in question was on her knees with one hand on her forehead.

"We need to get this ship moving," Jade told the nearest selkie. "Tell the captain to set a course for home."

The selkie nodded and dashed off to carry out Jade's instructions. Other selkies were already starting to clean up the aftermath with the help of the A-series. Jade hurried over to Isis' side, where Shae and Jensen already were.

"Dammit, Isis, what kind of trouble have you gotten yourself into this time?" Jade grumbled as she crouched in front of Isis. The experiment shook her head, swallowing.

"I'm bleeding out," she answered with her typical matter of fact tone. "Nick Chance was on the other ship. He, or one of his allies, stabbed me with a blade coated in co-ag."

"We still have the Tears of Betha," Shae mentioned hurriedly, but Isis shook her head again.

"The Tears of Betha doesn't work the same way on shape shifters as it does on guardians and it definitely doesn't work on experiments," she explained. "It won't heal me, no guardian magic will. It seals wounds but it doesn't repair them. Using it on me would likely go against some Meadows laws anyway."

"Do you really think we care about that right now?" Shae asked, looking over at Jade. The older protector clenched her jaw, knowing there was logic in her teammate's words. They only had a very limited supply of Betha's Tears and she didn't know how much Amethyst and Eshmun needed to treat the healers.

"As a protector, you have to," Isis replied.

"Girl has a point," Sly mentioned from nearby. "You lot have your hands tied. If you use too much of that sparkly stuff, it could be considered a treasonous act."

"Well we can't just let her bleed to death," Shae protested. Jade looked over at Jensen, who was strangely silent. One hand was resting on Isis' shoulder, keeping her steady. He was pale and she imagined his wounded arm was throbbing from the battle, judging from what Sly had told her. The experiments were quite good at fighting dirty and they could pinpoint any weakness within seconds. Then again, they all looked like they had seen better days. There was something else weighing on Jade's mind. She put her hand under Isis' chin and raised her eyes to meet her own gaze.

"Isis, what was that experiment talking about? What flashdrive?" she asked. Isis' glowing green eyes locked with hers and she let out a huff of breath, which might have been a laugh. Swallowing, she looked over to Jack when he approached. They exchanged one of those looks that Jade was convinced only experiments could read.

"Radar," Isis called, brushing off Jade's hand. "Give them the drive."

The young E-series quickly stood from where she had been working on her tablet and approached the small group by the side of the ship. She reached into a pocket and produced a small gray drive, which she held out to Jade. The older protector took it, trying not to shudder at how cold it was.

"Set gave that to me in Paris. It is likely video of Jack

and I in the field, probably some of our more questionable missions," Isis explained softly, glancing at Jade again. "He wants to make sure you know how dangerous we are. It's his way of driving a wedge between protectors and experiments, which would leave you at a severe disadvantage. But it's yours now. Radar will decrypt it for you, if you wish."

Jade furrowed her brow as she looked at the smooth drive with curiosity. Part of her didn't want to know what was on that drive. They already knew experiments were killers, both Jack and Isis had done morally dubious things at Grenich. But knowing something and seeing video of it were two different things. Jade bit her bottom lip, her mind racing as she tried to figure out what to do.

"Jensen, help her to the sleeping quarters. I'll meet you in there shortly," Jade ordered, rising to her feet and slipping the drive into her shirt pocket. "Radar? Can you contact the mansion?"

"On it," the experiment called back. Jensen was already helping Isis to her feet, allowing her to slump against him. Shae stood up as well, anger blazing in her eyes, but Jade ignored her for the time being. The other protectors had gathered around, waiting for her orders.

"The rest of us are going to help the selkies with whatever they need," Jade instructed. "There's a lot of clean up."

"Excuse me, Jade?" Reva's voice came from behind her and Jade turned, noticing the surviving A-series were standing nearby. "What would you like us to do?"

Jade rubbed her chin. "That's entirely up to you. You're now free, all of you. We'd welcome your assistance cleaning up and if any of you know about healing that would be a massive help, but you are under no obligation to do anything you don't want to."

Reva exchanged a look with Jo and then looked back to the other A-series who were milling about. Rami had rejoined them and Jade noticed he kept glancing back toward the sleeping quarters, likely noticing Mia's scent. After a moment, he separated from the group and made his way to the door.

"Jade," Shae started and Jade turned back to her.

"Shae, you need to relax. Trust me, Isis isn't going to die. She's more resilient than any of us. We'll have the selkie healer stitch her up and then when we get back to Earth, she can get a shot of adrenaline and she'll be fine," Jade tried to placate her teammate. Shae put her hands on her hips, obviously not thrilled with the prospect. It didn't surprise Jade. All four of them were protective of each other, but Isis and Shae had grown up together and therefore had a slightly different bond.

"I think the selkies would appreciate some help," Jade mentioned, nodding over to where the selkies were starting to clean the deck. Shae looked at Jade for another moment before turning and moving to help the crew. She playfully shoulder-checked Jack on her way, causing the experiment to look at her, puzzled. Shae couldn't help but smile faintly at the expression.

Jade rubbed the back of her neck, taking a moment to finally catch her breath. Long arms snaked through hers and wrapped around her waist. Jade smiled a little and leaned back, resting her cheek against Sly's, enjoying her closeness.

"You were missed," Sly whispered, kissing her neck.

"Getting sentimental?" Jade teased her, running a hand through her silky hair.

"Oh, I most certainly wasn't talking about myself. I'm still angry at you leaving me here to babysit this lot," Sly responded and Jade couldn't help but laugh. She looked out across the water, watching as the island got smaller in the distance. Jade knew she wouldn't relax until the island disappeared completely. Sly was quiet for a moment, gently pressing her lips to Jade's shoulder.

"So, are you going to hand that drive to Jet?" she asked softly. Jade dropped her head briefly, her shoulders slumping a little.

"I don't know," she answered honestly, her voice barely more than a whisper. A comfortable silence fell over the two women again.

"Come on," Sly urged. "Let's go get your wounds seen to before you drop. I'm not spending another minute in charge of self-righteous protectors and Nero."

Jade smiled again and allowed her lover to lead her to the sleeping quarters.

~~*~*~*

"He claims I threatened his life. Can you believe that?"

Jet sat in the healing rooms of the Meadows, helping his wife and Passion take care of the ailing healers. Passion threw a bloodied rag into a bucket with more force than was needed, almost knocking over the bucket. Jet looked over his shoulder to where Lilly was helping another healer drink a glass of water. She met his gaze, raising her eyebrows slightly.

"Mom, you did say you would end him," Electra pointed out from across the aisle.

"He threatened Isis. I'm not supposed to respond?"

"Yes," Jet and Electra answered simultaneously. Passion glared at Jet and turned her focus back to changing the sick healer's bandages. It had been a day and a half since the Four had gotten off the island. Jade had managed to contact Jet to let him know of everything that had happened. It sounded like they were fairly banged up, but they were alive and they had the Tears of Betha, but not the Box of Original Elements. Jade sounded exhausted, so Jet told her to get some rest. She could debrief him once they got back to Earth. Jet had come to the healing rooms after telling Artemis and Adonia what little information he had about the mission. They were currently with the High Council, figuring out what to do once the protectors returned home. The water guardians had submerged the Island of Avalon without issue and returned to the meeting soon afterwards.

Jet had left Remington in charge while he and Lilly awaited word from the High Council about what they were to do while waiting for the return of the Four. Many of the members were unhappy with the severing of the Leaves of Ivy, but the men were being the most vocal about it. The women wanted answers, but a few of the men wanted blood. Jet and Lilly both wanted to hear exactly what had happened before jumping to conclusions. They were also hoping Eris would lie low for a time. News of her escape would likely cause some sort of panic among shape shifters and that was the last thing they needed.

"I know I complain about Orion and Roan a lot," Passion's voice brought Jet out of his musings. "But honestly, I prefer their childish squabbling over the High Council's overreacting."

At that moment, the doors to the Healing Rooms were thrown open. Aneurin strode in, followed closely by Merrick and Artemis. Jet could tell that Artemis was displeased with whatever had happened and he straightened up, grabbing a nearby towel to wipe his hands clean. Lilly quickly moved to stand beside him, crossing her arms over her chest.

"Jet, Lilly. Thank you for your patience," Aneurin stated, looking around him, "And for your continued aid in here."

"Of course," Jet replied, noticing Donovan standing beside the door. He looked just as unhappy as Artemis did. *Uh oh,* Jet thought, knowing he wasn't going to like whatever Aneurin had to say, as usual.

"There's a slight change of plans," Aneurin began, smiling politely. "We're requesting Isis report immediately to the dungeons. There's going to be an inquiry into Eris' escape, but as the current evidence points to Isis having some hand in it, we would prefer to have her in custody. Just for our personal peace of mind."

Jet glanced at Lilly and noticed that she also looked rather surprised. He had certainly been expecting much worse. Looking back to Aneurin, he nodded.

"Of course. Once Orion looks her over," he began, stopping when Aneurin raised a hand.

"I'm afraid you misunderstand me. As young Isis may have engaged in treasonous acts, for your personal safety, we cannot allow any protector to approach her," Aneurin continued, unconcerned. "The guards shall take her to the dungeons immediately upon their return."

Jet had to bite his tongue and fight not to snap at the guardian. He knew that sentencing had been a little too easy.

"Why are you so certain it was Isis? The other members of the Four carry guardian silver on them. They had just as much opportunity," Lilly pointed out, resting a hand on her husband's back. Jet felt some of the tension leave his body, comforted by the nearness of his wife.

"The others don't have the same history as the experiment, do they?" Merrick countered. "Unless I'm unaware of something, I believe the other three can be healed by guardians."

Jet glanced over at Passion, who had approached the group while they were speaking, and wished he had told her all he knew earlier, because she wasn't going to react well to what he was about to say. Behind her, he could see Electra still helping with the healers, though she was looking over her shoulder every now and again at the conversing group.

"Aneurin, please listen to me. Isis was wounded and her healing abilities have been compromised as a result. If Orion doesn't give her a shot of adrenaline, she will bleed out," Jet explained calmly. "Please, the guards can watch them the whole time and then you can take her to the dungeons after."

Glancing behind him, Jet looked over at Passion apologetically. Passion's nostrils flared as she glared at him and Jet had a feeling they would be having a conversation after the members of the High Council left. Electra straightened up and turned her full attention to the group, trying to read what was going on.

"She should have considered that before unleashing the trickster on the world," Merrick stated, straightening up and practically puffing his chest out.

"Did I really just hear a guardian on the High Council suggest a woman should bleed to death as punishment for a *suspected* crime?" Donovan called out from where he leaned against the open doors. All the healers present in the healing wing looked up and turned their attention to the group, many stunned at Donovan's words.

"I would thank the night guardian to remember what the one we're talking about is," Merrick snapped.

"And I would thank the water guardian to look at the suffering that surrounds him before he inflicts even more upon us," Donovan replied, his tone just as sharp.

"The decision has been made. Isis shall be escorted to the dungeons, where a healer shall care for her under guard," Aneurin declared. "And I would thank both the night and water guardians present to keep a civil tone."

With that last declaration, Aneurin turned and left with Merrick following close behind. Artemis remained in the healing room along with Donovan, who watched both male guardians pass by before turning his attention back to the room. Electra was instantly at Jet and Lilly's side as Passion turned a furious gaze to her friends.

"You knew Isis was wounded and you didn't tell me?" Passion seethed. "How badly is she hurt? What happened?"

"Was it Eris?" Electra asked, obviously just as angry as her mother.

"It wasn't," Lilly answered, looking around the healing wing to where the healers had turned their attention back to their duties. "From what we understand, it was Nick Chance. We don't have all the details, which is why we didn't tell you."

Jet turned his attention back to Artemis. "The guardian healers are already stretched thin. They won't be able to help Isis and you risk more afflicted healers dying. Artemis, if Orion isn't allowed to see Isis, she will die."

Jet looked over at Passion and felt his heart break when he saw her eyes welling up, even as she kept her chin up. If they lost Isis again, he didn't know what it would do to Passion and Electra. Looking back to Artemis, he noticed that she was looking over at Amethyst. The head healer had been quietly watching everything unfold and it was very apparent the decision of the High Council didn't sit well with her. She met Artemis' gaze, subtly raising an eyebrow.

"Lady Amethyst, do you think you could see to Isis when she returns?" Artemis asked.

Amethyst crossed her arms over her chest. "I have my hands full, but I suppose I will be needed when the group returns with Betha's Tears."

Artemis lowered her voice significantly. "Do your apprentices still wear robes on occasion?"

Amethyst half-smiled and dipped her chin to her chest. "Not frequently, but yes they do sometimes. Am I to understand that this should be one such occasion?"

Jet felt relief swell in him and he looked over at Lilly, who smiled up at him. They still had to deal with the High Council, but at least this way, Isis would actually live to see that particular trial. Now they just had to figure out exactly what had happened on the Island of Avalon and prepare for whatever fallout might come to pass.

CHAPTER FIFTEEN

It had been quite some time since Isis had been unconscious and she didn't like it. The minute she had been brought to the sleeping quarters, she had passed out. She had only come to when the sun was rising and even then, her mind was hazy. Someone had changed her into looser-fitting clothes, thrown a blanket over her, and dressed her wounds, but the one in her back still bled. Though she would never admit it, Isis was exhausted. All her remaining strength had been expended on the island and then on the boat. She had pushed herself past her limits and it had drained her. Isis was uncertain whether she would actually make it back to the mainland.

When night fell on the first day of the journey back, Keane came to see Maeve, who had been hit with a co-ag round. Isis was dimly aware of their silent conversation, mostly because Maeve had a very pleasant soft laugh. Steve was dozing in the uncomfortable chair next to her cot, snoring softly in his sleep. The boat creaked every now and again. The waves had been much rougher than was typical for the Seelie Court, but it could be attributed to the sinking of the Island of Avalon. Isis was lost in thought, her mind racing, and she ached. Being wounded had made keeping her senses in check almost impossible, which meant even more discomfort.

Watching the elves converse gave Isis something new to focus on, even as she kept her eyes mostly closed. Keane glanced over his shoulder to where she was laying and Isis turned her attention to where Mia lay in a cot nearby. Most of the normals were sleeping on the floor so the wounded could have cots. Rami was curled up on the floor under Mia's cot, where he spent most of his time. She could tell from his unfocused eyes that he was in a meditative state.

Isis looked up when she heard Keane approach and pause next to her cot. In his hand, he held a bundle of bright purple and white flowers, which were smoking and giving off a pleasant subtle scent with a faint hint of sweetness to it. To Isis, the scent was similar to jasmine. Keane placed the bundle in a small bowl that was part of the table near her cot. The smell of the smoke relieved some of the tension and ache in Isis' body. It even helped make the assault on her senses somewhat bearable, much to her surprise. Hearing a scratching noise, Isis looked back to the elf who was now writing something on a small pad of paper. When he held it up in front of her, Isis studied the flawless elegant script on the yellowed page.

Elven blossoms, they have healing properties and my people believe they ease all hurts, whether physical or not.

Isis shook her head and looked up to him, making sure to speak clearly so he could see her lips. "You should save it for someone more in need. Your people are too hospitable, much too forgiving."

Keane looked puzzled as he studied her and then began writing something else. *It is not my place to judge another. You have shown just as much bravery as your team and helped save many lives. Why should you suffer?*

Isis turned her attention to the deck above her, too tired and pained to argue with an elf. It would accomplish nothing and was therefore utterly pointless. The feeling of a soft hand on her face brought her attention back to Keane. He smiled faintly at her and wrote something with his free hand, holding it up for her to see.

You are worth saving.

With that, the elf stood up and returned to the spot by Maeve's hammock, where she was dozing peacefully. Isis watched him, unsure what to make of his words. At some point, she lost consciousness again and when she awoke, Jensen was sitting in the seat next to her cot. He had a book open in front of him, which he stared at intently. Carefully turning a page, his eyes moved over the print as he read. There was a look of intense focus on his face as the book held his full attention.

"I don't understand you," Isis said quietly, unsure if he'd hear her. Jensen glanced over to her, smiling a little. He was the only normal she knew whose smile always had a hint of sadness to it.

"In what way?"

Isis swallowed. "I can't offer you anything that normals need or desire. I'm incapable of genuine love or affection. I don't experience emotions. The person you loved is gone; she isn't coming back. I'll never be the woman you remember and I won't ever be like a normal. So I don't understand why you enjoy my company. You get nothing out of it."

Jensen raised his eyebrows, but his grin didn't fade. "That's quite a lot of assumptions about me."

He closed the book and laid it reverently on his lap, turning his full attention to her. "I like you, Isis. I spend time with you because I want to. I consider you a friend and friends support each other. Even if you didn't need the occasional . . . ahem, adrenaline outlet, I would still enjoy your company. If you wanted to be strictly platonic, I would be fine with that. If you prefer things the way they are now, I'm fine with that too. I don't need you to be anyone other than who you are."

Isis turned her face to the thin scratchy pillow, folding

her arm under it. "I don't want you to put yourself in harm's way. I have read many accounts of your family, among others. The Aldridges were famed fighters, but many of them fell protecting those they were loyal to."

"We were a meddlesome bunch, steadfast to a fault," Jensen agreed quietly in an amused tone. Isis looked over to where Alex was sleeping on the neighboring cot. The Tears of Betha had been more effective for her and though her wound was serious, she wasn't in much danger of bleeding out. Isis swallowed and closed her eyes, tuning out the other noises.

"Being around protectors is exhausting," she spoke as though to herself. "You're too willing to die and you never seem to spare a thought for those you leave behind."

Jensen sighed and rose from his chair, sitting beside Isis' cot so that he was eye-level with her. He reached out and gently brushed the backs of his fingers down her cheek. She opened her eyes and looked at him again.

"It's unlikely we can defeat Set and I don't know how to neutralize him. Even if I make it through this trip, I . . . it's highly unlikely I will live to see the end of this war. I don't think any of us will," Isis paused. "I don't know what the point of fighting is if that is the inevitable outcome."

She grimaced at the ache in her body, which would flare up occasionally. Isis had decided that she didn't like being wounded and, if she were capable of hate, she hated co-ags.

"We fight because it's the right thing to do," Jensen replied, looking over his shoulder to Mia and Rami. "Look at them and the rest of the A-series and the humans — not to mention the healers back in the Meadows — all the lives the four of you helped save. We fight to help people like them."

Isis could feel her mind drifting further from consciousness and allowed it. Speaking, even thinking, was just too exhausting at the moment.

"As long as you're with us, Isis, we won't lose," she heard Jensen whisper softly in her ear before gently kissing her temple.

The next time she woke up, she heard an intense whispered conversation taking place on the opposite side of the room. Jack was sitting in the chair next to her, his arms crossed over his chest as he watched the conversation, which seemed unusually animated. Focusing her hearing on the voices, Isis soon identified all the protectors along with Alpha and Sly.

"They were able to contact the mansion again," Jack explained, his gaze not moving from the small group. "Apparently you and I are to be brought into custody immediately. They are not pleased that the doctor won't be allowed to see to you."

"Unsurprising, they likely suspect I let Eris go," Isis mentioned, closing her eyes again.

"If Orion doesn't see to you, you'll bleed out."

"That's certainly a possibility," Isis replied, unbothered.

Jack was quiet for a moment. "I've been sitting here for close to an hour, thinking about what happened. There are inconsistencies, some of which the normals have probably noticed."

He went quiet for a moment and then turned his gaze to her, his glowing brown eyes intensely serious. "Did you let her go, Isis?"

Isis opened her eyes and looked over at him, answering simply, "No."

Jack licked his lips and looked back to the arguing group.

"I know you have your own plan about how to handle things, but Isis, you can't fight a war on your own. Not against Grenich," Jack warned. "We do need their help."

"I know that, Jack. I have no intention of fighting Grenich, or Set, on my own," Isis reassured him. He looked over at her, his unnaturally glowing brown eyes brighter than even the light from the rising sun.

"Was it wise to hand over the flashdrive?" he asked. Isis shrugged and closed her eyes again, allowing the subtle scent of the flowers and the gentle waves to ease her back into unconsciousness.

~~*~*~*

Adonia was looking over documents in her office, resting her chin on her hand. Another healer had passed away the previous night: Lenus. He had been a promising young apprentice and one Eshmun favored. Feeling tears prick her eyes, Adonia let out a long breath and shook her head, clearing her throat. There hadn't been a guardian death since the War of the Meadows, except for Isis. But Isis had come back, whereas the healers in training and the other guardians they had lost would not.

Turning a piece of parchment, Adonia sat back in her chair and turned it so she could look out over the lands from her window. She had reigned for many years, longer than her mother had. It wasn't an easy job, but she felt a duty to her land and people, one she intended to see out. A knock on the door to her office brought her out of her thoughts.

"Enter," she called out, turning to face whoever it was. Phoenix, the young fire guardian, moved into the office and bowed her head respectfully. She was wearing an apron, obviously having been working in the healing wing. Many of the young guardians were helping in the healing rooms, which was much appreciated by Amethyst and Eshmun.

"Amethyst sent me to pick up the official notice for Lenus' father," Phoenix mentioned, brushing a few loose strands of red hair behind her ear. Adonia nodded to the neatly folded parchment that she had placed on the edge of her desk, secured with her official seal pressed into dark purple wax.

"How are things in the healing wing?" Adonia asked,

411

almost dreading the answer.

"Mostly quiet," Phoenix answered tiredly. "Many of the healers have been stabilized, for the time being. But Amethyst says she really needs the Tears of Betha. Apparently, this virus is more aggressive than was indicated in the old texts."

Adonia leaned back in her chair, turning her gaze up to the solar system that hovered high over her head. Things were going so wrong. It seemed like every time they cleared one hurdle, another two replaced it. Adonia looked over to Phoenix, who was tapping the folded parchment against her empty palm. The young guardian looked tired and the youthful exuberance was gone from her eyes.

"Worry not, young Phoenix. The protectors will be here in another day with the Tears of Betha," Adonia attempted to reassure the young woman standing across from her. Phoenix looked at her and smiled faintly, dipping her chin to her chest. She might have spoken more but the water in Adonia's fountain began bubbling violently. Smoke curled off the water, drifting gracefully down to the floor, and Adonia looked over to it. She hadn't scheduled anyone to contact her through the seeing pools, and neither had any other guardians.

After a moment, the smoke grew and formed a vivid picture of an elaborate room decorated in shades of blood red and gold. In the center of the scene, the smoke curled around and took the form of Set. He stood proudly with his hands clasped behind his back, one foot resting on an old wooden box. Behind him, on the lounge, sat Pyra and beside her, sat Eris. Pyra and Set were dressed in lighter colors, whereas Eris stood out in a dark purple shirt and black pants. Pyra had one arm draped over the trickster's shoulders and Eris leaned into her hold, obviously enjoying herself.

"Oh it worked," Set spoke eagerly, clapping his hands together. "Splendid."

Adonia immediately stood from her chair and moved

around her desk, forcing her expression to remain neutral. Inside, she felt a cold dread wrap around her. This shouldn't have been possible. Nobody could use the seeing pools outside the Meadows.

"Lady Adonia, apologies for the unusual method of communication, but we've only recently figured out how to tap into the seeing pools," Set continued happily, his eyes alight. "Thanks in large part to the help of young Eris here."

"Hello, grandmother," Eris greeted cheerfully, beaming as she waved. Adonia's eyes narrowed as she looked at her granddaughter. She genuinely couldn't believe what she was seeing. Eris had crossed plenty of lines in her time, but this was outright treason. That was something she hadn't thought even Eris capable of, but she had obviously been mistaken. Glancing over to Phoenix, she noticed the young guardian's eyes were wide and her mouth had dropped open.

"We can see you as well," Pyra mentioned, squinting. "Is that a fire guardian? Good lord, that line has not done well in my absence."

"What do you want?" Adonia asked Set, ignoring Pyra and Eris for the time being. Set looked back to Pyra and she stood from the lounge, approaching him. Eris leaned back and stretched her arms across the back, putting her feet up on the table in front of her. A small smirk played across her ruby red lips.

"As you know, I have a certain . . . " Set paused and rotated his wrist a couple times, "disdain for the ways of the guardians. Your primitivism and nostalgia have held you back from reaching your full potential. I merely wish to set you free, let you achieve the glory all of you are so capable of. Yet you would paint myself and my wife and partner here as villains. Quite childish if you ask me."

Adonia raised an eyebrow slightly as she continued to watch the scene. *Is he actually serious?* Crossing her arms over her chest, she cleared her throat. "Set, you are experimenting on innocent shape shifters. What you did to Isis is unforgiveable —"

"My lady, if you could refrain from interrupting me, it would be most appreciated," Set said with a hint of sharpness. "Now, you and your allies destroyed one of my facilities not too long ago. I lost some valuable information as a result, to say nothing of the weapons you had already stolen from me and continue to steal from me."

Set kicked open the lid of the box he had been resting his foot on and Pyra moved to stand on the other side of the box. Adonia put a hand to her throat, noticing the glistening bottles that were inside, arranged in neat rows. It had been decades since she had seen the Box of Original Elements, but it was something no guardian ever forgot. It was sacred to them, a gift from their ancestors and an important part of their history. Those bottles contained the remedies to many of the world's ills. Of the few memories Adonia had of her mother, the most vivid was when her mother had first shown her the box. The way her usually stoic mother had lit up with joy upon showing her young daughter the jars of sparkling liquid. It was one of the few times Adonia had seen her mother smile; a true honest smile and not a polite gesture.

Set crouched down and lifted up a bottle of glistening green liquid, which resembled grass and leaves. It was the lifeblood and essence of the first plants that had ever blossomed on Earth, something that could rejuvenate any and all plant life, should the need ever arise. Set twisted the bottle around in his grasp, nodding in approval, and then put it back in the box. Pyra crossed her arms over her chest, her gaze never straying from Adonia.

"History is a beautiful thing isn't it?" Set observed, trailing his fingers over the tops of the bottles. "The power in this box is simply extraordinary. Everything you'd need to bring life back to a decimated world. You could heal so much, help so many."

Set looked thoughtful for a moment and stood up

again, turning his attention back to Adonia. "But that's not the guardian way, is it?"

He nodded to Pyra and she formed a bright red ball of fire over one hand, slamming it down into the box, which combusted instantly. A billowing cloud of smoke rose as the fire consumed everything within the box, bottles bursting in the extreme heat. Set moved over to a large chair, sitting in it as if it were a throne and he a king. A malicious smile spread across his face as he watched the box burn, the flames climbing up and rising.

Adonia could feel the tears glistening in her eyes as she watched the priceless artifact, a cherished part of her people's history, burn in the unnatural red flames. A part of her wished the Four hadn't found it. Watching it burn was like watching a part of her soul wither and the crackling flames could have been the sound of her heart breaking. The fire was the same color as the flames that had nearly destroyed the Pearl Castle during the Changing of Seasons ceremony. She briefly looked over to Phoenix, who held a hand over her mouth. The young guardian looked horrified. Adonia turned her eyes back to the vivid picture in her office.

"I do believe we have upset the guardian queen, my love," Pyra spoke with morbid amusement as she moved to Set's side and watched the flames. He took her hand in his and gently kissed the back of it, smiling up at her with adoration.

Adonia turned her furious gaze to Eris. "Why?"

Eris arched a dark eyebrow. "Really, grandmother? You need to ask that after disowning me and tossing me in a cage like some wild beast?"

Adonia didn't speak as she watched her granddaughter.

"Whether or not you believe me, this isn't entirely about spite," Eris continued, a smile dancing across her lips as she tapped her fingers against the back of the lounge. "Though I admit, spite is a large part of it. But I can read a situation and I want to be on the right side of this war."

"You're a coward," Phoenix spat out from behind Adonia. Eris pursed her lips as she looked over to the young guardian, lifting her shoulders briefly in a small shrug.

"Perhaps, but I'd rather be a coward than a corpse," she replied, running her long fingers through her hair.

"Lady Eris is wise beyond her years," Set observed, looking over to her affectionately. "And I'm fully open to sheltering any other guardians who wish to pledge loyalty to me. Just come to Earth and draw the Grenich symbol on any paved surface or carve it into any wall you can find. A representative will come to collect you. I am very good to those who are loyal to me, as any of my allies can attest."

Set interlaced his fingers in front of him as he sat forward in his chair. "It is only going to get worse from here on out. I can get to you, no matter where you hide. There is no safe sanctuary that my forces can't breach."

Set smiled as he sat back and looked to the Box of Original Elements, which was now a large pile of smoldering ashes. "I have some tidying up to do and I imagine you have bodies to bury. So I bid you farewell for now."

The vivid image suddenly disappeared, vanishing back into the seeing pool. The smoke and bubbling stopped as the waters stilled once again. Adonia clenched her fists at her side, staring at where the picture had been just moments earlier. Licking her lips, she briefly closed her eyes and let out a calming breath. Turning to Phoenix, she smiled a thin, sad smile.

"I need you and Electra to find out how many guardians saw that message," she instructed, moving across her office and opening the door. There were a few messengers standing out in the hallway and Nemesis, who had been standing guard at Adonia's office door.

"All of you: send notice to the members of the High

Council that I'm calling an emergency meeting within the hour," Adonia instructed and watched as they took off to carry out her orders. Artemis and Passion, who had been coming up the steps, quickly stepped out of the way as messengers dashed past them.

"Mother, we saw the message in the seeing pool in the healing rooms," Artemis explained. "I . . . there must be some kind of explanation. Eris would never willingly ally with Set and the necromancers."

"Really?" Passion spoke as she leaned against the wall. "Because that kind of seems like exactly the sort of thing she would do."

"Passion, please," Artemis said quietly and Adonia massaged her brow, sensing an argument brewing.

"No! Mother, that woman stabbed my daughter — your granddaughter — in order to escape. There is no good left in her, something she has proven time and again," Passion said, anger seeping into her voice. "You'll excuse me if I don't hold any sympathy for her. I question why you still do."

"Did you give up on Isis?" Artemis argued without any hostility. "Because from what we know, she has possibly done worse than Eris."

"Okay, enough," Adonia commanded before Passion could react. "Artemis, I am sorry, but you know this looks bad. Even without considering Eris' history, this is treason and I cannot ignore that."

Sighing and putting her hands on her hips, Adonia looked between the two of them. "I am going to recommend not taking Isis into custody when she returns. However, I am going to suggest extending her sentence."

Passion didn't look happy with the decision, but she held her tongue. Artemis crossed her arms over her chest, her expression reflecting the worry she obviously felt.

"I believe Orion and Roan when they tell us that Set's afraid of Isis, as well as Jack and Dane," Adonia explained. "At the moment, that appears to be our only advantage over him. Now if you'll excuse me, I have a meeting to prepare for."

With that, she turned and moved the opposite way down the hall. Adonia held her head high and didn't think of the destruction she had just witnessed.

~~*~*~*

Isis completely lost track of the time and focused all her energy on putting one foot in front of the other, leaning most of her weight on Jensen. Earlier she had been leaning against Shae and then Alex. They had split up into smaller groups. Nero, Sly, Alpha, and Steve had taken the group of humans to the door that would open to Earth. They were going to be met by two of Nero's brothers, who would take them to a safe zone. With them were Jo and Reva, along with a few other A-series, who had decided to take an active part in the fight against Grenich on Earth. They would be staying with Shocker, who was not thrilled about having more visitors. Surprisingly, most of the A-series wanted to stay with the selkies. The two groups had bonded and grown attached in an unexpected way, enough that the selkies claimed the A-series as part of their family, something that had never happened before.

It had taken some negotiation, but in the end, the protectors didn't have authority over the Seelie Court. The fey never really cared about what the other groups did, so Titania and Oberon had given their blessing. Isis imagined their consent was in part due to selfish motivations: having experiments as allies was a valuable advantage.

They finally reached their destination after an agonizing amount of time and Isis could distantly hear Jade pound on the door leading to the Meadows. The experiment's vision was incredibly blurry and she felt like her legs could barely hold her weight, but she refused to be carried. She had made it this far, she could make it a few more steps. The door opened and Isis heard a muted conversation between Jade and Hecate. Glancing behind her, she noticed Radar and Jack milling about, patiently waiting to be allowed entrance. Maeve and Keane were just behind them. Even though Maeve was wounded and leaned on Keane for support, they looked no less intimidating or proud.

"Jade, remember to send a messenger back to the ships with the adrenaline for Mia," Isis mentioned, hoping she had spoken loud enough to be heard.

"Don't worry, Isis," Jade acknowledged her teammate without turning around. Soon, Isis felt herself being led forward again and she stepped into the hallway of doors. The familiar scent of the Meadows, which had a pleasant floral hint to it, filled her nose. The light was soft and gauzy, gentle to her sensitive eyes. She noticed Orion standing next to Hecate right as she started to fall forward. He hurried over to her and Jensen, a large syringe in his hand. Orion caught her, ordering Jensen to help hold her upright, and then he quickly jabbed the syringe into her upper arm. Once he pressed the plunger down and the liquid flowed into her veins, Isis felt a nice coolness race through her system. Letting out a sigh of relief, Isis leaned against the wall near the door, feeling her body gradually restart and begin repairing her wounds. She could feel warmth start returning to her body.

Opening her eyes, she watched Jade hand over the bag containing the Tears of Betha to Amethyst, who hurried away and soon disappeared down the long hall. Looking back to the doctor, she watched Orion hand a small bag to a messenger in dark robes, who stepped through the door and disappeared. The doctor next turned his attention to the wounded elf, looking her over and checking her wound, asking her questions in a soft tone. Isis turned her gaze to Hecate, who was watching her with an unreadable expression.

"Isis!"

Isis looked up to see her sister running down the hall to

her, with Passion close behind her. Electra skidded to a halt next to Isis, looking her over.

"My reparative abilities are working again," Isis reassured her. "Orion gave me the injection of adrenaline. I will be at full health in about an hour."

"Okay, well, you're awaited in the High Council chamber, all of you are," Electra reported, looking to the others. "Wasn't your group bigger?"

"The rest of them went to Earth to give Jet our report," Alex explained as Eir, who had come with Amethyst, healed her wounded shoulder. The color soon returned to her cheeks and her eyes weren't as glassy.

"Did they?" Passion asked with a raised eyebrow. Jade looked over at the guardian, mirroring her look and causing Passion to chuckle.

"Best not to keep the High Council waiting," Jade said, gesturing for the two guardians to lead the way. "Shall we?"

Passion and Electra disappeared in a flash of bright silver light and the protectors also disappeared from the hallway. Isis glanced over at Orion, who was still talking with the elves.

Isis disappeared from the hallway and Appeared in Electra's room. Moving quickly, Isis began to search the space. Opening drawers, careful not to disturb anything, she thoroughly went through everything. Dropping to the floor, she looked under the bed and pulled out a box, opening it and letting out a breath of relief as she found what she was looking for. Tucking the object into her belt, concealing it as best she could with her shirt, Isis stepped out into the hall and ran toward the High Council chamber, where the protectors were looking around for her. Remington had obviously met up with the other three outside the hall and was speaking with Alex, who appeared to be reassuring him she wasn't too badly injured.

"I apologize. My Appearing ability must have been affected by the co-ag," Isis explained. "I wound up in

Electra's room and it took me a moment to get my bearings."

"That's okay, no harm done," Electra said, but Alex was staring at her questioningly. Isis pretended not to notice as she followed the others inside the imposing chamber. The members of the High Council were already seated at the towering desks at the front of the room, waiting for them. For the first time, Aneurin wasn't looking over notes and pretending to busy himself, but rather watched as they entered. Adonia sat beside him, looking strong and regal. Donovan, as usual, was doodling on the parchment in front of him with Lucky sitting behind him. All the apprentices and assistants sat behind the guardian they served. Isis' eyes sought out Merrick, who was reading over something. As if sensing her gaze, he looked over at her and she held his hostile stare until he looked back to whatever he was reading. Isis sat back, watching him for another moment before looking to Adonia and Aneurin.

"Well," Aneurin cleared his throat. "That was certainly an eventful trip, from what little we know. I do apologize for our interference; rest assured the decision wasn't made lightly. Originally, we were going to take Isis and the other experiments into custody. However, we experienced a rather unsettling incident last night."

Isis heard Jensen lean forward in his seat and she also straightened up. Aneurin exchanged a look with Adonia, gesturing for her to continue. Folding her hands in front of her, she began to explain what had happened the previous day and Isis felt the wheels in her mind spinning. Set could contact the Meadows, but he obviously was still unable to physically enter the lands of the guardians. *Or he's unable to get his army here,* she thought and glanced over her shoulder when the door opened again. Jet and Lilly entered, moving to sit in the row where Jensen, Remington, Passion, and Electra were sitting.

Isis remained silent as Jade gave her account of

everything that had happened on the Island of Avalon, carefully glossing over a few incidents. Occasionally, Shae and Alex would chime in to clarify something or fill in a missing part of the story. Isis could feel some of the guardians looking at her, but she didn't speak as she tried to figure out Set's strategy. She knew he had to have some sort of plan for how to get into the Meadows. Much like experiments, the necromancer leader didn't make idle threats.

"The experiment is awfully quiet," Merrick observed in his cutting manner once the others had finished their account. Isis looked over at him expectantly.

"What would you like to know?" she asked. "I prefer to speak only when I'm asked a direct question. Otherwise I seem to invoke your ire or suspicion."

There was a quiet snort behind her, likely Passion, and Donovan chuckled quietly as he continued to doodle. Lucky started to smile, but quickly wiped the expression from his face when Merrick turned his glare over to the night guardians. A quiet murmur went through the other members of the High Council, but Isis kept her attention on the water guardian.

"Disrespect aside, I would like to know how it's possible a guardian, a normal as your kind terms us, was able to sneak up on you and wound you so grievously. Eris doesn't have your extensive training and experience," the water guardian explained, sitting back. "According to everything we know about experiments that should have been impossible."

"Unlikely, not impossible," Isis corrected. "I was in an unfamiliar environment surrounded by a massive amount of external stimuli, which proved to be slightly disorienting. She took advantage of the situation. If and when we encounter each other in the future, rest assured it will not happen again."

"The High Council will forgive me if I state that her explanation has not assuaged my suspicions," Merrick addressed the other guardians. "At best, she was incompetent and careless and her incompetence cost us a priceless sacred artifact, one which could have done a countless amount of good. At worst, she conspired with a traitor, which would make her also a traitor. It is my belief that the wisest course of action would be taking her into custody, at least until we have all the facts."

"Your concern is noted, Merrick," Adonia said softly. "However, as we discussed last night, we cannot afford to act only on suspicion and gut feelings. The only reason we have been able to fight back against Set is because of our allies, including the experiments. Unless we have concrete evidence of Isis engaging in treasonous acts, I will not approve her being imprisoned. The same goes for the other experiments."

"We are requesting the protectors keep a closer eye on them and a guardian shall be sent down to observe every month," Alister added from where he sat near Aneurin.

"We are also going to extend Isis' sentence another ten years," Aneurin continued, glancing over at Merrick briefly and before looking back to the hall. "Aside from that, the High Council is requesting a list of freed experiments, including what their abilities are and who will be taking responsibility for their rehabilitation."

"Sir, with all due respect, a list like that could easily fall into the wrong hands," Jade was quick to point out. "While I understand the purpose, I am concerned that the experiments' safety could potentially be compromised."

"Do you not trust the High Council?" Aneurin asked, tapping his thumbs together, which Isis recognized as an indication he was annoyed.

Jade shook her head, looking over at Isis briefly before looking back to the High Council. "It's not a question of trust. Even the most well-intentioned individual can make a mistake."

"Rest assured, we shall take every precaution to ensure the safety of the shape shifters on the list, which shall be kept in a vault that only Adonia and I can access. Now, if there's nothing else to be discussed?" Aneurin paused and looked over the High Council chamber, nodding in satisfaction. "All right, this meeting is adjourned."

Isis didn't waste any time as she rose from her seat and moved out of the well-lit chamber, hurrying out into the hallway. Jack and Radar were sitting on a bench just outside, patiently waiting for the session to end and probably listening closely to the proceedings. Radar was focused on her iPad while Jack had been leafing through an old book from the Meadows' library. He raised his glowing gaze up to Isis as she stepped past them.

"Radar, I need you to go home and tell Shocker and Coop about the High Council's ruling. Make sure any at-risk experiments are protected. We're not going to have much time, so you have to move fast," Isis stated with ease, continuing to move toward the stairs. "Make sure we can get in contact with them should the need arise, but for the moment they are to go underground."

"Isn't that going against the guardians' decree?" Radar asked. Isis glanced over at her and then to Jack, nodding over her shoulder. He gently put a hand on Radar's shoulder, leading her off to the side, disappearing in a flash of light. Isis noticed Shae approaching her, followed closely by Jade and Alex. The protector glanced to where Jack and Radar had been before turning her gaze back to her cousin, who was continuing on her way to the stairs.

"Are they headed back to the mansion?" Shae asked, following Isis down the stairs and the experiment nodded in response.

"Isis, I know you probably don't like the idea of a list of experiments," Jade began.

"You're correct, I don't. However, it's not unexpected," Isis interrupted her with a small shrug. "It's not the most pressing matter at the moment."

When they reached the bottom of the stairs, Isis led them through the bustling main area of the castle toward the healing rooms. She didn't need to walk around the messengers, who looked at her nervously and shuffled away from her. Once she reached the towering doors of the healing wing, which were open as they almost always were, Isis moved to the back of the room and observed the scene in front of her.

The moans weren't as loud, most of the afflicted healers were too weak to even cry anymore. There were buckets filled with bloodied bandages and rags at the foot of many of the beds. The sunlight beaming down from the windows highlighted the colorless features of the sick healers, many of whom had sweat beading on their brows indicating a high fever.

Eshmun and Amethyst were making mixtures as fast as they could at the other end of the room, which they would then pour into wooden bowls and set on a tray. Many younger guardians were helping to administer the antidote to the sick healers, carefully holding their heads up so they wouldn't choke on the liquid. Isis noticed Phoenix helping a woman in a bed nearby, speaking soothingly as she tipped the bowl up to help her swallow the concoction.

"Eir's the only other healer I see in here," Alex mentioned, looked around the healing wing. "Where are the other apprentices?"

Isis turned her attention to the door when Electra moved into the room, briefly smiling at her sister before moving to where Eshmun and Amethyst were still working on mixing the antidote. Isis noticed the bottles they had brought back from the Seelie Court. One was already empty and the other was only half full. That was all that was left of the gifts of the first guardians. Isis looked over to the door when more members of the High Council, mostly women, filtered into the healing rooms to help. Passion, Jet, and Lilly also entered.

"Ladies."

Isis looked over to Amethyst as she approached them. She had never seen a guardian look so exhausted and rundown. Amethyst's strawberry blonde hair was messily done up and wisps of it came out in all different directions. Her clothes were marred with blood and some vomit. She wasn't wearing a dress or robes, but rather a shirt and pants that allowed more range of motion. Isis moved over to the bench she gestured to.

"I want to thank you for what you did," she spoke softly, her voice hoarse from giving orders all day. "I know the High Council believes you were duty-bound, but you have saved us all. And I know it is not the first time."

"You needn't thank us, Amethyst. It's what we do," Shae replied with a small smile and Amethyst laughed softly, leaning back to rest her weight against the wall.

"How long will it take for the healers to recover?" Alex asked. Amethyst ran a hand over one side of her face, brushing some strands of hair away from her eyes.

"Physically, they'll probably have to spend a month or so in here," she answered, looking back out over the healing rooms. "I'm afraid their magic, what made them healers, is gone forever."

Isis' three teammates looked at the head healer in disbelief but she turned her attention back to the healing rooms, watching the young guardians work. She had suspected that the Tears of Betha wasn't the cure-all the others assumed it was. Isis scrunched up her nose at the vile scent of sickness that permeated the air.

"But you have the Tears of Betha," Shae stuttered, disbelief clear in her voice. "I thought that's what you needed to stop the virus."

"Oh child, the Tears of Betha kills the virus, this is true. But it cannot restore what is lost. The virus targets a healer's magic, destroying their abilities before killing the healer. They can be healed, but they will never be able to heal again," Amethyst explained. "We have saved them, but not their magic. They probably won't even be able to Appear again."

"But what will this mean for Earth?" Alex asked, trying

to mask the anxiety she felt.

"Nothing overly noticeable," Amethyst replied. "There might be the odd viral outbreak or new strand of disease, but nothing catastrophic. Those of us who weren't afflicted can do double duty for a time, until new apprentices come of age in a couple years. It is a minor setback, one that could have been infinitely worse. We were very lucky this time."

"What will happen to the healers?" Shae asked, her voice softer than was usual. Isis could hear that she was on the verge of tears, which was confusing. Amethyst rubbed the side of her neck, looking over the rooms again.

"I don't know. To be stripped of our magic, something that is so closely tied to our identity, is a very traumatic experience," Amethyst said. "I imagine most of them will want to journey past the mountains to the Land of Rest."

Isis looked over at Amethyst quizzically and the healer smiled at her.

"It's where guardians go when we retire," she explained. "It is reached only by a door within the mountains that separates the lands of men and women. Once you go there, you can never return."

Isis turned her gaze back to the room, watching her twin sister administer the antidote to a young man.

"A few may stay here and work as assistants, but that is entirely up to them," Amethyst finished. "I would certainly welcome the help. If you'll excuse me, I need to get back to work. There are many patients who require my attention."

Amethyst smiled and touched three fingers to her brow, bowing slightly to the Four in a sign of respect normally reserved for other guardians. Then she turned and moved back into the rooms, returning to her work next to Eshmun. Isis turned her attention back to her teammates, all of whom looked as if they had just been punched in the chest. Shae leaned against a heavy desk nearby and ran her hands down her face, obviously feeling some sort of grief.

"I do not understand your despondency," Isis commented. "The healers have been spared. We succeeded in what we set out to do."

"Didn't you hear Amethyst?" Shae asked, staring at her cousin in shock. "They've lost their magic, they'll never be healers. Isis, guardians are defined by their abilities and healers are born with a deep need to help people. They had that ability stripped from them and worse, it was stripped from them because they were doing what came naturally."

Isis looked between them, trying to understand their reasoning. The healers would live, which wasn't something that was expected before they set out. Hell, she hadn't even been sure if they would be successful in their mission. After a moment, she turned her gaze back to the healing rooms.

"I need the three of you to meet me at Sabina's rebel lair tomorrow night," she spoke suddenly, making a decision that had been weighing heavily on her. "There is something I must show you."

Turning back to the other three, she saw they were now looking at her curiously. Running a hand over her short hair, Isis turned and began making her way out of the healing ward, uninterested in answering what would likely be a multitude of questions. Orion was entering just as she reached the door and she paused, peering up at him. For a moment, it seemed like he was considering what to say.

"I don't suppose you'll tell me exactly what happened on Avalon," he said, a weariness seeping into his voice.

"You know what happened," she answered simply.

He laughed softly, watching her for a moment. "I know what you claim happened. I'm rather skeptical that is the whole story."

"Well, doctor, you have your secrets and I have mine. That is how we have always operated and that is likely how we will continue," Isis replied. Orion was quiet for a moment and she could swear he looked hurt.

"Whatever secrets I keep, I do so in order to keep the protectors safe."

Isis raised an eyebrow and turned her face slightly. "You think I do not?"

Orion opened his mouth and closed it again, hesitating. Isis looked back to the healing wing, watching the bustle of the room.

"You deny it, but you see me in a similar way as all the other normals: something dangerous that needs to be contained, and perhaps you're not entirely wrong," Isis remarked, turning her glowing green eyes back to Orion. "But you also need to be kept in check. You have been losing this war for as long as you have been fighting it. Let me do what I was trained to do and perhaps our combined efforts will result in victory."

Orion rubbed the bottom of his chin, closing his eyes briefly and nodding. "Very well, but Isis, don't try to fight a war on your own."

Isis rolled her eyes. "Why is *everyone* convinced that's what I'm going to do? It is an idiotic notion and one I have never considered."

She stepped around him, shaking her head as she tried to figure out where normals got such ludicrous ideas. Pausing, she saw Lucky hurrying down the stairs, his arm full of papers. She watched the young guardian as he hurried in the direction of the healing wing. Lucky practically collided with her, dropping an armful of papers everywhere. Isis knelt down and waved off his hurried apologies as she started scooping up papers, which appeared to be notes from the High Council session and some other notes about the War of the Meadows.

"Thank you," Lucky said gratefully as she handed the papers back to him. "Donovan would kill me if I didn't deliver this to Amethyst and Eshmun."

"The guardians don't believe in the death penalty. Even if they did, I don't think they would enact it for so small a mistake."

Lucky stared at her in confusion, squinting and opening his mouth to respond, then closing it. He glanced to the side when a messenger rushed past them, dressed in pale blue clothing.

"Um, that's not what I — I, uh," Lucky scratched the back of his head with one hand, almost dropping the papers again. "Shoot, I really need to deliver these."

Isis nodded and stepped out of his way, allowing him to pass by. She watched as the young guardian dashed off, nearly crashing into a few messengers on his way. Isis looked up at the high arched ceiling, running her hands down her face. Though it was impossible, or should have been, she suspected she was beginning to care about what happened to the normals. That was a truly terrifying notion.

~~*~*~*

Late the next night, Isis stood behind Sabina's rebel lair, patiently waiting for Jade and Shae. She arrived earlier with Alex, who was leaning against the wall of the towering building. Alex had been strangely silent all day and Isis could feel her teammate's eyes on her back. Adjusting the new sunglasses on her face, which concealed her brightly glowing eyes, Isis looked off into the peaceful night. She could hear cars peeling off in the distance, the roar of the engines as another race took place. The rebels did love their fast vehicles.

"Isis?"

Isis turned at Alex's hesitant voice, raising an eyebrow as she waited for her to continue. Alex looked off to the side briefly, biting her lower lip.

"Why did you Appear in Electra's room?" she finally asked.

"I explained that earlier," Isis stated. "I was recovering from the co-ag and my sense of direction was off apparently. The blood loss must have still been affecting

430

me."

Alex was quiet for a moment. "Okay."

Isis studied the woman, who obviously didn't believe her story. Out of all her teammates, Alex had often proven to be the best at reading experiments. Turning when she saw a light off to the side, Isis watched as Jade and Shae materialized a few feet away. Shae shook her head as though clearing it of cobwebs, whereas Jade just looked over at Isis.

"I am half-afraid of what you're going to do," Jade mentioned, adding under her breath, "Or did."

"The mansion's residents are asleep?" Isis asked and Jade nodded.

"Except for the experiments," Shae answered, shivering in excitement and practically beaming in anticipation. "Jack said he'll give us a ring should that change."

Isis turned and made her way to the back door of the lair, waving once at the camera located high above them. After a moment, the sound of locks turning sounded in the otherwise quiet night. The door swung outwards, revealing Ace. She sported a rainbow-colored fanhawk and a new lip piercing. Shae let out a high-pitched squeal and ran over to Ace, nearly knocking the smaller woman over as she embraced her tightly. Isis waited patiently as the other two women warmly greeted their one-time teammate.

"I hear the rebels need to bail your asses out again, typical," Ace teased, nodding over to Isis. "I knew shit was about to get wild when I got a call from Trouble over here."

Isis glanced at the rebel and tilted her head slightly. "Is that another nickname I was unaware of?"

"Nah, just something Orion calls you when he's riled up," Ace said, gesturing for them to come in. "I got the room set up, just like you asked. Nobody will bother you and Sabina was incredibly grateful for your generosity.

Fairly certain you could live here if you wanted."

"I have no intention of taking up residence here, but do convey my gratitude for the offer," Isis responded as they followed Ace through the back of the Lair, past the normally bustling kitchens. The young rebel laughed at the experiment's response, shaking her head in amusement.

As they continued down the hall, they could faintly hear the pulsing music pounding from behind the walls and the occasional muffled voice or a flash of brightly colored light. Ace pulled a ring with two keys out of the pocket of her jeans, handing it over to Isis.

"Elevator is at the end of the hall," Ace gestured. "It was lovely to see all of you again and I hope we can chat more in the future. Right now, it's a full house and I am working the bar in five minutes, so I'm afraid I must be going."

With that, Ace put her palms together and nodded at them before moving quickly back the way they came. The other three looked over to Isis, who was making her way to the elevator. Pressing the button, which lit up with a dim orange glow, Isis patiently waited for the doors to open. Once they did, she stepped inside the brightly lit car and waited for the others to do the same. Running her eyes over the buttons, she found the keyhole toward the top and placed the small irregular key in it. The elevator doors closed and the car started to ascend.

"I needed a place that the guardians didn't have any reason to watch," Isis explained, taking off her sunglasses and resting them on her head. "You'll understand why soon enough. Radar dug up some funds, which I used to rent the penthouse at the top of this Lair indefinitely."

"Radar dug up some funds," Jade repeated, rubbing her eyes. "Christ, please tell me she didn't rob a bank, Isis."

"No, that would have been foolish. She merely found a few nest eggs that Grenich had hidden, likely for missions, and discreetly borrowed from them," Isis explained. "The E-series are good at finding things and covering their tracks, so I assure you there's nothing to be concerned about."

"We'll see," Jade replied, looking around the medium-sized elevator car. The higher up they went the softer the music from the main floor became. Isis didn't look away from the numbers overhead, watching as each one lit up.

They soon reached the topmost floor and the doors opened to reveal a mostly empty space. There were a few chairs scattered about and a futon against one of the walls. The towering windows were concealed behind curtains and heavy drapes, all of which had been drawn. Isis moved over to a dimmer switch on the wall, switching on just enough lamps to navigate the area safely. Her eyes traveled to the center of the room where a full-length mirror in a dark frame stood. Isis quickly approached it, running her fingers around the smooth frame. *Perfect. This will definitely work,* she thought. Turning back to her teammates, Isis studied them briefly. Jade did not look thrilled, but Alex and Shae both appeared rather curious. Shae was definitely excited, judging from her fidgety body language and happy expression.

"Understand that what you see here tonight cannot leave this building," Isis began to explain as she moved around the space and pushed the chairs closer to the mirror. "I know that you will likely be unhappy with me afterward, but I need you to let me explain."

"That's reassuring," Jade said dryly, looking over to the mirror skeptically.

Once she had arranged the chairs, Isis gestured to them, inviting the other three to sit down. As they approached, Isis turned her attention back to the mirror and pulled a sheath out from where she had tucked it into her belt.

"There are so many things I'm imagining right now," Jade grumbled. Isis drew the knife from its sheath, studying it for a moment and then looking to the clean surface of the mirror. Reaching up to the top of the standing mirror, Isis used the tip of the dagger to scratch a name into the glass, toward the top. The blade pulsed with light as each letter was written and continued to glimmer once Isis had finished. Taking a step back, Isis tapped the flat of the blade on her palm.

"What are you doing?" Alex asked and Isis turned around, noticing the protector was leaning forward in her chair. Alex never could conceal her curiosity about things. She enjoyed mysteries and puzzles, so this was definitely something that would peak her interest.

"Contacting someone," Isis replied as she sheathed the knife again. "It might take a few minutes for her to reply. I confess, I have never done this before."

"Never done what?" Shae asked. "Who are we contacting? Is this like a Ouija board but with a mirror?"

Isis opened her mouth to respond, but was interrupted by a voice behind her. "Ooooh, nice ass. Now, do you think that's from the shape shifter genes or the guardian ones? I'm torn."

"What the fuck?" Jade and Alex shouted simultaneously. Isis turned around and saw Eris seated in a bedroom decorated in various shades of purple. She was wearing a thick fluffy white robe with matching slippers. In one hand, she held some sort of tropical drink, a piña colada from the looks of it. She sipped from the straw, smiling when Isis looked at her.

"And you brought friends. Hello ladies!" Eris greeted with a wave, setting her drink off to the side. Isis looked back at the other three, unsurprised at the disbelief plastered on their faces. Jade also looked infuriated, whereas Alex appeared to be completely taken aback. Shae leaned back in her chair, throwing one leg over the arm.

"Gotta say, of all the things I was expecting, *this* was certainly not one of them," she commented after a moment, doing her best to stifle a laugh.

"Oh, now I have *got* to hear the explanation for this," Jade commented, a hint of anger in her voice, which gradually increased in volume. "Because there better be a pretty goddamn good reason for working with a traitor. One who attempted to fucking kill you, by the way!"

"Isis, what did you do?" Shae asked, still trying not to laugh as she shook her head. She appeared to be resigned, too tired to even begin trying to unravel the experiment's motivations.

"Jade's being completely overdramatic, as usual," Eris answered, glancing at her perfectly manicured nails. "You know, for a team who is supposedly trained in espionage, three of you can be quite dense at times."

"Eris is going to be a double-agent," Isis explained to the other three. "She's working for me, though her going off script did almost torpedo the whole thing before it even got started."

Eris rolled her eyes up to the ceiling and groaned. "I had to sell it, sweetheart. A shoulder wound most certainly would not have done that."

"Well, stabbing me in the chest almost killed me," Isis responded, crossing her arms over her chest. "Have you figured out how susceptible the higher ups are?"

"Second generation onwards is putty," Eris reported, resting her chin on her hand. "The first generation is a bit trickier, requires some extra elbow grease, but still susceptible to my abilities. Revenants, forget it. I have no control over the dead, which I suppose partly explains your immunity."

Isis shook her head. "No, Jack wasn't affected by your abilities either, nor was the 8-series who attacked you. It's a fairly safe assumption that other experiments will also be immune to your abilities, so avoid them."

"Not a problem," Eris replied, sipping at her drink again. "They basically have me lounging around looking pretty. Oh, and pissing off the guardians. It's a dream existence, or it would be if there weren't so many necromancers. They all smell of death, it's disgusting."

"You destroyed the Box of Original Elements," Alex

stated and Eris laughed.

"Tell me which is worse, baby protector: the annihilation of the guardians, their followers, and probably millions of lives in the subsequent chaos or an old box full of stuff that has never been used before and likely never would be," Eris responded, turning her attention back to Isis. "Oh, by the way, darling niece, thank you *so* much for insisting I remove the Tears of Betha. That sentimental decision nearly cost me my head."

"You're good at getting out of dicey situations," Isis said, unconcerned. "It was a necessary risk."

Eris made a noncommittal noise in response, sipping at her drink again. Isis stood to the side of the mirror. The three protectors still looked as though they couldn't believe their eyes.

"Eris will act as our eyes and ears inside Grenich. With her on the inside, we can attack the Corporation from within as well as outside," Isis explained. "Set and Pyra are susceptible to her powers. That means we now have a significant advantage over them."

"But we can't trust her, Isis!" Jade protested. "She has betrayed her own people time and again. What makes you think she won't do it again?"

"For one, she owes me her life. Her sense of honor might be different from yours and perhaps somewhat skewed, but that doesn't mean she doesn't have one. For another, she knows I won't pursue her after we destroy Grenich," Isis said calmly. "I will not return her to the dungeons in the Meadows and I will not allow anyone else to either. After she finishes with this, she will have earned her freedom."

"And being a secret agent is sexy as hell," Eris added, stirring her drink.

"And what about all the lives she has destroyed in the past?" Jade asked and Isis looked over at her.

"What of my own past?" Isis pointed out before glancing at the mirror again. She turned her attention back to her teammates.

"I had considered keeping this arrangement between the two of us," she began.

"Which would have been the wiser course of action," Eris mumbled as she finished her drink.

"But if anything should happen to me, I don't want Eris to be stranded in hostile territory," Isis finished. "It is wiser to keep the three of you in the loop. But we cannot tell Jet and we cannot tell the guardians. This must remain a secret shared by the four of us."

"Why?" Alex asked as she stood up from her chair, studying the mirror.

"Because, darling bookworm, Set has a couple allies in the Meadows," Eris replied. "He has mentioned at least two in passing and your comrade suspects a member of the High Council may also be on the necromancer payroll. His reach is *quite* impressive."

Isis turned back to Eris. "Remember what your objective is: get the information I told you about, keep me apprised of anything the necromancers figure out or are planning, find the Dagger of Oriana, and try to find out exactly where Set's desert world is located."

"Yes, yes, yes," Eris said with a dismissive wave, glancing over her shoulder then looking back to the mirror, a sharp smile spreading across her mouth. "Well, I've got a massage scheduled and glowing eyes there probably wants to get back to fucking her shape shifter pet or blowing some shit up or whatever it is she does in her free time."

Isis raised an eyebrow. "Eris, if you feel like anything is off, if you even suspect you might be in danger, I want you to contact me immediately. I can extract you in minutes."

"Will do, lamb. I'll give you a call when I find something interesting."

Eris lifted a knife and scratched a line at the top of her mirror. The glass instantly went cloudy and only cleared once Isis scratched a line through Eris' name at the top of her mirror. For a moment, she stood and looked at her brightly glowing green eyes in the clean glass, considering her words. Isis put the knife back in its sheath and looked over at Alex.

"You were right in your suspicions about my Appearing in Electra's room. I needed to steal this," Isis explained as she held up the knife in its sheath. "Eris has mine."

Jade was standing with a hand over her eyes, her other resting on her hip. Shae started snickering and Alex seemed to be thinking over what had just been revealed.

"The guardians are going to have your head when they find out about this. You realize that, right?" Jade finally spoke, running her hand over her forehead. Isis studied her for a moment.

"I don't think my sentence will be quite so extreme, though I do agree I will probably end up in the dungeons when the guardians find out about this," she said.

"Isis, you can't leave her in there. She doesn't have any training or experience in this sort of work," Shae pointed out.

"She is better equipped to do this than any protector would be," Isis countered. "And whatever happens, it will be beneficial to us. If she remains embedded, we get invaluable information that will allow us to dismantle Grenich. If the necromancers harm or kill her, the guardians will have no choice but to take an active part in this war. Necromancers are powerful, but they're still no match for the guardians."

Isis was quiet for a moment and then looked over at Jade. "What did you do with the flashdrive?"

Jade swallowed and shifted her weight, crossing her arms. "I threw it into the Seelie Court Ocean. I know what Set's trying to do, driving a wedge between allies, and I'm sure as hell not going to let him do it."

"We all decided it was the best course of action," Alex mentioned from where she still sat. Isis looked over at her and then looked back to Jade, surprised. Of all the things she had anticipated her teammate doing, that possibility had never even entered her mind. It was probably the smartest course of action. Isis swallowed and glanced down at her feet briefly, trying to figure out what to say.

"Thank you," she said softly and it was one of the first times she could remember genuinely meaning those words. When Isis looked up again, she noticed her three teammates were watching her expectantly.

Isis put her hands on her hips, looking to each one of her teammates. "I am sorry for keeping you in the dark about this, but now you know. If you tell the guardians, they will extract her and we'll get nothing. If we leave her there, we have a very real chance of actually succeeding in defeating Grenich. I'm still trying to understand your definition of team but I think that we should all agree on a decision like this. If you ask it of me, I will extract Eris immediately, but I feel it would be wise to at least try this."

For a moment, the four women stood silently in a circle. Then Shae nodded her agreement.

"As long as you can get Eris out if she should get into trouble," Shae said. "Then I'm in."

"I guess I'm in too," Alex said with a shrug. "I just don't know if we have any other chance against Grenich."

Jade dropped her head when they all looked to her. "There are just so many ways I can see this going wrong or blowing up in our faces, not the least of which is Eris being the most untrustworthy individual in the history of the world."

She glanced over at Isis, who watched her. After a moment, Jade looked up to the ceiling.

"Fine, I'm in too. Guardians have mercy on us," she reluctantly agreed.

TO BE CONTINUED

ACKNOWLEDGMENTS

Thank you so much to my friends and family, who are continually supportive of me. Thank you to my parents for their endless patience, love, and support. Thank you to my brother, Michael, and Mom for being great proofreaders.

Thank you to my amazing editor, Rose Anne Roper. Thank you to my cover artist, Najla Qamber.

Thank you so much to Crimson Fox/Snowy Wings Publishing for helping me achieve a dream and providing support, as well as helping immensely with marketing. I must give a very special thank you to my good friend, Lyssa Chiavari, who invited me to join Snowy Wings and for being one of the absolute best people in the world. It is truly an honor to know you and call you a friend.

Thank you so much to all the wonderful professors in my life, who have taught me and continue to teach me to this day. Thank you so much, Alex and Jess Hall for your continued knowledge of all things concerning mythology. It is an honor to know you both. Thank you, Marco Benassi and Alexander Bolyanatz, for never giving up on me and providing advice when needed. Thank you Ángela Rebellón (the best ASL teacher there is). Thank you to all the professors and teachers who I've thanked in previous novels. If you enjoyed this novel, it is thanks to them. Any success I've experienced is thanks in large part to the dedicated professors and teachers I've had the privilege to learn from.

Thank you so much to all the incredible asexual artists

who I have met through Asexual Artists. Thank you to my dear friends, Joel Cornah, Darcie Little Badger, and T. Hueston. You put such beautiful art into the world and it inspires me so very much. I love you all.

Thank you so much to my friends for providing me with the support I need to continue on the rocky path that is writing. Thank you, Billy Payne, for coming to my first reading and making the experience a lot less terrifying. Thank you Robyn Byrd, Emily Kittell-Queller (extra special thanks to you and your housemates for being a safe haven on the holidays), Julie Denninger-Greensly, Ryan Prior, Puck (my wonderful cosplayer), Taia Hartman, Emmy Jackson, Leigh Hellman, and anyone else who I'm forgetting (and will undoubtedly feel just awful about later). Your love, kind words, encouragement, and support make a world of difference in my life.

A special thank you to Becca (who gave me the most wonderful compliment a writer can ever hope to hear) and Susan Sandahl, who continue to be active on my author page and are some of the most awesome people I've ever had the pleasure of meeting.

Again, I must thank all my readers. Thank you for your kind words and gestures. Thank you for getting lost in the crazy world I created. Thank you for continuing to be so generous with your time. I cannot begin to express my gratitude to you all. You continue to humble me and I hope this book lived up to your expectations. Thank you all, so very, very much.

ABOUT THE AUTHOR

Lauren Jankowski, an openly aromantic asexual feminist activist and author from Illinois, has been an avid reader and a genre feminist for most of her life. She holds a degree in Women and Genders Studies from Beloit College. In 2015, she founded "Asexual Artists," a Tumblr and WordPress site dedicated to highlighting the contributions of asexual identifying individuals to the arts.

She has been writing fiction since high school, when she noticed a lack of strong women in the popular genre books. When she's not writing or researching, she enjoys reading (particularly anything relating to ancient myths) or playing with her pets. She participates in activism for asexual visibility and feminist causes. She hopes to bring more strong heroines to literature, including badass asexual women.

Her ongoing fantasy series is *The Shape Shifter Chronicles*, which is published through Crimson Fox Publishing.